"Many are the attempts to create fictional accounts around the life and times of Jesus of Nazareth but few stand up to any kind of historical scrutiny. As a historian and archaeologist of the period I usually avoid such productions. Clearly The Judas Case is a happy exception. Graham has dug deeply into what we know of the history, culture, and geography of the times, his writing is so contemporary and engaging one feels transported into the past—with lively characters that are believable and ring true. And the plot—gripping from the first chapter. You won't be able to put it down."

James D. Tabor
University of North Carolina at Charlotte
Professor of Ancient Judaism and Christian Origins

Nicholas Graham grew up in West Cumbria and spent his youth among the mountains of the Lake District. He has worked for an international airline, a long-standing mutual organisation, various governments and several leading universities. He was a member of the Sidney Sussex College team that won BBC2's *University Challenge – Champion of Champions* series. After living for many years in the south of England, he returned to Cumbria with the aim of writing fiction. He lives with his partner in a remote coastal village close to a decommissioned nuclear power station, a location he regards as being at the heart of the realities of the age.

THE JUDAS CASE

NICHOLAS GRAHAM

The Book Guild Ltd

First published in Great Britain in 2022 by
The Book Guild Ltd
Unit E2 Airfield Business Park,
Harrison Road, Market Harborough,
Leicestershire. LE16 7UL
Tel: 0116 2792299
www.bookguild.co.uk
Email: info@bookguild.co.uk
Twitter: @bookguild

Typeset in 11pt Adobe Garamond Pro

Printed and bound in Great Britain by CMP UK

ISBN 978 1915122 520

British Library Cataloguing in Publication Data.
A catalogue record for this book is available from the British Library.

For Margaret, Harriet and Beatrice

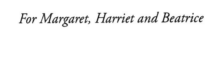

JUDEAN HILLS
1ST DAY OF THE WEEK,
DAWN

It was the still time between first light and sunrise, on a spring morning after the double Shabbat of Pesach, and I was lying in the arms of my beloved – she had just murmured "No" and turned away, then placed her right hand upon my thigh; my left hand was still beneath her head – when the hammering began upon the farmhouse doors.

I sat up. Five beats. The hammering stopped. No voices called out. Then the beating began again: one, two.

"Solomon…" Zenobia stirred and ruffled the black length of her hair across her face. I slipped from beneath the pelts, reached out for my knife and strapped it to my left calf. Slowly, one hand on the side of the bed, I stood, naked and armed. Zenobia opened her eyes.

"You look ridiculous."

I raised a finger, enjoining silence. Then I padded across our room and tilted the shutters. Outside, our vineyard had vanished: the air of the Judean hillside was full of a soft mist, one of those fine pervasive films that sit like gauze upon the landscape so that the first rays of the sun illuminate the air in a mantle of soft fire. A storm had broken on Preparation Day and curtains of rain had wrung themselves out across the skies.

The hammering returned. Five harsh, deep, deliberate blows. Then two more. My ears caught the sound of metal upon metal somewhere in the mist: a horse's bridle at the gateway to the home field. So, our visitor understood enough about movement in silence to approach us with the care of a professional, but we had not yet been murdered in our beds. The hammering began a third time. Five knocks, and two, to the same rhythm. Behind me, I heard my beloved stir. She rose from our bed naked, drew across her shoulders the wrap of rich red Damascus work and secured it with the Isis brooch. Then she opened the inner door and stepped out onto the gallery at the head of the stairs.

"Abi? Stephanos? Will you see who it is, please? We'll be down in a moment."

"Yes, mistress," a voice called out from below. And I heard the light bustle of reassuringly purposeful movement from Abi, then Stephanos' thumping tread upon the flagstones.

Zenobia turned to me.

"If it's day-labourers looking for work, you can tell them to come back at vintage time. We're not carrying anybody. Not this year."

"That's not someone looking for work. No-one hoping for employment would announce their arrival like that."

The hammering began a fourth time, and then the sound of a male voice, interrogatory, first in Aramaic, then in everyday Greek. A soft, slightly tremulous response, also in Greek. Yes, we've gone so far up in the world that even our domestics can't bear to be addressed in Aramaic. Abigail pretends not to understand what's said to her in her own mother's tongue. She speaks Greek to the goats and Hebrew to the chickens. Zenobia has been teaching her Sahidic. I've no idea who or what she'll speak to in that tongue.

My beloved and I dressed in silence. When she put on her shift and tied the cord beneath her breasts, I brushed my hand against her, but she smiled, looked down and turned away.

2

"Come on, Shlomo. We have business." And she began combing out her hair with the ivory and antelope brush she had bought on the wharf at Caesarea the previous week.

An uncertain knock at our chamber door and Abi was standing beneath the lintel, wide-eyed fear upon her face.

"What is it, child?" Zenobia held her by the arms. The girl was trembling.

"If you please, ma'am. High Priest's messenger. From the Temple Guard."

Zenobia looked at me.

"The master. He said he wants to speak with the master."

I put my hand on her shoulder.

"Don't be afraid, child. He can do you no harm. Not in this house."

Abi nodded, but still trembled.

"Go and ask him if he would be so kind as to wait for us in the courtyard. We'll be down in a short while," Zenobia told her.

"Yes, mistress."

"And offer him a bowl of fresh goat's milk, some flatbread and a piece of honeycomb," Zenobia called after her. "He must have set out early."

Zenobia looked at me, eyebrows raised. I shrugged and pursed my lips.

"I have no idea," I said. "Honestly. None at all."

"Well, then." She stretched the cover tidily across our bed. "We'd better make ourselves presentable, hadn't we? First we confuse the enemy, then we deceive him. Isn't that what you do?"

"Let's just be hospitable and interested, shall we?"

"At this hour of the day?" At last she smiled and kissed me. "I may just be able to manage that. For a while."

In the recess at the far end of the chamber I washed myself with the chill water from the ewer, tied back my hair and oiled my beard. Then

I dressed in my best working tunic and a heavy pair of breeches made of good-quality cloth from Aleppo. Wolfskin boots, scuffed but clean. Gentleman farmer. That was what I was aiming for. Doing nicely but not too well. Our vineyard is our livelihood, not some business speculation or a rich man's amusement. I shivered. The mist was seeping into the chamber. Cold points of light glinted upon the empty bedstead.

The messenger from the Temple Guard stood in the centre of the small walled garden that we keep at the rear of the farmhouse. Our paradise. It nestles behind the living quarters, enclosed on two sides by the house, on a third by the wall of the press room and wine cave, to the rear by the rock of the Judean hillside. A fountain, fed by a clever device of my own design, plays in its centre: four culverts lead the water out between the flagstone paths. Palms and succulents of Zenobia's choice push up in half-forced luxury into the cool air. The walls and their orientation are cleverly designed too: even in high summer it is a place of cool shade.

He was young. One of the new ones, I supposed. He wore the blue and white uniform – new for the last ten years – and the brass and leather warrant satchel across his left shoulder that told everyone he was an official messenger. Rather a conspicuous way of advertising your official business, I always thought. Still, it showed confidence. They were known in the Service, but not to their faces, as "angels" when they were first recruited. Messengers. Bringers of news.

This one knew how to command an audience. He stood apart, at the centre of my garden, just in the spot where he was impossible to ignore. No scroll, so he was a memory artist. With a pressing mission. The milk, the honey and the bread were lying untouched. Stephanos was standing by, staring at him, his hulking body taut and ready. I put my hand on his shoulder.

"Thank you, Stephanos. You may leave us. You have done your duty." He grimaced and stomped off to the house, jarring the flagstones at every step.

I turned to our guest. He had the poised stillness of someone who knew how to move swiftly and no doubt with violence too when required. So, he had been a soldier. But his skin was smooth, his head and neck without scars. If he was a soldier, then he was either a very lucky soldier or else a very skilful one. I deduced the private guard of a great man. His body had the confidence of someone used to being associated with power.

"Shalom." I opened my arms and embraced him. He bent forward stiffly.

"Shalom."

"Forgive us for keeping you waiting."

"Please," said Zenobia, "eat and rest after your journey."

"You are Solomon Eliades, the oenarch?"

"I am."

"I am commanded to bring a message to you." He glanced at Zenobia for the first time. "For your ears only."

"My wife and I have no secrets. You may speak in her presence."

"I was ordered to speak it to you alone."

"You may speak in her presence," I told him. "Recite."

He looked down as if reassuring himself that what he was about to do was against his better judgement. Then he began. To my mild surprise, he spoke in Hebrew not Greek.

"Solomon ben Eleazar, your uncle Yehonatan sends you his greetings. He is engaged in the purchase of some land for a vineyard. But the price he is being asked is too high. He requests your personal advice in the matter of the negotiations. The vineyard is a walled field in the Vale of Eshkol. The price is seven talents per *semed*."

My mouth must have hung open long enough for our guest to think either that he had misidentified his target or else that he was dealing with an imbecile. I was still struggling to arrange the latches in the box of memory – the Hebrew form of my name, the non-existent Uncle Yehonatan, the vineyard, seven talents – and turn them into the expected response when Zenobia broke the silence.

"Look. If you want something from my husband, why not just ask him? I can't be having these childish games. We have a farm to run."

The messenger looked at her for a moment and then gave me his attention.

"I was ordered to receive an answer."

I drew my nails across my scalp. Yehonatan. Eshkol. Then I spoke.

"The price he is being asked is too high. That land is not suitable for vines."

His expression did not change.

"Will that satisfy you?" Zenobia asked. "Now, please. Don't offend me any longer. Take some refreshment in my house."

The messenger looked again at the honeycomb and the warm milk.

"I was ordered to return with an answer. And also with you. There are two horses at the gate of your farm."

"Tell your principal that he's not my uncle and that I will conduct the negotiations in person."

Zenobia sighed. "Solomon, my husband, we've still not agreed what to do about the lower block."

"Please," I said, touching the messenger on his shoulder. "Eat. Drink. Rest for a short while."

He stood there, eyeing the bowl of milk. He must have been confident of my agreement.

"I need to discuss the care of the vineyard with my wife," I told him. "You'll excuse us." Finally, he reached out for the food.

In our chamber, Zenobia closed the door and turned to me.

"I don't suppose that all that nonsense gave you a clue what they want you to do?"

"No. That's just how the Service lets you know that they know you."

"You mean games for boys with under-occupied intelligence."

6

"They did say that they might be in touch. If they ever needed me."

"I don't believe a word of this. You're not being honest with me, are you?"

"They want my advice. On an important matter. But only my advice. Nothing more."

"That's what you think."

"That's what the message said."

"That's how it starts, isn't it? First, advice. Next, a favour. Then it's an obligation."

"Advice. That's what he said."

"And I thought you said that you were finished with them, that you were never going back?"

"Yes, I did."

"And so?"

"Everyone always says that. It's what you say."

"I'm not interested in everyone. I'm not married to everyone. I'm not running a vineyard with everyone. I'm running a vineyard with you. What about you? Why you?"

"They told me when I left that there might come a time when they would send me a message. This must be the time."

"Why does it have to be you?"

"Now, where's my prayer shawl?"

"It's wherever you left it the last time you used it. Remind me – when was that?"

I stopped my search through the second of the wooden chests at the far end of the chamber, stood and looked back at her.

"That was last winter. When you were ill."

We glanced at each other and then our eyes very notably failed to meet.

"What about this?" I held up a heavy Parthian cloak from the bottom of the chest.

"Completely impractical, husband. Besides, nobody's been seen wearing one of those since Old Herod died."

7

"The monster."

"The monster," she responded. "They'll think you're an enthusiast – or a madman. They'd be right about the last bit."

She moved towards me and touched the side of my face.

"The vines need you more than they do."

"It's a duty."

"Your duty is to us, and to the vineyard, my love."

"I cannot refuse."

"Then you'd better go. Hadn't you?"

"Though I can't imagine what sort of help they would want from an old, retired farmer who spends his time pruning vines and pressing grapes."

Our foreheads touched and she smiled, her hand in my hair.

"You'd better come back quickly."

"I promise I shall."

She closed her eyes.

"Men's promises. They mean nothing, my sweet. Now go. Go on, just go. Go, before I lose my patience entirely."

So there was an end to the appearance of the gentleman farmer, the Judean estatesman. I took off the rough boots, the tunic and the breeches and put on my travelling clothes. They were still unwashed after the journey back from Caesarea on the Western Sea five days before. Red mud had dried to the calves of my riding boots. The heavy tunic was rank. I pulled on the old breeches of weathered camel-skin and they hung on me like dead things, clinging to my thighs. I drew the traveller's cloak around my shoulders and tied a square of folded cotton over my head. Then I squinted at the great sheet of high-polished copper that Zenobia kept against the wall on her side of the bed. I looked, I thought, like a great brown and grey behemoth, some hairy abomination without boundary or form. It occurred to me that I really could have no certain idea when I would return to my vineyard and my wife.

In the atrium, my messenger was standing by the great doors, his cloak drawn about him, impatient for his mission. Abi stood in the shade at the rear of the light-well. Stephanos scowled from the shadows. When I came to Zenobia, she thrust a packet into my hands: meat and bitter sauce, wrapped in flatbread, tied in a bundle of leaves.

"For the journey," she said, and embraced me. I looked back to the rest of the house. Abigail handed me a goatskin full of fresh water and I slung it over my shoulder. I looked again to the house. Zenobia gripped my arm.

"Come back safe, master," said Abi.

"Of course I will."

I turned to Stephanos.

"The vineyard and the house need you. Be on your guard. Watch at night and protect the mistress. And your wife." Abi clung to him. He nodded glumly and scowled again at the messenger.

Then I kissed my wife gently on the lips, broke from her and strode back into the depths of the house.

"Where are you going?" the messenger demanded.

"Leave him," Zenobia said. "He has something to do."

I returned to our garden, walked past the fountain and the gorgeous, clinging plants and stood in front of the far wall. There I knelt and put my cheek against the cold rock that covered the grave where our Benjamin and Eleazar lay buried.

I breathed as deeply as I could, twice, and began to recite.

"May His great name be exalted and sanctified, in the world that He created as He willed…"

And I stopped, my words falling upon the stone. I had no voice. For I have no sons to leave behind me any remembrance of my name. My sons have gone down to Sheol, the land of the dead.

I stood up and smeared the tears across my cheeks. Then I walked back to the house, the cold air of the atrium, and my wife standing in the flame glory of her Damascus cloak, and Abi and Stephanos, and the messenger and his summons from my former employers in Jerusalem.

"Your name, brother?"

Messengers, of course, are only supposed to speak their messages, saying no more than is needed to deliver them and elicit their answer.

"Cassiel."

Of course. A summons from an angelic being.

"Well, then, Cassiel. Let us go to Jerusalem."

I embraced Zenobia and walked out of my house. We had lived there since the day that I left the Service. Seven years.

Cassiel's horses were tethered at the gate of the home field. They were sweating in the cold mist and bare of any blanket on their backs. He really must have been confident that he would not be kept waiting. Each horse had a red fox-brush tied to the straps of its bridle and hanging down upon its forehead – the old peasant's charm for sure-footed speed. So, my messenger was superstitious.

"Do the priests allow those things when you're on official business?" I asked him.

He shrugged.

"Well, you know the priests…" he said, and took the reins.

We mounted and rode down into a thicker mist, where the rows of vines vanished from sight after three paces and drops of water hung upon every shoot and leaf. The blocks are extensive, all set to dark grapes, and we have, in the last years, found the trick of making good wine. In the first summer the shoots were blasted by the heat and we did not understand the business of irrigation. A clue to making a profit in the wine trade: find someone else to grow the grapes for you. But, if you must grow them yourself, be a patient student, be a fast learner, and have a deep purse.

After a summer-hour of silent riding we turned the spur of a rocky hillside and emerged onto the Joppa Road. Five days earlier, when Zenobia and I had returned from the coast, the road had been full of pilgrims going up to the city for Pesach. We had turned left at "our" dirt track, as we thought of it, and vanished into the hills with a sense of relief. We go to Jerusalem little enough and during the weeks of the festivals not at all: three times a year the city becomes a close-packed menagerie of people, the streets clogged, the open spaces bursting with bodies. And the Temple courts are simply impossible. I have not been what you would call diligent in my observance of the Law since my early manhood, and I feel no compulsion to keep the festivals there. Zenobia, for reasons of her own, has no wish to spend time in a city where she formerly lived an entirely different life. We lock ourselves away during Pesach, overlooked and forgotten by the nation and the world, and then we address ourselves to the serious work of the vineyard at blossom time.

The stench of Jerusalem came to me long before the city walls emerged from the mist. The stench of the Hinnom Valley, deep and urgent, and further off in the mist the fires of burning filth from the city's rubbish heap. Dogs howled below us and the beast beneath me spooked. I gave him a tight rein and pulled him to an inelegant stand. Then we heard the hammering of iron on timber carry across the dead air. Voices called out to each other, a sharp order – "Brace them!" – and a man singing in Aramaic:

My love, come away,
Let's go down to the country at the start of the day…

with a voice light and perfect in its sweetness.

Someone unseen shouted, reminding the singer that this was a military detail and work songs were forbidden. Figures moved in the mist ahead of us. One seemed to float above the rest before he dropped gently to the ground, stood up and began to untie the rope around his waist.

Three carpenters, under the command of an auxiliary officer, were dismantling a group of crosses. An ox-cart stood by the roadside to take the timber away. There is nothing half so melancholy as a place of execution after the awful business has been finished, the crowds have all gone home and only the workmen remain. *What do they do with the old crosses?* I had once asked my mother. *Do they chop them up for firewood to keep the poor people warm? Hush, my child* was all she said. *What a curious mind you have.* Now, of course, our good friends reuse the crosses over and over again. I looked at these roadside gibbets. They were worn deep where the ropes had been run to lift and lower them. The foot-ledges and the ends of the beams were stained deep and dark with sweat and blood. They must have been used many times. How admirably efficient our good friends had become. I squeezed the flanks of my horse and we trotted on down the hill.

At the Joppa Gate the dark stone of the Phasael Tower loomed above us. I stood my horse and turned to look back into the mists that enshrouded our hills, back towards my vineyard and Zenobia. Cassiel's horse stirred, as impatient as its rider. We turned and entered the city.

Inside the gate we dismounted and watered our horses at the pools by the new aqueduct. Then we led them down into the lower city. There was something wrong: it was obvious to me as soon as we passed beneath the high walls of Young Herod's palace. It was the eyes. They were on every street corner. We had reached the far end of the raised pavement and were about to lead the horses through the smiths' market before I understood. Someone had posted lookouts at the regulation fifty paces, covering lines of sight from street corners and across squares. The city was still beginning its week encumbered by the memory of the double Shabbat of Pesach. The observant were contemplating their duty; the sinful were, presumably, still coming to terms with the consequences of their actions of the night before. The market stalls were still shut up. But the eyes were there, at every corner. The city might seem to be slumbering: on the street it was tense and unready. The eyes watched us as we passed. I detected no reassurance in the fact that one of us was visibly identifiable as travelling on the High Priest's business.

12

We skirted the smooth bastions of the Antonia Tower and came to the building works at the north-western end of the Temple. There we found ourselves on the wrong side of a great flock of the new season's lambs being driven up into the holding pens. Their bleatings were harsh; their stench was ripe with terror. They moved together, paused, trembled, turned and flowed along the side of a stacked wall of wicker baskets full of the anxious, confined flutterings of perfect doves. Whatever the fear in the streets, the life of the Temple was carrying on. Just as I was remembering why I disliked the noise and smell of Jerusalem so much, we came to an open space before a high wall of well-dressed white marble. We tethered the horses at a messengers' post where a dozen runners in their blue-bordered shifts were awaiting instructions. The despatcher, an old man with a stark black beard and squinting eyes, was flinging scrolls at them and calling out destinations – "Siloam. Upper City. The Pool. West Gate. Zion Pavement. Bezetha, fifth entrance" – with an intensity and speed that bordered upon panic. Very obviously, something had gone wrong. Cassiel and I passed onwards unnoticed.

One thing in the city was unchanged this morning: gathered around the despatch post was the usual crowd of the ill and the more or less possessed, men and women whom the rustic holy men had failed to cure with their quackery and who eventually found their way to Jerusalem in search of healing. Now they spent their days strutting and gesticulating in imitation of the men engrossed in the business of the state, entranced by the purpose and bustle of the messengers, imagining that the comings and goings bore with them who knew what sign of reassurance or release from the suffering of their diseased minds. Beyond them a man lay beneath a canvas awning. He was thin to the point of emaciation, his nose and his chin cut through the air above him, his eyes were sunk deep. Attached to the loose belt at his waist was the small, intimate spade of the Essenes. He must be an outcast of the sectaries, expelled by his spiritual masters for some disobedience but still bound by his oath to eat only in the company of his fellows. In previous years the square had supported a succession of such wretches, starving to death in observance of their oath.

By his side was a young boy, as ragged as his master. When he looked up he stared through me.

"What's your name, boy?"

"Bannus, lord."

"Well, Bannus, keep an eye on my horse, will you?" I reached into my purse and took out three coins. "Get some water for your master. And some food if he'll have it."

Bannus stared at the coins with the same blankness.

"Yes, lord," he said at last.

To the left of the messengers' post was a bronze door, small enough for one man to pass, cleverly recessed against the white marble of the Temple's wall in a way that made it difficult to notice until you were directly before it. Cassiel thumped his fist upon it four times and stepped back. It opened in silence from within. At the barrier inside we paused and signed the day-scroll. When he saw my name, the doorkeeper looked up in surprise and his eyes darted, seeking to find in his memory something about my face, my eyes, my beard, my mouth.

"Shalom, Zev," I said. The old man's features softened and he breathed in, delighted.

"Ah. Sir, sir, Lord Solomon sir, welcome back. This is a wonder for us all. We never thought that we would ever be seeing you again."

I was back indeed. I breathed deeply, walked past Zev, and entered the shadows beyond.

TEMPLE MOUNT
1ST DAY OF THE WEEK,
5TH HOUR

The room had not changed in seven years. The great memory box of pigeon-holes, shelves and lockboxes that occupied the height and length of the rear wall was still bursting with the scrolls and parchments that made up the established records and memories of the Service. The box had been built by Theodore the Indexer, a Greek cataloguer in the library at Alexandria who had come to work for the Service in the time of Old Herod. According to Service legend there were secret chambers and spaces within it that could only be opened by pressing upon the wooden panels in a particular way. I had tried to find them many times, without success. A fetcher stood by the door of the metal cage that surrounded the box, ready to retrieve scrolls and bring them to the desks that lined the long wall. To the right, the steep interior steps that led up to the barracks of the Temple Guard were still giving the unfortunate impression of being a ladder to oblivion. It has always been a disconcerting comfort to me that when, a generation ago, we decided to embrace the inevitable and become the new best friends of our good friends in Rome, we should have flattered them to the extent of acquiring that most imperial of state organs, an efficient and complex bureaucracy to minister to the needs of our state's masters. The Service was part of this organisation from the beginning. Under Old Herod it had acquired an unfortunate reputation (ill-deserved, some would say). In the aftermath of the old monster's death we persisted as a discreet department of the Temple Guard. The priests did not want the Herodians to have us at their disposal, nor did they wish our good friends to have a monopoly in the information trade. The High Priest and his family recognise a useful asset when they see one.

And the noises of the room were still the same. From behind the walls and beneath the flagstones at my feet came the sound of water cascading within the system of pipes and conduits that drained away the blood of the sacrifices on the Temple's high altar, far above. The Service offices were contained within what had formerly been an ancient cistern of the old Temple. Herod's architects had designed the water supply to run above, behind and below us. The Service was, you could say, continually washed by the blood of the beasts sacrificed above us.

The only thing quite different from the day seven years earlier when I had last stood in this room was the man who had summoned me. He sat behind the widest desk of them all, at the far end, on the raised dais just outside the metal cage of memory. My successor (or was he my successor's successor? I had made no effort whatsoever to keep up) rose to greet me. I thanked Cassiel for his company and walked across the room.

The man at the desk was in middle life. Barely more than thirty. Dark, curling hair. The beard of a philosopher. Brown eyes and oddly soft hands.

"Shalom."

"Shalom."

"Philo Aristides," he said and embraced me. "It's an honour, sir."

He sat down, indicated with a generous sweep of his arm that I too was permitted to sit, then put his hands together in front of him and leaned forward.

"We met once, at Tiberias. You were delivering a class on logic as an investigative tool."

That could have been at any time in the last three decades. When we were making sure that the Service shed the dark reputation it had gained during Old Herod's years. Science and logic were to be used in place of violence and terror. And we succeeded, to an extent.

The great desk was admirably free of clutter. A clay lamp, an inkstand, a stylus. And a single canvas bag of scrolls. He raised his left hand and beckoned. A young, dark-skinned Arabian boy – a Mariby, I would guess – stepped out of the shadows at the long side of the room carrying a copper tray with a clay jug and two mugs of lemon-milk. The boy served us, bowed and returned to the shadows. The drink was cool and sweet with the odour of almonds and honey. Philo soon put his aside. He was, he repeated, very glad that I had agreed to come here.

"I am an old man, Philo. Of an age to be deep in my decades of wisdom. Why do you drag me away like this from the farm that earns me a living and allows me to keep my wife in good health?"

"I would like to ask you for your help."

"Whatever help that might be must be extraordinarily urgent if it requires a summons at dawn after the Pesach Sabbaths. What possible help can a private citizen give you?"

"The Service wishes one last favour."

"If it's a memory from the old days, then they're all up there." I indicated the memory box. "Everything that I ever did is on those shelves."

He took two scrolls from the satchel on his desk, unrolled them and read.

"Solomon Eliades. Hebrew name Shlomo ben Eleazar. Tall. Broad-faced. Dark complexion. No blemishes or distinguishing marks. Recruited from the School of Athens in the year 21 of the Temple. Trainer and recruiter for the Service. Liaised with the Prefect's office for three years. More recruitment. Spent ten years running our network Spikenard in Arabia from a spice warehouse at Pera. Ran our operations here in Jerusalem. I could go on. Our most outstanding officer. And you retired with a pension and honours in the year 41 of the Temple. The consulship of Marcus Agrippa, as our good friends would call it."

"That scroll's the chronicle of a wasted life. I would have made an outstandingly good teacher of logic and rhetoric in Athens. But I chose the path of service and duty."

"Among your recruits," he went on, pulling sheets of papyrus from the satchel, "were four young men of exceptional promise. This cadre was known as the '*hayyot*'. Service names Eagle, Ox, Lion and Man. Do you remember them?"

This was the point at which professional standards dictated that the proper response was to deny any knowledge of those names, to tell him that none of those people had ever existed, and to add that even if they had existed and I did remember them I would not be inclined to discuss any aspect of their entirely hypothetical activities and lives.

"Of course I do," I told him. "I recruited a lot of people, but those four were the best I ever found. Hence their Service names. The beasts that guard the throne of the Lord God of Israel."

"The one known as the Lion? Do you remember him?"

"Of course I do."

When he was a child, he had wanted a sword. He had always wanted a sword. I remembered a young man of medium build, barrel chest and very considerable physical strength. Red hair and freckles. From his father, I supposed. And a mind with a faultless, all-consuming memory. Numbers, faces, names, facts. He could preserve whole documents in his mind, eat entire muster rolls and balance sheets, then recall them at will. A wonderful asset in an officer. He was far too clever for the kind of work we gave him. I breathed his name. A wisp, a fugitive trace of air.

He had first come to the attention of the Service when one of our officers had pulled him out from beneath the bodies of his mother and his father, and of a hundred of their fellow villagers, who had been driven into their synagogue and slaughtered by a detachment of militia during the insurrection that followed Old Herod's death. His father had apparently been one of Herod's personal guards who were recruited from Gaul, or the islands beyond the Ocean. He had converted to the faith when he married a Jewish woman, and then retired with a grant of land that would be the death of him. The militia was one of the rag-tag religious groups who were opposed to Herodians, soldiers and the families of settlers of whatever sort. The young boy was perhaps seven or eight years old. For weeks, he would speak only two words – his name and the name of his village. The officer fed him, gave him water and a blanket, talked to him. His mop of red curls had been full of lice. The officer cleaned and washed him. This care from a stranger was the making of the lad. Otherwise, who could tell what might have become of him? The Service liked its dangerous young men to have no ties to community, family or friends. With this one we had been lucky. First he was put to running errands and passing messages. Observing the enemy was his next task. Soon, he had made himself indispensable. And, at last, he had spoken.

"I want a sword." These had been his first words. "I want a sword, like my father."

"What will you do with a sword?"

"Kill them. Kill the enemies."

"This is the Service," the officer told him. "We don't use swords. Here, we defeat our enemies with our brains."

"Then I want to learn."

And he did.

A few years later I picked him out to be a member of the "*hayyot*" group. "Yehuda from Kerioth", as he first identified himself, was the best we had ever found.

"Sir?" Philo reached out, his hand upon my arm.

"Forgive me. Where were we? What has happened to our Yehuda?"

"He was found dead in complicated circumstances early last night, just after the end of Shabbat."

I breathed out and looked down. Yehuda. Dead. Then I looked up at the high ceiling and wiped my sleeve across my eyes. I would have said *My sympathies to his people*, but of course he had no family.

"What circumstances, exactly?"

"Someone found him on wasteland south of the city. Hanged. Very possibly not by his own hands."

"You mean you don't know?"

"There is no certainty."

"And this was in the course of duty?"

Philo took the stylus from his desk and began to rotate it around the fingers of his right hand.

"He'd just completed a long and complicated piece of work. He'd achieved a very good ending for us. Or so it seemed."

"And what had he been doing?"

"He was our eyes and ears among the followers of a popular holy man. His reports told us that his mark intended to overthrow His Highness, install one of his followers as High Priest and set himself up as king of the nation." Philo's eyes strayed upwards to the ceiling, as if our words could possibly be heard far above us. Then he went on.

"He came down to Jerusalem for the festival with his holy man a week ago. That's when things began to go wrong, the way they do at festival time. Five days ago he signalled for an urgent meeting and we decided that we had to act quickly, before Pesach. Yehuda helped us to bring in the holy man before his supporters caused any more trouble. And that was when it all went down to Gehenna."

"How, exactly?"

"An object lesson in the dangers of reacting to circumstances rather than pursuing policy goals. That, I believe, is how you would characterise what happened next."

"Which was?"

"When our colleagues in the Temple Guard had the holy man safely under lock and key, our good friends decided to involve themselves. The man's entourage had camped outside the Residence and were not going to move. Well: the public execution of a popular holy man when the city's full of pilgrims, including all the usual religious enthusiasts. You can imagine just how keen the Prefect was about that."

"But he went ahead? On Preparation Day? The eve of Pesach?"

"He did. He had the man executed on Preparation Day. Three days ago, and our source at the Residence tells us he's been spitting nails about it ever since. Insists he was bounced into a course of action not of his own choosing. By precisely the people who are supposed to be his partners in maintaining good order. That would be us. Of course, we don't see things in quite that way."

I could not help but smile.

"Of course. And we still have a pair of eyes in our good friend's private office?"

"One of our best."

"He needs to be. What is our assessment of the current Prefect?"

"Pilatos is unpredictable, impulsive. We cannot hear what he thinks. He would be easier to deal with if there was an imperial legate in place in Damascus. When I briefed the High Priest I told His Sanctity that my view was that without the reassurance of someone in Damascus to whom he could refer matters, the Prefect was likely to exercise his authority in unpredictable ways. Insecurity feeds his anger. Usually, he solves problems by summary execution."

"Just like his predecessor."

"Worse. Anything complicated, he doesn't seem able to take decisions, so he puts them in chains and sends them to Damascus to await the arrival of the legate. The pits there are full of cases he's sent up. Assuming any of them are still alive."

"How are you handling him?"

"We're taking steps, very careful steps, to encourage a well-balanced humour on his part. The best thing that our good friends could do for us now is insist that someone takes up the legate's chair in Damascus."

"When I rode in this morning there were watchers all over the city. Eyes on every street corner. What sort of trouble are you expecting?"

"Our good friends are convinced there's going to be another general uprising. His Sanctity seems untroubled by this now that he's got his holy man out of the way. I've got every man – all but one of them – from the uniform branch, from the reserves and the rest of the Service out on the streets to stop any trouble before it starts. Everybody we have is committed to the operation."

"And who was it who gave the orders that set this sequence of events in motion?"

"That would be me." Philo resumed twisting the stylus.

"An officer dead in questionable circumstances, relationships with our good friends at a low point, and the city about to revolt. You have a problem. I understand completely." So they send a messenger up into the hills to ask me to drop in to the office and could I possibly offer them some advice? "What was your plan for ensuring that our Yehuda was safe after the arrest of this holy man?"

"He was told to disappear from the scene as soon as he could. Vanish for a few days. Then come in for debriefing."

"But there were no specific arrangements for his safety?"

"He was expected to rely on his own resourcefulness. Never a problem in the past. I expect that he went to the usual place for a couple of nights."

The usual place. No doubt he did just that. I thought of my Zenobia at our farmhouse deep in the hills. Now she would be walking the vineyards. Examining the buds and blossoms for damage in the rain.

"When was he last seen?"

"At the arrest."

"Where exactly was that?"

"An olive grove on the other side of the Kidron. After that he seems to have vanished, as expected. Then nothing. Till late last night."

"Was it his choice, the location for the arrest?"

"Yes, it was his specific recommendation."

"So he must have known the ground and had an escape route in mind?"

"That's reasonable."

"But you did not explicitly discuss and agree one with him?"

"No. We did not."

"This holy man that Yehuda was watching. Who was he?"

"Yeshua from Nazareth."

"Never heard of him."

Philo raised an eyebrow.

"Should I have?"

"He had followers. Lots of them. Not just the usual fanatics from Galilee. He'd gone a long way beyond that. They were all over Judea. A lot of them here in the city."

"My wife and I live a quiet life at our vineyard. We go down to the coast twice a year. I don't keep up with preachers and magicians. I leave that to the labourers. And their wives, mostly."

"Then you should have come to the city for Pesach. Why did you not?"

"My wife is unwell. She cannot travel."

Philo looked at me in the interrogator's way that told me he did not believe a word of this.

"Never mind. This Yeshua was the sole subject of interest in the city last week. He even has followers in Young Herod's household."

"Please. Tell me that Young Herod's not involved in this."

"He's kept well away from it. Our good friend the Prefect tried to palm Yeshua off on to him after his arrest on the grounds that a Galilean criminal came under his jurisdiction, but the sly one was having nothing to do with it. Sent him straight back to the Antonia dungeons with his deepest regrets."

"How very astute of him."

"Precisely. He's still terrified of another disaster like that business with the Baptiser."

"What was his thing, this Yeshua?"

"His thing?"

"His appeal."

Philo frowned. "The urgent need for the people to live as the Almighty commanded. Conjuring tricks for the peasants. Miracle cures for the women. Brotherly love for the troubled." He glanced up towards the ceiling, paused and waited. I wondered, for a moment, if Philo's wife had been one of those to whom all this had appealed.

"None of that is criminal. It could even be said to be admirable. Why would the Service take an interest?"

"The imminent arrival of the end of the world. He had convinced himself, his followers, and half the population of the city that the Almighty's rule here on earth was about to begin. Here in Jerusalem."

"Long overdue. When was this going to happen?"

"At Pesach."

"Well, that would provide our good friends with a problem. And the High Priest too. Inconvenient for all of them if it ever actually happened."

Philo looked at me and his fingers stopped mauling the stylus. He seemed unsure whether I was being serious, a question I was not about to help him with.

"Did we find out anything about him that made him any kind of threat?"

"He's a descendant of King David in the male line."

"So are half the population of Sepphoris. Or they were until Old Herod died and our good friends massacred half of them and deported the rest. What was so special about Yeshua?"

"His family had a pedigree. Certified by the Temple's office of records. He was touting himself as king of the Jews. We investigated his family background when he first came to our attention. The pedigree was real enough. His father was a timber merchant. The mother remarried after he died. Second husband was a builder, younger brother of the timber merchant."

"And a builder's stepson was enough to panic the High Priest?"

"You can see why he would be concerned. Can't you?"

"I can see why Young Herod might be. And our good friends too. Straightforward sedition. Wait, when he was king, who would be High Priest? Not His Sanctity Caiaphas ben Ananas, I take it?"

Again, Philo glanced upwards to the ceiling, as if he was expecting the priests in the courts above to hear us.

"Our Yehuda believed that Yeshua had someone properly qualified by birth and physical perfection conveniently ready in the background."

I paused for a moment as the next idea formed.

"Tell me. Was there ever any suggestion, from his despatches or his debriefs, that our Yehuda might have started to believe in this Yeshua himself?"

"What?"

"It's not unknown, when you're undercover. Identification with the mark. Crossing the river, we used to call it."

"I don't believe so. You can read his despatches for yourself. There's nothing in them that would make me think that."

"Yet one of our people is dead, and we do not know why. We don't even know if it is suicide or it is murder."

There was silence between us. Then Philo looked me in the eyes again.

"This is why I sent for you. There is no-one else to whom I can entrust this task at such a dangerous time."

I thought of my Zenobia again, walking through the rows of vines, lying warm next to me in our bed, her body full of the scent of sandalwood and traces of tragacanth in her hair. I could choose to return home to her tonight.

So I spoke the words without hesitation.

"What do you want me to do?"

"Find out what happened to our man. If he was killed, find the man who did it. If he killed himself, find out why."

"How long have I got?"

"I have audience with His Sanctity in four days' time. I'd like to present him with the result."

The weekly audience had, for a while, been my burden: interminable sessions of flattery and reassurance from which nothing good ever came.

"Why are we uncertain about the means of death?"

"The man who found the body could not tell."

"I'll question him. Where is he? And where's the body now?"

"Akel-dama, the pottery kilns on the south side of the Hinnom. The man is still there. So is the body. I've got two men guarding it."

"It's not been taken down and buried?"

"I thought you would want to examine the scene yourself."

"I'll need an assistant. Someone who's smart, someone who understands intelligence work and deductive reasoning. Not just an enthusiast for enforcing the Law. And I'll need to look at Yehuda's reports. Everything you've got – interviews, debriefs, despatches."

Philo dropped the stylus, walked around the table and embraced me.

"Shlomo, my friend. I knew that you would not let us down."

"And I report to you personally. I don't want any interference from the priests."

"You'll act with my authority. Officially you'll be assisting the Temple Guard with their investigation of the murder of one of their officers."

I put down my mug.

"In reality," he went on, seeing the expression on my face, "they are of course entirely at your disposal."

"And I'll need a messenger. Someone who really is entirely at my disposal."

Philo looked across the room towards Cassiel.

"You're to assist my colleague with whatever he requires," Philo told him. To my pleasure, Cassiel smiled.

Philo beckoned to the fetcher who was standing by the memory box. "Micah, the bundle on Yeshua from Nazareth if you please. Our colleague can look at anything that he wants to see. No restrictions. Except for the Ur-Thum series." He smiled as he said this. The Urim and Thummim scrolls were the internal record of the Service's observations of the priests themselves. I wasn't leaving my vineyard just to waste my time with that sort of nonsense.

Micah the fetcher unlocked the cage, slid aside the latches of the door, and leaped in a movement of speed and grace onto the great wooden ladder that stood at the right-hand side of the memory box. Like all the fetchers, he was lithe and light-boned. Then he turned the wheel that propelled its runners across the face of the box. He was soon at the position – high up on the left-hand side, above the middle of the wall – that he sought. Easily balanced, he slung the satchel containing the scrolls over his shoulder and slid, hands and feet clamped to the ladder's sides, down to the floor. It was almost like old times, to be watching the quiet style of the manoeuvre. Micah locked the iron cage behind him and deposited the satchel on the desk closest to Philo's. Tactful, I thought.

"Great honour, sir." Micah's words were pure lower city Jerusalem, the sort of speech that goes looking for trouble.

"I have to go up there" – Philo indicated the steps that vanished into darkness behind the arch – "and arrange for your assistant to be released."

"Released?"

"Don't worry. Please. Sit down and familiarise yourself with the case. This won't take long."

He vanished through the arch and I watched his feet departing, upwards, into darkness. Then I looked across at Micah the fetcher. He smiled. I smiled back. He was watching me with curiosity.

I walked over to my successor's desk, held out a mug and said, "If you please," to no-one in particular. The Mariby boy emerged from the shadows and poured. Good. Some things had not changed. Then I opened the satchel and sat down to work.

Three sets of documents: a commission record, a sheaf of reports in double-transposition cipher with their transcriptions in plain, and a series of scribal records of personal debriefings. All in everyday Greek.

The commission was of the usual sort. It recorded that on 5th Ab in the 46th year of the Temple, the Lion from the *hayyot* cadre, trading under the name of Yehuda from Kerioth, formerly watcher of the renegade priest Yehonatan the Baptiser, that mission completed, was to watch the object of investigation Yeshua from Nazareth in Galilee and report what he saw and heard until further notice. The verbal recognition codes, arrangements for communication of messages and details of the standard cipher followed. A Jerusalem drop-point was specified – an olive grove over the Kidron, six trees down and seven across from its upper wall. Each of the coded reports was a single papyrus sheet, covered in carefully arranged blocks of characters, six in a group, in standard Service code. The encrypted characters were Greek cursive, but they meant nothing to the untutored eye. There was no indication of Yehuda's personal cipher. I wondered for a moment what he would have chosen. For a long time, verses from the Greek translations of the books of wisdom or the prophets had been used. My own cipher, back in the days of the spice merchant's at Pera, had been something entirely personal. *My vineyard is my own to give.*

Then the decrypts: scribbled down in plain Greek on a second set of papyri. At their head, the brief descriptions of the individuals he was observing, identified in the way that a court of law would recognise: age, height, colouring, face, eyes, distinguishing marks. A long list. Most of them with no recognisable features whatsoever.

And the reports. I held them up, hands trembling, and to my astonishment began to weep. Written in his own hand, the odd, angular cursive with the long tails to the *psi* and *chi*. I had taught him to write, to encipher and decode. At first he had hated the idea of scholarship – *Not going near no kahal-house ever again, Mister Shlo.* But I taught him the secrets of knowledge and power. A spy must be literate. *Look*, I told him – *See these?* A set of reports very like the ones before me now. *You think they're some sort of witchcraft? Spells to conjure the dead? This is what will give you life: knowledge; power over your enemies.*

Secrets? Give me. I want to learn. I want to write.

So I taught him. And he learned, faster than any boy I ever trained.

I wiped my eyes and read on.

Yeshua bar Yussuf. The craftsman. Tall, broad face, dark eyes, brows like a cliff's edge. Bad teeth in lower jaw. No other marks. But he has changed since our time with the Baptiser. The desert: it changes you, even on a slight acquaintance. And he spent a long, long time out there, after the Baptiser's death.

I waved Micah over to the desk.

"Another record, if you please. The subject's previous assignment: file on this man the Baptiser." And he strode off to the cage door, thrilled to be helping me.

I returned to the reports, picked out a handful and scanned them: Yehuda was telling me how he had got close to Yeshua's inner circle, had gained his trust, and then made himself indispensable. Soon he had become the holy man's principal assistant, his fixer, treasurer and steward, his gatekeeper and watchman. My heart swelled with delighted pride: this was an example, practically perfect in its execution, of how to penetrate a group and influence a target. I had taught the boy well. Other decrypts recorded Yehuda's thoughts on the holy man's closest followers and his family. They replayed accounts of his travels, his conjuring tricks, his healings, his teachings and his disputes. Yehuda had got close, admirably close: whole papyri described private conversations with Yeshua. I put these aside – if they were likely to throw any light on the case, then I could return to them later. What I was looking for now was the formal record of the urgent meeting held four days earlier. With the imprecision typical of the Service, this turned out to be at the bottom end of the scroll in the satchel's secure pouch. Gently, I removed it, snapped the seals, and unrolled the cloth. What I read there astonished me.

Yehuda described a day-long riot in the Court of the Nations at the Temple, quite clearly deliberately provoked by Yeshua. Yehuda said nothing about his own actions but I could not imagine that such a well-trained man would have been a passive observer of this violence. And they had been aided by the pilgrims, who had torn into the merchants and the money-changers with real enthusiasm. One could not, in all conscience, feel any serious surprise. Then the Temple Guard had arrived and, typically, done their best to provoke further violence by knocking heads together. The fighting had spread to the inner courts. The transcript noted that five men died in the course of the day. It was not clear whether this was down to the enthusiasm of the guards or the indignation of Yeshua and his followers. It may even have been the pilgrims themselves who were to blame. For some of them, no visit to a festival in the city is ever complete without a riot of some sort. There was no mention of what our good friends had been doing while all this was going on. In fact, they were very noticeably absent from the scene.

Then Yehuda described a discussion between Yeshua and his followers later that day at a place he called "Yussuf's house".

He said that everything was happening as it was intended. He means to declare himself. On Preparation Day, at the sacrifice, he means to declare himself.

Decision: immediate arrest. The writing was in Greek, in the margin of the scroll. There was then a long account of how Yehuda's controller – this must have been Philo – wanted this to happen. How many officers of the Temple Guard were to be assigned. What weapons should be issued. According to Yehuda, the target's followers had two swords between them and violent resistance was expected. Philo seemed to be extremely anxious about the possibility of their arresting the wrong man. Someone called Yehuda-the-Twin – not our man, obviously – was mentioned. Then our Yehuda offered a plan, a time, and a place for the identification.

Plan: agreed. The scroll recorded that Yehuda had drawn a sum of money from Treasury for unspecified expenses in connection with the operation. The record ended with his signature against the receipt. The scroll must have been a verbatim scribe's record of the conversation. Where you would expect the post-operational debriefing to follow, there was nothing. The scroll of his life in the Service ended with a half-baked plan. Our Yehuda had pulled off the finest work of his career. Two days later, he was dead. What had gone wrong?

I put the scroll down, leaned back in the chair, looked up to the ceiling, and despaired, not for the first time in my career, of the competence of my Service. Yehuda's reports were exemplary. But there was no idea, no hint, not a suggestion of a thought, as to how he was to make himself safe at the end of the operation. No protection. No place of refuge or escape route. Just "the usual place". Philo seemed not to have given this any consideration. The Yehuda I knew would have insisted. The first principle of any operation: to protect your own people. I looked over the record of the meeting again, and again I despaired.

The cage door rattled shut and Micah returned with another satchel.

"Sorry, boss."

This one was light enough to be empty. A papyrus with the High Priest's seal told me that the contents had been removed and sent to

Caiaphas ben Ananas for the attention of Young Herod's personal secretary.

"We still send them whatever they ask for?"

"And we never get it back, boss. Not from that lot."

I examined the interior. Inside the cipher pocket, there were two sheets and a crumpled, folded papyrus. I removed them and handed the now definitively empty satchel back to Micah.

Philo emerged from the dark stairway opposite the desk. I indicated the papers.

"Two questions."

He sat down.

"Yehuda was probably our best officer. In my day we sent men like him east to Parthia or Babylon. What were you doing wasting him on fanatics in Galilee?"

"You've been away a long time, haven't you?"

"Seven years."

"These days the priests are asking us to do a lot of things that we would not have concerned ourselves with in the past."

"Such as?"

"Observance. Opposition."

"Then they are fools."

"That opinion is, certainly, not without its adherents. But they are fewer than you might imagine."

"This nation – what's left of it after Old Herod – used to have important uses for us. Listening to our good friends, to Parthia, to whatever was going on in Babylon. If we were really short of work, we would pretend to keep an eye on the Samaritans. We'd not be worrying ourselves over a collection of brigands and fanatics up in Galilee."

"Of course, I cannot disagree. But that was precisely why Yehuda was so useful to us."

"Why?"

"Galilee is one place that hasn't changed for the better since you've been away. You must remember it? Villages fighting for generations.

If you live on the wrong side of a hill, then you might as well be from Samaria. Walk across the wrong field or speak with an accent that's not from the right village and it'll get you killed. You can't buy intelligence up there. Sometimes you can rent it for an hour or two, if you get lucky. That's why your Yehuda was so valuable. He could pass for a local."

"He was a local."

"Exactly. We were lucky to have him. And time spent observing those fanatics you're so contemptuous of turned out to be well spent."

"Did it? Why did you not just have this Yeshua discreetly assassinated while he was still up in Galilee?"

"That," said Philo, "is what I proposed myself. It would have saved us so much trouble."

"Then why not?"

His eyes looked up, almost imperceptibly, towards the ceiling. Above us came the sound of the waters rushing through the conduits. Then another sound from the floor above, that of a door being opened and chains being dragged across stone. This time we both looked upwards.

"He'll be with us shortly," Philo said, "your assistant. I've told him that officially you're here to liaise with the Temple Guard, support their investigation and provide them with advice and expertise. Officially. Unofficially, you have absolute freedom to call on whatever resources you require."

"Except that you can't spare me a single man from the Service and the guards are over-stretched with surveillance." They were handing me a junior, an inexperienced innocent, someone whose feet I'd need to wash and beard I'd have to comb. "He's a probationer, isn't he? You're giving me a trainee."

Philo shook his head and smiled.

"Not exactly."

"What, then?"

"He's actually one of our brightest talents. He had a very fine reputation as a student. I would have kept him in the Service. But he chose the official branch."

"What would make him do that?"

Philo glanced upwards again and began to twist the stylus round his fingers.

"You'll find him very useful. He's been liaising with our good friends at the Antonia barracks and at the Prefect's office. He understands them. But there's something you should know. He went back to general duties in the uniform branch last winter, at his own request. Lots of enthusiasm but not many results. He was involved in the operation to bring in this Yeshua, and he didn't distinguish himself."

"In what way did he not distinguish himself?"

"He abandoned his post."

"So you're giving me an incompetent. Or a coward. What did he do? Or fail to do?"

"I think you'd better get him to tell you about that himself. Be careful with him, will you? He needs a chance to show his worth. I'm giving it to him now."

"You want me to rely on someone who's got a point to prove? And if he's a religious enthusiast he'll just get in my way."

"He's intelligent and he's committed. And he's all that I've got. I suggest you watch him. Tell me anything about him that concerns you."

I stood up.

"Right. Let us begin. We'll start with the body. Your man says he can't tell how he died?"

"Yes."

"Cassiel – I want you to find my old and dear friend the surgeon Nicanor from Alexandria. Message for his ears only. Memorise. To my old friend, greetings. I have an urgent need to consult with you on a matter of great importance to me. Your friend, Solomon Eliades.

Ask him to meet me at the pottery kilns south of Siloam as soon as he can get there. Now, recite."

Cassiel repeated the message.

"Good. If he's still enjoying his well-deserved reputation, you'll find him at this time of the day at the Residence examining the Prefect's morning specimens. I do hope that he's not detected anything worrying about our good friend's health. No: don't go there yourself. Go to my old friend's house up in Bezetha – it's above the third entry, just off the west side. You can't miss it: there's more gold leaf on the doorposts than is strictly decent. Tell one of his domestics to go to the Residence and inform his master there's an emergency at home. Bribe him if you have to. But don't go to the Antonia yourself – I don't want our good friends to know anything about this business."

I turned to Philo.

"I assume that our good friends don't need to know that we've lost someone in the course of an action that's an embarrassment to us and to them?"

"I'll be pleased if they never hear so much as a whisper about this."

"Cassiel, after you've ensured that my friend is on his way, ride back to my vineyard and greet my wife. Tell her that I will not be home tonight and ask her, out of the goodness of her heart, to send me three days of clean cotton and a pair of sandals. And this," I added. I took a piece of papyrus from the pile at the top right corner of Philo's desk, wrote a few lines upon it, folded it twice and then sealed it with wax from the brass well. My ring left a pleasing impression – an intaglio with the name of our vineyard in Greek and Hebrew. *Solomon Eliades. Oenarch. My vineyard is my own to give.*

The sound of a door being unlocked came down from the upper stairs. We both looked at the arch in the opposite wall. A pair of feet appeared in my line of sight, and stood still upon the step. Their owner was obviously delayed by something. I noticed that the feet were shod with light boots that had built-up heels. They gave their wearer two fingers' breadth of height that was not his own.

The feet resumed their descent. It became apparent that their owner was bandy-legged. More of the coat appeared. It was spotless, bright, stiffly starched and creased, as if being worn for the first time. Beneath it, I could see quite clearly the long-fringed prayer shawl of the conspicuously observant. I sighed, far too audibly. Philo had sent me a religious enthusiast after all. Finally, the coat's owner emerged into the light beneath the arch.

He was short, and his legs splayed widely outward at the knees. He seemed to inhabit his new coat like an ill-designed tent. But it was his face that compelled attention. He was bearded, and had long, curled hair as if giving the appearance of someone who was simultaneously a philosopher and a teacher of Torah. His eyebrows curved black and intense in a single arch across the breadth of his brow. His cheeks and his forehead were bruised. A livid welt ran across the bridge of his nose. Both eyes were blackened, as if he had been punched twice, precisely, by blows of equal force. The eyes stared at me, challenging me to ask him how he came to have these wounds. He stood tiptoe in his built-up heels, erect and leaning forward.

"This is your assistant," I heard Philo say, carefully avoiding any suggestion which one of us he was addressing.

"Xaire," I said in Greek to the newcomer and leaned down to embrace him. He looked at me as if I had flung dirt in his face. His arms stayed firmly by his side.

"Shalom," he said.

"Shalom," I replied. "Shalom aleichum."

It seemed that my investigation was to be conducted in the language of piety.

AKEL-DAMA
1ST DAY OF THE WEEK,
8TH HOUR

The red clay of Judea hardly seems made of earth and water. It is an element entirely to itself. Beyond Jerusalem's southern walls, the fields of the potters were a sucking, glutinous morass. We left our horses at the end of the road and began to struggle towards the kilns. My assistant had barely spoken during the journey, either to his horse or to me. His name was Saul. *Sha'ul. The prayed-for child.* Perhaps the child of aged parents. Prayed-for, to be a comfort to them. Not prayed for by me. When he had condescended to speak to me at all it had been in the faultless Hebrew of piety.

"And did you study in Athens?" I asked him in Greek. He grunted and looked away. His bruised face was hurt and resentful.

One rule of interrogation, even the friendly sort: you wait until your informant is ready to tell you whatever truth is burdening his soul. All you need do is prepare the circumstances, and wait. Whatever it was that my assistant wanted to tell me about himself I would find out when he was ready.

Above us the kilns glowed deep against the darkness of the valley sides. Mud clung to my boots, every step adding a fresh layer. The last heave up to the charcoal stacks was a mimed toil, each movement more exaggerated than the last. I looked back. Saul was struggling twenty paces behind, a permanent scowl part agony, part outrage, all indignity, twisted across his face. I had draped a white shroud from the Temple stores around his neck and he was very obviously terrified of polluting it.

"Come on," I shouted in Greek. He glanced up at me, and slipped, one knee smeared in the morass. Then I turned back to the kilns and looked upon the scene of death. Beyond the stacks of charcoal was a single shuttle tree. A body hung from the third branch. The rope was short. The man's feet were barely clear of the ground. Pink blossoms, battered and sodden by the days of rain, were smeared around him. I held back: the first impression of the scene of a crime can yield clues in the moments before your mind rearranges what it sees for the first time into familiarity. The body turned slowly in the damp wind. The morass beneath the tree was darker than the mud through which I had struggled. I wiped my eyes and looked again. Our Yehuda was dead. He had gone down to Sheol.

The men posted to guard the body were slouched by the last kiln. Their presence was a rather extravagant precaution: no-one would willingly approach that tree. They shuffled forwards, looking foolishly under-employed, and I thanked them for their vigilance.

"Has anyone approached the body?"

No. Nobody had. The potters had kept their distance too.

"And the body is just as you found it?"

"Yes, master," the taller of the two finally spoke.

"May we be relieved, master?" the smaller one asked.

"No." They both visibly drooped. "You've done well to stay at your posts, both of you. I'm grateful for your service. You'll be commended to Lord Philo. But we will need your assistance in removing the body."

They glanced at each other, appalled by the idea. Old, simple men for whom the prospect of defilement by touching the dead was a humiliation and a horror.

"I'm sorry," I added. "But we must. Now, take me to the man who first found him."

Down the slope, Saul still laboured with the shroud he was carrying around his shoulders.

"Come on," I shouted.

The man who had found our Yehuda was caked in clay slip, his rough garments clarted across his skin. Hands, arms, neck and face were covered in the cracked and dried substance of his trade. His hair was singed, the parts of his face that were bare were blasted red with the heat of the kilns and his fingers were blistered into deformity. Beneath all this, he was a boy. Perhaps as old as fourteen. His eyes watered red, and he stared at me in fear.

"What you want, then?"

"I'm looking for the man who found the body of my friend. I want to thank him for his trouble."

With the maximum fuss that was reasonable, I took the purse from the cord at my waist and began to extract a single gold coin. I had his attention.

"I want to know: was he like that when you found him?"

"Course he was. You don't think I'd touch a thing like that, do you?"

"Of course not."

"When are you taking it away, then? I suppose that you're going to." He glanced over my shoulder. "Your friend's having some trouble, isn't he?"

I looked back. Saul was at the top of the slope, gripping his thighs with both hands and pulling each time he raised his foot.

"Don't worry. We'll take it away. When did you find it?"

"When I got here, of course."

"And when was that?" He looked at me and his eyes distrusted me again. I held up the coin and offered it to him.

"Early," he said. "I got here early. I can't let the kilns cool down and break up, can I, just because of some extra Shabbat the priests decide we've got to have."

"How early?"

"Early enough," he said, and his eyes were looking over my shoulder at Saul.

"Yesterday?"

"Nah. I was early, but I wouldn't do that, would I?"

"What?"

"Break the laws of Shabbat? Not me, boss." He took the coin. "Tell your friend that."

The sound of squelching mud behind me announced the arrival of my assistant. He was standing there, mud up to his thighs. He unwound the shroud, the boy saw his Temple Guard tunic and distrust returned.

"He means you no harm. You're a good boy, I can tell. I'm sure you've not broken Shabbat." I showed him the purse. "We'll talk again, yes?"

"Yeah. Whenever." He turned back to his kiln.

"What's your name, friend?"

"Levi."

"Thank you, Levi. Come on." I grasped Saul by the arm. "Cover up your tunic. You're frightening people. We've got work to do. Let's examine the body, shall we?"

"Must I allow myself to be defiled?"

Yes, I thought to myself, you must. This is the Service. What did you expect?

"You have a tablet? And a stylus?"

"Of course."

"Then use them. Take down everything I say. Word for word, while I examine the body. That will be helpful."

I walked up to the tree. Fifteen years and the violence of death had changed his appearance, but it was him, of that I had no doubt. The same red hair, now streaked grey at the sides. The same freckles, still visible beneath the dried blood that caked his face. But his eyes were a mess where the birds had been at them and his cheeks, chin, neck and ears were swollen with black blood down to the line where the rope cut into his skin. It was the engorged face of a man who had suffocated under his own weight. A vile way to die; no-one who understood that would have chosen it. And he had understood about death. Flies darted across his face. I looked up at him, bloody, beaten, encrusted, choked. Then the body turned in the wind and swung away from us, and I wept. When I mastered myself, I spoke in Greek.

"Are you ready?"

Saul scowled. I began. "First day of the week. 17 Nisan. Year 48 of the Temple. My name is Solomon Eliades, temporarily attached to the Service of the Temple Guard in Jerusalem and commanded to investigate these matters. These are my true words, describing what I see and hear. The body is hanging from a tree in the fields of the pottery workers about a Shabbat's journey beyond the city walls. The tree is a common shuttle tree and stands one hundred paces from the roadside to the south. I hereby identify the body as that of Yehuda from Kerioth, also an officer of the Service."

Silence. I looked round. The stylus and tablet had dropped from my assistant's hands and were lying in the mud. Saul was staring in appalled fascination at Yehuda's face. The body, turning on its rope as I had been speaking, was facing him. Close observation, the first element of any investigation.

"Look, Saul," I said gently. "You'll need to get used to this."

"It's really him, isn't it?" he said, half in a whisper, half in horror. "Yehuda, from Kerioth. He helped us arrest that Galilean magician."

He picked up his stylus and the tablet, from which he began to wipe the mud with fastidious care.

"Philo said you were there. What happened?"

"What did he tell you?"

"He said it was a difficult operation."

Saul looked away from the body and stared down.

"You can tell me," I said. But I was too soon. He chose silence.

"Very well. Let us begin."

I began my observations; he began to scratch.

"The limbs of the body are stiff, indicating it has been dead for some time. It is impossible to tell for how long, but the odour that I can detect with my own nostrils tells me that death did not occur in the last few hours. The hands…" I tugged the fabric of the sleeve up Yehuda's bare arm until it lay against the fringes of his shawl. "The man's hands have been bound at the wrists with cord. If we look, very carefully now, it is clear that the nails of both hands are damaged, far more than I would expect even for a peasant who lives by manual labour. There are violent injuries to the fingers and the thumbs. The nails are torn and full of blood. On the right hand they have beneath them what looks like fragments of cloth fibre, dirt, and… in the case of the forefinger and the second finger, human skin and flesh. The same is true of the left hand. Deduction?" I looked across at Saul.

"This man was bound while still alive. He struggled. He was taken against his will." He was speaking Greek at last.

"And?"

"This is not a case of self-murder. Obviously, he was killed by someone."

"Anything else?"

There was a pause.

"We should be looking for someone with injuries to his own body?"

"Good. Let's see what else we can learn, shall we? Are you ready?" I looked down at Yehuda's feet and the ground beneath them. I swallowed, turned my face away, breathed in, and went on.

"The man's legs and his cloak are fouled with excrement, which has dried. The skin of his ankles is blistered and cut, with deep bruises. Deduction?"

"His feet were bound too."

"And?"

"He was carried here against his will."

"Good. He was immobilised, certainly. Perhaps held prisoner somewhere. Are you ready?"

"Of course."

I looked back and forced myself to continue.

"The ground beneath the tree has been fouled with excrement too. This has soaked into the soil, but has not been washed away by the rain. It is bland, and is mixed with the mud and clay at the foot of the tree." I breathed out, bent down, and inhaled. There was a rank and oppressive quality about the stench that met my nostrils, the smell of some vile and dangerous vegetation. "It would be difficult to say what caused this – I may detect the scent of a herbal purge – but the man voided his bowels either at the moment of death or shortly before. Conclusion?"

No reply came.

"Conclusion?"

Silence again. I turned round, expecting a new loss of nerve, but Saul's attention was on the road. Voices called out to us in Greek. A closed litter with white drapes, carried by six slaves, had come up the lane from the city and was now jammed in the gateway to the field. The slaves were struggling to release their burden and were shouting at each other and waving to us. One of them seemed to be gesturing at the curtains and carrying on a conversation with the burden they were carrying. The curtains drew back and an arm emerged. At the end of the arm was a clenched fist. It was being waved at the slave. The slaves put down the litter, gathered at its side and formed a sort of cradle with their arms into which a corpulent old man with short grey hair and a grizzled beard eased himself as he emerged.

"I recognise him, don't I?" said Saul. Suddenly he was smug.

"That's my old friend Nicanor of Alexandria," I said. "The Service's doctor. He's arrived at just the right moment."

I had first encountered Nicanor in the course of my professional work. An Alexandrian Jew, his expertise had been retained by a very private establishment in the Upper City that the Service found it useful to cultivate. Esther's house occupied an old Hasmonean-era palace and its owner – I was certain that Esther was not her real name – was notorious for her ability to find and recruit into her trade astonishingly beautiful girls, in particular young women who bore a tantalising resemblance to the women of Old Herod's family. Esther's was open to all who could afford the experience. For a small fortune, anyone could enjoy the favours of a girl who looked just like the princess Salome, or Pan-Nyches, the old monster's legendary mistress whose energy and enthusiasm had given her the name by which she was remembered. (The rumour that Salome's mother Herodias had once persuaded Esther to let her spend a night providing the entertainment there herself was, so far as I could find out, probably untrue. Or so Esther assured me.) At festival times, when the Prefect's court came down to Jerusalem from Caesarea, business boomed. The establishment could afford its own doctor, and Nicanor was assiduous in ensuring the health and well-being of the girls. For Esther this was a sensible business decision, a deliberate means of placing her house at the very top of the profession, rather than a sentimental dedication to the welfare of the girls, who were, for the most part, her personal property. But Nico's involvement seemed to benefit all concerned – girls, customers, business and proprietress alike. The bearer of this universal good was a rotund, stubble-bearded man of about my own age who had arrived in Jerusalem some years earlier and showed every sign of a profound reluctance to return to his native city where, I have no doubt, the clientele would have been far richer and the fees from his practice far more lucrative than in Jerusalem. Quite why he could not return to Alexandria was a subject even I had never been able to draw him on. But he had been of immense help to me in numerous operations both at Esther's and in the world beyond that establishment.

And it had not been long before word spread, by whatever unacknowledged channels of female understanding, that an absolutely first-class Alexandrian gynaecologist was plying his trade in the city, and Nicanor found himself with a list of patients that stretched the length and breadth of the Upper City, even as far as the new mansions that were going up in Bezetha. At the Feast of Tabernacles, he was called upon to attend the Prefect's wife and found himself being expected to interpret that lady's intractable, recurring nightmares. "Mumbo jumbo, old son," he'd said to me and winced. "Not the sort of thing a scientific man like me should get involved with. I'm not a magician, am I?"

I should add that Nico never availed himself personally of Esther's girls, even when their astonishing good health made them generously well disposed towards him: his own tastes were inconspicuously directed towards young men from the Antonia barracks. "Just doing to the Roman army today what Gnaeus Pompeius the Butcher did to my country ninety years ago," he would reassure me when another conquest staggered back to barracks. The centurion of the resident cohort was a regular dinner guest at his house in Bezetha.

I said nothing of this to Saul. He was a pious boy and would probably denounce my friend to the priests.

The slaves halted at the edge of the morass, refusing further progress. Raised voices floated through the damp air. Nicanor jabbed his left hand in our direction and with very obvious reluctance the slaves began to carry their master through the mud. I noticed that my friend had changed in the year and a half since he last attended Zenobia at our vineyard. His beard was slightly greyer, his face somewhat redder, his belly far greater.

Nico eased himself down from the arms of his slaves and gestured to one of them, who removed a canvas bag from his shoulder and handed it to his master. He looked around at us, took in my assistant, the tree and the body hanging from it, and then he embraced me, an extravagant smile splitting his face.

"Solomon. My old son. How are you?" Then he stood back, looked at me and leaned forward, lowering his voice.

"How's your Zenobia doing? Is she coming along? Back to her old self?"

"We take things slowly. One step at a time."

"Good. Good." He smiled again and squeezed my arm. "You must send for me, you understand? If there's anything, anything at all I can do to help things along?"

"Of course."

He squeezed my arm again and looked around. His words spilled out breathlessly, followed by that characteristic exhalation, almost a wheeze, at the end of each sentence. His teeth had deteriorated dreadfully.

"Good. Good, my old son," he repeated and looked at Saul directly for the first time.

"My associate Saul," I said.

"Didn't expect to see you here. You're in the Temple Guard now, eh? Never mind. Now then, Azizus, dear," he waved an arm in the direction of the slave who had handed him the canvas bag. "Now, let's see what this tells us, shall we? What's the story?"

He faced the body and looked it up and down.

"Dear me. What a mess." He turned to me. "I came as soon as I got your message. Rather enigmatic, by the way. So I knew it must be something important. How long has he been here? When was he found?"

I told him what I had learned from Philo, from Levi and from my own examination.

"Good. Well done. Now tell me, did you touch the body yourself?"

"Of course not. Only the clothing."

"Good. Let's get to work."

He handed the bag back to the slave.

"Specimens, please, dear. Mouth, eyes, nostrils, ears, don't forget beneath the fingernails. And the lower openings too."

Saul and I stood back from the body and watched as the slave addressed as Azizus took a set of small clay jars from the satchel, along with a metal probe flattened at each end, and began to poke, scrape and smear whatever he could find on the body into the jars. Nicanor stood back too, supervising the work, while being careful not to have any direct contact with the body himself. After some time, Azizus halted his work and spoke.

"Too late, master," he said. "Too dry. He has been dead too long." The slave was a young African man of considerable beauty, dark-skinned, shaved bald and smooth. There were traces of cosmetics around his eyes. Nicanor beamed at him.

"What about his guts?" Saul asked, indicating the ground beneath. "Couldn't he have been poisoned?"

Nicanor looked round at him sharply.

"Let us listen to the evidence before we diagnose, shall we? We'll have to be very careful about that." Nicanor turned to Azizus. "The lower body too, if you please."

Azizus handed the clay jars and the instrument to a second, younger slave with a charming smile.

"If you please, Sosthenes." The slave scowled but took the instruments.

While this was going on, Saul gave his attention to the rope from which the body hung. He walked round the bole of the tree, put a foot and one hand against it and his eyes followed the line of the branch out to the point where the rope was looped. Azizus and Sosthenes continued their examination of the body.

"Did you find anything on his clothing?" Nicanor asked.

I stepped up to the body and forced myself to touch the fabric of the clothes. Yehuda's pockets were empty. He was carrying no satchels or pouches on his shoulders or at his waist. There seemed to be nothing concealed in any of the usual hiding places and sewn linings that a spy would use to keep things privately about his person.

"Well, that's unusual," I said.

Azizus offered me a cotton towel at Nicanor's bidding. It was best Egyptian, close-weaved threads.

"Thank you. I'll wash properly later," I said. "When we're finished."

"What's odd?" Nicanor asked.

"This man, Yehuda from Kerioth, I know him; he's an old colleague. He drew a large sum of money from Treasury a day or two before he died. And his cover gave him control of the common property of the group that he had penetrated. Now there's not a single copper obol on him. He's been cleaned out. In a manner of speaking. Deduction?" I asked Saul.

"I would think that was obvious. We must find out where the money went and that will lead us to his killer."

"Very good." I turned to Nico.

"I take it you don't think this is suicide any more than I do?"

"Can't rule it out yet, old son. I've seen more peculiar scenes of death than this in my time, and some of those have turned out not to be telling us what we thought they were at all."

We looked at each other and then looked up at the body. Saul had climbed up the tree and was sitting astride the branch, the bowing of his legs providing a reassuringly effective way of securing his balance as he reached out.

"What on earth is that boy of yours up to now?"

"No idea. Are you finished with the body?"

"I've got everything that I need. You said he was one of yours? From the old days?"

"Yes. I'm afraid he was."

"I'm sorry, old son. Very sorry indeed." He beckoned to Azizus and Sosthenes and ordered them to step back.

"Now," he said, "once the formalities are observed, will you dine with me? I want to know what really brings you back to Jerusalem, and how long you'll be staying. Azizus does an outstanding job in the kitchen."

"Nico, my friend. I would really like to know how our man died. If he was poisoned, then I'd like to know the substance he was poisoned by. That's why I'm in Jerusalem. Can you do that with those specimens?"

"It's guesswork, old son. I don't know if I'll be able to tell you anything certain if Azizus says he's been here too long. It's a messy one. Sometimes we can tell from the stools, sometimes not."

"Then I'll accept your kind offer of supper tonight."

"Shlomo, my friend. It'll be like old times. And you'll need a place to stay in the city, won't you?" He grasped my arm. "Stay with me as long as you're here."

"Thank you." Nicanor's hospitality was a far more welcome prospect than a makeshift bed in the dormitory of the Service barracks. I looked up at Saul.

"You can cut him down," I said. "We're finished."

"No, we're not. Look at this."

Nicanor, Azizus and I stared up at the branch.

"What is it?"

"The rope. You should look at the rope." Saul looked down at us, his sullenness now replaced by a rather bumptious superiority. Already I preferred the silence and the scowls.

"So, tell us."

"This is a fresh rope," he announced. "Never been used before. And when they hung him from it he was already dead."

"Don't deduce just yet! Give me the observation and the evidence."

"Steady on," Nicanor wheezed softly beside me. "He's trying to be helpful."

"Look." Saul leaned ever more alarmingly along the branch. "There's no play in the rope. And there's no sign of any fibres being shed. It's not rubbed against the branch at all. If he'd struggled when he was hanged, then the rope would have rubbed against the branch and the bark would be worn. There's no sign of it. He was already dead when they hauled him up." Saul inched backwards along the branch and then clambered back down the trunk with swift agility.

"It's builder's rope," he added when he once again stood next to us. "Never been used. Nice piece of work. So perhaps it was bought for the purpose. Quite different from the stuff they tied his hands with, by the way. That's just an old bit of boatyard twine."

"Good work. Close observation," I said. Saul had taught us something and was delighted with himself. "Tell me, how do you know all this?"

"That's easy," he said. "My family are in the tent-making business. I learned how to twine rope and plait cord when I was a child."

His father had been a lucky man: one of his sons had lived long enough for him to teach the boy a trade.

"One other thing," Saul went on. "The man who strung him up on the tree didn't know what he was doing. He couldn't tie a noose properly."

"Now he informs us," I said to Nico. "We could tell that from the state of the body."

"But the man who bound his hands must have been someone different, because he knew exactly what he was doing. That's a proper fisherman's knot."

"Thank you," I said. "Now, if we're all agreed that there's nothing further to be done?" I looked at Nicanor and Saul. Both nodded. Saul uncoiled the shroud cloth from around his shoulders and handed it with obvious relief to the two old men, who had observed our investigations with unconcealed disgust. They stirred into movement and spread out the shroud between the tree trunk and the mess on the ground. Then I ordered them to cut him down.

Saul clambered back up the tree and severed the rope. The body of Yehuda from Kerioth fell onto the red clay of the Judean hillside with a final splattering thud, and toppled, rigid, straight onto the shroud. For a moment I admired the deftness of it. Chance, of course, but nicely done.

"Untie the rope, please," I asked as Saul shifted his weight for the descent. He looked at the carelessly hitched rope and sighed.

"The other end too." Azizus looked at his master and, at a nod, bent over the body. Then he beckoned to Sosthenes to work the noose over the swollen flesh of the neck and jaw. I took the rope from Azizus and turned to Saul. He was looking back down the hillside towards the city.

"I want you to go to the marketplace," I told him. "Find out who sold this rope and who he sold it to. Full description and identification."

I dismissed the two watchers, walked back along the line of kilns and called the boy Levi to me. The kiln master was there in an instant.

"Make it quick, brother. The lad has to work his shift."

I took another gold Tyrian from my purse.

"You can earn yourself some more money."

He replied with an obscenity. "I'm not that kind of boy."

"I'm not that kind of man." I tossed him the coin, and it vanished into his cloak. "I'm not Temple Guard either," I told him. "Do you understand? I'm not interested in whether you were breaking Shabbat law at Pesach. Whatever you tell me, it's a matter between you and me." He looked at the kiln master. "Your master has nothing to fear either. He'll not be in trouble."

At last the lad looked up and met my eyes.

"What do you want to know?"

Good boy. I smiled. He smiled back.

"When you came to work that day. At the end of," I stopped and corrected myself. "Towards the end of Shabbat, wasn't it? Were you alone?"

He nodded, and looked back to the kilns again.

"And you found the body of that man, hanging on the tree down there?"

There was silence. No movement of his eyes or his hands. The noise of the furnace crackled in my right ear. At last he spoke.

"No. He wasn't hanging there when I arrived."

"Are you sure of that?"

"Course I am."

"So what happened? What did you see?"

"I was there." He pointed to the side of the kilns. "I'd just come up from my *satva*'s shack by the back way at the end of the day. He makes me rake out the kilns" – he indicated the kiln master – "and get them ready to fire up after the break, yeah? You understand?"

"I do."

"That's all I was doing, yeah? Not proper work. Understand?"

I told him again that I understood. Raking out the ash and the charcoal dust from below the furnace's grating. Not proper work. If the lad was lucky, it might be another Shabbat year before the charcoal dust blinded his eyes and coated his lungs. I reached into my purse and found another Tyrian for him.

"And what did you see?"

"I saw them. Three of them, dragging the poor man up the hill from the road. The rain had stopped by then. But you could hear the noise that they made in the mud. They dragged him to the tree, and they beat him. Just down there."

"And what did they look like, these men?"

"Nothing special."

"But you did see them?"

"Yeah, I did."

"And?"

"Two of them looked like they were soldiers."

"How could you tell?"

"They had proper boots, didn't they? Who else has got proper boots?"

"Was there anything else about them?"

"Their tunics. Military-like. And a scar. One of them had a scar. On his face."

"And what about the other one?"

"His clothes didn't fit him. Dressed like a peasant. But he didn't look like one."

"What do you mean? Describe him."

"He was different from the others. That's all."

"And there were three of them?"

"I told you. Listen, will you? One of them shinned up the tree and slung the rope. The other two made the man stand up and tied the rope round his neck."

"Did you hear them speak?"

"They never stopped, master. They were arguing all the time."

"What were they saying?"

"How should I know? They spoke Greek, didn't they?"

"Are you sure of that?"

"Course I'm sure."

"And none of them spoke Hebrew? Or Aramaic?"

"I told you. They spoke Greek the way soldiers do. Sharp and barking. The bastards."

"So they were Syrian?"

Levi shrugged and looked away.

"Foreigners," he said. "Not our people. Foreigners who're supposed to keep our laws if they're living in our country. But they don't, do they?"

"All right," I said. "You've done well." I gave him the second coin. "Tell me what happened next."

He looked down the hill towards the tree.

"They pulled on the rope till he was stood upright on his toes. Then they pulled some more. He was thrashing about, but it didn't do him no good. They pulled on the rope till he was up by the branch. Then the two that were down on the ground got hold of his legs and they pulled him back down till he stopped thrashing. That was the end of it, master."

I looked down at the ground and then turned to stare at the tree. I should take Saul's observations with some scepticism in future. But that was the end of it. The end of our Yehuda.

"Thank you," I said. "You're a good lad. What did they do after that, these men?"

"They ran off, the three of them. One of them barked something in Greek to his two mates."

"And he was in charge, was he?"

"He gave them orders, the way soldiers do."

"A soldier. And what sort of accent did he have, this solder?"

"Master, I told you, didn't I? I don't know Greek. It sounds like dogs yapping, that language."

"Well, perhaps it is, my brother. Did they see you?"

"No. I was crouching there." He pointed to the side of the kiln. "They never saw me."

The kiln master loomed around the furnace side. It was time for Levi's work to begin. I turned back to the boy.

"And has anyone else been here to ask you about this business?"

"No, master."

"Good." I gave him another coin and spoke clearly enough for the kiln master to hear me.

"Share this money with your grandmother. She's lucky to have a boy as good as you to look after her." He bowed, and glanced at the kiln master. He could not be the boy's father – no man would set his own son to cleaning out kilns.

"Thank you, my brother. He's a good boy," I said to the kiln master. "Give him easy work, will you?"

"Aye, aye," said the old man, and spat on the side of the kiln. His spittle sizzled in beads upon the clay, and vanished into air and light.

When I returned to the tree I heard our horses' bridles chink and the sound of a distant snorting down at the end of the lane. Saul was staring at the road. Beyond the gate, where Nicanor's litter was still jammed between the stone posts, a fat, bald man in a white tunic was riding a grey horse with a Roman bridle and harness at a leisurely, unconcerned walk, turning his shining head left and right, then looking towards the potters' kilns. This was what I had wanted to avoid.

"I know him," said Saul. "It's Marcus."

Of course it was Marcus. Marcus Varro. The Prefect's head of intelligence. One of the Service's very best good friends. Out for a casual ride that just happened to bring him past our field. I looked round at the slope behind us. We were beneath his horizon. Perhaps, from his position, he could see a group of men taking a body down from a tree. Perhaps not. I sighed.

The horseman came to the field gate and looked about him, paused at the litter but did not give it a second glance. Then he examined our horses. They were messenger's mounts, obviously from the Service. Then he sat his horse and watched us for thirty heartbeats. During this time we did nothing but look back at him, without movement, without sound. His forehead shone across the expanse of mud between us.

He squeezed his horse to a walk and went towards the city without looking back. Finally, we stirred ourselves to movement. Nicanor's slaves picked up the enshrouded body of Yehuda from Kerioth and began the precarious business of carrying it down through the mud. Behind us Levi was loosening the fire-door of his kiln and throwing bundles of fresh charcoal onto the blaze.

As we moved off behind the body, Nicanor was by my side.

"I see Marcus quite often at the Prefect's," he said softly.

I glanced across at him.

"Do you think that he'll have forgotten?" I asked, not taking my eyes off the now distant horseman.

"No. He's not forgotten."

"I didn't think he would. That's not Marcus' way. He never forgets anything at all. Whether he ever learns anything – well, that's a different matter."

CITY WALLS
1ST DAY OF THE WEEK,
11TH HOUR

We buried Yehuda from Kerioth in the Service tomb between the Kidron and the city walls reserved for those who die in the course of duty. Three of us mourned him: Saul and Nicanor were alongside me. Under the low sun we recited the Service prayer:

> *In the world that will be renewed, and where he will give life to the dead and raise them to eternal life... may His salvation blossom and His anointed be near.*

I could not speak the words, even for Yehuda. And I found the silence of my ears filled by my companions' voices. Nico pronounced the Aramaic with the clumsiness of an educated man; Saul, oddly, with the accent of the north, of Galilee.

At dusk, as the horns on the Temple walls announced the start of a new day, Saul went back to the Temple barracks and Nico ordered Azizus and the other slaves to take the litter home, with instructions to prepare food and wine for our arrival. We hired a torch-bearer and walked through the city up the long street that divides Mount

Zion from the Temple. Our way was jammed with pilgrim crowds, prominent among them the Service's eyes, though the tension and the watchfulness of the morning were not so sharp in the coolness of the night air. Another festival day without public violence, but Jerusalem could still not be mistaken for a city at ease with itself.

As we passed beneath the aqueduct, I said to Nico:

"How do you know my new assistant?"

"The Prefect's Residence last autumn. He was the Temple's liaison at Pilatos' office. Odd choice for the job, I thought. But he seemed to keep the old man well disposed."

"That boy was our liaison? With our good friends?"

"He was. You might think that he's quite the fanatic with that long prayer shawl. But when he was in front of the Prefect you'd think he'd crossed the river. Do you know what they called him? Behind his back of course. The ambassador to the nations."

Once, the post of liaison with the Prefect's office had been a highly delicate position, entrusted to a senior member of the Service, rarely with positive results. If you finished your term with only an occasional massacre to show for it you were considered a notable success.

"And what is he doing in the Temple guards?"

"He's a youngest son. And you know what the youngest sons of rich men are like. They have the luxury of being able to pursue the truth, if they chose to trouble themselves with it."

"The third generation. They study Torah."

"Or, in your case, philosophy."

"Logic and rhetoric. In Athens. How did you come by all this?"

"He consulted me."

"What about?"

Nico laughed softly. "Can't tell you, old son. He was my patient."

"Then you'll know where he got those black eyes?"

"You should ask him."

"I'd rather ask you about Marcus, and how he already knows what I'm doing."

"Marcus has got fatter. He never takes my advice about diet."

"Is he any better tempered?"

"No, he is not. He fell out with the Prefect last week. Worst row they've had for a year."

"And what was that about?"

"I'll tell you while we're eating. Now, where has that Azizus got to?"

We passed through Damascus Gate and came to the upper streets of Bezetha. While Nicanor paid off the torch-boy, I admired his new residence.

"Very lavish, Nico. Doing well?"

"Booming, old son. Is there good health in the city, and it is not my work?"

He excused himself and went with Azizus into what he described as his consulting room to examine the specimens he had taken from the scene of Yehuda's death.

"Sosthenes will take you up to the roof, and bring you some refreshment. We'll not be long. A guest will join us after we've eaten. He'll interest you."

The youngest of Nicanor's domestic slaves, the one who had helped his master most diligently across the mud of Akel-dama, led me up the steps to the roof terrace. The boy was another Egyptian, perhaps fourteen years of age, with full lips and a mole to the side of his left eye. He had the soft, withdrawn servility of one for whom your needs are everything and at the same time nothing: as if his true self had withdrawn far too deeply behind his eyes ever to be reached. On the terrace I looked back at the city. To the west, Herod's theatre and his hippodrome, unused for entertainments in twenty years, were lapped by the dark hides of pilgrims' tents. The lights and the noise from the buildings below were oppressively loud compared to the stillness of my vineyard in the hills. I should be labouring there with Zenobia. Instead I was returning to the craft of detection, the painstaking recreation of a now unreachable past, the world as it had been a day or two before I arrived in the city. A time when our Yehuda still lived and breathed and walked in Jerusalem, following the hidden art of his trade. And all my craft could never return him to us.

I sat down beneath the awning and opened the satchel of documents from Yeshua's file. At the head of each bundle of encrypted messages was the seal of the High Priest and a note in Hebrew explaining that the encryptions were not sorcery, nor did they contain spells for conjuring up the dead, but they were a dialect of *koine* Greek, known to the Temple Guard, and its use was acceptable in the sight of the Lord. We had found that civilian eyes trying to read a coded despatch would often conclude that it was a necromancer's spell-book and that the act of touching it would defile his hands. Someone passionate for the Law might risk bringing such a thing to the attention of his local synagogue. Once someone did just that, with catastrophic results. A boy from the village where one of our officers worked saw him hiding a message, removed it from its place of concealment and showed it to his father, who could read a little... Witchcraft, he decided, and brought it to the village elders. They dragged our man to their synagogue, where he was condemned and stoned to death. That's Galilee: a place where ignorance and stupidity walk alongside righteousness and observance.

First, I took the crumpled sheet that was all that remained of the Baptiser's file. It began mid-sentence.

fisman, one of his chief organisers and errand boys. No mistaking him, in any crowd or company. He's compelling, more so even than the Baptiser. Tall, powerful build. Hair never cut. Forehead like a cliff. Enormous hands. Bad teeth. Not that you'd need a description to identify. He can draw attention to himself by silence and stillness. Three days down in the dust at Machaerus before I came to his attention. Instantly, he's utterly absorbed in me, as if no-one could be more important. He's noticed that I keep away from synagogue.

"You hang back. Why? Don't you want to learn?"

To my astonishment, I find myself telling him. About the synagogue at Kerioth and the day that the soldiers came.

"Three days before they pulled me out, from beneath my parents' bodies. My mother and my father were butchered for trying to protect me."

He stood up and he embraced me. A huge, engulfing hug of power and strength.

"I'm sorry for you. And this was when Old Herod, the monster, died?"

"The monster. Yes."

"Let me tell you what happened to my family when the soldiers came to our Nazareth." Silence, for a long time. Then he spoke.

"When I was a child in Byblos, I would dream every night – every night, without change – about my parents leaving Nazareth. Which is odd, because I could have no memory of such a thing, I was not even born then. I may have been conceived, but I was not born, so how could I remember it?"

"Perhaps your parents told you stories?"

He didn't like this. No. The dreams were always the same. "I saw it every time. The soldiers. Their officer taking the women and the young girls aside to the walls by the goat-bield. He had the pelt of a big cat across his shoulders. He took every one of them. Now why should I dream that? Me, a boy?"

I was about to tell him that at least his parents had lived to look after him, but this was not one of his riddles about prophecy. He was weeping. I opened my arms and embraced him.

Later, he told me about his childhood.

"When we were growing up in Byblos, my brother Yehuda and I, the Greek children would mock us for being Galilean.

Even our fellow Jews mocked us. And I wondered what sort of wonderful place our Galilee and our Nazareth must be. And I wondered about the welcome we would get when we went back to our own people."

This was the time, he explained, when the magic started. He found that simple tricks would distract and enthral. Making an egg disappear, swallowing flatbread from the bakery next door, then pulling it out of the ear of the owner's daughter were ways of turning hostile bullies into a fascinated gang of followers. Soon he had a little band, the children of local craftsmen, who followed him around, agog for the next trick, none of them aware that they were being deceived by someone too smart to let them know the truth.

"Then it all ended the year before I became a man. They allowed us to go back to Nazareth. And I wondered what a welcome we would get when we came back to our own people. We came back to hatred and mistrust. My fellow Galileans mocked my accent — my words were all wrong. The children called me a sorcerer who could bring back the dead to life when I did tricks for them, because everyone knows the best sorcerers come from Egypt. That was when the trouble started; they'd bring dead animals to me. Bring it back, they said. Make it live."

He's a child of war, as am I. A child of civil violence, like all of us. But I look at us both and realise that I am the lucky one.

I turned the papyrus. On its back, two scribbled decrypts in another hand.

The followers are still waiting. The group has been paralysed since the Baptiser was arrested. Nobody knows what to do. They've established a line of communication into the fortress at Machaerus by which the Baptiser issues orders to his followers. But they're showing more enthusiasm for arguing about his instructions than for following them. No leader has yet emerged from among the followers, which suggests they are either expecting Young Herod to release him – or else they are waiting for the intervention of God.

They had been disappointed, on both counts.

A group of the Baptiser's followers has split off, left the area around Machaerus and vanished into the desert. Their leader is one of the Baptiser's lieutenants – a craftsman called Yeshua. Deductions from the messages carried out of the fortress indicate he was not one of those expecting Young Herod to release their leader. He argued that intervention would come, but not yet, and not in time to save the Baptiser.

A note beneath – *Have him watched.* The scroll went on to describe arrangements for Yehuda to begin his new mission. This involved getting back his old job as clerk-of-works at a boatyard in Magdala. Apparently he had been a very good clerk-of-works and they were delighted when he returned. I knew Magdala. It reeked of fish. You could smell the place half a day's journey off.

Then the first of Yehuda's reports from Galilee:

The poverty becomes noticeable as you travel north from Beth-shean. Houses abandoned. Animals starving on their tethers. The peasants have had their debts bought up by the rich and are being set to work in the fields they themselves owned before last year's so-called harvest. The men who went for soldiering have returned, with nothing to show for it but fresh wounds, empty purses and a rage against Herod. Some of them are mad with hunger. They live in dried-out river-beds and sleep beneath walls or by wayside wells. The roads are lined with beggars. Then, half a day's journey south of the lake, the smell of fish begins to infect the air.

There's a problem brewing in Capernaum and Magdala, in all the villages around the sea. Ownership of land is one thing; no-one's yet worked out a way of owning the waters in the lake. So the fish wholesalers and the sauce-merchants in Magdala keep driving prices down. The fishermen need bigger catches. Bigger catches need bigger boats. So they go into debt and pay the yard to build. What will happen when they haul the last of the fish out of the sea is something no-one dares to think about. Already the smaller operators, out at Kinneret and Capernaum, are mortgaging their boats to the sauce-merchants against future sales. I've sacked one of the journeymen who was selling terebinth over the fence to some friends of his from Capernaum. I've put the balance sheet and the timber stock into good order. There are still problems with the nail-makers: we're being cheated. They cannot imagine how they ever managed to run the yard without me.
Seven days working in the boatyard. I can still smell the fish. He has not yet returned. Gone to Sidon to buy Lebanese cedar for the winter building season. There are questions about the Baptiser and his arrest. They all seem to believe that I was lucky to escape being taken by Herod's men myself. The hatred of Young Herod and his people hangs in the air whenever the Baptiser is mentioned, which is often. Andros-the-Man, our best customer, is most fervent of all. And the most delighted that I've found my way here.

"He's changed," Andros told me. "The desert changed him. You weren't there."

Andros-the-Man: a great, calm lunk without a hint of the violence that's brewing in some of the others. Lacks Yeshua's intelligence and charm though. He could never beguile you. Tight-curled black hair, big build, lopsided face. A livid scar on his right arm where someone took a knife to him in a fight over a girl. He's an absolute, straightforward passionate believer in anything Yeshua tells him. Got his name when Yeshua tried to teach him Greek but he got stuck after half a dozen phrases. One of them really stuck. I'm the man. Andros, Andros-the-man.

He came back from Sidon, astride an empty ox-cart. Mistress Mariam and Little Yeuda were with him. Mariam looked furious. And not just because I was back. What happened next explained everything. He jumped down from the cart, walked straight past his family, Andros, Shimon-the-Rock, Yakoub and the rest of the hands, and embraced me.

"You're back with us!" He took my arm and dragged me into the boatyard. "Come on. There's no time. I need your help." He leaned against the keel of the new boat and turned to look back at me. He had that smile in his eyes, the one he keeps for teasing the followers with difficult questions of law.

He picked up a toolbag that someone had left hanging on a thwart and rummaged in it. Then he picked up a piece of wood and jerked his hand, miming a splinter. He looked up to me while my attention was on his hand. "Your eye," he said. "There's something in it." His hand on my brow and fingers gently pulling my lower lid.

"Look up," he said. I looked and he took away his hand.

"Got it." He grinned and held up his hand, a splinter of wood the length of a finger on his palm. "It's a wonder you could see anything." Before I could say a word he smacked his palm, full and open, against his own face, on his left eye. Then he shook his head, groggy and drew his right hand across his brow, pulling out of his own eye a length of four-by-two terebinth that grew and grew, getting larger and longer, until it extended from the side of his face to the cuff of his tunic at the end of his outstretched arm. Now, I thought, that really was clever.

"Tell me, Yehuda, when is Purim?"

"Two Shabbats off. The village idiot knows that."

"We're starting after Purim. I've a task for you."

"Starting? Starting what?"

"The end."

"What?"

"Of everything."

"At Purim?"

"After!"

Really, I should have known better to echo his questions, but his sudden anger (another new thing – he's never previously been impatient with people who can't keep up) was just as suddenly replaced by another sudden smile and laughter. But then the family and the hands turned up, demanding to know why he had not come back from Sidon with any timber.

"Timber?" he demanded. "Timber? From now on, none of us will be needing timber."

Then, the shouting started. Shimon-the-Rock loudest of all. In the end, he could only calm them by calling them all out to the lakeside and practically forcing them to sit on the rocks and pray. The prayer was the one we used with the Baptiser. But this time he added new words and we all stumbled across them.

"What was that?" I asked him afterwards – none of the others dared.

"What?"

"The words. They were different."

"Oh, that?" And his eyes shone, delighted to have the chance to play. "Well, that was just something I learned in the desert."

We're not going to be laying down keels any longer, however much the family want to keep their business. Nor going out in the boats either.

There was another page of debrief, dated Pesach in the year of the Temple 46, in plain.

Dawn, or just after. My cloak and my hair soaked with dew. The left side of my face pressed against the timber thwart. I drew my arms together and shivered: my head, neck, belly and chest were hot with sweat. My eyes opened: the heels and ankles of a pair of legs were pushed up against the other side of my head. Then I moved, and regretted it: as soon as I was truly awake, the pain began. A head with seven spheres of agony, each grating against its neighbour. A mouth full of dust and a desiccated tongue. Then I turned, and I regretted as a long-lost content the muffled discomfort of my half-waking mind a few moments before.

The heels and the ankles moved and dragged themselves across my face. I grunted. Then I looked up.

It was him. He was lying half across me. We were in a boat. That was bad. The boat was on land. That was reassuring. But the land was swaying, wildly.

I turned away, faced the stern, sat up and ran my hands through my hair and my beard. My hands trembled as they met. Behind me, I heard the sound of vomit splashing upon the ground and the retched gulping in of breath. I looked round. He was wiping his mouth.

"Work," I said. "We have to work. Purim's gone."

He laughed.

"Purim was gone two days ago."

Thaddeus bar Ptolemai's head appeared above the gunwale. He was making a careful attempt to seem sound in body and in mind. He's an irritant, bar Ptolemai. Always acting up. Over-compensating for being the only one with an education – or so he thinks.

"All right, are we? So. When do we start for Nazareth?"

I leaned over the gunwale and my stomach heaved.

"What happened?" I asked, myself as much as him.

"Purim," he said. "Purim happened." Purim. We had celebrated Purim and we had lost two days of our lives.

He stood up, stumbled, and jumped out of the boat, holding tight to the side of the hull. His face appeared above the taff, next to bar Ptolemai's.

"We learned a lot about you at Purim."

Fear closed around me. Betrayal. What had I said, in the depths of the wine? With exaggerated care, I hauled myself out of the boat, and faced him.

"What? What did you learn?"

"A lot." He clasped me by the shoulder and pulled me to him. "We learned that you can keep a secret. I learned that I can trust you. That you can organise things. Not just the business of the boatyard."

"What do you mean?"

"Don't you remember what I told you? I need someone," he went on, "to make sure that we have a roof over our heads each night, food in our satchels, and wine and water in our goatskins. Someone to raise funds and oversee their distribution to the poor – that most of all. I need someone who can organise all this."

There was none of his playfulness now. For once he was being practical. This was far better than I had imagined possible. And it got better as he went on.

"None of the others – Shimon, Yehonatan and Yakoub – can do this. Oh, they can catch fish. I'd ask my brother but he has no skills with anything except stone and mortar. My little brother would think anything as practical as organising ourselves was an affront to his scholarship and piety. Yehuda, you are the only one that I can trust with this. Do you understand?"

We began our celebration of the story of Queen Esther, the good man Mordecai and the evil Hamman two days earlier. At noon he told the men to stop working on the keels. We followed him along the side of the lake till we were out of sight of the road south and the only sounds or movements were the wading birds out towards Capernaum. We formed a circle, looking inwards, and we prayed the way that we had learned to pray when we were with the Baptiser. New words again, but this time no-one stumbled. He makes this a daily habit, always in a remote, quiet place. Then we reflected, in silence. By the time that we returned to the boatyard, the family had arrived, riding in an ox-cart with two great red amphorae of wine wedged upright in the back. Yehonatan and Yakoub, the two bad lads, glanced at each other, and smiled: divinely sanctioned oblivion beckoned.

This time his family was there. His mother must have been beautiful in youth. In age, there's a closed off harshness to her features. Pinched skin, sharp lines. She orders and organises with the certainty of a woman who has not had to defer to a man for a very long time. The hands refer to her as "Mother" Mariam, to distinguish her from "Mistress" Mariam, the wife. The distinction is not all light-hearted – some of them resent her. She draws a regular slice of the boatyard's surplus. Her second husband left her wealthy enough, by local standards. The two girls, Salome and Little Miriam, are modest but beautiful. Of an age that you would think they were now ready for marriage, but they remain scandalously unbetrothed: nobody quite good enough for them in this part of Galilee. The youngest son is a surprise: Yakoub is pale, skinny, practically lost in the long shawl of the ostentatiously studious young man. It's a poor family that cannot afford to support at least one scholar. There's a moment of real pain: he obviously adores his elder brother the woodworker, but his naïve revulsion for the excess that awaits us is obvious too. He withdraws with his mother as soon as the meal is over. But the real shock comes in the shape of the other adult brother, the stonemason from Sepphoris.

He enters the boatyard while I'm filling up the last bag of the bad iron nails.

"Yehuda." He calls my name. When I turn, for longer than I imagine possible, I am completely taken in. This is Yeshua, isn't it? He grins and opens his arms. We embrace. Something is

different, but it has nothing to do with touch. And then I realise that this is not Yeshua at all.

"Shalom," he says. "Yehuda."

For a moment there was the embarrassment of mistaken identity. Surely I am Yehuda? But he smiled, and I understood. This was the twin brother, also called Yehuda.

"Yehuda," he repeated. "Yehuda-the-Twin."

When they greet each other, the twins, they have an odd little routine, one that probably goes back to Byblos. First they embrace.

"Split the wood," says one.

"There you will find me. Cleave the stone," says the other.

"And there I am."

I watched them together as carefully as I could without giving any obvious sign of interest. I wondered whether, as we became drunk enough to be unable to distinguish the evil Hamman from the good Mordecai in the tale of Esther, the way you're supposed to at Purim, I would remain sober enough to be able to distinguish Yeshua from Yehuda. The moment of realisation came early in the evening at the common meal, as he passed around the cup. It was obvious, and I reproached myself for not realising it earlier, when I took the cup from him. The key to their identities was there in their hands. Both of them have the thick, muscular wrists and forearms of craftsmen who have spent their lives working with difficult materials. Yeshua's hands have the calluses of the woodworker: shattered nails, fingers and palms riddled with the gouges and holes of cedar and terebinth splinters. His right palm is a great callused pad of flesh and skin grown hard from the force of pushing a plane. The hands of Yehuda-the-Twin are quite different: the swollen joints and knuckles of a man who wields mallet and chisel. Stone dust packed deep in every grain and crevice of his skin. A wide ridge of white skin just at the base of the fingers of his left hand. It's odd that it took me so long to realise when one of the first things I noticed about Mistress Mariam was that she's lost two fingers on her left hand and half the forefinger of her right – result of gutting fish on the wharf at Magdala. After a few moments of observation, it is obvious that no-one could doubt who is who. But the followers don't seem to have got the hang of this basic fact. They're not a bright bunch, really. I make sure that I publicly and very noticeably mistake Yeshua for Yehuda now and then, just like the rest of them.

After the cup has passed the second time, both Mariams, Mother and Mistress, and the young ones leave. Yakoub the young scholar goes with them and he departs with a look of reproach and regret at his eldest brother, who wastes no time broaching the second amphora. Shimon, Yehonatan and Yakoub are delighted in a rough, ragged way. They're already far gone in their pious and lawful drunkenness. We all are, though I'm trying hard to keep well behind their pace. After an evening of the second amphora, none of us remembers very much at all. Until I wake up in the boat, with his feet on my head.

Now it is two days later. My head feels no better. The trembling and the sweats have ceased. I still have no idea what the secret is that I'm supposed to have kept so successfully through the night of drinking. We leave for Nazareth in three days' time. I'm to be his quartermaster and fixer. That's a good start.

I must have fallen asleep beneath the awning: Nicanor came up the steps and roused me.

"Well?" I asked. "What did you find?"

"In a moment. First, we eat."

Azizus and Sosthenes brought flatbread, roasted chickpeas and hot sauce, and a stuffed chicken. The younger slave carried a tray with a ewer and a set of silver bowls, the grandest of which was set before Nico. Engraved upon it was an image of a naked man taking his pleasure with a youth. They were both attached, in complicated ways, to an apparatus of ropes and slings. My own bowl was unadorned.

"A gift from a grateful client," Nico said when he noticed my gaze. Then Azizus poured, and I knew the scent that rose from the ewer as my own wine. Azizus joined us. Sosthenes stood back, smiling shyly, holding the ewer.

"Nico, tell me straight. What happened to him?"

"Azizus dear, tell Solomon what we found."

"We know that, when a man is poisoned, his stools will often have a characteristic odour and consistency. It is not pleasant, but it is distinctive. This man's did not have them. He was not poisoned by any of the potions that are typical of the Herodians. We first noticed this when examining the remains of a man poisoned by one of Young Herod's people – a dispute over a mistress, I believe. Or possibly over a husband. I know Young Herod's chef," he added. "He shares his recipes with me. Very enlightening."

"And you're absolutely sure?"

"Of course I am," Nico snapped. "Not a trace of anything."

I sat in silence for a moment, chewing a mouthful of chickpeas. They were beautifully scented and steeped in a slightly sweet sauce of pepper and tamar dates.

"I thought that I could smell something, a purgative, when we examined the body," I said. "There was the scent of it, I was sure."

Azizus went on. "There are some poisons that have their source in the earth, not in vegetable matter. They are made from ores and metals. We have found that the stools and hair and nails of a man who has been poisoned with these will burn with a characteristic flame. Sometimes white, sometimes green. There was no trace of these poisons in this friend of yours."

"Sorry, old son," Nico said. "Whoever killed him did it the crude way. Hands on."

He raised his mug of wine.

"Now tell me. What had he been up to?"

"Our Yehuda was watching a holy man from Galilee. He came down to Jerusalem last week and caused quite a stir – or so I'm told. I've been down on the vineyard too long to bother myself about what goes on up here."

"You mean Yeshua? The Galilean conjuror?"

"That's him."

He whistled softly.

"He was supposed to be good. Very good indeed. Never seen him perform myself, but apparently he did the lot: lepers, madmen, the blind, even the recently deceased. Women's problems too. One of my own patients wanted to consult him. I tried to dissuade her, obviously. Have you ever seen a country healer performing?"

"Of course."

"Sheer force of personality. That's what does it. And a patient who truly wishes and believes that the man is able to heal her. What I can't work out is how he managed the recently deceased. I heard about a man over in Beth-Anya last week. Dead for three days. Down in Sheol with his ancestors, sleeping the long sleep. This Yeshua brought him back to life. Now, if a healer needs a patient who wants, desperately, to be well and healthy, then how does he manage when the patient is dead – or at the very least unconscious? I don't understand it. Most of my patients – apart from the obstetrics, obviously, that's quite different – I don't think they actually want me to make them well at all."

"What do you mean?"

"They want to be told that their suffering matters," he said after some hesitation. "They have diseases of the soul that I cannot hope to heal, unless by chance or good luck. Their physical symptoms I can do something about, at least for a while. And they get my attention. So they depend upon me for that, but the real malady escapes us all. Do you know something?"

"What?"

"They're rich, the ones with distempers of the soul. The poor don't get ill in anything like the same way. With them it's poverty, starvation, ignorance and childbirth. Hence the need for men like your Yeshua."

"He wasn't my Yeshua."

"I'll tell you what. When you've finished your investigation and I can get a day off from examining the Prefect's turds, we'll go to Beth-Anya and we'll ask for the man who died. Oh, he's alive and well, apparently, eating and drinking like you and I. You question the family; I'll examine the patient medically. Ten'll get you five Tyrian shekels that he's a rich man with something chronically and undiagnosably wrong with him and he'll be dead again within a month."

I raised my bowl. "Let's do that before I leave. But I'm not betting against a professional."

"He was a lucky man, your Yeshua. Most doctors would kill to have a list of clients as dedicated to health and well-being as that man's patients must have been. Mine spend all their time languishing between house calls and drinking themselves into oblivion."

"You sound as if you envy him."

"Of course I don't," he snapped. "He's dead."

"I meant professionally, not philosophically."

"Shlomo, I'm a graduate of the academy at Kos. Don't insult me by comparing me to a country magician. Drink your wine, old son."

"It's mine, by the way. This wine."

"Then don't insult one of your best customers," he said and burst into laughter. Azizus giggled, his hand over his mouth.

"I recognised it as soon as I could smell it. I can also tell you that it's not the vintage I gave you last year. This is older. Where did you get it?"

"I bought a couple of amphorae from a merchant who was heading south to Arabia last autumn."

"I don't sell to the caravans. Did he tell you where he'd bought it, this merchant?"

"He said he'd got it in Caesarea. Said it was the best wine he had ever found west of the river and north of Arabia. Of course, I didn't believe a word. Then I saw your seal on the amphorae and I knew it would be good."

"And did he say what he had done with the rest of his stock?"

"He claimed the rest of it had already gone to the High Priest, Young Herod and your good friends in the Prefect's Residence. I was lucky to get the last two amphorae. You've got a very distinguished list of customers there. Very grateful too."

"How wonderful," I said. "Why should they be grateful?"

"It turned out to be the best business investment I'd made in years. Half of my clients are convinced your wine is a tonic for every malady you can name. Don't worry," he added when he saw the look on my face, "I tell them they should use it for their stomachs, nothing more. Azizus believes them, though, don't you, dear?"

Azizus looked down in embarrassment. "We have noticed all sorts of improvements in patients who take it," he said.

"Azizus thinks your wine is a genuine cure-all. You should tell him about the vineyard and the press house. He'd love to hear, wouldn't you, dear?"

"I would," he said. "Your wine is remarkable. I would love to know everything. From the planting, the soil, the irrigation, to the pressing and fermentation."

So I told Azizus about the vines and the vineyard, about how Zenobia and I had found the farm in the cleft of the Judean hills, and how we had transported rootstock from the vineyards of Tirazis in Parthia, where they really do make the finest wine between the River Oxus and the Western Sea.

"I used the eastern caravans of the spice merchants who had been my couriers when I worked in Pera. But the cuttings had withered when they arrived from over the Jordan; the rootstock was dry."

"What happened?" Azizus asked.

"We planted without hope, and we waited in despair. Do you know what a healthy grape looks like? Black but lovely, with a sheen on the skin. You leave them till they are shrivelled with ripeness before you pick. The smallest grapes are the most powerful, and they make the finest vats of wine." All this was a gloss of course on the dreadful problems that Zenobia and I had in the first two years when the vines had withered, before we had learned the tricks of irrigation.

"Some advice," I said to Azizus, "if you ever own a vineyard. Make sure you have access to a reliable water supply. And make sure you have deep pockets and an even more reliable source of easy credit. Because you'll need both."

"And how is business now?" Nico asked. "How are you both doing?"

I ignored the second question. "If my wines are being bought by the High Priest and our good friends and you're prescribing them for the health of your clients, Nico, then I'm in danger of becoming too successful for my own safety."

And I told him how three weeks earlier Zenobia and I had hired four ox-wains, loaded them with close-packed double-handled pitchers out of the wine cave and driven them down to Caesarea. I had picked out the best amphorae by smell alone – beyond a certain point there was barely any need to taste the wine itself. My wine has the perfume of Cyprus plums, balsam from En-Gedi and Jezreel figs. I thought again of Zenobia and regretted our untimely awakening at dawn. The scent of my beloved's body was sandalwood, wild thyme and the sweetness of honeycomb.

At Caesarea we sold five-sevenths of our entire vintage to Ariel on Cyprus Wharf. Zenobia had negotiated a price higher than I had imagined possible. From the very beginning of our joint enterprise, my wife has been an astute businesswoman, sensing the value of a product, the keenness of the prospect and always knowing just how far to push the price before agreeing to sell the goods. It should have been no surprise to me from her previous life, this calculation and expert playing of the mark. And now we were doing something right in the vineyard.

"I'd always thought that Ariel sold the wines on to merchants in Cyprus and Rhodos. Maybe even Sicily, and beyond. And now I wish he had," I added. "Do you know what he said when I asked him who our customers really were? He said they were people who pay cash, on the nail. People who come back every year. That's what you want: people who'll forgive you for the occasional difficult vintage. But we've not had any more of those." I turned to Azizus. "It can be a dangerous thing to have a business that's successful so close to Jerusalem. Do you understand?" Azizus raised his brows. He did not understand. "You come to the attention of people who will want to know more about you. Then someone, perhaps a friend of the Prefect, or a cousin of the High Priest's wife, will offer to help you by investing in your farm. A generous investment. And you are under an obligation. Before long, they wish to buy it – for a fraction of its worth. Do you see?"

Azizus nodded. Nico looked away and drank from his silver cup. "Long life," he said. "And many more wonderful vintages to come, old son. Vintages more wonderful even than this."

I did not mention that this year we had a surplus from our sale sufficient for Zenobia to spend a morning in the textile warehouses. I had put a small sum that we did not need for the vineyard into Ariel's hands to buy a piece of a ship's hold sailing beyond the Pillars to Lusos and Pretanya. "Tin," he told me, "that's where you want to be. Cassiterides. It's the future, that place." I thought it likely this was the last I'd ever see of the money but Zenobia approved of the idea. On the way home we agreed that we were in some danger of becoming modestly prosperous.

Sosthenes and the domestics began to clear away the bowls and platters. A tray of melted cheese and pastry soaked in warm honey appeared. Sosthenes brought us three small bowls of a sweet white wine.

"From Cyprus," Nicanor said. "You'll enjoy it." I did: it was smooth and full and perfectly satisfied all the senses of my tongue and nose that the honey and cheese had already aroused.

"Now, will you need to stay in Jerusalem for long?"

"I'm leaving as soon as I can. The vineyard needs me." Nicanor nodded. "And so does Zenobia."

"You're welcome to lodge here for as long as you please."

"Thank you, Nico. I'll be gone as soon as I've finished with this business. A day or two, I'd hope. The end of Pesach at the latest."

"As long as you need." Then he asked me, "How are things? At home?"

I put down my bowl and pushed the plate of cheese and honey aside.

"Truly?"

"Yes. Truly. I want to know how things are now. How long has it been?"

"Almost two years."

"And?"

"Truly, Nico: I've taken to wondering which one of us I should be the more worried about. She's absorbed herself into the work of the vineyard – completely and utterly. Nothing else matters to her. She's vanished into it. Without a trace of her former self." I paused and looked down, wondering what further truth I could tell him. When he said nothing, I went on.

"Of course, she's done wonders for the vines and the business. And I ought to be there. But we're partners in a business now. Not man and wife. If you understand me?"

"Yes, I do, old son. I'm sorry. I'm very sorry indeed."

"Still, it's better than the first six months."

The time between the months of Ab and Tishrei two years earlier. When she could not rise from bed, would not eat, would not wash herself, would not even think about the farm. My darling, my bride, had disappeared into herself and could not be reached, spoken to, caressed or held. She did not eat, or drink or take any account of her appearance. It was as if she too was a dead thing, or about to become one along with our infant sons. She had been that way through the year's vintage and fermentation. I had worked the vineyard and the cellar myself, with the help of the hired men, through to the winter pruning, while Abi had cared for her mistress. Then, one morning, sometime around the first Shabbat of Marcheshvan, she appeared downstairs for the first time since the previous summer. Her hair was a thick, matted mess, her face caked with dirt and the sweat of months, her hands were trembling and her shift was stained and stiff with filth.

"Solomon," she said, "enough of mourning. Let me cut your hair and trim your beard. You look dreadful."

Then she walked out of the back door of the farmhouse, past the line of astonished and shamefaced labourers, took a pruning hook in her hands and started to hack at the front bush in the first row of vines. I walked past the labourers and placed my hands on her shoulders.

"Zen? My darling?"

She turned to my arms and collapsed in a wailing, trembling sack of bones and skin. Gently, I removed the pruning hook from her hands, passed it to Abi, who was standing, terrified, just out of arm's reach, and walked my darling wife back indoors.

"What will you do?" Nicanor's voice came to me across the table.

"I'm sorry," I said, looking up at him at last. The bowls and platters of cheese had been removed.

"What will you do?" he repeated, more gently.

"I'll finish this case, this Yehuda business, for the Service as soon as I can. And, of course, you and I will go to Beth-Anya to take a look at the man who died."

"I meant about your family, about Zenobia?"

"I was just about to say," I went on, "that I'll go back to my farm and set my shoulder to the winepress and work alongside my wife. At least we can do that together."

There was a knocking at the outside door, and Sosthenes announced the arrival of Nico's expected guest. He was one of our very best good friends – Nico's in particular. Quintus Cassius, centurion of the resident cohort of guard at the Antonia. Like every soldier I have ever known, Quintus drank deeply and quickly. A lesson of mess halls and meals interrupted by unexpected violence. And he barked his Greek in foreshortened, elliptical periods with the rounded twang of the Latins, as if conversation was a series of imperatives only interrupted by drafts of wine. But he complimented me upon the wine in a straightforward way that had no hint that I would have to send him an amphora as a gift. Perhaps he had ample opportunities for extorting favours elsewhere.

While Azizus was pouring, Nico mentioned that "the Ambassador", as he called him, was one of my colleagues.

"Saul? Knew your friend when he was attached to the Prefect's staff. Thought he'd gone to the Temple Guard. Working for you now?"

"He's assisting the Service."

"With what?"

"I'm curious to know how my colleague got on when he was at the Prefect's office."

"Why?"

"There seems to be some mystery about why he returned to uniform."

"No surprise. Lad's an enthusiast. On official business. If you can imagine. Convinced the world is about to end. Tried to convince us all. Old Marcus found it funny – at first. Soon stopped."

"And what happened?"

"His Excellency had one of his fits of anger. Happens more often these days. Your friend was asked to leave, quietly. What's he doing for you now, your Saul?"

"One of our comrades was murdered during Pesach. He's helping me find out who killed him."

"Fortune may not smile on you. Two hundred and thirty-five dead bodies. Fifty-three public brawls. A riot in the Temple of your

God. And the usual executions. That's what you get when the Prefect and his staff come to town and imagine they can exert some kind of control over three hundred thousand pilgrims from all over the world. They create the problem they're brought here to solve. This is the second week of the worst fortnight of the year in Jerusalem. You think that Sukkoth last year was bad? This is the worst Pesach I've known in nineteen years. Do you know what I spend my time doing, from one festival to the next?" He went on before I could answer. "Fixing the damage done by the last one. I've got eighty men fit for active service. That's twenty on a watch. To keep the peace in Jerusalem, day in, day out. Festivals are worst of all. Your friend, he must have done something to help us when he was at the Prefect's office. Difficult to imagine, but things actually got worse when he left."

"How was that?"

"That was the odd thing. Marcus thought that he could understand them when he talked to Saul about his people."

I looked up at this and waited for a moment before I spoke.

"Did Saul talk to Marcus often?"

"Your friend was in and out of Marcus' office all the time. It's barely stopped since he went to the Guard. That's when he wasn't up at Young Herod's palace or in front of the Prefect every morning."

"For which the Service is very grateful," I said quickly. "I've always thought it a sensible thing for the Service to be close to their good friends. Saul and Marcus must have worked together very closely."

"They did. Do you know the story about Marcus?"

"We've all heard the story about Marcus," I said firmly and without curiosity. I was quite certain that I already knew what story that would be.

"You should tell Solomon about the riot last week in the Temple court," said Nico before Quintus could speak.

"I came to Jerusalem late," I added when I saw Quintus' surprise. "My wife is unwell."

Quintus drained his bowl and wiped his lips, then looked across at me.

"Each year, we march a little bit closer to catastrophe," he said. "I keep order with a single century of men from Chislev to Nisan, every year. And everything's quiet. Public business goes on. Every day Augustus' sacrifice to the One God is made for us all. The lads go back to the Antonia at the end of the day and the city is at peace. Your enthusiasts in the synagogues and the yeshivas may not be happy about our presence here in the first place, but they're all too busy arguing about the Law to bother about us unless we do something egregiously stupid. And I make sure that my boys, every one of them, are smart and respectful and understand the rules. And they do. A single century to look after a city of thirty thousand men women and children. We cover everything from the top end of Bezetha down to Siloam, from the Joppa Road to the top of the House of God. How much trouble do you think we have?"

I opened my arms, palms upwards.

"Tell me."

"Damned little. Half my lads are married to local girls. Some of them are God-fearers and go to synagogue on Shabbat. Do you think they want to see trouble here? Relationships with the locals are very good indeed." Here he raised his goblet and grinned at Nico. Azizus scowled.

"Festival time, my lads have two problems: the pilgrims, and His Excellency's boys from Caesarea. They turn up three times a year and none of them have learned a thing from what happened the last time they were here. My lads spend their time dealing with the drunks and the rapists – all of them wearing our uniform. The pilgrims are less trouble. And then there's His Excellency. Never known to execute one man when ten will do. Do you know what happened this Pesach? With that holy man of yours?"

"I wouldn't say that he was my holy man, particularly. Though we take an interest."

"Well, it seems that we must have been taking an interest in him too."

I put my goblet to one side. "Of course you did," I said, and waited.

"A disaster. Two days before the Pesach sacrifice. Late afternoon. Polite request from Temple Guard. Your lot. I'm to provide an escort for a squad going outside the walls after sunset. Ten men required. An arrest, after the business in the Temple the previous day. More trouble. We stand to an hour before sunset, and we wait. And wait. Nothing comes down from the Temple. No sign. At last, when the lads have stood in the courtyard for a couple of hours, the sun's gone down and we're all feeling the cold, we're stood down. One of Marcus' errand boys comes running down from the Citadel and tells us we can go back to quarters. Not needed on detail, thank you very much. His mob are handling this one."

"So. What happened?"

"Marcus' boys get the honour of the arrest. Biggest catch from among your troublemakers in years. All done without too much trouble, too, from what I hear. Even if they did let their other target slip through their fingers. Very careless. Amateurs, letting him get away."

"What do you mean they let him get away? They arrested him, didn't they?"

Quintus swirled the wine in his bowl, looked down, and drank.

"Of course they did. Your boys. They got the holy man. Though I could wish that they'd let him get away too, after what we had the next day."

"What do you mean, get away too?"

Another pause.

"I heard that Marcus' boys were looking for someone else. And he got away. Your friend the ambassador, he may know something about it. I heard he chased someone, and lost them. Very careless, if he did."

"I thought that the Temple Guard took him, this Yeshua?"

"Of course they did, officially. And our friend Marcus thought that he'd got a catch. Until it turned out that His Excellency was incandescent. Didn't like it. Don't ask me why. I don't understand them up in Damascus and Caesarea. Playing another game. And it's nothing to do with keeping the peace."

"And?"

"And nothing. Marcus suddenly decided that he had to find some way to keep His Excellency sweet and reasonable. So who do you think had to deal with the mess that our visitors made?"

"Quintus Cassius?"

"You understand. Quintus Cassius, the servant of peace. The next morning Marcus sends his errand boy down to the barracks again – the same little smooth-arsed Samnite as the previous day – and tells us that the arrested man's been condemned to death and we'd better make the usual arrangements. Execution set for noon. Detail to parade an hour in advance. Thank you very much." Quintus drank. "Two of Marcus' boys came down and got him ready for the show. We took him up to Golgotha. Seen many, have you? Crucifixions?"

Of course I had. They had been the roadside distractions of childhood journeys to Jerusalem. In the days when I asked my mother what would become of the leftover timber.

"This Galilean, the magician, the charge on him was sedition. King of the Jews. Marcus left it to us to drag him off to Golgotha and put on the show. Know what the crowd were like?" This time he did not wait for my response. "Impossible. It was the women, the women and the girls who were the worst. Most of the men and boys still had some kind of dignity. The women, they spat at us. They threw stones and goat shit at us. Olives and rotten pomegranates. The lot. We got him through Joppa Gate and on the road to Golgotha and that was when things started to change. You know what they were expecting? Everyone in the crowd, even some of my lads, it was the same: your holy Elijah, he's going to come down from heaven and rescue him. The heavens are going to open and the world is going to end. Your Yeshua, he didn't last long, I'm pleased to say. Any longer and we'd've been finished. The crowd would have torn us to pieces. He was in a bad way by the time we got him to the place. Kept falling down. Have you seen what the whip does? I don't mean the wounds and the bleeding. I mean what it does to the mind of the man being whipped. This one had gone far, far off. When we pushed him down and stretched out his arms, he came back to us, just a bit. He looked up at me, from wherever he had found away from the agony and he whispered, a single word.

"'Elijah?' he asked.

"'There's no Elijah here,' I told him, and I hit the nail. Then we hauled him up and stood there, waiting for the end of the world. I can tell you: there were a lot of people in Jerusalem who were relieved when they realised it wasn't going to happen and they'd all be sleeping in their beds that night. Except for the lad on the cross: he was still expecting it. He cried out to your Elijah again. Heard him myself. Terrible disappointment for him, to die like that."

From good-natured tricks with planks of wood to the end of the world and the horror of a humiliating, agonising, public death, in a year and a half. A disappointment. Quintus drained his bowl.

"And I thought: that's Marcus and the boys from Caesarea for you. They get the arrest and the conviction just in time for a peaceful Pesach. They don't have to deal with all the goat shit and the rotten pomegranates. We come along and do that for them. Very obliging."

He raised his bowl again.

"To Marcus and his boys," he said.

"To Marcus," I echoed back.

Later, when we stumbled out of the room at the end of the evening, Quintus turned to me.

"You said you were looking for somebody?"

"I am. I want to find the people who took my colleague and murdered him."

"Where and when?"

"We lost him the night before Preparation Day. His body turned up at the pottery kilns at the start of the week. Between that, nothing. Three days of lost time. We need a sighting, an incident, anything."

Quintus nodded.

"Let me see what we've got."

"It's possible that the Service has already made the request."

"I'll ask the lads. They remember things that don't turn up in reports."

"Thank you."

He grasped my arm.

"For a friend of Nico's."

As I turned towards the sleeping quarters. I stopped and said to him:

"When I get home, I'll send some of the oenarch's wine down to the barracks."

Quintus' face assembled itself out of a stupor and into a slow smile.

"Thank you, Solomon. You're a good man."

"But favour me, will you? Not a word to Marcus or anyone on the Prefect's staff about this."

"What?" He seemed puzzled for a moment. Then he understood.

"If they hear that you've got some of my wine they'll all be wanting their own private supply."

"Marcus? We can't have that, can we?"

"No," I said. "We really can't."

We retired at a dreadfully late hour for a countryman, that must have been some time well before the second watch of the night. Sosthenes guided me by the light of a taper to a little room at the rear of the house. It was set above the slaves' quarters at the opposite end of the long upper gallery from Nicanor's own chamber. The room's walls were a deep red. From the ceiling there hung an odd contraption of ropes and wood that looked very like the device in the scene that was engraved on Nico's silver cup. This must be his guest room. Unusual choice, I thought, even for Nico.

As I was gently prising the rough cloth from my body, there was a light knock at the door and Sosthenes entered the room. He brought with him a ewer of water, an empty bowl and a sponge that he placed on the wooden table at the foot of the bed. Then he turned to me, and waited. After a few moments he spoke.

"Will you be requiring anything else, lord?" His skin was dark and his eyes shone in the taper's light. Shadows cast across his arms and chest.

"Thank you, Sosthenes. There will be nothing else."

The boy bowed, and withdrew. My limbs ached and my ears buzzed with the wine. Sleep eluded me in this unfamiliar bed, without the reassuring bulk of my beloved's body by my side. The noises of the night-time city were not the sounds of the Judean hills. The life of the house, too, was carrying on beyond my door. I heard footsteps padding along the gallery and a door opening slowly. Then silence, and a voice crying out. Much later, the light of a taper swept by, throwing a dim glow beneath my door. I pulled out the satchel of papyrus and read through Yehuda's account of the early days again.

They've got a pedigree. An official document, sealed and signed in the Temple. They're proud of it too. The mother most of all. Look, she said to me. Look at this. I read:

Given at the office of records. The Temple. Jerusalem. 20th Ab, the 26th year of the rebuilding of the Temple. This is the descent of Yeshua from Nazareth, son of Yussuf, of the tribe of Yehuda.

The scribe had done a thorough job. It went back to our first father. I was careful to read every line in the list and commit each generation to memory. There were a lot of them. I stopped twice at King David and his son Nathan to be sure that I had the details. Then I looked up at her. Mother Mariam explained to me that the family had the document drawn up when they returned from exile in Egypt. I watched her closely and memorised her precise words. Yeshua was with us, but not Yehuda-the-Twin. Wood not stone. I was being introduced to family secrets, which meant that I was being trusted. I was inside – though it felt like a test.

"When we were all allowed to return from Egypt," she explained, "my boy was twelve years old. We were poor in those days, very poor. When I took my boy to the Temple to redeem him under the Law we could not even afford the two lambs that Moses commands us to sacrifice. We had to make do with pigeons. Pigeons! Can you imagine the shame of it?" I nodded, but she was not expecting sympathy. "We had to establish his right to the timber yard. It was ours, before the Herodians came and took it away from us. There were difficulties. It was a dreadful time. They would do nothing without this, this certificate." She gestured. There was unease as well as pride in the movement, in the official acknowledgement of her eldest son. Her features did not soften during any of this. Her face was closed up, the skin nut-brown and drawn tight, her eyes small and sunken.

"Yehuda, the other one, he was apprenticed to my second husband's trade. The brother's trade," she added, as if it was somehow less worthy. "They were difficult times for us," she repeated. "You will help my boy, won't you?" I agreed. What else could I do? Yeshua was staring at me for once, giving no sign.

"What happened?" I asked. She leaned back, pushed the certificate to one side and let out a long, slow, rhythmic moaning.

"It was when the old king died," she said. "There was trouble, such trouble. Our own people, we thought that they would help us. But instead, one day, the soldiers came to Nazareth. When they had finished with the people in Sepphoris." She paused, pain

and bewilderment in the memory, and the silence went on. Her eyes were on me when she spoke, but they were staring through me to some other place. Yeshua reached out and enclosed her hands, which were twisted around each other, the fingers snarled against the joints, with the great splintered pads of his own palms.

"The soldiers went from house to house," he said. "Looking for the young women and the girls. Do you understand?"

The mother looked down in shame and it was a long time before she spoke again. "The next day, the militia arrived. Our own people. We thought that they would help us. But no. They took all the young men to the far end of the village. My husband was old. So they let him come with me. With the other women, and the children. They would not let him take anything from his workshop. He had to leave behind his tools, his plane, his chisels, everything. How can a man live without a trade? What can he teach his sons? The chief soldier told him that his chisel was a weapon. How can the thing that puts bread in the mouths of our children be a weapon?"

"Mother." Yeshua's hands tightened around her fingers. She was shaking, and her breath came in heaves.

"He dragged me to one side, the soldier. When it was over, he let my husband take the donkey from the field. Then they drove us out. They told us we were to go to the south. My husband helped me up onto the beast. The pain when I sat upon the back of the beast. I shall never forget that pain. Never. Do you understand? He had no idea where we would go to that night. He was an old man, driven out from the soil of his people."

Mother Mariam fell silent. I looked at her. It is impossible to tell the age of a peasant. She could be thirty or she could be seventy.

Yeshua leaned across the table.

"We spent ten years in Egypt. Ten years! With twin boys. Do you understand what that means for a family of the soil?"

I looked back at his eyes. They were blazing with anger. The mother looked down at her hands, still enclosed by her son's. Yes, I thought: I know exactly what that means. When I spoke it was to her, not Yeshua.

"I can remember the day that the soldiers came to us in Kerioth, when the old king died. I was seven years old. My family hid in the synagogue. Bad choice. It was three days before anyone came to pull out the dead. Eventually, they found me. I was curled up beneath my parents' bodies. My mother and my father had been protecting me."

She raised her eyes and looked at me. There was a look of shared horror. A long, dreadful keening welled up from her throat and her hands broke free from her son's grasp and began rhythmically smacking the sides of her head. Her son took her hands and grasped them more tightly within his own.

"Mother," he said again.

That's it, I thought. I'm in.

I looked at her. "Take it," she said, and pushed the certificate of descent into my hands. "He will need this. Won't he? When his time comes? It will tell them that he can be king." I looked at her again. For the first time, it occurred to me that she could not read it. The peasant's incomprehension and awe of written documents. She knew that they were important, but had no understanding of why.

Well, I thought. Give this to our good friends and they'll conclude that your son's a seditionary, that he wants to proclaim an independent monarchy. And there's only one way they'll deal with that.

"I'd better take good care of it," I said to her.

She disentangled her fingers from her son's embrace and reached out to me.

"Thank you," she said. "You are a good man. My son, he trusts you. You will not fail him. I know you will not fail him."

*The pedigree, when the time comes: all you need do is give
it to our good friends and explain what Davidic descent means.
Evidence of seditious intent to proclaim a monarchy without the
authority of Rome. They'll not waste any time.*

*Later, in the boatyard office, Yeshua came up to me. He was
carrying a hemp bag full, judging by its weight, of Tyrian silver.
"She's given me these. She was keeping it for my sisters. Enough
to carry on the work we started with the Baptiser. Enough to last
us."*

"Till when?"

He grinned. "Until none of us need it any longer."

"Yeshua," I said, as quietly as I could.

"Yes?"

*"Your mother. How old was she when all that happened to
her?"*

*"She thinks she must have been twelve years old. As far as
she can remember. She knows that it was two Shabbats past her
betrothal to my father."*

Finally, deep in the night, I fell asleep, and the dreams came. I stood
upright in a narrow room with dark red walls, though I knew it was
not the room in which I slept. I looked, and saw my Zenobia, sitting
on the bed, her shoulders bare, the deep red cloth of her Damascus
cloak thrown back. She was giving her breasts to our Benjamin on
the right and Eleazar on the left, and she rocked gently backwards
and forwards as they sucked. I looked at her and she closed her eyes,
her head tilted back, the sound of a sonorous humming coming from
her throat. Then the babies cried out. I looked down. Benjamin's
mouth had come away from the nipple, spilling drops of milk across
my beloved's skin. Eleazar's hand reached out, the red thread of the
first-born still wrapped around his wrist, and clawed at the air. A
light, treble keening of grief and agony came to my ears. They were

screaming. I looked down again and saw the skin of their arms and their backs began to slough off from their tiny bodies, in moist scales. They breathed in and the screaming began again. More skin, more scales, fell from their flesh. Now the legs and the feet, now their heads and lips and nose, now their bellies and their loins. My boys looked back at me, their features convolved into tiny masks of pain, their exposed flesh glistening unprotected in the agony of the air. They breathed in, barely paused, and the screaming began again.

I tried to look into my beloved's eyes but I saw only the red darkness of the room. Then I awoke, bolt upright, and the screaming still sounding in my ears was my own.

BEZETHA
2ND DAY OF THE WEEK,
FIRST LIGHT

Before dawn I slipped down to Nico's courtyard and sat on the bench that gave a view across Bezetha to Mount Zion. The stones were beginning to glow with that soft yellow tone that morning light gives the city in spring. I re-opened the satchel that contained Yehuda's despatches, and read on. The next report described what happened when they went back to Nazareth.

> *The homecoming went badly. The eyes in the street: long stares. First, bewilderment and memories half-stirred, then slowly the recognition. And the moment at which the stares turned into something else: the timber merchant's son, the one who couldn't make his claim to the family business stick, come home again with some new friends. By the time that Shabbat came and we went to the synagogue, there was enough hostility in those eyes to make any other man think better of it. But he went ahead. Before it all started, I was waiting at the synagogue door.*
>
> *"I know," he said, "but I want you to come inside for once. Support me." Another test. I could not refuse.*

The arguments came soon enough. Then the shouting, and the raised fists. It was Yehuda-the-Twin who made the suggestion to me. "The door," he hissed. "Now. Help me get him out." Our leader was surprisingly reluctant to move. In the end we had to manhandle him outside. Then there was neither doubt nor argument: we ran. And ran. The shouting took a very long time to recede. It dawned upon me, when the first of the stones hit the ground to my left, that they were actually running after us. So we ran too. Predictably, Shimon-the-Rock was in the lead. Yakoub-the-Thunderer yelled out in pain. Finally, when my chest was aching and my legs felt like water, we all simultaneously came to a halt, bending down, panting agonised, visions of oblivion in our eyes. A final stone raised dust fifty paces back. We were still panting. We stared at each other, not quite believing that we were all here. I looked back towards the village: Nazareth was a distant haze of brick, mud and canvas awnings. What a shithole, I thought. Full of peasants. It was Thaddeus bar Ptolemai who broke the silence.

"I say. Just wondering. But aren't we almost a Sabbath day's journey from where we've come? Just to let you know."

We're stuck here, I thought. Unable to move on. Unable to turn back. And it's not even noon. I squeezed my water-skin, and it sagged. We turned and looked at our leader.

He stared into the dust, in that way he has when he's thinking, and then he looked up at us, smiling in that sweet, playful, clever way.

"Shabbat was made for us, lads," he began...

Whether it was made for us lads or not, it was the women who rescued us. Mother Mariam and young Salome: we saw them from far off, walking across the broken ground. They brought us goatskins. Mother Mariam dropped them at his feet.

"Running away. Is that what I taught you?"

Then another papyrus.

The money has gone, more quickly than I'd imagined, on food and drink. It's not simply the poverty: the boats can't afford anything but to sell the fish they catch to the sauce-makers. They can't afford fish sauce themselves, of course – that goes down to the coast for export – and bread is still just about cheaper than fish or else they'd eat the fish themselves. It's the rest of the countryside that can't afford food and is falling sick. So he announced a distribution of food. Would people donate bread? The crowds that came to us were, for the first time, unmanageable. He couldn't speak to them all, let alone control them. Not enough donated food – stale bread and the remains of someone's catch that the sauce-merchants had thrown away. Yeshua turned to me and this time there were no smiles. "Yehuda," he said, "time for you to astonish us all." It could have been worse: he could have invented some new nickname or asked me a riddle. "Leave it to me, boss."

The shopkeepers down in Magdala saw me coming, but I cleaned them out of every scrap of leaven and cured fish I could find. By the time I was done prices had doubled and the purse was light. I had to hire a herd of donkeys to carry the food down to the lakeside and half the crowd were out in the water. I was greeted with cheers and applause. Then the distribution.

It ended badly, of course. We fed everyone. Yeshua was delighted. "They'll expect this every week now," I told him. He laughed. "Of course they will. And we'll give it to them."

"Boss?"

He laughed again. "You'd better find some more fish."

Then the family arrived. Bad move. Mother Mariam, Salome, young Yakoub. Mother Mariam, incensed.

"You've brought shame on me," she told him. "I didn't give you family money to throw it away like that. On what? On peasants."

It was little brother Yakoub who tried to make peace. "God enjoins charity, mother."

She could not bring herself to rebuke the boy. Yeshua laughed. "Then I'd better find myself another family." Gasps, and then silence. Yehuda-the-Twin held the old woman as she began to weep. "Shame on you, shame on you."

"Come on," said Yeshua, "we'd better go across the water. They'll want us there."

That was when I understood he really is serious. Whatever he's expecting to happen will change everything. There'll be no return. Not to Nazareth, not to Magdala.

A long gap in time, then another debrief of Yehuda when Yeshua and his followers came to Jerusalem for the festival of Sukkoth. Things were different.

Now we are armed. We have a sword. He performed another cure two days ago. This time I witnessed it myself. A young girl, perhaps seven or eight years old, daughter of a soldier. He's a centurion, retired with full honours from the Syrian legion. Married a local girl when he was garrisoned at Caesarea and converted to the faith. The house is five doors from the end of the village of Nain, on the west side.

His approach is the usual method for any country healer or rural magician. He leaned over the corpse and looked at it for a very long time. Then he touched the body. There was a moment of silence and shock at the deliberate act of defilement. Then a gasp from the girl's father and wailing from her sisters and her mother. He laid himself flat upon the body, pinched the girl's nose, and breathed three times into her mouth. I shivered at the horror of this. We all stood back, disgusted. The touch and the proximity of cold flesh must have been a revolting thing to endure, but it was nothing to him. Then he breathed deeply and called out the name of God in a long, deep, agonised cry. The effect on those around him was extraordinary. We all felt a moment of intense awareness, our sense heightened and sensitive to the slightest movement or sound.

At last he stood up, leaned over the girl and called out her name. The centurion looked at him. The mother's eyes never left her daughter's face. Silence. Then the girl stirred, and her eyes opened. A cry of shock and wonder, half-strangled and amazed, came from her mother. Then the girl spoke, "I'm hungry," and chaos broke out.

Later on, when he was already quite drunk, the centurion brought out his sword. His elder son was sent into the hut and returned with it, wrapped in a length of oiled canvas. It was, very obviously, the most valuable object in the household. The soldier presented it to Yeshua.

Take it to the Temple, Yeshua told him. Use it to buy a lamb, and make your sacrifice of thanks. The centurion shook his head. It's yours, master. Take it. Sell it and give the money to the poor. Yeshua glanced at me. The centurion held out the sword. It was a terrifying piece of work, a real legionary gladius, and he had kept it bright and sharp. The sort of steel that the soldiers had carried when they came to Kerioth when I was a child.

Usually, he orders gifts handed over to me. But with this sword he hesitated, and you could see why. Yehonatan and Yakoub, the two thugs from the fishing boats, were eyeing the weapon with indecent need. You could see that there would soon be arguments over whose turn it was to carry it today. Then there would be an unspoken competition to see which of them would be the first to draw it on someone. Perhaps some idiot small-town teacher who failed to show their master sufficient respect. He looked across the table at the two of them and recognised the problem. Of course, if the centurion had two swords that he could give us the problem would have been doubled, not solved.

"Shimon-the-Rock," he called out. The old roughneck put aside his wine and walked round the table.

"Take it," said Yeshua. "And look after it for us."

The two thugs stared at their cousin with unconcealed loathing.

Shimon-the-Rock. Andros' brother. A roughneck and a blusterer, so the rest take their cue from him. The trouble is, when Yeshua's absent, even for a morning, Shimon tends to take his cue from whoever's spoken last. When Yeshua first addressed him as Shimon-the-Rock I asked Andros what it meant. He looked uneasy. Later, when we were alone, he told me. One winter's evening, years ago, Shimon had been at the helm of the family's best boat as they approached the wharf at Capernaum. There's a shoal there, a big rock that's well above the waterline. Everyone knows about it. Shimon had set his course straight for it. Andros and their father cried out. Shimon, the rock. Shimon, the rock! He held his course, oblivious to their cries. The boat foundered. The catch was lost. The next day, he went down to the boatyard with all the family's wealth around his waist, to ask Yeshua to lay down a new keel. And exactly why did his family need another boat? Yeshua asked him. This is an abiding source of ribbing and humiliation to him. And he's not a young man. To receive that from his younger companions is a shame he should not have to endure. It teaches him humility, Yeshua said, when I asked him about it. He takes an odd delight in giving them nicknames, just short of outright humiliation, but with such good-nature none of them – not even the Thunder Brothers – dare object.

They have a second sword now. Gift from another centurion, another convert. This one came to us on the road. An old bruiser. He had a scar across the left side of his neck that ended at his ear. He told us his child was sick. He looked at Yeshua, who said nothing. The silence went on until it became an embarrassment. Andros-the-Man fixed his eyes on the dust between his feet. Yakoub *and Yehonatan looked at each other. Bar Ptolemai watched him. Then Yeshua looked up to the sky and let out a moan of quivering agony and distress. "Go," he said at last. "Your child will be well. She will be well." The man breathed out in a deep, vibrantly mournful sigh. And he turned away from us. He was weeping.*

The sword arrived in the hands of a slave later that afternoon. We never saw its previous owner again. He was, the slave told us, celebrating with his family.

"Tell your master to give the thanks and offerings that the Law prescribes," Yeshua told him. But he still took the sword. Another gladius. Another family treasure.

The effect upon Yakoub and Yehonatan was pitifully obvious: this was their turn, wasn't it? Now that we have two swords, each will have his own. He'll tell Shimon-the-Rock to surrender his to Yakoub. Yehonatan will have the new one. Of course he will. I've never seen two men more thwarted, more agonised in their disappointment. They dared not contradict him. He's taken to teasing them. For anyone else this would be a dangerous business, the only outcome violence. Children of Thunder, he's started calling them. Their anger at the state of things consumes them. They act as his muscle, his protection. If anything, they're closer to his person than Shimon-the-Rock and Andros-the-Man. Some of the time they're closer to him than I am. You can understand why he'll not give them arms: they'd be cutting people to pieces within a winter-hour. But he'll need them, one day. And we all know that.

Andros-the-Man got the second sword. The brothers glared: there's something that goes back to childhood here, or perhaps some disagreement years ago on the boats. They'll never be satisfied. Andros makes a hash of strapping the buckler round his waist. They're on to him immediately.

"He's not confident, is he?" (Yehonatan)

"Never handled a blade for anything other than gutting fish. And that's women's work. You can tell." (Yakoub)

"Ignore them," I said to him. And for a while, he did. It was late in the afternoon when they started again. This time, a confrontation. Yakoub to Shimon-the-Rock. Yehonatan to Andros-the-Man.

"You're never going to use that thing, are you?"

"We can tell. You'll not know what to do, will you?"

"When the moment comes."

Shimon-the-Rock stirred at last, and you could see the speed of his anger.

"And what moment would that be?"

"The one he's promised."

"Promised us."

"Us, Shimon. Promised us."

It's an oddity of the two brothers that Yakoub, the elder, is just a little slower than Yehonatan. He's an echo and a reinforcement of all his brother's words.

"And what is it that you two think you've been promised, exactly?"

The Thunder Brothers look at each other. There's some doubt. What, I wondered, has he said to them when they're alone? Behind me, I could hear footfalls in the dust. Shimon and Andros did not look round. We were all waiting for what would come next.

"You'd not have the courage, would you, to use that in the way you should. If the High Priest himself was standing here in front of you."

"And what, exactly, would you do?" asked Shimon. "If you ever had this in your hand? Which you never will."

"Don't you know?" said Yakoub.

"I'd cut him," said Yehonatan. "That's what. Cut off his ears and send him back to his palace carrying them in his hands."

"And you think that's what we should do?" Shimon asked them. "Has he spoken to us about this? Has he? Ever? Have we heard those words on his lips?"

"*We heard it from the Baptiser. Didn't we, Andros?*"

"*He told us how in the old days King Antigonus stopped the high priest Hyrcanus from making the sacrifices.*"

"*Don't you know? Antigonus called him into his palace, had him put in irons and then he got his sword and he cut off Hyrcanus' ears.*"

"*Cut 'em right off,*" said Yakoub smiling and nodding. Then he looked at his brother. "*Why'd he do that, then?*"

"*Why did he do that? You don't know the Law, do you, eh? A high priest's got to be perfectly formed. That's what Moses told us, isn't it? Perfectly formed.*"

"*What, perfectly formed – like Thaddeus bar Ptolemai, you mean?*" he said so quietly that I barely heard the words. They glanced at each other, grinned in a shamefaced way, and then looked up at the Rock and the Man.

"*I don't think that our friend Shimon-the-Rock has got what it takes to use that sword the way it's supposed to be used, do you? When the time comes? When he gives us the word. In Jerusalem. In the Temple. Do you? Eh?*"

Then he looked beyond me, a frown on his face. The sound of footsteps squirming in the sand behind us. I turned, expecting to see Yeshua, come to silence them with a word, the way that he always does when this sort of thing happens. But it was bar Ptolemai. Perhaps he had heard his name mentioned, and wandered over? Yehonatan's frown creased into a reassuringly modest smile.

"*All for your benefit, priest-boy. When the time comes.*"

He's paired us up and sent us out, six partnerships, on a mission to the lost sheep of the nation. Partly, it's in practical response to the problems of the last month: the crowds are now unmanageable. They're forcing their way into the houses where we stay; he's taken to addressing them from a boat off the shore of the lake. This *hasn't stopped them from swimming out to us: two men drowned last week, and Shimon had to haul a child out of the water. Suddenly, nobody in Galilee seems to be doing anything but coming out to the lakeside and listening to what he has to say. That'll change come harvest time.*

And he has chosen. Shimon-the-Rock and Andros-the-Man, obviously. Yakoub and Yehonatan, the thugs: nobody else would wish to be the companion of either one. There's the inevitable argument about whether Shimon and Andros should be taking both the swords with them. It's decided with anger: he commands them yes. The Thunder Boys show no sign of shame. The rest of us are shaken: there was no playfulness in his command. It was genuine rage, to the core of him. We move on: Yehuda-the-Twin with Yakoub his younger brother. It is made clear to the Twin that he's expected to ensure no harm comes to the boy. Phillipos and Levi: that's clever – a radical alongside the most compromised and conventional of us all. The other two: they'll make up in enthusiasm what they lack in intelligence. The message will be safe with them. Repent: the kingdom is at hand. But whose kingdom, exactly? He's been surprisingly sketchy about what the kingdom will actually be – so far. It's something he's deliberately keeping from us, I'm certain of it. He'll speak when he decides that we're ready. Last of all – I get Thaddeus bar Ptolemai. Envious looks from some, relief from others. The priestly posh-boy goes with the money. Stick with him, Bart, said Phillipos. Make sure he gets you good scoff and a decent bed. The rest of them stirred and grunted. Then he stood up and addressed us.

"You'll each carry no more than a day's food with you," he told us. "You'll take lodging with the people you speak to. You'll rely only upon their charity and their goodwill."

Yehonatan and Yakoub looked at each other. They were going to have trouble sustaining the good will of anybody they encountered, and they knew it.

Then he addresses me.

"Yes, master?"

"Give me the purse."

I untie the bag from my belt and hand it over to him instantly. A full account, from memory: 13 Tyrian shekels, 25 denarii, 36 obols and copper coins. 18 sesterces with Caesar's image on them. A handful of Babylonian chalkoi. 13 Parthian coins of various incomprehensible denominations. At least one that I've never seen before, small and bronze. From Africa, I think. It seems that we are in good health, financially. Though most of this is already marked for distribution to the poor, the bereaved and the infirm. "Thank you," he says. "You've looked after it well." I feel lighter on my feet already, the weight of the purse gone. The rest of the followers relax. Glances are exchanged. At least I'll not be running off with the funds. But it doesn't stop Shimon and Andros clutching their swords as if, after all, they might be the next ones called to surrender.

Afterwards, I asked the question that none of the rest had dared to put to him. "What are you doing?" I said. "While we're on this mission?"

That smile again, confident, but also completely disarming in its self-effacement.

"I'm going to Sidon," he said, "with Mistress Mariam and the boy. Family," he added, as if this explained everything.

An odd thing: he always refers to her by that name and title when he speaks to us of her.

Another question. If I didn't know now, I never would. It was then or never.

"Master – when it comes, at the end, the day that the world comes to Mount Zion for judgement and Elijah comes down from heaven. What about the dead?"

Silence.

"The dead who died in holiness?"

"What do the sages tell us?" he asked at last.

"They… they say that the righteous dead whose bodies were broken for their beliefs, their bodies will be remade by the Almighty, in physical perfection."

"And?"

"And they will be brought back to us, to live righteous lives."

We walked on in silence. At last, we squatted down and we prayed together. It was only much later, when we walked back, that I realised he had told me nothing new. I had told him his own words, while I was looking elsewhere.

It's the optimism that I find unbearable. The insouciance. The lack of care. The trust.

He made us draw lots for our missions. Much complaining from the usual quarters. Suggestions that the lots have been rigged: Thaddeus bar Ptolemai the priest and I have drawn the northern part of Idumea, well away from the others. So, we set off to the south: three days' journey and our own wits to feed and house us. Sorry, the charity of our nation. We step as lightly as we may. After a morning on the road we pause and look back. Something cold grips my bowels and I look across at my companion. There is something not quite right about his relentlessly optimistic demeanour. Too keen to ingratiate himself with Yeshua by imitating him.

The village we came to was a snug, opulent place, a sudden green slash on the fringes of the desert. Water, and a grove of balsam trees by a stream. The synagogue a brown mud-baked block at the centre of the street. None of the buildings were made of anything other than mud and reeds, but still it looked far too prosperous to greet us with any enthusiasm. We need a slightly desperate poverty for the message to stir hearts. At least we do in Galilee. But here they listened, they understood, and they opened to us.

At the Shabbat meeting, the president of the synagogue asked bar Ptolemai to read from the Prophets. To proclaim the favourable year of the Lord, to comfort all who mourn. While he spoke, I looked down at the faces. It was hope that filled their eyes, need and hope. Hope that we were there to, in some way they did not yet understand, set everything about their lives right, and make all things the way that they should be. I could reach out and wring it from the air between us. And we gave them back their hope, we filled their need. Repent. For the Kingdom of God is upon you. And we are its messengers.

These, I thought, are the first signs of crossing the river. Our Yehuda becomes a true follower of Yeshua, whether he wishes it or not. His observations become less precise; he begins to omit matter that may be important.

Afterwards, hope is transformed into adulation. We are welcomed into houses. Whatever they have, however inadequate, is ours. We come in the name of God. I begin to understand how Yeshua must feel when he has spoken to the crowds and they surround him with their pleas, their needs, their adoration. It is a far more dangerous intoxication than anything you endure at Purim. He cannot experience this and remain the same man as he was in the boatyard.

At the meal, someone came to us. An old man, leaning on a stick.

"Brothers," he said, "my wife is sick. Very sick."

"My friend does the healing," bar Ptolemai told him. "I just speak to the people."

I looked across at him. There was no possibility of escape. So I turned to the old man and put on my best open-hearted, optimistic smile, the way that I'd seen Yeshua do it. An instant transformation, so quick that even I could not see the join. The old man, deep in his fear and need, was convinced there and then.

His own house was a squat mud block at the end of the street. To my horror, the crowd followed. I indicated bar Ptolemai must remain outside and to my relief he squatted down in the dust. Outside, I heard the press of bodies scraping against the mud wall.

The woman was sick to the point of death, that much was obvious, even in the light from the clay lamp. She was woefully frail and her eyes were an absence. Her lips sucked over sunken teeth. What was she dying of? Everything, I suppose.

"Lie down, mother, rest for a moment." I helped the old man to lie her down on the mud floor and cover her with a ragged fleece. She breathed more deeply for a while and then opened her eyes. They were vacant still. I leaned over and looked straight back at her. What, I asked myself, would Yeshua do? What could I do? I had spent much of my life up to that moment trading upon being something other than myself. And it had saved my life on many occasions. Why should this be any different? There was no avoiding the act. I had to do something. Anything would do. And everything would fall short. So I leaned more closely, brought my mouth to hers and did what Yeshua would do. I closed my eyes, breathed as deeply as I could, and spoke the holy name of God, as deep and sonorous as I could, into her mouth.

The old man wailed in horror. At last, I opened my eyes. The woman was staring at me. Her eyes had cleared. She was staring with an intensity that was part shock, part overawed ecstasy. Then she grasped my arm and began to pull herself to her feet. The old man's wailing stalled and began again. He was in a sort of ecstasy too.

"They must see her," he said. "They must see."

They'll see her die, I thought. Much better to tell her husband to say the prayers ordered for a return to health and leave as *quickly and quietly as we could. But her husband was beckoning. "We must," he repeated. "We must." This trust in whatever I had done was written on his face. And then I realised: this must be the most wonderful thing that had happened to him in his entire life. His was the face of someone whose prayers had been heard by God. And I had done it. We opened the door. The crowd fell silent and after a moment people began to fall to their knees. This is what it must be like for him, I realised. How can he remain in possession of his own self when people react to him like this all the time? This once was enough to shake me utterly. How could Yeshua possibly endure it day after day?*

"She'll not last the week," I told Thaddeus bar Ptolemai. "You do realise that?" Next day. We had left the village early, at my urging. Our knapsacks were stuffed full of offerings from the villagers. Bread, fruit, dates, dried kid's meat. We walked on.

"Did you know? That you could do that?"

I looked at him as if he was a madman: half fear, half pity, all understanding.

"I did nothing. Don't you understand? Nothing."

"But it was just as he told us it would be. It worked. It actually worked. The man's belief healed his wife. His belief in us. In you."

I looked away. It seemed to me far more likely that the woman had found the strength for one last rally and that the attention I had paid her and her husband's expectations had forced her to leave her bed. Tomorrow that last rally would be the death of her.

On the last night, after we had eaten and prayed, bar Ptolemai asked me:

"What do you talk about, when you are with him?"

I had to admire the sheer nerve.

"We pray," I said.

"Money, I suppose? Who has given. How much they have given. How our funds are to be distributed among the poor, the widows, the orphaned."

I grunted. I could tell him exactly how much had been given to us, by whom, when and where; and how much we had given away, to whom, where and when, from the ledger of my own memory. Down to the last clipped copper obol. But I wasn't about to do so. I could also reassure him that as Yeshua's treasurer I was not becoming rich. You don't with this sort of religion. Unlike the priests.

"Of course," he went on, "when the time comes, you'll have the Temple treasury at your disposal, won't you? Think what you could do with that."

This genuinely astonished me. It was the sort of stupidity that you would expect from the two Sons of Thunder. Coming from someone sophisticated as bar Ptolemai it was a shock that reduced me to a wary silence.

"We talk of the folly of the priests," I said, as evenly as I could. "That's all."

We met him and the rest of our fellows down by the river the next day, at the cave that the Baptiser once used. The air within was chill, and we huddled together in the damp. It seemed a melancholy place for a reunion. As if we had come to an ending and were looking back.

The others had fared far better than bar Ptolemai and I. I deduced from this that the name Yeshua from Nazareth and the message must already be well known throughout Judea, Samaria and the Ten Towns. Only Yehonatan and Yakoub had failed to gather any kind of support. We looked at each other when they told us about the idiocy and dullness of the people in Gaulanitis. Of course, they may have been uniquely unfortunate in their given territory.

Yeshua was subdued. Not the happy receiver of the good news of our travels that we had expected. After prayer he took me outside and led me deeper into the hills. It was dusk. A dangerous time – wild animals would be about. I could feel the eyes of the followers on my back as we vanished into the twilight.

We knelt and prayed the prayer together. A long silence. Then he spoke.

"They want me to stop, Yehuda."

"Who do you mean?"

"The family. They want me home. They want me to provide. To teach little Yeuda the Torah, to teach him a trade, to teach him to swim in the lake."

This must be Mistress Mariam. It hardly seemed likely that his mother and his brothers would try to persuade him a second time.

I said nothing. I could hardly offer him advice on being a father to his son. I looked up into the night air and shivered, then I closed my eyes. Perhaps I gave him the impression of looking to the hills or the heavens for help.

"Yehuda," he said, "I rely on you. You organise me. You raise money, give out charity. You find a roof for our heads and bread and wine for our bellies. Every day."

"Our Father in heaven," I said, "is the one who provides. It's him you should trust."

"He provides for us through you, Yehuda."

At last, the smile and the open, easy beguilement is back. For a moment I think that he is going to say something excessive, the way that he does, to tell me that he has decided that I am acting as some kind of messenger from the Almighty. He is staring at me in an intent, inquisitive fashion, searching for something.

"None of this would have been possible without you," he went on. "So I ask myself: my friend Yehuda – what would he do? Would he go on?"

That really is a stupid question to ask a man with no children, no father, no mother, no family or friends but the Service that he works in, none but the control he serves.

I realised that I could end it there. I could tell him that he should go back to Magdala and build boats on his slipway. Take his plane and his saw and his plumbline and his labour. Teach his child a trade. Love his wife and make more children with her. The way that any good man would. Go up to Jerusalem three times a year. Keep Shabbat. Grow wise. Grow old.

I groaned. He looked sharply at me. I had only to say it. The Service would thank me. A dangerous man turned deftly into the way of silence and a blameless life. Another danger made harmless. I looked down at the ground between us. Finally, I looked up and met his eyes. What should Yehuda do?

"Master," I said, "you told us that at the end of the world, when Elijah returns to us and the Almighty begins his kingdom, the people of the world will come to Jerusalem. And the dead, our fellow Jews who died for their faith, will return to us, their bodies restored."

He looked straight back at me.

"Is this true?" The question direct. This time he made no effort to turn it.

"It is."

I stared back at him for a long time in silence.

"Take me with you," I said at last. "I want to see your rule begin."

And I want to see my parents.

The account ended there.

It had happened, even to him. Our Yehuda had crossed the river, for an illiterate magician from Galilee. I dropped the papyrus into the satchel, lowered my eyes, and stared into the dust.

"Lord Solomon?" Cassiel bowed before me.

"Shalom." I indicated that he should sit. "How is my wife?"

"She is in good health. And she sends you this." He laid at my feet a satchel: three cotton tunics, two pairs of leather sandals and a second cloak, much lighter than the Parthian cloak I had taken in such haste the previous day, its lining neatly sewn with pockets and pouches.

"This too," and he handed me a papyrus with the wax impression of our vineyard's seal. Within, in my beloved's own hand:

Be back in three days, my sweet, or not at all. Z.

"Is there a response?"

"No. No response." I screwed the papyrus into a rough ball and tossed it into the satchel. "Take this, if you please," and I handed him the satchel full of despatches. "Keep it safe for me. I am old, and it is heavy. And I can't have you carrying a parcel full of my clothes around, can I?"

Nicanor and his slaves were at the front of the house, preparing the litter for his daily procession down to the Residence and the Antonia barracks.

"Duty calls," he said when I greeted him. "Examination of His Excellency's turds."

"How is he these days?"

Nico turned from the litter.

"Understand this, old son: Philo has not indicated to me that I should share information about the Prefect other than with him alone."

"As a favour? To an old friend?"

He licked his lips and wheezed softly. "I'm sure that I won't tell you anything at all. And what I don't tell you, you will not happen to hear. Strictly about the state of the Prefect's turds, that is."

"So how have they been for the last few days? Since Pesach? The Prefect's turds?"

"Angry. And his wife will want me to interpret her latest nightmares for her. She does keep on about them. I tell her I'm a man of science, not a charlatan, but she won't have it."

"Will Marcus be there?"

"He never misses the daily greeting."

"Then give him mine, will you?"

"I don't think that would be a wise thing for me to do. Not a wise thing at all."

"And what are you going to tell him, if he asks?"

"About yesterday?" He fell silent. "I was doing a favour for an old friend. An interesting case. That's all. Now, business." He waved to his slaves and eased himself gently into the litter. Azizus and his colleagues wilted.

"Prefect's Residence. And hurry."

We watched the little procession disappear around the corner at the bottom of the street.

"What are your orders today, sir?" Cassiel asked.

"Is there a good man among us?" I said. "Then let him go to Jerusalem."

At the Service office, Zev was still delighted by my return. The old days were coming back to us, he said. There would be a Herodian king again. I sincerely hoped not, but said nothing. Philo demanded news.

"What did you find at the scene? How did our Yehuda die?"

"Beaten, strangled, hanged. It's complicated. Do we still use poison?"

"Of course not. We leave that sort of thing to Herod's family. It's a woman's trick."

"Nicanor told me he found no sign, but cannot rule out that our Yehuda's killers may have used some new substance."

Philo frowned, walked back to the table's edge, and sat on it. His eyes focused on the wall of the memory box.

"The Herodians would have no reason to be involved in anything like this," he said at last.

"Nevertheless, I would like to question the household."

"Impossible. Now, or any other time. I can't send you over there while Young Herod's in residence on some kind of expedition. He'd have the High Priest down here within an hour, and that would be that."

I tried for a moment to imagine Caiaphas ben Ananas in his *ephod* with the Urim and Thummim jewels across his chest coming down the staircase into the Service's office.

"But you said that our Galilean magician had followers in Young Herod's household?"

"Let's see if we can find a more fruitful line of enquiry, shall we? Our man was murdered by people who have covered their traces. What do we know about Yehuda's movements before his death?"

"Nothing. Tell me, you had eyes and ears on the streets when I arrived. Were they out before Pesach too?"

"Yes. But in their usual numbers. We only swamped the city on Preparation Day."

"And over the double Shabbat?"

"Of course not."

No, of course not. At one time, when the Service watched over the city, it never slept.

"We must ask them if they ever saw our man between Preparation Day and the first day of the week. Any sighting at all. We've a city of half a million pilgrims. One man with red hair and freckles." In spite of his remarkable ability to fade into the background of any situation, somebody must have noticed him somewhere at some time in the two days of his life that were lost to us. "What were you expecting them to watch for, by the way?"

"What do you mean?"

"All those eyes and ears on the street. What were you expecting to happen?"

"Nothing good."

"But you were expecting something?"

"What are your next steps?" Philo stood up. "I have to go: meeting with the High Priest."

"He's aware of this case?"

"He knows nothing about it. And that's the way I hope it will stay. Special audience," he added with the slightest trace of satisfaction. I had attended those meetings, in the days of Caiaphas' father-in-law. They were interminably dull.

"Well, can you ask him to return the records of the Yeshua trial? That would be useful."

"Whom do you intend to interrogate next? How far off is the end of this investigation?"

"I want to find everyone that Yehuda may have spoken with between the operation in the olive grove and the potters' kilns. I'll start with the usual place, this afternoon."

"You think he went there?"

"Where else would he go if we had no plan to protect him?"

"Well, give her the Service's regards."

"And I want to talk to someone who witnessed the riot in the Temple last week."

"Why?"

"It was the last public action involving our Yehuda and his mark, and it convinced you to act. I'm sure we can learn something from that."

"Promise me you're not going to go off and try to talk to Young Herod's people?"

I reflected on this idea just long enough to irritate him.

"Solomon? Are you?"

"Let's wait, shall we? I'm sure I'll be kept busy enough without needing to involve them."

Micah the fetcher was by Philo's side. He greeted me with an enthusiastic grin and began loading scrolls into Philo's arms. "For the attention of the High Priest," he said. "These are the records that were asked for."

One scroll had the distinctive metal clasp of the Urim–Thummim series. The priests must be busy spying upon each other. Keeps them occupied.

"Report progress to me personally tomorrow," said Philo.

"The Yeshua trial records," I said. And he was gone, through the arch and up the inner stairs, to his special audience.

We found Saul at the side of the fullers' workshops, where the air was puffed up with the sour, clawing stench of vegetable dyes and their fixings. He looked away when he saw us across the sacks of madder roots and moved to hide the rope that he was carrying. He failed, convincingly.

"What have you discovered?" I asked him when we had greeted each other.

"Nothing. It's just standard builder's rope, the sort you'd find on any construction site. Nobody knows it for their own. Nobody remembers selling something like it to anybody other than their usual customers."

"And their usual customers? Who are they exactly?"

He waved northwards, towards the Temple walls.

"The masons and the carpenters, up there."

"And what about the twine?"

"None of them make anything like that," he said. "You don't need fishing line up in the mountains, do you?"

His anger at his failure was no surprise. In spite of the truculence and smarting, he really was keen to impress me. Time was the Temple Guard went into the marketplace to look for someone and people were practically arresting themselves and confessing to any crime you mentioned, they were so keen to help. Now we can't even find the right end of a piece of rope. What had he spent his time doing when he was liaising with our good friends? Did he ever find out anything useful at all?

"Give me the twine. You can keep the rope, for the moment." I slipped the twine into a pocket in the lining of my new cloak. "And don't reproach yourself. Your time's not been wasted. We'll come back to the murder weapons later."

"And what about the samples that Nicanor took? What about that murder weapon?"

"Our Yehuda wasn't poisoned. Nico is sure of it. He died of strangulation. The mystery is this: who put him there? And why?"

"What do you propose?"

"Have you eaten yet?"

"No." Well, he had been keen, then, to go through the market at this time of morning without food in his belly.

"Come and eat, then." And I indicated the covered way that led back up towards Mount Zion. "There used to be a place that you can get refreshment up there."

We found the little shop in the shadow of the Temple walls with trays of honeyed cheese arranged outside, the first bake of the morning, and sat down where we could watch the street, just beneath the sign that said "By the Curtain Wall" in Hebrew and "Curds and Whey" in Greek. Beneath it someone had scrawled "They make good cheese…" in Aramaic.

It was the place that Zenobia and I had visited, years earlier, the first time that we had arranged to meet out in the streets. A sullen girl in a dark robe brought us fermented milk, nuts and honey.

"We cannot discover anything about our murder weapon," I said to Saul and Cassiel, "But we can trace Yehuda's movements between the arrest of Yeshua and our man's death down in the potteries some time on Shabbat."

"Preparation Day, Pesach Day, Pesach Shabbat. Three days," said Saul. "Anything could happen."

"I have a suspicion about where he spent some of that time. But it's too early in the day to be troubling the people who can help us with that. Though they're usually well disposed to the Service and eager to please."

Cassiel caught my eyes and smiled at this, but Saul looked blank.

"We're going to question the man who was the last person that we know who saw Yehuda alive. I want to find out what he knows."

I should really have asked him about this the day before. Now his recollection of the details that would reveal to us some truth were a day less fresh, fitted together from their ill-remembered parts into something that he thought he should remember, not what he had actually seen and heard.

"Cassiel, make a record of this conversation, if you please."

I turned to Saul.

"Let us begin."

"What?"

"You were involved in the operation to arrest Yeshua under the guidance of our Yehuda on the night of 13th Nisan, weren't you?"

"I was. But—"

"Then the last person we know of who saw our man would be you. The Service needs your help, Saul. What you can tell us may be very important."

To my pleasure, he relaxed at these words. Hope returned to his eyes. At last he was going to be useful.

"Yes. I want to help. Let me tell you what happened."

I dictated the usual opening of a witness statement to Cassiel, speaking slowly at first but then more quickly as I saw how rapid he was in his transcription. Unusually for a former soldier, he had a small, precise hand in Greek letters that covered the tablet with ease.

"I am Solomon Eliades, charged to investigate the death of Yehuda from Kerioth. This is the account of Saul an officer of the Temple Guard, as told to me the 18th Nisan in the year 48 of the Temple's restoration." I turned to Saul. "Tell me in your own words, the events of 13th Nisan, what you saw and heard during the operation. From the beginning."

He fell silent for a moment. Then he stretched out his hands palms down upon the table, looked up at me and spoke.

"It was a little after dusk, at the beginning of the day, and I had just begun my duty with the night watch. There were twelve of us, in the barracks room on the north side of the Court of the Nations. An urgent message came that we were to assemble in the Service's office below. Lord Philo was there. The man with him was the one that I know to be Yehuda from Kerioth."

"Describe him."

"You could never mistake him. His hair was the most peculiar colour of red. Like the hero Achilleos' must have been. And he had freckles on his face and neck. His beard was an even darker shade of the same colour. Middle height. Broad face. No marks or disfigurements. A long-fringed shawl. He seemed very strong. Solid."

That was my Yehuda, as I remembered him. With hair like the hero Achilleos. Gone. Gone down to Sheol.

"How did Yehuda seem?"

"He was calm. Philo spoke first. Our task was to take into custody this Yeshua from Galilee, for his own safety. Yehuda would lead us to him."

"And how was Yehuda going to do that?"

"He told us that Yeshua and his followers would spend the first part of the night at prayer in a quiet place outside the city. He would take us there. Once in place, he would personally identify Yeshua for us. We would do the rest."

"How was identification to be made?"

"He would greet him and embrace him."

"Anything else?"

"No."

"Why was this personal identification necessary?"

"I'll come to that in a moment," Saul said with just the slightest return of the previous day's bumptiousness. "Yehuda warned us that the followers were armed. Two swords, he said. Carried by Yeshua's bodyguards. He would point them out to us. I asked Philo: what should we do? He smiled at this – they all did – and he said that he had made arrangements for assistance. They laughed."

"They?"

"The rest of the night watch. The day watch too. Some of them were still in the barracks at the end of their duty and Philo had ordered them to come down too."

"I don't understand. What did Philo fear?"

He did not answer. His comrades had laughed when he asked what they should do about two peasants armed with swords.

"We were issued clubs from the armoury," he said. "Every second man was given a naphtha torch. Then we filed out. Yehuda was in the lead with Captain Malchus. I was just behind them."

"Where did you go, exactly?"

"Down to the Kidron Gate. We halted just outside and waited for a long time."

"Why? What had gone wrong?"

"Nothing went wrong. We were ordered to break ranks and to sit down and wait. I moved a little way off, and I prayed. Then I looked across the Kidron to the opposite bank and wondered where Yehuda was going to lead us. They must be up there, somewhere. Then the soldiers arrived."

"What?"

"The soldiers. Twenty of them, with their officer. Swords, shields, torches. Backup. That's what they said."

This matched Quintus' account, but why had Philo not mentioned these soldiers to me? And the record on Yehuda's case scroll said nothing about our good friends being involved. There had been a long discussion about what to draw from the armoury. No mention of any backup.

"Twenty soldiers. And twelve of you from the night watch? That's a lot, to arrest one holy man."

"He had his followers. And they were armed."

"Of course they were. But you were expecting trouble?"

"No."

"Tell me about the soldiers. You've spent time liaising with our good friends, haven't you?"

"Oh yes. They were from the 3rd and 4th."

"So they were known to you?"

"No. I didn't recognise any of them. They weren't Quintus' men, from the garrison. They were the Caesarea boys. They'd come down with the Prefect last week."

"Now think very carefully. Were any of them Marcus' men?"

He looked at me and he understood why I asked. There was a moment's silence.

"No," he said. "I know who you mean, but they weren't there. All of them were regulars."

"Well done. What happened next?"

"We waited. Captain Malchus and their officer went down to the streambed. They talked for a long time."

"What did they talk about?"

"Couldn't tell you. Once or twice their voices were loud enough for us to hear. They were arguing. Malchus waved his arms about and pointed back to us."

"An argument before an operation. What did you think?"

"As far as we were concerned, Malchus was right, whatever it was about. He's a good man. Properly observant. That's why His Sanctity thinks so well of him."

"How long did this go on?"

"About... as long as you could say your prayers twice over? The moon had moved further over above the Temple wall."

"And then?"

"We moved off together. Night watch in the lead. The soldiers behind us. We went down to the Kidron, crossed the stream at the Beth-Anya road, then we climbed up the hill."

"What was the mood?"

The mood, he told me, was changed. Men fell silent and moved with care. Torchlight danced on their faces. At a gatepost on the left of the road, Malchus raised his hand and they came to a halt. Saul heard Yehuda's words. "He's close. Over there." He indicated a grove of olive trees. "The top end. By the wall. That's his usual place." Malchus turned round and pointed with his right hand and then waved ahead. Two men peeled off from each side of the group and vanished into the trees. The rest waited. Malchus gestured, his hands palm-side down. They dropped to the ground in silence.

"I remember the moonlight. There was a light wind from the south, blowing up the valley and a cloud moved across the moon. It was low in the sky by now. Suddenly, even in the torchlight, we could see each other's faces quite clearly. I shivered."

The scouts returned, whispered to Malchus and nodded to Yehuda. Malchus raised his hand and swept his arm upwards in an extravagant, all-embracing fashion. The men stood to.

"How did our Yehuda seem? What did he say?"

"Yehuda turned to me," said Saul, "and he handed me his torch. 'I won't be needing this,' he said. I took it and for a moment did not know what to say. Then he disappeared beneath the trees."

"What happened next?"

"We waited. At last the soldiers stirred and moved off into the trees: one group to our left, by the wall, the others to the grove above us. I was surprised by how silently they moved. Someone was going to be surprised. Malchus waved us forward."

He paused again.

"And?"

"Suddenly, we were there: an open space at the heart of the olive grove."

"How many of them?"

"Twelve. Thirteen if you include our man Yehuda."

"And did you observe him? How did he behave?"

Saul paused for a moment and drew his hand across his beard.

"He was calm. Matter of fact. It was almost as if you would barely notice him."

I smiled. Perfection. Slipping into the background and going unnoticed at the moment of crisis.

"Yehuda walked towards them. The two at the front faced up to him but he walked past them and for a moment it was as if they opened to him, the line of bodies parted. At the back of the group three men stood together. And what do you think? One of them was a priest."

"How do you know that?"

"I'll tell you in a moment. That wasn't the only surprising thing about the magician. Yehuda stepped towards the man on the right, opened his arms and embraced him. And that was the moment when I understood why we needed someone to identify the man we were going to arrest. It was extraordinary. I don't think I've ever seen anything like it."

"What do you mean?"

Saul put down his mug.

"Didn't you know?"

"What?"

He smiled at me again, that trace of self-regard in his knowledge.

"They were identical. Yeshua and the man who stood next to him. You could not tell them apart."

"But Yehuda could?"

"Of course he could. He went straight up to the man on the right, took his hands in his own, and he kissed him. He knew exactly what he was doing."

"And what did Yeshua do?"

"He returned his greeting."

"And what about the other one?"

"The priest?"

"No, the other man. The one who looked like Yeshua."

"The twin, he held Yeshua's right hand in his. It was a very strange grasp. As if the other man held Yeshua to restrain him, to keep him out of trouble."

"They were twins?"

"They were twins."

"Well, that explains the need for a personal identification from someone close to the subject. Twins. Do you know what that must mean in a place like Galilee?"

"What makes you think that I would know about a place like Galilee?"

"I've known sophisticated women in Jerusalem who've given birth to twins and their husbands – and they were educated men, philosophers – have been convinced that they've had the seed of two men inside them. Doctors reasoned with them night and day to persuade them that it was natural, something that happened in the course of nature and not a sign of betrayal." I paused and drank again from my mug. "And that was in a city like Jerusalem. What do you imagine must have happened to their mother? In a peasant village in Galilee? She'd be lucky to escape with her life. That's if the local synagogue was sensible and well disposed. And when was that the case in Galilee?"

Cassiel raised his stylus.

"Shall I take this down?"

"Yes."

"Can I go on?" Saul asked.

"Tell me about the priest."

"He was young."

"How did you know that he was a priest?"

"He was wearing linen. The way priests do."

"And what happened next?"

"We moved forward. The magician's followers drew in around him. One of them, a big roughneck with arms like timbers, turned Malchus round and slashed at his face with his sword. Malchus screamed – and then I saw him clutching the side of his head, with blood running down his arms. I wondered where the soldiers were – what had happened to them? At last two of the night watch laid hands on the magician. Then the soldiers arrived, more slowly than you would ever think possible, though the trees." He looked down at his hands and fell silent.

"Go on. Was that the end of the action?"

"Almost."

"And what happened to Yehuda?"

He shook his head and looked down again.

"Now there were soldiers everywhere. I took hold of him. By the shoulders. He stared at me, straight into my eyes. Fear. I saw fear in them. Nothing but fear. Then he was pulled away from me."

"Who pulled him away?"

"It was the young one, the priest with the linen robe." He frowned again and looked down. "That was the end."

"Are you sure?"

He looked up at me. The mug trembled in his hands.

"Saul, the Service needs your help. What happened next to our Yehuda?"

He said nothing, but shook his head once.

"Saul," I began again, more gently. "How did you get those black eyes? What happened?"

"Look," he said, "we obeyed our orders. We finished the task. But I..." and he fell silent.

"Yes?" I reached out my hand across the table.

"We took hold of the magician," he said. "Me and two of the watchmen dragged him away from his twin brother. Malchus was crawling away to one side, blood streaming from the side of his head. A soldier was shouting at the roughneck with the sword. He stepped backwards, but the sword was still in his hands. Then I fell to my knees. My head ached and my left eye felt like burning metal. I decided that I needed to stand up. I caught hold of the man in front of me. It was the priest. He grabbed our man Yehuda and threw a punch as he turned him round. I tried to push him away. Then there were soldiers, everywhere." Saul looked up at me. "I tried to protect our Yehuda. Believe me, I did."

"And what happened to him?"

"He vanished. Out into the darkness. I never saw him again."

"You are absolutely sure of that?"

"Of course I am. I was there."

And he was gone from out of our sight and care, vanished into darkness and heading to his death. Our Yehuda, gone from us.

"Thank you, Saul."

He slumped back into his seat and looked at the empty mug. I called the girl over and ordered more curds, and some honeycomb, for us all. We drank in silence. At last, I asked him.

"So how did you come by the black eyes?"

He looked defeated, emptied out of any fight or will or purpose.

"I don't know," he said. "It must have been the two bruisers. When I had hold of the priest."

"The bruisers? Who were they?"

"There were two of them. Big. Not as big as the one with the sword. They had the same look about them. They both had the same thick hands, the same low brows. Typical Galilean. They smelled of something, both of them. One of them hit me. I lifted up my arms. But they kept on hitting me."

He looked down again.

"Then I ran. I fell over Malchus. I caught hold of the priest again. I caught hold of his tunic and his shawl. He pulled away, and I heard the fabric tear. I kept on pulling, and he kept on running. Everything slowed down again. Someone hit me on my left cheek. I felt fists beating on my back. I pulled on the cloth, and the priest kept on trying to run. Then he was free. He ran off, naked, into the trees. So I picked up the linen and I ran after him. Away from Yeshua and his followers. Away from the two bruisers. I stood up, and I ran away."

Saul was looking at me, shame and disgust upon his face.

"I ran away. That's how it ended. I ran away."

He stood up, drained his mug and walked out of Curds and Whey. I stretched out my arm to Cassiel.

"Watch him," I said. "I'll follow."

MOUNT ZION
2ND DAY OF THE WEEK,
6TH HOUR

We followed him as he climbed the steps of Mount Zion to the Upper City and turned towards the Temple bridge. There were Service eyes by the western gate, watching pilgrims enter and leave. I had seen no other observers, not even at the messengers' post outside Caiaphas' house. We passed beneath the great cedar gates of the outer wall. Above us, sentries were encamped upon the Temple's curtain walls, which served as billets for the Damascus cohorts when they came to the city at festival time.

The Temple's Court of the Nations was in a state that I had never imagined possible. The merchants' stalls were a chaos of shattered timber, torn canvas and wrecked tables. Signs lay torn and trampled on the stone flags. The stalls by the western gate had rigged up temporary boards showing the prices offered for everything from silver sesterces to the Babylonian stater and Antiochan tetradrachm. The pigeon, flour and wine merchants were still in the shade of the southern colonnade. The pens of the livestock merchants were on the eastern and northern sides of the court. I gazed in wonder and confusion. This must be the wreckage of last week's riot, instigated by Yeshua and our Yehuda. Only one thing indicated that the normal daily life of the Temple really did continue amid the chaos: by the west side of the inner wall a group of duty priests were distributing to the poor the meat butchered from the pure white bull sent each day by the Augustus to be sacrificed to our God. Some of the stalls' billboards had the owners' names on them. "Open for business," said one in Greek. "As usual," said another in Hebrew, "still in business".

Saul went to the *mikvah* pool at the entrance to the Court of Israel, washed himself, and entered the great cedar doors, above which was written:

Only Jews are permitted within. Greek or foreigner, whoever passes within these walls, will only have himself to blame for his death.

I turned to Cassiel. "Let us not disturb his devotions. Give me the satchel; I'll read while we wait." And we settled down beneath the awning of an abandoned stall.

When we came to Lake Huleh, he asked us the question for the first time. We had spent the day on the road from Bethsaida and were exhausted. We were all there. Shimon-the-Rock. The two thugs. I was present throughout the conversation. Thaddeus bar Ptolemai followed us and lingered uninvited until Yeshua ended his misery and beckoned to him. The look of relief. He was in. He needs watching.

We crouched down on our heels, facing inwards.

"Who do men say that I am?"

Usually, when he sets us these conundrums the spark of playfulness is in his eyes, there's a sense of mischief. This time, he looked down at the ground and poked the sand with a stick, the way that he does. He was serious.

I looked at him. Yakoub and Yehonatan looked at each other. They had no idea what this was about. Bar Ptolemai was looking at me. The silence went on too long.

I spoke just as Shimon-the-Rock was raising his right hand in that irritating way that he has.

"They say that you are our king."

The brothers stared at me in astonishment. Bar Ptolemai's gaze never left me.

"… the One…" said Shimon a moment later and looked at me, the way he always did, as if he wished for praise or a reward for his agreement. "That's what they say," he added, "I suppose, like."

"And what do you say?" His eyes were dull and his face without expression. This question, even if it was something that he had rehearsed in his own thoughts, was costing him something unmanageable to ask us.

"Well, Yehuda?"

I looked at him. The others looked at each other. Shimon-the-Rock was staring at the ground as if it would give him the answer. Just before Shimon raised his hand again I realised, too late, that bar Ptolemai still had his attention not on Yeshua but on me. I spoke anyway.

"You are our king of Israel," I told him. On cue, Shimon-the-Rock's words fell into the dust.

"… the king…" he whispered.

Yeshua raised his gaze from the ground between his feet and stared at me. For the first time in days, he smiled. The rest of them were staring at me too. Bar Ptolemai longest of all.

Beneath this, the priestly hand had written:

This evidence has no value in law. What do we pay the Service for?

I turned to the next sheet.

The circle of those to whom he'll talk in private has shrunk still further. It is me. Alone with him. And he asks me the question.
"Am I him? The chosen?"
Not "Do you believe that…". The question direct. Am I?
So, of course, I told him.
There was silence between us for a long time after that.
Then, at last, he spoke again. And there was just a suggestion that his gloom had lifted.
He leaned forwards, placed his hand on my head, and asked me softly:
"Then, Yehuda, what is to be done?"
"Master?"
"When we began, people would ask me why this was done. What did I tell you to tell them? The blind see, the lame walk, the sick are healed. All this means that the Kingdom of God approaches. My question, Yehuda: what is to be done to bring us to that day? What must I do to make this happen?"
I looked at him. He was serious, so I responded as lightly as I could.
"Master, you told me once that it was sinful for us to tempt the Lord God. To commit an act that gives the Lord no choice but to intervene. It shows that we do not trust him as we should trust a father."
I could tell immediately that I had misjudged him and the moment. There was another long silence between us.
"I want you to help me, Yehuda, do you understand? I want you to help me with the work I must perform. To help me to bring about the kingdom."

The priestly hand had written beneath this:

Why are we employing the Service to produce this kind of nonsense? Evidence of blasphemy, or sedition. Where is it?

I am certain that a final deed is being prepared. The talk hasn't ceased since the business at Beth-Anya two days ago. He healed a man. The first healing that he has performed in months. We all thought that things were about to return to the way that they used to be up in Galilee. Folly. The man had been three days in the grave, when he brought him out of the tomb at the north end of the village. The stench was insupportable. Even for someone used to the smell of the fish-wharf at Magdala. And the man walked out of his own tomb. I saw this with my own eyes. It was not one of his conjuring tricks. The dead man lived. I cannot speak of this. It is beyond my ability to explain.

This was the man of whom Nico had heard. If we went to Beth-Anya, across the Kidron and up the hill, what would we find there now? We were supposed to be dealing with evidence here, a firm basis to protect the nation, not folk-tales and conjuring tricks. How could you conjure a dead man? If the High Priest had wanted to use Yehuda's account to condemn Yeshua on a capital charge of necromancy, of raising the spirit of a dead man back to bodily life, he could have done so without a second thought. But he had not.

He knew exactly what the effect of this deed would be. They came to us from out in the fields. By nightfall people were making their way up the hill and over Mount Olive to find us. They wanted to see the man who had died and then come back from Sheol. It was like the old days in Galilee. Crowds everywhere, and no space to move. If there had been a lake in Beth-Anya we would have climbed into a boat and rowed out above its deeps.

I talked to the man who had died. He was young. Of an age with Yeshua. What had Sheol been like, I asked him? He looked at me and there was horror mixed with pity in his eyes. The land of the dead, he told me, was dark and cold. Grey shadows bound him in. He had been unable to move. He had been scarcely able to think. Had there been others there, I asked him? Had his family been there, his parents? Had he seen his mother and his father? Surely his parents had been there? Had he seen them?

Perhaps I asked him the question with too great a vehemence. Perhaps he was still too terrified of what he had seen and heard in Sheol. He looked away from me and shook his head. "No," was all he said. "I saw no-one, do you understand? Not my father. Not my mother. Not my brothers." And he wept.

I turned away from him and looked across at Yeshua. He was staring at me with a look I had never seen before. There is something within him of which he will not speak. There are moments, at the end of evening prayers, when he sweats and cannot look at us, a look of horror and fear in his eyes. Philo: you need to understand – I cannot discover what is burdening his soul. But he intends something, something that is dark and full of horror.

This was followed by a further passage. Someone had written at the top:

Transcript of our man's interview of 11th Nisan. To be used, with care.

He came to me yesterday evening, in the courtyard of the sisters' house in Beth-Anya. We had just returned from prayer at dusk in the olive groves down the hill. His face was closed to me again, his eyes dull. His brows dripped sweat, though the evening was chill. He reached out and grasped my arm. He trembled when he spoke.

"Yehuda," he whispered, "I have to tell you what is going to happen."

"Master?" It wasn't a question that I asked, or an expression of bewilderment. I reached out to him, in pity and in love.

"When we go to Jerusalem—" He stopped and he looked me directly in the eyes. It was a look of torment.

"When I go there," he said, "the time will come." He paused and looked at me. "The kingdom," he said. "The kingdom is here; the kingdom is now. And I will bring it about."

"How?" And I thought of the man who had died, found Sheol empty, and came back to us from the land of the dead with nothing but silence and horror. "How will you do that?"

He took my arm.

"Yehuda, the occupiers of our land will not allow anyone the right to be king. They will kill anyone who proclaims himself. And that is what I intend to do."

The light of horror was still in his eyes, but there was a lightness to his words.

"What do you—"

"I want you to help me, Yehuda. None of the others will understand. You saw how they acted, heard what they said. You're the only one I can trust, to help me make this happen."

I looked away. He continued to talk to me, to tell me about what would happen at Pesach in Jerusalem. He really does believe that what he set out to me at the very beginning in Galilee – the Kingdom of God, here on earth, here in Jerusalem – is going to happen. In our time. This week, at Pesach. Elijah will come down to him, here on this very ground, and the rule of the just and the righteous, his rule, will begin on earth. We're not in Galilee any longer. We're not feeding starved peasants and curing the sick. He charmed and entranced us all with his words, until we were close enough to see what it meant.

"Will you do this?"

Of course. Give that pedigree to our good friends, the one he gave me for safekeeping back in Galilee. Did he know even then? Give it to them and they'll not hesitate.

My advice: take him into custody. For the whole week. I can arrange it for you. Easy as you like. Then send him back to Galilee. Nothing will happen, and his appeal will be shot. We can all go back to spending our time on some more serious threat to whoever's interests we're supposed to be protecting. I despair of this work. I despair.

Beneath this, a hand that I guessed to be Philo's:

What would happen? Nothing good, if you're one of our good friends?

Philo added, as if in afterthought:

Not to be shown to the High Priest or the court under any circumstance.

Yehuda went on:

Because, if there is any truth in any of his words, then there is nothing that you, Philo, the priests or the Prefect can do. Not the Romans and their army can stand in the way of God. Not the Temple itself can stand. The end of all things. When the people of the earth will come to Mount Zion and stand before God. If he is wrong, then his followers will desert him soon enough. But, if he is right, then there is nothing to be done by any of us. I can no longer serve any useful purpose. I want to be released, whatever the outcome. I wish to leave this posting. As soon as you've taken him into custody. For his own sake. I want to be released.

Beneath this, Philo:

Agreed. Get him out. First arrest and hold the Galilean. If no obvious danger, release after Festival. Threat discredited without disturbance. Best possible outcome.

And then the priestly hand:

Hopeless. We cannot use any of this. Possession? Impossible. If he
does not incriminate himself, then our only course is to release
him. Prefect's temper always short at Festival time.

At last Saul returned from the inner courts. Prayer had done him
good: he seemed at peace, his brows unfurrowed for the first time
since we had met. He even seemed prepared to tolerate my company.

"Are you ready to resume our investigation? Because there's a
contact of mine that you should meet."

Cassiel, Saul and I clambered up onto the wreckage of a stall and
surveyed the south-western quadrant of the Court of Nations.

"There's our man." A hand-written sign upon a broken pole.
IRAKLEIDES OPEN.

We descended the steps, climbed over the wreckage of beams and
ripped canvas, waited to let a group of Egyptians go past, then skirted
a pile of ruined brass scales, reed baskets and hides. Irakleides was
standing between two of his slaves, whose eyes were upon the line
of customers waiting to change their coin. In the past they had kept
wooden clubs beneath their tunics, ready to deal with complaints
about exchange rates. Today they openly held swords. One of them
had a wide gash on his forehead; the other a gleaming bruise around
his left eye.

"Leave this to me," I said.

We joined the line of pilgrims. Irakleides wore the great leather
girdle pouch slung around his waist, supported by two straps upon
his shoulders that crossed his chest and his back. The stamina of the
man was a wonder. Tyrian shekels in stacks of five in each of the
pockets along the straps. Pouches for the customers' currency at his
waist. The leather of the straps was more highly polished and more
deeply worn than when I had first made a friend of him.

"What will I get for ten staters?" I asked.

He sighed and then looked up at me.

"Shlomo? Try Perez's stall. Over there."

Then he stepped towards me and his voice softened.

"What can I do to help you, Master Solomon? It's been a long time."

"Seven years."

"You've not changed."

"It looks as if things have changed here, my friend." I indicated the slaves with their swords.

"The boys? New rule from the priests. It's all right to wear them in plain sight. We don't want another riot like that last one, do we?"

"I heard you had some trouble. What happened?"

"Best riot we've ever had, those Galileans last week. Didn't seem like it at the time, I can tell you. Can't speak against them. Not now. The High Priest's office says they'll pay for the repairs. In full. Send in the bill; they'll sort it out for you."

"Congratulations. That's very generous of them. Now, remind me, how did it all start?"

"Galileans, that's how it started."

"They're good for one thing," said Saul, and drew back. "That's nice stitching on that belt, by the way. The man who made that knows his craft." Irakleides and I looked at him in astonishment.

"My junior," I said. "He's here to help."

"I'm sure he is, Shlo."

"I heard it went on all day, this riot."

"They took their time, Shlo. They didn't just walk in here and start throwing punches. They went round every exchange, talking to all of us, asking about our prices, rates and charges. And how much for a new-season lamb, best Judean hills bred. That was what they wanted to know."

"And they came and asked you?"

"Course they did. Just before it all started. I'd seen them coming. Perez there came over in the second hour and told me what they'd asked him."

"And?"

"Just the same as everyone else. What rate for ten Tyrian shekels."

"Who was asking?"

"Their leader. The one who died. Tall lad with the long face and the forehead like a cliff's edge."

"Anything else?"

"He asked the lad next to him who was carrying a purse to take out a coin. He held it up between his fingers till it shone in the sun and he screwed up his eyes and took a good long look at it. Then he held it out in front of me so that I could see its face. And I thought, we're in for some conjuring now. This lad's reputation, he'll make this thing vanish and then he'll ask me for my purse and it'll turn up in the fold of my change pouch. Some sort of business like that."

"His friend with the purse. Describe him."

"He was an odd one. Red hair and freckles. Stocky."

"So, what happened?"

"He hadn't come to play tricks after all. Must have kept that for the peasants back in Galilee. He had two of his big lads about ten paces away on either side, keeping their eyes peeled for trouble from the Temple guards. Not watching what he was doing; they were keeping an eye on anyone trying to get close. Standard street con-artist's setup. They knew exactly what they were doing. They both had swords. Kept them under their cloaks, but you could tell by the way they walked. Another of his friends was right in front of him and looking backwards, behind him – he had his eyes on the soldiers up on the walls."

"What did he do?"

"He looked at this coin and he looked back at me. 'See, lads,' he says, turning to his friends, 'look at this coin here.' Then he turns to me. 'What's this on the coin?' he asks me. It's a Tyrian shekel, palm tree, of course, so I tell him. Wrong move. Suddenly we're not conjuring any more.

"An idol's image in the Temple," he says. "You take money from the poor and the widows. And what do you give them in return? You're bandits, the lot of you." And he throws the shekel at me. I duck and it hits the back of the stall. And that's when it all starts, the performance. He's kicking down the tables, his friends are pushing people away from the stalls, they're pulling the booths apart. He doesn't waste any time on us after he's pulled down the awning, he's off to Perez's stall and the rest of them down the south side of the court. It's a free-for-all. Jubilee's come early. Fill your wolfskin boots, lads. Half my best customers of the morning are piling in and helping themselves. Six months of stock's gone in the time you can say your morning prayer. If it wasn't for this" – he tugged the straps of the great money-belt with the palms of his hands – "I'd've lost the takings too and we'd be destitute, me and my family. I had to tear one of them off my chest and give him a kick. Little lad, curly hair. Then they moved on. The magician, the one they nailed up – quite right too, if you ask me – he was off."

"What do you mean?"

"He vanished. Clever trick. For a Galilean."

"How very convenient. And sensible. Where did he go?"

"Over there." Irakleides indicated the far side of the colonnade that led round to the wall of the Antonia Tower. "He stood up on the steps by the *mikvah* and he started talking to the crowd. Not that he got much attention. Over here it's still mayhem."

"And what about the short one? The one who attacked you?"

"The priest? He was joining in too."

"What do you mean, the priest?"

"He was a priest, this lad. He was the one encouraging them. The crowds, I mean. Not that they needed any of that."

"A priest, among his followers? Not the magician himself?"

"I told you, Shlo."

"You did. And he was encouraging them. Encouraging them to do what, exactly?"

"That's easy. After the magician had gone off to the north end to do his preaching, the priest-lad was busy leading them all from one stall to the next. He was telling them to smash the place to bits. Very polite, like. And would it be too much trouble if you smashed up this stall next? And holding their cloaks while they did it. And he was a priest. Never seen such a thing."

"How do you know he was a priest?" I looked round. The words came from Cassiel.

"He was dressed like a priest, wasn't he? Best Babylonian linen. It had seen better days, mind. Rough old state: looked like he'd been sleeping in the desert. But he was a priest all right. No doubt about it. Educated accent. Spoke Greek and Hebrew like a proper scholar. Not so keen on the things he was saying, mind."

"How would I know him, this priest – if I happened to see him?"

"I told you. He was wearing linen, like priests do."

"I mean his appearance."

Irakleides shrugged. "A small one, that lad. Very slight. Something deliberate about everything he did. Like it was rehearsed. Brownish hair. Thin cheeks. And he had a gash on his eyebrow."

"And you're sure he was a priest?"

"I told you."

"Marvellous," I said. "Thank you, Irakleides."

"Pleasure, Shlo. Any time."

"And didn't the Temple Guard put a stop to this?"

He looked at Saul. "Your lot were of strictly limited use, as usual. No offence, brother. No sign till it was all over and they turned up in time to knock some of the pilgrims on the head. The ones who'd been stupid enough not to get out of here with their loot."

"And how long did it all go on?"

"It went on all day. Till dusk. What do you think kept them from coming in and dealing with it, I'd like to know?"

"And what about our good friends…?" I glanced upwards to the soldiers on the colonnade. "Why didn't they march down the steps and knock heads together?"

"Funny you should ask that, Shlo – they did nothing at all. They sat up there in their billets and they had their breakfast. Porridge, apparently. Then they marched along the colonnade to their posts. Perfect spot to watch what was going on down here. And they stood and they watched."

"All day?"

"All day. The priest set the two lads with the swords and some of their friends to go and stand at the gates. Nobody was getting out. Nobody was getting in, either way. About noon, I see the Prefect's people turn up at the gate on the bridge and guess what happens?"

"Surprise me."

"The priest walks over to them, calm as you please, and has a word with the Prefect's man, who's standing there. And that was it. They all stand down and go back to eating their porridge. What were they waiting for, a message from Damascus? Rome or Capri, more like. Must have been good porridge that, Shlo."

"And what was happening down here by then?"

"The magician had gone up to the north end with a crowd of his friends. Perez reckons he was telling them that the world was going to end at Pesach." Irakleides paused and he looked away from me. "Well, we're still here, aren't we? And he's gone. All those friends of his – do you think someone was paying them to turn up?"

"What makes you think that?" Saul asked.

"I don't know, friend. Just a thought."

I looked at the wreckage of the stalls. I had, in the course of my work, witnessed unrest in many cities, from Alexandria to Babylon. Those experienced in the stirring of disaffection all know about the point of crisis: the day when their command of the streets matches the command of the magistrates. The centurions are not given their orders. Authority vanishes. There is anarchy in the city, and it is the work of the Lord. The soldiers do nothing. The magistrates flee. The people command the city.

"And his friend with the red hair and the freckles. What was he doing while all this was happening?"

"I told you Shlo, I don't remember seeing him after that first business with the shekel. He just vanished. I suppose he must have been over there listening to his magician friend telling everyone the world was going to end when Pesach came. Never saw him again."

"You're quite certain of that?"

"Of course I am. If you find him, you can tell him from me to come and help us fix the mess he left. Now that his carpenter friend's not around to help."

"I'll bear that in mind. Thanks, friend. Shalom."

"Shalom, Shlo. It's good to see you again."

I wished him well with his business when the booths were repaired.

"And if you do remember anything else. Anything at all. Especially about our friend with the red hair. Let me know, will you?"

We clambered back over the wrecked timber, Cassiel leading, Saul behind, and ascended to the colonnade where we walked between the double line of pillars, the sun on our heads followed by the cool of the shade in gentle succession.

"Nice stitching?" I said to Saul. "You're some sort of stitching expert too?"

"My people were tent-makers," he told me. "At Tarsus on the Orontes. My father sold hides and canvas to the caravans that passed through the city. He was the best. And there were a lot of caravans that passed through."

I was prevented from hearing more: a squad of our good friends sprawled between the pillars of the colonnade, stood down from whatever light guarding duties they may have been performing. They looked up at us and turned away. Then one looked back, and his eyes lit upon Saul's uniform.

"Temple Guard? Go on, then..."

They slouched and made a hand's-breadth wider space between the columns. We picked our way around them and I kept my eyes on their officer as we did. None of them returned my gaze. At last we came to the eastern end of the colonnade, and the high place of the Temple walls.

"I used to come here," I told Saul and Cassiel. "When I needed to reflect, to tease out the intricacies of a case. For some reason the view always helped. Of course, it was lower and less ornate in those days."

I looked down. Below us, the Kidron valley receded and for a moment the stream's waters seemed to rush backwards and the banks moved. Saul stood to one side and looked out across the valley.

"Show me," I said and pointed to the slopes across the valley. "Show me where you made the arrest."

"You mean the place where I failed to pursue a fugitive?"

"I don't think anyone would hold it against you that someone slipped away. Someone of no importance to the case."

"How can you be sure?"

"Perhaps the interesting question is why the followers of a rural magician from Galilee, even one who taught Torah and had ideas about the end of the world, should include a priest. We'll come back to that another time."

Saul reached out his arm as if encompassing the Kidron below us and indicated the sparse greenness of budding trees upon the lower slopes of Mount Olive and the road to Beth-Anya. I thought of Nicanor and his story of the dead man who had been returned to life there. We must go, I decided: we must go and investigate the case of the man who had come back to life, if only to satisfy our own curiosity, whether medical, legal or philosophical. Coming back to life: it was a trick of the old prophets. You didn't see so much of it these days, however much the enthusiasts for national destruction in the name of religion might wish for it and use it to encourage the uneducated. Our good friends, with their admirable efficiency, have ensured that it simply no longer happens.

The olive grove looked well set out and tended. The slope faced westwards and the trees would wait until late in the day to receive the full light of the sun. In the cool of the evening it must be a quiet pleasure to walk beneath the trees. I wondered how many *metretes* of oil its master must get from it.

"Who owns the olive grove?" I asked.

"I have no idea. But I will find out. Why?"

"Your squad and our good friends went onto the property to arrest a man. I thought the name of the owner might have been mentioned."

"No. I don't believe that it ever was."

"Never mind. A farmer's question, that's all."

"Oh?" Saul looked up at me.

"When I left the Service, I bought a farm up in the hills and set it to vines." I let that settle in his mind for a moment but it was obvious that he had never heard of Solomon the Oenarch. But he seemed eager, and this would be a moment to find some common interest or experience. Zenobia had learned in her former career that there was nothing men liked half so much as to talk about themselves.

"Did your father teach you the trade of wine-maker? I thought that you said that you were a scholar?"

"I was," I said. "And he did not. My people owned land in the Jezreel Valley. But I was the youngest son and there was no room in the family business, so they invested in a more than usually expensive education for me. Scholarship didn't quite work in the way that they hoped. Though I don't believe that I ever brought any shame upon them. Do you know what made me want to follow this trade? It was Pesach, in my eighth year. My family had assembled for the festival meal, here in Jerusalem. I was the youngest child present. So I knew what I had to do. I had to ask my family the question – *Why is this night not like other nights?* And they answered. At that moment, I knew what I wanted: to discover the truth about things. I realised that I could find out the truth, by the power of words and logic. It was Pesach, the festival of our liberation from slavery, that made me a detective. Years later, I studied philosophy for a short while in Athens before I took employment in the Service. I studied rhetoric too. Rhetoric and philosophy teach you the most important skill that you will ever need in this life: to discover the truth, and to recognise a lie. Beyond that, nothing matters."

"Nothing? But our Law is the only truth, the only good. You must know that. The Law of God is all we need to know or understand."

"Let me tell you something. I studied the Law too. When I was young, Old Herod awarded me a shawl of excellence for my scholarship. Meeting him was the most terrifying moment of my childhood. Of course, he was no judge of scholarship. Or of truth. Did you know? He had his own very practical way of finding out the truth. If a cup of wine was thought to be poisoned, he would haul a prisoner up from the cells to offer him either immediate execution or a chance of freedom. I believe the prisoner usually risked drinking the wine – and usually died. But Old Herod, the monster, found out the truth. Practical? Perhaps you are lucky, and the truth you know is so great that it fills every moment of your time, occupies every space and every action of your life. Every half-begun thought—"

"You're insulting me," his voice rose, "insulting the Law."

"Saul, let me tell you how the Service used to work. In the days of Old Herod, we had a reputation for terror. Why? Because the old monster would not trust us. He had no time at all for reason and logic. Each time he sensed a threat he went and called in his favourite troupe of magicians from Mesopotamia. He ordered them to predict the future for him, when all the while he had the finest philosophers and logicians at his disposal. The magicians' methods were all sorts of superstition and nonsense. Tests of guilt that involved terrifying their victims. All very well for peasants, but in a modern state, part of our good friends' settled peace, this sort of nonsense was unnecessary. But he listened to these charlatans, and as a result half his court died agonising deaths. We have moved on, do you understand? We must use reason to find out the truth. We cannot allow ourselves to return to those days."

I paused and looked at him, eyebrows raised. An interrogation technique that never fails. And he opened: I was granted a sort of entrance. His face shone with pleasure and he even managed to extend his height beyond the assistance of his built-up boots by bobbing onto the tips of his toes with the rhythms of his words.

"My father decided that I should study too, and he sent me here to Jerusalem. There was no place for me in the family business either. Though I could spin rope better than any of my brothers. I could cut canvas and hide quicker than the craftsmen in my father's workshop and my stitching was faster and more accurate than my brothers' work. Do you understand?"

"I don't doubt it."

"When I was a child my brothers and I would compete to see which one of us could spin hemp into rope the quickest. None of my brothers could equal me. Can you imagine that? The old craftsmen of Tarsus would come to ask my opinion of their work, and the young masters would bring their best pieces to me for inspection and ask me which hides were the most suitable. While I was still a boy. Do you understand?"

I understood well enough that this was the sort of story I had heard from many young scholars in my own youth, and from craftsmen of all sorts when in old age they were looking back and comparing their own efforts with those of the pupils of the day. Saul must truly believe he was the first person to whom this immoderate piece of boasting could apply.

"And what happened when you became a scholar?"

He beamed.

"I was unrivalled! Of all the scholars I was the one whose knowledge of Torah was agreed to be outstanding. I outstripped them all. Gamaliel, my good master, was astonished by my learning."

There was much else like this too, as we watched the sun begin to illuminate the olive groves across the Kidron and the shadows folded themselves beneath the trees. At last he paused and I was able to ask a question.

"What happened when you were appointed to the Prefect's office to liaise with our good friends? Remind me – when was it?"

"Last year," he said. "For three months."

"And?"

He looked down at his feet.

"It was obvious to me, from the very beginning."

"What was?"

"That they did not understand."

"And?"

"And I soon understood that my task was to be with the Temple guards. To ensure that the people are able to live their lives in a good and holy way. And I could not do that if I was spending my days waiting on the Prefect, could I?"

"No. I don't suppose that you could."

"And when I was assigned to the Temple Guard, at my own request, you can imagine how it was. The officers," he announced, his eyes shining again, "were always consulting me on matters of the Law and the correct interpretation of Torah. Me! Not Captain Malchus or the priests, but me. Do you understand? I had the respect of good men in our work of ensuring that the people and the city were kept holy and pure."

He fell silent, turned away from the view across the Kidron and looked out over the great roof of the Temple where the dark smoke of the afternoon sacrifices rose into the air.

"I was the one," he repeated. "Can you understand what that means? To direct people into a good and holy way of living. To help our people live every moment of their lives in full view of the Law of God."

I decided that I preferred Saul bumptious and enthusiastic to his despair of the morning and that we had his piety within the Temple to thank for this. Observance had its uses.

"Cassiel, what hour of the day would you say it is?"

He shaded his eyes.

"About the tenth hour, sir."

"Just the time," I said. "Our next step is to pay a visit to the place that I believe Yehuda went to after the arrest. Come on."

"Where are we going?" Saul asked.

I said nothing. Let him understand and be shocked in his own time. I led him back along the colonnade where the soldiers again grudged us space to pass, and we returned to the Court of Nations and the western gate. As we descended into the depths of the lower city, my knees resumed their aching and Saul was soon beside me, supporting my arm.

"Have you ever worked under an assumed name?" I asked him. "A false identity?"

"No." He was offended again. "I am Saul, of the tribe of Benjamin. That sort of work is only for—"

"I have. A long time ago. It can be dangerous work, to penetrate a group of people, to become one of them. The fear of exposure runs deep, believe me. But that is not all. It can also be destructive of a man's true self. To live as someone else for a long time wears out a man's sense of who he is. Often, it can destroy him completely."

"I see." He very obviously did not, but I went on.

"When you are given this kind of assignment, you must be very careful to become entirely the person that you seem. Entirely, you understand? Your life, your self, your childhood, your family, your father, your mother, they are all invented. They all belong to this person you become. You must forget your own childhood, your family, your mother. You must forget your true self. When I was recruiting young men to work for the Service I found that it was wise to pay attention to a man's background and his sense of who he was. A long period of living like that can destroy a man."

We stepped down from the stairs and walked to the left, below the aqueduct and the Temple bridge.

"What were these hazards, exactly?"

"Have you heard the expression *to cross the river*?"

"No. I have not."

Another disappointment. Where had the boy spent his time as a probationer?

"We use those words to describe what happens when someone who is undercover identifies too closely with the person, or the group, whom he is watching. He becomes so much a part of their world that he forgets his duty to the Service. I suspect that is what happened to our Yehuda. There are other dangers too. I knew a man once who, when he came back, no longer knew just who he really was. He had lost any idea of his own true self."

"What happened to him?" There was both horror and a very plain fascination in Saul's eyes.

"He killed himself. It was a dreadful thing. I should never have allowed it to happen. So I decided, from then on, that every member of the Service who returned to us from such an assignment was given whatever help they needed to avoid such a thing happening."

"And how did you help them?"

"I decided they should find that the change from one life to another – the return to their old and unfamiliar life – was arranged for them. We tried many ways of doing this before we found the right one. You can, perhaps, imagine it as helping them to feel the way that a man might feel after he has been cleansed of a devil that has possessed him. If that helps." It did. There was disgust and revulsion in his eyes.

"One of our people told me that what he wanted, above all else, at the end of an assignment, was to feel the drunkenness that a man should feel when he is celebrating the feast of Purim. To be so drunk that he cannot tell who or what is good and who or what is evil, then awaken a day or two later and remember nothing of what he has experienced except that the nation has been saved through his efforts. He has to feel as if he is new again, as if the old life, his real life, has returned."

Saul tilted his head, as if pretending to consider the idea, in a more convincing fashion this time.

"We soon found that there was one experience that worked more effectively than any other in securing such a state of emptying out your life."

We turned a corner into a street of gaudy opulence just below the north-eastern slopes of Zion Hill. We were outside an old palace of Hasmonean times that must once have belonged to a rich and powerful family of priests.

"We found that our men needed to return to the world through this doorway," I said. The door was of old, green-tinged bronze. Above it, carved in relief upon the stone lintel, was a single Aleph in Hebrew, a single Alpha in Greek. Saul looked up at the sign and the look of revulsion returned to his face. Cassiel was grinning. He knew what was behind the door.

"Shall we go in?"

"No," said Saul. "Oh no. You cannot make me set foot in such a place."

"Duty," I told him. "We must." And I struck the brass door with my fist, five times, paused, and then twice more. The hammering echoed through the halls of the building and fell silent. Then we heard footsteps within.

UPPER CITY
2ND DAY OF THE WEEK,
10TH HOUR

"We're closed. You hear? Closed."

The voice rasped through the gap in the door. It came from a face half in shadow. The face bore a dark mole across its visible side, from forehead to cheek.

"May we speak with the Lady Esther?" I asked.

"Never heard of her."

"Who are you? And what's happened to Epaphroditus? Why isn't he on the door?"

"Never heard of him either."

At that moment the eye caught sight of Saul's tunic and realised that it was dealing with the Temple Guard.

"If you've come for another bribe, you can stuff it. The lady dealt with all that before Pesach."

"Listen, whoever you are, don't waste my time. I know Lady Esther and I know this place. Just take me to her."

The eye looked me up and down. Contempt, not fear.

"Get me Epaphroditus," I told him. "Now." It was at that moment that Esther's new doorman tried to shut the door upon us.

I heard the scream before I saw the movement. And I barely saw the movement at all, because I was knocked back by the door swinging open and I fell against Saul. When I looked, the door was wide open and its keeper was decisively on our side of it. He was pinned to the stone column by Cassiel's left hand. Cassiel's right hand held a knife at the doorkeeper's bare throat. My messenger's action must have been extraordinarily swift and well disguised because I saw it neither begin nor end. I was about to order him to put the man down and put away his knife when I heard shouting inside the house. A pale bulk of flesh and fabric filled the corridor within. Its head was bald and plump, sweat glistened at its temples and its eyes seemed to be popping out of the deep folds of flesh that engulfed them. The scream rose as the flesh approached, and suddenly fell silent. A fat round fist, knuckles glistening, filled my vision and came to a halt within a finger's breadth of my nose.

"Lord Solomon, sir." The voice was far more squeaky and excitable than I remembered. "We didn't recognise you for a moment."

I was embraced by the mass of flesh in front of me. It seemed to have neither form nor end. Saul looked away. The doorkeeper's throat crackled and squeaked. At last, I stepped back.

"Epaphroditus, my friend. We've come to pay a call upon your mistress. Purely business."

"You are always welcome in the house, sir." He glanced at the doorkeeper, who was still pinned to the pillar. "You must excuse Ev; he's only just joined us."

I tapped Cassiel on the shoulder and he relaxed his grip. Ev the doorkeeper stepped away, his breath coming in stertorous gasps. He did not take his eyes off Cassiel. My messenger stared back at him. The knife had already slipped silently into the folds of his robe. I did not see that movement either.

Saul was hanging back, still half in the street.

"We must do this for our Yehuda," I told him. He scowled and shuffled forward. When we moved on, I said softly to Cassiel.

"Where did you learn that?"

"I was with Young Herod the Tetrarch's personal guard before I joined the Service." His lips barely moved and his eyes never left the backs of Epaphroditus and Saul.

"Thank you," I said quietly. "I'm in your debt."

"A pleasure, sir."

"Philo chose well."

The trace of a smile passed over his lips.

"He did say that I might find it a change."

"Watch our friend Saul, will you? He may not like what he sees in here. I don't want to be distracted by any displays of piety."

The atrium announced itself to my nostrils five paces before we entered the room. Resin of sandalwood and steeped violets masked the smell of human sweat and semen that leaked from all the inner chambers of the house. It was late afternoon and the great open space at its centre was still full of the smells and signs of enthusiastically pursued and very expensive pleasure.

The room was a wide oval, its floors polished marble, its walls ornamented with false columns and friezes. When I last set foot in here, it had been painted in the Back-to-Alexander colour schemes practically compulsory in Herodian times. Now it was decked out in a style that you might call New Parthian Exotic if you were a craftsman trying to sell fashion to a client with more wealth than taste. There were, of course, absolutely no figurative representations of anything in the Almighty's created world anywhere. The copulating men and women, ecstatic beasts with thrashing limbs and enormous organs that pleasured the eyes in a Greek brothel were not to be found here. Esther's was a brothel, certainly, but it was a respectfully observant Jewish brothel and images of any sort were strictly forbidden.

At the end of the colonnade there still stood the famous column decorated like a ship's mast festooned with ropes and manacles, and a tub of beeswax at its foot. An arm's breadth away a highly foreshortened ship's prow tapered exquisitely into an alarmingly smooth wooden phallus. Recreating scenes from Homer had always been a favourite diversion for Esther's more sophisticated customers. Saul stared in horror.

"Don't worry," I said. "Sirens don't work at Pesach." The poor boy looked terrified. Outrage and shame were palpable in his trembling hands. In the past I had never lingered long in the public rooms: the business that brought me here had always been conducted in the privacy of one of the upper chambers. Always a very particular chamber, cleverly designed and arranged with some help from the carpenter's guild.

A voice called out from the far side of the room, and Epaphroditus bowed low. Esther's wig had assumed even more elaborate dimensions since I last saw her: two long braids on either side of her neck, the rest gathered and teased out into cascades of elaborate ringlets. Face powdered white and a thick line of kohl around her eyes. Impossible, beneath all this, to guess her age or health. This was not the Esther of previous years. We were not offered wine from the bowls on her table, though I could tell from a single breath of the air within her office whose wine it was and the year that I made it. After a polite enquiry after my wife's health and sending her greetings from all the girls, Esther pointed out that she could not possibly have done anything wrong this Pesach, the Service must be here for a favour, so could I please tell her what I was looking for as quickly as possible?

"What is it? A girl? Or a customer?"

"I need to trace the movements of a colleague. Someone who was here before Pesach."

"Shlomo darling, your friends were in and out of here until the moment Pesach started. Since then, not a trace. They've all vanished. I was expecting them to turn up again yesterday morning but you're the first. Should I be worried? Oh, don't look so surprised. They've obviously decided to stay away. I do rather wonder why."

"The man I'm looking for had just finished doing a job for us."

"Oh. One of those."

"And I wondered if he might not still be here, enjoying your hospitality?"

"Darling, if he'd tried to do that I'd have kicked him out. You know my girls don't work Shabbat. Not even at festival time. You can tell that to your friend from the Temple Guard too, by the way."

"That is not my concern. Nor his, if he has any sense."

"Describe him, this colleague."

"Red-haired, stocky. Freckles. Red beard too. He may have caused you some trouble."

"That one. Came in on Thursday night, spending money like a drunken camel-driver after eight months in the desert. Two of my girls said they'd never felt so sore in their lives. He must have had a lot that he wanted to get off his mind. Shall I send you Nicanor's bill?"

"How long did he stay?"

"He left in a hurry with some of his friends."

"He came here with friends?"

"Madam," said Epaphroditus, "may I speak?"

"Go on, you. You've got something to spit out, haven't you?"

"The gentleman arrived alone. Some people called for him."

"Who were they, these people?" I asked. "How many of them?"

"Look, Solomon, why don't you just ask the girl he was with? Will that satisfy you? Don't detain her for long, you understand? I've got some rich Parthians coming in and they're expecting entertainment. Epaphroditus?"

"Madam?"

"Remind me. Who was it that Lord Solomon's friend, the red-haired man, was with the night before Preparation Day?"

He consulted the third of the long scrolls that were strung vertically on a winding mechanism on her desk. Five turns of the lower spindle took him back to the night.

"It was Rahab, madam."

"Rahab?" I asked, in polite incredulity. "Her name is Rahab?"

"Of course it is, dear. And she's very popular with the pious. The priests will keep asking for her. Now, do you want to speak with her or don't you?"

Beneath the dome the girls were beginning to gather for the evening's business. I caught Cassiel's eye. He indicated Saul. My assistant was standing apart, between two pillars, his face turned to the wall, intensely ignoring his surroundings.

"Is he all right?"

"No trouble. Not yet, anyway. Another moment, perhaps…"

I put my hand on Saul's shoulder. His eyes were full of loathing, mixed with a pleading. *Take me away from this. Save me.*

"Are you ready to go upstairs?" Epaphroditus guided us to the steps on the west side of the rotunda. Cassiel walked behind. We came to a narrow passage lit by triple candles held in sconces on the walls. In a Greek brothel they would nestle atop sculpted penises: no such representation of the human form here.

Epaphroditus put his hand on a door. The room was pitifully constricted. And it now contained a bed, a girl, Epaphroditus, Saul, Cassiel and me. We crowded together, unable to avoid contact. The air was solid with the stench of sweat and sex, softened by a phantom trace of sandalwood and rosewater. Rahab lay on a wooden truckle piled with pillows and scarlet cloth. She was clothed, but her *peplos* was falling open. Saul gasped in disgust. She stirred on the bed and stood up. A smile of welcome spent some time assembling itself across her face and then turned into a grimace.

"Well. This is unusual," she said. "An old man, a High Priest's messenger, a eunuch and the Temple Guard. What would you like me to do exactly?"

She spoke, but I barely heard her words. I was looking at the room: the wooden bed, the painted walls, the high slit window onto the street below, the concave ceiling. I knew this place. Saul shuffled and looked down at his feet.

"Or would you really just prefer to talk?"

There could be no doubt that I had been here before. Eight years earlier, in this very room, those had been the first words that Zenobia had spoken to me.

It was to have been a simple entrapment, overhearing the pillow-talk of the Greek Secretary of Gondophares, King of Parthia. We sent in men from the stonemasons' and carpenters' synagogue to knock out the wall between the place of entertainment and a listening room next door, and to build a partition of laths and animal hides, disguised with plaster and wash. The Greek Secretary was understood to have an enthusiasm for light-skinned blonde women and, astonishingly, Esther had managed to find one – a voluptuous Goth from the plains far north of the Pontus who traded as "Chione" and had been made to understand that she should draw out her man and take a close interest in whatever was troubling him. Then we arrived at Esther's well in advance of the Greek Secretary and discovered that, in the confusion of the preparations, nobody had told the girl who normally worked in the room next door to leave.

Her beauty was as exceptional and unexpected as her presence. Dark skin, voluptuous body, and her face had none of the crude makeup that Esther encouraged her girls to use.

Zenobia looked at me. Her hair shone in the candlelight and I was thrilled, for the first time, by the sheer luxury of its body and its length. She raised both her hands to grasp the thickness of it and move it round so that it fell over her left shoulder and covered her breasts, her belly, her waist, her hips.

"I suppose," she said, "that you'll just want to talk?"

"Didn't anybody tell you?"

"What? That my next customers were going to be an old man and a scholar?"

My junior, a young man from the school at Tiberias called Boaz, looked down and clutched his tablets.

"No, they didn't," she said before I could respond. "So what happens? You make the noises and he writes it all down? Because I have to warn you. I'm not a screamer. Unlike that Goth next door."

"We are here to listen." I tapped the false wall, which rattled alarmingly.

"Oh that," she said. "Just so long as you've not brought any of those carpenters or plasterers with you."

"What's wrong with them?"

"Their manners are crude. And they smell."

"I apologise for them. We're here to listen."

She curled her lips. "You're spies, aren't you? What's your name?"

"Shlomo."

"Solomon? Coming in peace, are you? Telling me your real name in a place like this can be a foolish thing. Are you sure it's Solomon?"

"And what's yours?"

"You can call me Zenobia."

"And is that your real name?"

"I borrowed it from a girl I used to work with. Of course it's my real name. The customers call me Aurora Pan-Nyches."

"All-Night Dawn? I don't believe you."

"Very wise of you, Solomon."

So we listened together. When I sat in the narrow space, my ear to the wall, she sat in front of me, listening too, a look of mischief and delight in her eyes. Then she raised her eyebrows and her cheeks dimpled. Her eyes were a deeper brown by far than the brown of her skin. Pocks of darkness littered the upper part of her right cheek. Her hair fell down around her neck and shoulders, encompassing the world. Through the wall there first came voices and then the sounds of pleasure. She was right about Chione.

When Gondophares' Greek Secretary's hopes, fears and policies, his problems with his wives and with his various mistresses had been recorded upon Boaz's tablets, the sounds from the adjoining room returned to incoherent ecstasy before he took his leave of Chione. In the silence, Zenobia looked at me and took my hands in hers.

"You really are a good listener."

She leaned towards me and I could feel the softness of her breath upon my face. The cloak of her hair enclosed us. "And now," she said, "I'm going to tell you a story."

I signalled to Boaz that he could leave.

Three months later I used a very considerable portion of the money that I had accumulated in the spice merchant's business at Pera to purchase Zenobia from her mistress. Esther demanded a very high price. The same day, I emancipated Zenobia and married her – the first time I had troubled to do anything of importance strictly according to the Law for a very long time. The purchase of the land for my vineyard took far longer. The seller was a rich man called Yephthah who wished to enter the community of the Essenes in the final years of his life. In preparation he was selling all his possessions and giving the money raised to the poor of Jerusalem. His children were horrified at the idea of losing the family's land and put all sorts of obstacles in the way of the sale. At last we agreed a price, far in excess of any value, and Yephthah, angry that his family had delayed his embrace of piety, agreed that I buy the land in perpetuity, without reversion at the next jubilee year. The vineyard would be ours and our family's for ever. I left the Service and on 9th Ab in the 41st year of the Temple Zenobia and I travelled up into the hills to begin the planting of our vineyard.

Same room, different girl. Rahab was slight, and far younger than Zenobia. Her features had a compact look arrested in a state of artificial prettiness. The look stopped at her eyes. They had a jolting avidity: she was weighing up exactly what each of us would be good for. Saul could not meet her gaze. Epaphroditus spoke.

"These gentlemen are friends of the Lady Esther. They want to ask you some questions."

Rahab's eyes moved from my loins to my face and back again.

When she spoke, it was with a trace of Mesopotamia: the burr of the rivers to the east. People think it means rural idiocy.

"What'll you give us, then?"

I took out my drawstring purse and placed a silver Tyrian shekel on the table by the bed. It sat there next to the sponges on sticks, a wad of soiled cotton, and a bowl of last season's lemons.

"A deposit."

She looked at it, then back at me, at Saul, at Cassiel, and finally at Epaphroditus.

"Gentlemen pay in advance, don't they, Eppy?" Her eyes settled on my purse.

"The Lady Esther will be pleased if you can help," Epaphroditus said.

I pushed a second Tyrian shekel onto the table.

"That's payment in full."

"And what are you doing, my love?" Cassiel had taken out his tablet and stylus.

"No. Memory, please. We'll make a record later." I turned to the girl. "Esther tells me you had a customer the night before Pesach."

"His name was Yehuda," said Epaphroditus.

She smiled a smile of pity.

"Do you think that I ask them for their names? Give me yours if you like, but I don't imagine it'll be the one that you're known by."

"You'd remember him—"

"There were lots of them that night, darling. You'll have to jog my memory a bit, won't you?"

"You'd know him. Red hair. Freckles."

"The redhead? Looked like he'd been singed in the fiery furnace, that one." She looked over my shoulder at Epaphroditus. "Official Service, was he? Thought so. I was asked for special, by madam. Left me feeling sore, he did. Rachel too, while she was with us."

I was about to frame a question in a stupid way – "What did he do?" – and thought better of it.

"How," I asked her, "did he seem to you?"

"The way they always do, darling. Like they want to unburden themselves. Sometimes their minds seem somewhere else entirely."

"Tell me," I said, "and when we're finished you'll get double, but not till then. Tell me everything you remember about him."

"He turned up late, well after the middle of the night. Helped himself to three bowls of wine before madam asked him what he thought he was doing. He was very free with his hands. I don't like that sort of uncouthness in a man. We get enough of that from them Latins."

"Were there any Latins here that night?"

She laughed out loud.

"What do you think? Crawling all over us. Busiest night of the year, apart from Purim. They just maul you. If you're lucky."

"And our friend? The one with freckles?"

"He was sweaty. And drunk." She wrinkled her nose. "Madam told me to keep him happy. Well, I just do what I'm told – don't I?"

She looked round to Cassiel and Saul. Saul stared at the door.

"Go on," I said.

"He told me he'd met two of those Latins outside. Made a nuisance of himself. Madam doesn't like that sort of thing happening down in the salon, so I took him upstairs and I calmed him down." She giggled. "That took till well after the sun had come up, I can tell you. He was quite excitable, your friend. I asked Rachel to come in and help." She smiled again in that mockery of appeal. "We took the edge off him all right. Would you like her to tell you about it herself?"

"No thank you."

"Well, suit yourself. You don't know what you're missing."

"Tell me about the rest of the time he spent with you."

"After Rachel left?"

"When was that exactly?"

"About midday. She went off to watch that execution. She wanted to be there to see Elijah come down from heaven and rescue the holy man on his cross. So she said. She likes a good execution, our Rachel. She's quite common that way. Me, I'm a more refined kind of girl."

Zenobia once told me that many of her fellow workers had a certain enthusiasm for attending crucifixions. They were a good source of trade. Apparently customers were particularly keen after watching a man die in agony. Esther's girls regarded this as something for the street whores and the tarts from the cheaper houses – uprights and cross-beams as they were known. It was beneath the dignity of Esther's girls to show too much enthusiasm for that sort of spectacle, or that sort of customer.

"So she left you, but he stayed?"

She grinned. "He started up again the moment she was gone. Wouldn't leave me alone. Like it was the last time he'd ever do it. Frenzied, he was. Do you like frenzied?"

Her features twisted into an arrangement of breathtaking harshness. She went on in a sullen, matter-of-fact way, all playfulness vanished.

"Rachel came back later in the afternoon. Your friend asked her what had happened. So the world didn't end, then? That's what he said. What? No. He died. That was all. Died like all the rest of them. The way they do. They're always such a disappointment, aren't they? He went very quiet for a long time after that, so Rachel went back downstairs. He was all closed off and distant. As if he was barely there."

"And what happened afterwards?"

"I woke up in the night and felt him move. He was sitting just there, by the shelf. There were five piles of coins, all neat and counted out next to him, and he was scribbling on one of those tablet things. Then he looked round when he heard me and I got out of bed. There was voices from outside." She nodded towards the high slit in the exterior wall. "Then there was a stone hit the side of the wall and someone called his name. *Yehuda.*"

"What were they speaking?"

"Greek mostly. There were three of them that I heard. One of them did most of the talking. The other two just chipped in. And he talked back."

"What did they say?"

"Didn't catch much, did I? The one who talked most had a northern accent, Syrian or something. The other two, I couldn't tell you. One of them, he sounded foreign. The last one was educated, like he was confident and in charge." She stopped.

"The one in charge," I asked her. "He spoke Greek?"

"Greek. Proper refined, he was."

"And the other?"

"A Latin. Dull, dull, dull. Like all that sort."

"Did you see them?" This was from Saul. We all looked at him. Rahab laughed.

"Through a hole that size? I doubt it." She looked up at the narrow opening from her workplace to the world outside Esther's. I took out my purse and counted out two more silver shekels for her to see. I glanced at the table but kept them in my hand.

"One more thing. What exactly did you hear them say?"

"They wanted him to come down. Said they had to talk to him. Some business. Important business."

"What sort of business?"

She shrugged, pursed her lips and looked charmless again.

"It was nothing much. They wanted to talk to him. That refined one, he said he needed him to identify someone. That got his attention."

"And what did he do?"

"Suddenly he was all bright and hopeful again. *Your friend, he wants a word.* He just cleared out. Left me with a pile of silver. Said to give half of it to Rachel. Very generous of him."

I stood up and laid the final money down.

"Thank you," I said. "You've been extremely helpful."

She smiled again, suddenly bashful and coy.

"I hope I've given good service, sir. Come again, won't you, my love?"

"We're finished," I said to Epaphroditus. "I must thank your mistress before we go." Then I turned back to the girl.

"One more thing. Remind me. When did your friend Rachel leave you alone with him?"

"I told you. She was off duty, wasn't she? Gone out with her common friends to see what would happen when that holy man got nailed up. They'd got this idea Elijah was coming down and the world was going to end."

"Thank you. And you said that, when his friends came for him, it was in the night?"

Rahab twisted her hair and pouted.

"Dunno. Might have."

"You said that you remembered it was deep in the night."

Fear and regret covered the harshness of her features.

"Don't worry. I am not interested in whether or not you were working after Shabbat began. That is no concern of mine. Nor of my friend here from the Temple Guard. I'm sure that Esther has already paid generously to avoid coming to their attention, and my friend will respect that. Won't you?" No sound came from Saul. "Won't you?" I repeated. At last a long exhalation of breath in the depths of which I could detect a syllable of agreement.

Epaphroditus led us from the room. As I turned in the doorway I glimpsed Rahab pouring the money into a canvas bag and sliding it beneath her bed. We were already forgotten. As we walked back along the corridor I touched the eunuch's shoulder.

"How long has that new doorman been with you?"

"Ev? He's quite a rough boy, isn't he? A few Shabbats. But he came recommended. There's been a lot of trouble in the street."

I wondered if the trouble had not become even greater since Ev started work, but did not ask.

When we returned to the main room, the party for Esther's Parthians had already begun. Cassiel took it all in with undisguised boredom. He must have witnessed far greater depravities as a member of Young Herod's personal bodyguard: those men never left the fox's presence, night or day. But Saul was visibly upset and, to my surprise, I felt sympathy for him. He trembled at the sight of flesh.

"They should not be doing this," he muttered, and moved into the shadows between the line of pillars.

Epaphroditus was at my side.

"The Lady asked me to give you this," he said, and pushed into my hands a canvas bag within which I felt the outline of three or four small objects. "Your friend left it behind." He hurried us onwards, stretching out his great arms to encompass Saul on one side and Cassiel on the other. There was no sign at the door of Ev and I had the sense to hand the bundle to Cassiel.

"In your Service satchel, please. Material of interest. Not to be opened till we are back at the Temple." He slipped it into his bag just as the door creaked open and we stepped out onto the street.

"You're coming with us," someone shouted in coarse Greek.

Hands pinned my arms to my sides and dragged me sideways. I was aware, far to the left of my vision, of Ev the doorman's face: he was laughing and the few teeth in his mouth were shining in a ferocious way. Saul was lifted off his feet and turned on his back. In the middle of the street, Cassiel was being professionally beaten by two big men in tunics. For some reason, it struck me that they must be Syrians, and I wondered why soldiers were patrolling the streets out of uniform when something hard collided with my head and I saw the stars of the Empyrean and the city's lights spangled across the paving stones against which my face was being dragged.

We were forced onto a bench, our heads bent down, staring at the scrubbed wood of a table, Cassiel on my left, Saul on my right. The men who had taken us stood on either side, blocking any possible movement. One of them had oily, black hair. The other was bald. He had a deep scar down the side of his face. There was a wall behind us. I looked at the scrubbed wood of the table. Beyond it, I heard the clack and swish of a curtain's beads.

"Now then. What do you think that we're going to talk about?"

I looked up.

Time had spoiled him. His skin had sagged and his features, once sharp with a dispassionate ugliness, were now overwhelmed by an integument of fat. There was nothing sleek about him anymore. His lips and jowls were bloodless.

"Hello, Marcus," I said.

"This is outrageous. We are officers of the Temple. You cannot do this."

I kicked Saul hard beneath the table with the heel of my right foot. He gasped and bent low.

"I deal with this. You say nothing."

To my left, Cassiel was staring at Marcus without a sign of emotion. Messengers are trained to deal with interrogation. Saul, I was certain, was not.

"I'm sure that the good envoy is quite entitled to express his dismay at the trouble that you've led him into, Solomon. Saul, I can well understand your distaste for the vile place that he's just forced you to endure. That's one thing about Eliades. He never cares whom he degrades." Marcus' smile became mournful. On cue, his guards leaned forward across the table, balling their fists. How dreadfully predictable.

"Very good," I said. "Do you get them to practise that, Marcus?"

Marcus' eyes moved across us from left to right.

"Young Saul. Former representative at His Excellency's office. Now inexplicably pretending to be a religious guard. Solomon Eliades, inveterate interferer in matters that are none of his business. And some roughneck who was thrown out of Young Herod's personal guard in circumstances that have never been quite clear enough to reassure us. Now." He paused for a moment. "These three are suddenly running around Jerusalem poking their noses into matters that cannot possibly concern them. Tell me, Solomon, what am I supposed to make of that?"

I wondered how long a silence would truly anger him. First rule of counter-interrogation. Second rule: only ever answer a question with one of your own. At last, I spoke.

"Marcus. You're not confessing your ignorance, are you? Now what does that mean, I wonder?"

Marcus' lips became even looser and his skin had the paleness of a fish in moult. At the side of his jaws something was throbbing, a light, fluttering pulse. He swallowed, and pressed his lips together.

"I'm wondering, Solomon, why you are taking such an interest in the body that was found down at the kilns the other day. Is there anything I should be hearing from you?"

"So that's what you're troubled about? I wouldn't be worrying yourself with that, Marcus. Why should you?"

"Take care. We had to deal with one of your Jewish seditionaries before the festival. His Excellency was livid." He turned to Saul. "Yes, you know what I'm talking about, don't you? You can see the sense of ensuring religious festivals are carried out in an orderly way and do not become an occasion for disagreement. Almost made a career out of that point of view, didn't you?" He smiled, a thin, bitter slit opened between his lips, then vanished in an instant. "And now, Eliades of all people turns up in Jerusalem and starts poking around."

"Marcus, you don't really think I'm interested in that Galilean magician you decided to execute, do you? Is that what you think?"

"What am I to make of your taking such a close interest in his treasurer and fixer? Also recently deceased, from what I understand."

"His fixer? Who might that be?"

"You were observed at the potteries yesterday."

"That business down by the kilns? Are you quite sure about that? I never knew that he was the Galilean's financial backer. Now that does come as a surprise. You're very helpful, Marcus. Thank you."

"I said he was the man's fixer, Solomon. I never said that he was his financier. Though, if that's what you believe about him, that's of some interest. Assuming that that is indeed what you believe? Do you believe anything at all? No? Oh well. There's little enough difference between your being obtuse and your being mendacious." His lips tightened to the point of invisibility. The skin on the side of his jaws was pulsing. "Solomon," he went on, "let me make one thing absolutely plain to you. I will speak directly, without any ornament. Do you understand?"

"I'm sure."

"The Prefect will not tolerate any further outbreaks of religious enthusiasm of any sort whatsoever. Are we agreed?"

I bent forward and folded my hands together across the table, as if I was paying attention.

"Marcus, I'm retired. I'll grant you that the Service may no longer be quite what it was in the old days…"

The old days were never a good idea with Marcus.

"Listen to me, Solomon. I think your employers knew exactly what they were doing when they sent that magician to His Excellency. Speaking personally, I'd've thrown him in jail till the festival was over and then sent him on his way with a really first-class whipping. His Excellency has had quite enough, just between you and me, of being expected to sort out your own intractable problems for you. Religious fanatics are supposed to be your problem, not ours. Do you understand? And what happens? We find you and your new friends sniffing around the corpse of the man's number one helper."

He leaned back.

"Listen to me, Solomon, if there are any further outbreaks of enthusiasm among your people and I find out that you've been involved, then I'll have you and your friends here arrested on a charge of sedition. And you know what that means, don't you?"

"You can't do that!" Saul wailed. "I'm a citizen."

I pushed my right elbow into his ribs to shut him up, never

taking my eyes off Marcus. Saul cried out, spluttered and collapsed across the table, clutching his left side. There was blood on his lips and his beard. He tried to breath in and a stertorous groaning came from his lungs. Then he sat up, gasping, and fell off the bench.

Marcus turned to his thugs. "Marvellous. They're beating each other up in order to assist us. At least it spares us the trouble. Sort him out." Then he stood up and disappeared through the beaded curtain to whatever arrangements he had waiting for him away from the place of interrogation.

We laid Saul gently on the bench and waited for his breathing to become uncomplicated by bubbling and hacks. At last, he opened his eyes. They were still full of reproachful terror.

"Thank you," he said.

"Forgive me. Can you sit?" I was repelled by the idea that I had to prepare him for whatever would happen when Marcus returned.

"Forgive me," I repeated. He inclined his head.

"Don't be concerned. You did not know." He looked up towards the ceiling. "It was those two animals at the arrest. When they beat me. They smelled of fish," he added.

In the time you might say your morning prayers ten times over we raised him upright and the two thugs permitted him to walk backwards and forwards to ensure that he could move freely and that his head was clear. In all this Cassiel was as attentive and gentle as Nico's assistant Azizus. At last, Saul nodded.

"I am ready."

We sat down on the bench, just as we had been when I made my foolish attempt to stop him from speaking. The two thugs took up their position at either side of the table, the bead curtain swished and clacked as before and Marcus returned.

He turned his eyes upon Saul. "You see, my dear envoy, what happens when you are involved with people of this sort? Solomon here has a long and regrettable history of not caring whom he inconveniences, whom he damages, or whom he betrays when he is pursuing one of the goals that he has selected for himself. Haven't you?"

I looked into his eyes and said nothing. To his credit, he held my gaze while he spoke.

"The magician we executed on Friday. The one that your man turned in—"

He was looking at me. That look – I've not often seen it – that tells me he knows something that I don't.

"He was buried in a tomb down the valley from the southern gate. I thought you should know." The fat of his jowls trembled and his smile became smug. "There was some trouble over there yesterday morning. Someone robbed the grave."

"Marcus, you're showing outstanding ignorance for someone who pretends to understand my people. We don't bury our dead with grave goods. Unlike you Latins, who will believe anything. Our God can't be bribed."

Marcus smiled. That look again.

"You're not listening, Solomon. I did not say that goods had been stolen. Go and see for yourself. The tomb is empty. Someone has stolen the body."

I looked across at Saul. The disgust on his face was painful. Marcus went on.

"Don't you hear? I'm giving you an opportunity. If you want to do one of your famous analyses of the scene of a crime, then I suggest that you get over there while you've still got the light of day. I've put a guard on the tomb." He looked across at Saul. "Apparently your people are too fastidious to go anywhere near it."

Then he turned to his guards.

"You can throw them out," he said. "I've finished with them. For the moment."

TEMPLE MOUNT
3RD DAY OF THE WEEK,
1ST HOUR OF DARKNESS

"It's a provocation," I said as we helped Saul down the steps of the Upper City. "Marcus would never think of doing me a favour. Our good friends have set a trap for us."

"Why?" Saul was still wheezing. "Why should they do that to us?"

"Why do you think?"

"He hates you, your good friend Marcus, doesn't he?"

"Very likely."

"Why? They're our good friends, aren't they? Marcus was always straight with me. When I was at the Prefect's office," he added softly.

"I'm sure that he was."

"So why does he hate you?"

Saul would not understand the meaning of what I could tell him about Marcus. And he would be revolted by the details. An episode of my life in which, to this day, I cannot take pride or comfort.

"Another time," I said.

"You're patronising me. How dare you treat me as if I cannot understand."

He stumbled, and in a moment was bent double, breathless. Then he sat down in the street.

"That settles it," I said. "We're taking you to Nico."

"I'm not letting that man or his slaves touch me," he wailed. But Cassiel carried him, unresisting, to the house in Bezetha where, to my relief, we found Nico and Azizus. They examined the patient, whose resistance had now collapsed, in a brisk, unanswerable manner. Soon he consented to lying flat on a table, removing his shawl and enduring the prodding of his sides by the Egyptian slave.

"You're fine, my lad," Nico said at last. "You'll be back to ambassadoring in a week or two."

"That may not be fast enough."

"I'm doing all I can, old son. Azizus too. He's having a wonderful effect on the patient."

Saul spluttered and finally dragged himself off the table. Nico made him drink a sedative decoction of Arabian herbs and led him to a couch in a curtained alcove.

"He'll sleep late tomorrow," he said. "Now, you and Cassiel are my guests. We must eat."

Much later, when the household had retired, I beckoned to Cassiel.

"You've kept the contents of that satchel safe from our good friends, for which the Service is grateful. Time to examine it ourselves."

He unlaced its clasps, took from it the objects that Epaphroditus had pressed into my hands, removed the rough hemp covering and spread them out before us.

"No sign of his purse," I said. "Perhaps he took it with him when he left the room. Here we have—"

We had a sealed tablet and stylus. Three sheets of papyrus, rolled up and tied with a thin cord. And, to my delight, Yehuda's Service cipher block.

"See," I said to Cassiel, "we have prevented our good friends from getting their hands on a set of our encryption tools. That alone is a good day's work. Well done."

To one side, wrapped in a small square of cotton, was something light and soft. I gently removed the cloth. It contained a piece of unleavened Pesach bread wrapped around a slice of lamb still moist in its bitter sauces. Someone had taken a single bite out of it. The teeth marks were clear.

"Someone's Pesach meal was interrupted and never finished. That's bad."

I wrapped up the remains in the cotton and put them to one side. Then I untied the papyrus sheets. Two were blank. Then a third had the start of a message, in plain:

I have discovered something extraordinary about one of my fellows. Details as usual or by word of mouth –

No indication of what that extraordinary thing might be. I sat back.

"I am weary. I may sleep long in the morning. Before you go, a favour if you please. When you wake I want you to go back to Lady Esther's. Do whatever you must to get past that new doorman. No doubt he'll tell his masters that you have been visiting the establishment. When you are inside, give Epaphroditus my greeting, and tell him you have a message from me for the Lady Esther. He will take you to her. Tell the Lady that her new doorman is working for our good friends. That is all. Just give her the information. You are to make no suggestions about the action she will take. Do you understand?"

"Of course."

"After you leave, she will dismiss him. Watch for his departure and follow him. Do what you must, within reason, to find out the truth from him about the men who called out our Yehuda. And anything else that he observed or knows about our man. But be careful: I do not want him dead. If he really is in the pay of our good friends, they would treat that as a very serious provocation, one that we could not justify. If it's simply the case that he loses his job watching our brothel because he has become too noticeable, then they will treat it as part of our game."

"A game? Forgive me: it did not seem to me that the Prefect's adviser was treating this matter as a game."

"Marcus plays it very seriously. Nevertheless, a game it is."

"And what will he think when I interrogate his watcher?"

"I don't think that I really care one way or the other what Marcus thinks about that, or what he thinks about anything at all." The look on his face, even in exhaustion and under lamplight, said that he did not believe me. "All that matters for the moment is whether that doorman knows anything at all about our Yehuda."

I slept long and woke to the sounds of Saul's still-drugged sleep in the alcove. Nico and Azizus must have departed to the daily inspection of the Prefect's bowels. On the roof, Sosthenes was waiting with fresh water, cool cotton, clotted milk curds and whey, flatbread, and a length of honeycomb that glistened in the morning sun. I muttered thanks to the One God for my life and my manhood, and ate. This was the hour at which Zenobia and I would walk the vineyard, examining the buds as we passed through the rows of vines, from the lower gate to the east wall; from the eastern corner to the middle block. I swallowed the last mouthful of curds and honeycomb and stood up.

"When my friend wakes, tell him that I have gone to the offices of the Temple Guard." Sosthenes inclined his head.

"The master said that our guest would sleep till nightfall. He should not be disturbed. The master also said that I should give you this." He handed me a folded and sealed papyrus sheet. The message was from Quintus. Unsigned, but its content identified the sender. In rough everyday Greek, it read:

There's a soldier called Demas at the Antonia. Syrian. Scarred face. He can help you.

I walked to the city among crowds of wealthy pilgrims who had kept the festival in Bezetha. At the end of the lane sunlight bounced off the limestone walls, and the air was a coarse, dry shroud. I stood above the Hinnom Valley, not far from the spot where our father Abraham is supposed to have met Melchizedek the priest of Zion. The spot looked down into the depths of the Hinnom and it was only now, with the view of the valley and the Joppa Road leading up into the western hills, that the latches of my own memory box arranged themselves and released the name of the place. This was Golgotha. Below me, between the houses and the roadside, was the place of the skull.

Years ago, when they were first beginning to develop the city's northern suburbs, some builders unearthed the petrified bones of one of the great beasts that had perished in the Flood. This discovery caused both fascination and revulsion, and the priests were called in to examine the remains of the creature cursed by God. Of course, they could not agree among themselves. Some of them announced that it was the skull of one of the giants, some the skull of our first father; others decided that, whatever it was, it defiled the place. Then Young Herod sent his men to claim the object. I believe he had it shipped to Rome as a curiosity to ingratiate himself with whoever was Augustus at the time. After this the place never quite lost its association with the sinister and the accursed. The owners of the land never built their houses on the site, and it was sold on to a speculator who went bankrupt. A few years later our good friends, realising the potential of a prominent location not far from the Joppa Gate, close to a busy road and just above the city's rubbish tip, decided to use it for their executions. The owners of the neighbouring houses complained about the noise, the smell and the inevitable crowds, but our good friends, with their usual consistency and enthusiasm, did nothing about finding a more suitable spot for their justice. The executions continue to this day, with no sign that the morale of the neighbours has improved.

"It's a dreadful place, isn't it?" A hand grasped my arm and I turned to find Philo was alongside me. "Our good friends. I've tried to suggest more suitable places to them. But they don't listen to us. My ability to influence them is limited. Do you hear?" He relaxed his grip. "You know the most unfortunate thing of all? The women's quarters of my house. Up there." He indicated one of the larger buildings further up the hill with a rather self-satisfied sweep of his arm. "Just there, do you see? They look directly onto the place. Golgotha: my wife and my daughters have a perfect view. They find it intolerable. They really do."

The house was no more than a hundred paces from Nicanor's entrance. They could consider themselves neighbours.

"It must be terrible for them. For everyone," I agreed. Old crones and young girls, mothers and wives fighting their way to the front of the crowd, to watch the agony. Respectable women would never be caught watching such a thing. Even from behind half-closed shutters.

"Have you found them yet?"

"Investigations are proceeding."

"So, there's no change from yesterday?"

"Two areas of interest. Our Yehuda knew something about one of his fellows in the Galilean's entourage. Exactly what, I don't yet know."

"And?"

"And I want to find the owner of the linen tunic that Saul acquired in the course of the arrest. We should return it to him."

"Anything else?"

"Someone in the Antonia barracks."

"What?"

"One of the visiting cohort."

"Do we know him?"

"Syrian. Scar on his face."

Philo stopped in the middle of the street. A line of investigation that led to our good friends was as welcome as asking questions of Young Herod.

"Solomon, I need you to finish this as quickly as possible."

"What has happened?"

"You know what is happening. At the end of the week, the city will empty. Whoever did this will be halfway back to Babylon. Or off to Egypt. I want someone caught. Even if we're no longer faced with an imminent general insurrection. Do you understand?"

"Then help me. What have your eyes discovered? I asked for sightings of our man."

Philo paused and breathed out. "He was everywhere. All over the city. A red-haired man stole someone's water-skin outside Joppa Gate. Someone saw a red-haired man drinking whey and honey at a stall by the Siloam pool. Apparently Jerusalem was full of red-haired men at Pesach. There must have been thousands of them."

"Yehuda could go anywhere and you would never notice him. He drew attention away from himself, very effectively. None of these reports sound like my Yehuda."

"At least five people claim to have seen him in the crowd at Golgotha watching the Galilean's execution on Pesach Eve. We have a statement from a woman that one of the other men executed alongside Yeshua meets the description of our man: red hair, freckles, a strong body. Up there on the gibbet next to him. So of course it must have been our man. Up there, on a cross."

"That was my boy. He could blend in anywhere."

"Solomon, I don't think we need to give this sort of nonsense a second thought. There are two or three sightings that might be your man. Someone saw a red-haired man arguing with three Greeks outside a brothel in the Upper City in the early hours of the morning. The same man was seen being frog-marched towards the Antonia barracks. Then nothing. The last sighting, if it's a sighting at all, is of a red-haired man with blood on his face being helped up the hill in the direction of Beth-Anya on the afternoon of the first Shabbat of Pesach."

"During Shabbat?"

"That's what they said."

"And the Temple Guard didn't notice?"

"Apparently not."

"But he was being helped?"

"That's what they said. Helped."

"Who? Who described it?"

"Some pilgrims from over the Jordan who were delayed on the road and kept Shabbat in Beth-Anya."

"And he was being helped. Thank you."

We walked on in silence.

"There's another thing," he said at last. "I've had a representation from an old acquaintance of yours."

"You mean Marcus?"

Philo gave no sign but spoke softly.

"He wants your investigations stopped right now."

"My investigations? You mean the Service's investigation?"

"The Service's. Of course."

"And what did you say to him?"

"I let him watch me reflect upon his generous advice. And then I told him that his counsel, as ever, was of great value. And that I looked forward to some quite different occasion, in the near future, when I would be able to express my agreement with him."

"Thank you."

For the first time in the conversation, he smiled. "I cannot give Marcus the idea that he can tell us just what we can and can't do, can I?"

"I did not give him that impression either, when he questioned me."

Philo stopped again. "He questioned you? When?"

"He picked me up on the street. No, it was nothing serious." And I gave Philo a short, entirely artless account of my conversation with him. Second rule of the man in the field: share everything, finally, with your control. I said nothing about my assistant.

"And Saul?"

"He found it uncomfortable. I'm sorry. The boy has much to learn."

"Does Marcus think that we are at all close to finding the people that killed Yehuda?"

"I doubt he formed that impression. One thing puzzled me about the conversation. Why would Marcus be interested in this holy man's body? Keeping an eye on fanatics is our job. Not a proper job for an intelligence service, in my view, but it's the one that we've got. So why would Marcus be interested in such nonsense?"

"I'll have to find another occasion on which to understand that, Solomon."

"Then how long have I got?"

"You have no time at all. I don't want Marcus thinking that he can insist on you stopping immediately. But I doubt I could persuade him for very long. Do you understand?"

"Yes."

"Do not give him any occasion for intervention, do you understand? Just find the killer before Marcus approaches me again."

"One more thing. You told me when you first asked me to investigate this case that we have one of our people in Marcus' office. You said he was one of our best."

Philo said nothing and we walked on.

"So who does Marcus have in ours?" I asked him.

He stopped short. We looked at each other for a long time before he spoke.

"I could not possibly ask you to investigate such a possibility. Do you understand?"

We passed the north side of the polished bastion of the Antonia Tower, skirted the bulwarks of the Temple wall and came to the

Service door. There Zev greeted us, convinced that, with the Lords Philo and Solomon working together, the great days of the Service were about to return.

When Philo went to his desk I wandered over towards the memory box. Micah beckoned me from the shadows and informed me that nothing had come back from the High Priest's office.

"But there's something else you should know."

"What?"

"My oppo in Treasury Records says our good friends have been all over his scribes this last day and a half. Wanting to know about land registered in the name of ben Eleazar, Solomon. Seems they're interested in a vineyard."

"Our good friends?"

"That's what he said."

I stood back and looked up to the vaulted stones of the roof. *And the locusts shall possess your vines, and the fruit of your land.* Where was Zenobia? She should be here, in the city.

"And what have they found?"

He laughed softly and shook his head.

"They're stupid as Latins, our good friends. Property scrolls are ordered by the name of the owner at the last jubilee year, not the current owner. Anyone knows that. Anyone but them. That's years gone. Old Herod's time, and then some. Don't worry, sir. I told my oppo that this was no time to be enlightening our friends about the workings of the Law. He's a good lad. I taught him everything he knows about good order in the catalogue. Strict Alexandria fashion. All the scrolls and all the information beyond them are all in the right place. He'll not give them any more help than he has to."

"Thank you, Micah." I offered him a gold Tyrian.

"Keep it," he said. "My knowledge is my own to give." We laughed, and I called for a mug of lemon-milk. Before the second mouthful, there came the noise of another arrival at Zev's barrier. Cassiel stepped forward from the shadows.

"The Lady Esther thanks you for your advice regarding her staff. She'll be employing a new doorman."

"Good. What else did you learn?"

"Our friend was eager to help us. Once he understood what it was that I wanted. He gave of himself. Fully. And I heard him."

"Could he identify the men who called at Esther's?"

"They weren't enthusiasts from Galilee, I can tell you that much. There were three of them. Two of them were soldiers with Damascus accents. The other was somebody that knew our man, and our man knew him. He was very clear about this. 'Oh, it's you,' he said. 'Again.' That's what he said."

"Was there anything else?"

"'Shouldn't you be with them?' Those were the words that our friend says he heard. 'Again. Shouldn't you be with them.' That was all."

"And?"

"And they took Yehuda. In the street outside Esther's house. In the small hours. I doubt that anyone else saw what happened."

We stood in silence for a short while.

"Thank you, Cassiel," I said at last. "That's a job well done."

Again, there came the noise of a new arrival at Zev's post. A familiar voice was shouting that he had been abandoned. Philo got up from his desk. A shadow fell across my mug. I looked up: it was Saul.

"Awake already? How are you feeling?"

"How dare you?" he shouted. "How dare you desert me?"

"What?"

"You abandoned me, alone, in that nest of sodomites. That house of filth."

"Please. Softly..."

"You abandoned me!"

I stood up.

"As if it was not enough for you to take me into that disgusting place, your Lady Esther's."

"Saul," I ordered him. "Sit down. Right now." He looked at me in astonishment and to my very great surprise did as he was told.

"Understand this: Nicanor is a very fine doctor indeed. The finest in all Judea and Syria. Probably the finest in Alexandria. When you fell ill, I took you to him as quickly as I was able. His skill has brought you back to us. As to Lady Esther's – that was Service work, an investigation."

"It demeans me. It makes me defiled."

"Saul, we are all defiled. This is what our work means," I said. "I was asked to look after you. And I have done so, as well as I am able."

He looked away, back towards the door and to Philo's desk in entreaty and disgust.

"Now," I went on, "we should talk to Yehuda's former friends among Yeshua's followers and find out what they can tell us about his last hours. Do you agree?"

Saul gave no sign.

"Good. You told me you'd acquired a cloak that belonged to one of Yeshua's followers when you arrested him. Have you still got it? Bring it to me."

Saul turned away, his eyes looking to Philo for reassurance as he went to the barracks stairs.

"I asked you to be easy with him."

"And I asked you for a competent assistant. Someone suited to this sort of work."

"Keep him with you for another day. That will be all you need, won't it?"

"Philo, Saul takes everything that happens to him as a personal affront. He cannot see things as they are. I do regret taking him to Esther's. But it's wrong for him to be angry about Nico: he did him some good."

"In what way?"

I gave Philo a full account of yesterday's interview with Marcus. "It wasn't Marcus' thugs who hurt him. It was me – and a bruise from the fight he got into at the Galilean's arrest. I asked Nico to treat him."

"And his prognosis?"

"As you can see, the patient is back to his usual health. And sense of righteousness."

An opening door echoed from the barracks above, Saul's legs appeared, bent at the same alarming angle as before, and began their descent. He moved freely, I was relieved to notice, and he carried a garment sashed in his arms. At the table he laid it out unfolded, and stood back.

"There." He had brought us something that demanded our attention.

The garment must once have been an expensive and cherished article: seamless, double-weave. Now it was muddied, torn, repaired and torn again, and it had the sweat and dirt of long-repeated wear upon it. It was linen, undoubtedly. Why would anyone choose to take fine clothes with them when they decided to follow an itinerant holy man committed to conspicuous and common poverty? Unless he wished the garment to say something about who he was.

"It must be the property of a priest." I turned to Saul. "There was a renegade priest among Yeshua's followers. And you tried to arrest him. Now why would we do that?"

"We had orders to arrest the man that your Yehuda identified for us. That was all. It was the soldiers who joined us who went for this man." He jabbed his finger against the cloth. "Not us."

"Why would our good friends turn up and want to arrest anyone other than Yeshua?" I asked Philo.

"I do not know."

"So, remind me. Help us, please: what exactly happened at the scene of the arrest. Think very carefully."

Saul opened his mouth and drew in breath. Then he paused. At last, he breathed out again, and spoke.

"It was as I told you. Yehuda approached his friends. There were two men. Identical appearance. He took the hands of one of them in his own. Looked at them, and then he kissed him in greeting. Then one of his followers, the old one, the one with a sword, went for Captain Malchus and cut his ear off."

An act of defiance and despair. We cannot remove the High Priest from office by maiming him, but at least we can maim one of his people, the captain of his guard.

"Why did the man with the sword not attack our Yehuda? It would have made sense for him to do so, wouldn't it? Think how the man must have felt. You've been itching to use this sword for half a year. Your friends have been goading you, telling you that it's all for show, that you don't have the courage to actually use it. So why not revenge yourself on the man who's just betrayed your master?"

"It's obvious," said Saul. "You attack the captain of the guard and hope that you can free Yeshua."

"And our Yehuda thought that the sword would be used on him. But it's not, and in that moment he slips away. But this still does not tell us why our good friends then set hands on one of the other followers, the one who is a priest. Why would they want to arrest him at the moment that we arrest his master?"

"If he's a priest and what Yehuda says is true – that Yeshua was expecting Elijah to come down from heaven and help him to set up the rule of the Lord over our nation – then our new king would need a High Priest by his side," said Saul.

"So why do our good friends arrest the priest and leave it to us to arrest our would-be king? I would have thought the responsibilities would be other way round. We deal with the would-be High Priest; our good friends deal with the king."

"Would-be king," said Saul.

"Would-be king. Of course."

"But they did deal with him. They dealt with Yeshua."

"Yes they did. Though that was an unintended consequence. We arrested him for his own protection, remember? Didn't we?"

"And we did not deal with the would-be High Priest. In fact, we knew nothing whatsoever about him. Unless you bother to read every page of our Yehuda's reports."

"What did Yehuda think of him?"

"He didn't like him. He thought he was too curious. Always asking questions."

"And why would he be doing that, do you think?"

"He's studious, a good pupil. He puts questions to his teacher."

"I don't think they were that sort of question."

"Yehuda's accounts mention two swords. Did the man in the linen cloak have a sword? Did he attempt to attack you, or attack our good friends?" Philo asked.

"No," said Saul. "He did not."

I sat down and moved the linen across the table.

"And you are absolutely certain that there was no question, on our part, of arresting anyone other than Yeshua?"

Philo spoke. "There can be no doubt. He was the sole target of our operation."

"So why would our good friends be so interested in arresting a renegade priest?"

"If that is what they were trying to do," said Saul.

"Well, that was what you said in your own account, my friend. Or is there something that you may have forgotten? Some detail, in all that chaos and confusion, that may have escaped your memory?"

To his credit, he took this suggestion as seriously as I had offered it to him.

"No," he said at last. "There is nothing. It happened just as I told you. The soldiers tried to arrest another man, I barred his way; we fought. He escaped me. I'm sorry. Forgive me. I failed."

"Well, then," I said, as I folded the linen tunic into a neat square, stood up, and put it under my right arm. "I think it's time that we took this garment back to its owner. Don't you?"

MOUNT ZION
3RD DAY OF THE WEEK, 8TH HOUR

"Master?"

"Saul?"

"How will we arrest them? There are ten of them. And three of us. They have swords. Two of them. And they'll use them."

We were outside the Alabarch's office at the city's southern gate. When Saul spoke, he sprang upwards on his toes as if looking down upon me from a position of inferiority. More than ever, I wished that I was with Zenobia among the harmony and slow purpose of our vines.

"Saul, if you would rather go back to the barracks and discuss this with Philo and Captain Malchus, I will not stop you."

"Never. Never."

"Good. Are you ready?"

Cassiel grunted. Saul scowled.

"Let's find these Galileans, shall we?"

Two soldiers jostled us on their way to the gate. Two of their comrades were loitering outside one of the walled gardens that lined the road down to Akel-dama. The soldiers went through some very informal exchange of duties and in a moment their comrades strode back up towards us in no kind of military style. Guard duty must be a slow business in festival week. The garden was one of those where the tombs of the rich nestle beneath the southern slopes of Mount Zion, the place to which the nations of the world will make their way, answering whatever summons the Lord will send us all, at the end of the world. The wealthy will arrive first, of course.

"Pay attention," I said to Saul as we turned back towards the city. "Our Yehuda's despatch was clear. We should follow the water carriers. What can we deduce from this?"

"That the place we are looking for does not have its own water supply?"

"And?"

"It won't be a house built for the rich families of Babylon or the Western Sea, up at the top of the hill. We're seeking a modest lodging house, close to the gate. Perhaps one of the old synagogues that were built before the aqueduct."

"Good. Well done."

We watched the women who were hauling double-handed pitchers from the pool by the gate. Then I emptied my goatskin into the dust and joined them. At first the accents were Judean. Soon I caught the sounds of Nabatea and Ashkelon, and at last, close to the gate, the twang of the north.

"Favour me, my sisters," I said, "I am old." And I held out my goatskin. They laughed, looked at each other as if to let me know that I was nothing of the sort, and covered their faces. Then a brown arm stretched out towards me from a sleeve of rags. There were streaks of ash upon her skin. Her face was pained and exhausted.

"And why would a man of strength expect a woman to serve him?" Her voice was pure Galilee.

"Sister, I thirst." There was more laughter from the other women. She did not smile, but pushed the goatskin down into the pool, hauled it up and handed it to me.

"Where do you stay in Jerusalem, my sister?"

"The place that my husband found for our family," she said, hefted her pitcher onto her left hip and turned away into the crowd.

I stood back, slung my goatskin on my shoulder and watched her go. I caught Cassiel's eye and indicated the departing woman as she passed to the left and climbed up the steps towards the slopes of Mount Zion. We lost her, took a left turn back towards the walls and found ourselves in an impasse: the last two water carriers of the afternoon, one of whom might have been the woman at the pool, vanished into a building at the end of the street.

It was a synagogue and lodging house of quite sprawling opulence. We were among the rich. Above its door was an inscription in Greek and Hebrew:

This synagogue, this lodging house and its garden were built and endowed for the benefit of the craftsmen of the Temple in stone & in wood, in the third year of its restoration, by Iosefos from Arimathea, the president of the synagogue, son of a synagogue president, grandson of a synagogue president.

"If this Iosefos had the resources of a guild of carpenters and stonemasons at his disposal, why couldn't he arrange his own water supply from the aqueduct?"

"There were riots," said Cassiel. "People objected to the aqueduct. They said it defiled the city. They flung themselves into the pits of its foundations and fought battles with the builders."

The man who opened to us seemed far too young to be the president of a synagogue. He was younger than Philo, and he wore the long prayer shawl of the conspicuously pious. He saw Saul's Temple Guard tunic and something blossomed when he realised that Cassiel was a messenger.

"We are seeking the followers and family of Yeshua from Nazareth," Saul announced before the young man could greet us.

"Thank you, Saul." I pulled him back, my hand on his shoulder, and introduced myself by name. A trace of recognition passed over the young man's face. He was full of expectation. "We wish to speak with the synagogue's president."

He must have understood the doubt. "You are speaking with him. My name is Iosefos, son of Iosefos. I have authority here. Now: do you have news for us?"

"News?"

"You have found his body? And the men who stole it?"

Silence.

"We told you: we are seeking the followers of Yeshua from Nazareth," Saul repeated too loudly. I gripped his shoulder again.

"May we speak with you in private?"

The hope fled from Iosefos' eyes and he looked down in silence. "You are welcome in this house," he said at last. "All of you."

As we climbed the stairs, the latches of memory finally fell into their slots. "Aren't you the son of old Yussuf?" I asked the young man. "I knew your father." The boy looked round at me sharply, eyes overflowing again with hope. "He did me a favour once," I told him. "He loaned me a couple of men to knock down a wall between two rooms. I've much to thank him for."

Iosefos glanced backwards and spoke softly. "Are you from the Service? Because my father once told me that Solomon Eliades was a man who could find out the truth of things. If you can, then you really are welcome in this house."

We passed a door from behind which came the sound of sonorous chanting with many voices on a falling cadence in prayers for the dead.

"I'm grateful, my friend. Your father was always generous, a friend of the Service. Is there anything that I can do to help you and your people?"

We came to the head of the stairs and walked out onto a wide roof with a view across the lower city, the slopes of Mount Zion and the valley below. Iosefos looked at me for a long time in silence.

"The body of the man whose family are my guests here at Pesach. Our Yeshua. It has vanished from his tomb. We buried him on Preparation Day. By the end of the double Shabbats, the tomb had been opened and his body removed." He looked at Saul. "I've been asking the Temple Guard to send someone to find the body and arrest whoever took it for three days now. It would be a comfort to us all. And it would stop the women." He paused. "I went to the Prefect's staff when I got no answer from the Guard. Marcus Ulpianus sent two of his men to guard the tomb. That was practical, don't you think? Guarding the scene of desecration after the crime?"

Marcus had already goaded me to this distraction. A mystery without a future, one that would lead us away from the truth about our Yehuda.

"And it hasn't stopped the women," he went on. "They cannot understand that he is dead. They imagine that it cannot have happened."

"What has happened?"

"I told you. And I told the Temple Guard. A crime. Down there, at my family's tomb. Please, investigate it and tell me what you find."

Saul's squirming became insupportable. He stood up and flung out his arms as if he was about to suffer another collapse.

"We are here to question the followers of Yeshua from Nazareth," he shouted.

The chanting ceased behind the door. Silence. Then slow movement, whispers, and another silence before the voices began again.

"We have come to return some property to one of them," I added quietly. "But first, may I speak to them? In particular, to the keeper of their common purse."

Iosefos looked at me sharply, and we stood in silence for too long. At last, he spoke.

"Our guests are below, mourning their dead. They have been there since the end of Shabbat. Except for the time that the women went to the tomb. I should never have permitted that. I will ask them if they wish to speak with you." He turned back towards us at the top of the stairs. "But if I were you I would not repeat your question about Yehuda, the keeper of their common purse. Unless you know where they can find him."

Again, the voices vanished into silence below. Then there was the sound of argument, men shouting at each other, and a woman keening. Someone female was refusing to go back to Galilee. She had to stay here in Jerusalem until he was found. At least two were insisting that they would go home as soon as Pesach ended. And then the woman again: they have not found him. They have not found him. And the male voice: he told us to go back home. He told us to go to Galilee.

Footsteps sounded upon the stairs. I moved smartly over to the other side of the roof, and gave my attention to the city walls, the hillside gardens, the Siloam road and the potters' kilns beyond.

"Boss." Cassiel touched my arm. Iosefos had returned.

Four peasants filed onto the roof behind him. Each was at the extremes of exhaustion and grief. They had the same look of frayed absence, the vacancy in their eyes, that Zenobia had endured in her mourning. Their beards were wild, their hair tangled with filth, their faces withdrawn into emptiness and sorrow. They were present, but hardly with us at all.

The first was tall and broad-shouldered, his beard and his hair smeared grey and white. His face looked as if it had spent its entire existence battered by wind, rain and sun. Behind him came two dark-haired men who must have been ten years younger, if it is possible to judge the age of any peasant who has survived his second decade. They were squat brutes, their features caved in, and they stared at me with exhausted violence in their eyes. The last of the four was taller than the first by a span: his hair hung long upon his shoulders and his beard reached down to his chest. His face was a cliff, a dark, overhanging brow, eyes sunk deep. Of the four he was the one who carried himself with some dignity. He stared at us, void of either hostility or expectation. My eyes scanned them a second time and I forced myself to gather the treasure of first impressions before they were destroyed by gesture and speech.

"Peace upon this house," I said to them in Aramaic. "We are sorry for your grief, my brothers. We would bring you comfort in your mourning."

They stared straight through us, across the roof, to the outside air, the gardens and the tombs below us.

"Shlomo bar Eleazar," I said, inclining my head respectfully. "My brothers in toil," I nodded to either side. The four men stared at me, their exhaustion outweighing any hostility.

"Shimon bar Yonah," said the big man. He glanced to his right. "Yakoub and Yehonatan. My cousins."

"Yehuda bar Yussef," said the fourth man, and barely inclined his head.

The old roughneck. The two thugs. And the twin brother. All from our Yehuda's account. The twin's hands were lost in the folds of his robe. I took the linen cloak from around my shoulders. Then slowly, with the care of the old, I squatted down on my haunches. They squatted too, in a circle, looking inwards. I looked at Saul. Saul followed. Cassiel stood upright, just behind me.

"We wish to return this garment to its owner, one of your brothers."

"And how did you come by that?" one of the two thugs asked. Perhaps it was Yakoub. Before I could answer, the other looked up, suddenly hostile and alert, and said to Saul:

"It's you, is it? You're here for some more, are you? Well?" His teeth were broken and yellow. Shimon-the-Rock stretched out his arm to calm him.

"Brothers," I said, "we are here to restore this thing to its owner. We mean you no harm," I said to Iosefos.

"I could have saved you time, my friend. Thaddeus bar Ptolemai's not here," he said.

"You want the priest-boy?" Yehonatan asked.

"He ran away," said Yakoub.

"Gone and left us, didn't he?"

"Where may we find him?"

"He told us that he was going to Emmaous."

"Emmaous?" Saul asked. "Why would he go there?"

"Let me ask the questions," I said to him quietly.

"Was he sick?" Saul asked.

They laughed. Emmaous was a place where the rich went in search of healing from the hot springs that welled up from the world below. The town's brothels did a roaring trade – except at festival time, when everyone came to Jerusalem. A Jew journeying to Emmaous mid-Pesach would be remarkable, a priest unthinkable.

Yehonatan went on: "He said he was going there for healing. Said he had to go back, to be with his own people."

"And who were they?"

"He ran away. Not the only one, was he?" he added, looking at Shimon-the-Rock.

"What do you mean, eh?"

"You ran away," said Yakoub, "didn't you?"

"… ran away," Yehonatan echoed.

"And now you're all for running away again, back to Galilee."

"… back to Galilee."

"And what about the women, eh? How are they going to finish burying him?"

"Enough," said Yehuda-the-Twin. "We agreed we would consider that tomorrow. Didn't we?" Yakoub looked up at him. Yehonatan rocked backwards and forwards on his heels, bobbing his head, saying nothing.

"Aye, like, we did," said Yakoub. "He said he was going back to his own people. Whoever they might be. He's an odd one, the priest-boy."

"Always hanging around with that Yehuda," said Yehonatan.

"And where's that Yehuda got to? That's what we'd like to know."

Shimon-the-Rock leaned forward, his hands pressed together and looked straight at me. He was taller and broader than Cassiel.

"Well, look, lad" – he must have been ten or fifteen years my junior – "this coat of his, we could look after it, see? Look after it for him, sort of style. Save you the trouble, eh?" He reached out towards the linen.

"Aye, we'd make sure that he got it back, like," said Yakoub.

"Thank you," I said. "I'll return it to him myself."

"What? You told us you were bringing it here to give it to him. Didn't you?"

"Of course," Shimon said to me. "Of course, lad. It's better that you do that. Give it back yourself."

Yakoub snorted. A moment later Yehonatan, rather more softly, snorted too.

"Thank you," I said to the Twin. He shrugged and waved a hand in dismissal. "When do you expect him back?"

"Well, now, how should we know?" Shimon said. "How should we know anything, eh?"

"You're Temple Guard, aren't you?" Yakoub asked. "You should know. You've got your eyes everywhere."

"My brothers," said Iosefos, "we should resume our mourning."

Shimon-the-Rock and the two thugs stood up with some show of grace. Our interview was at an end. I rose unsteadily and stretched out my arms in front of Cassiel and Saul as they stood back. Yehuda-the-Twin did not move.

"We have also come to ask you about another matter," I said.

Shimon turned back. He at least wished to be helpful. The two thugs gave no sign. Iosefos spread his arms. "Of course."

"The man who kept your common purse. We would like—"

Yakoub laughed out loud, a long, cracked, derisive hoot. Iosefos was frowning in anger. Shimon-the-Rock looked completely defeated and horrified by this question.

"That bastard?" said Yehonatan. "You're asking us about that bastard?"

"Don't you know?" This was Shimon, and he spoke to Saul. "You were there, weren't you? You saw what happened? Our fixer and our best friend, our Yehuda from Kerioth, he turned the master in, didn't he? You saw it. He was with you. You, the Temple Guard. What had you done to him? He was always good to me, Yehuda. Couldn't do too much for you, that lad. He loved the master; he was always with him. What did you do to him? To make him change? What did you do?" I was relieved of the necessity of responding to this by one thing: Shimon-the-Rock was addressing not me but Saul, the representative of the Temple Guard, in his uniform. Then Yakoub addressed me.

"You should ask him yourself, shouldn't you? Why don't you? Bring him along here and let's hear what he's got to say."

"We would have done so," I said. "But, unfortunately, that won't be possible."

"Why not?"

"Because Yehuda from Kerioth is dead."

The instant of the first impression is always the truth. They had no idea. It may have been welcome news, but it was still a completely unexpected shock to every one of them. I said nothing more, and stared back. At last Yehuda-the-Twin spoke.

"What has happened to him?"

"He died sometime between the start of Pesach and dawn on the first day of the week."

There were no glances at each other. They looked straight at me, without words.

"He was murdered," I said.

"Who did this thing?" Yehuda asked.

"This is the rope that he was hanged with," Saul shouted, and threw down the length whose origins he had been unable to establish in the market place two days earlier. The four men looked down at it without any sign of recognition or understanding.

"Don't you know it?" He picked it up and pulled it taut. His hands were trembling.

There was a far longer silence than I had expected at this. Shimon-the-Rock looked across at us with loathing. We've lost them, I thought: whatever help they might have been inclined to give us, even without their being aware of it, was lost. The whole thing was going down to Sheol in darkness and despair.

"Did any of you," I asked, "see your brother Yehuda from Kerioth after the arrest of your teacher?"

They sat mute.

"Either that night or on Preparation Day?"

Nothing. Saul stirred at my side.

"That's builder's rope," he said.

"Yes. We can see that," said Iosefos. "Now—"

"What's your trade, brother?" Saul asked the twin.

"Stonemason."

I grasped Saul's shoulder. To my relief, he crouched down again and said nothing.

"May I see your hands?" I asked the Twin. With reluctance, he lifted his arms and turned out his palms to face me. They had the deep grain of sand and masonry dust in every line and callus. "And your brother – he was a carpenter?"

"He was."

"Thank you," I said. "You have been most helpful, my brothers. You should go back to your prayers and comfort the women in their sorrow. I'm sorry for your family's grief. May you be comforted among the mourners." I looked at Yehuda-the-Twin directly. His head and shoulders were illuminated by light from the western side of the awning. This would have been the same face and body as his late brother. A big, burly presence, a firm, rounded chin and a long face with brows that hung like a lintel above his eyes. Solid, unanswerable strength.

I took the short length of string from the inside of my cloak, where it had been since Saul had given it to me, and I held it up.

"One other thing," I said, "that you may be able to help me with. Do you recognise this at all?"

Silence again, broken only by their breathing: deep, sharp intakes, each fuller than the last. What do you say to people who have watched their teacher go to his death? Perhaps they have even encouraged him in his choice. Imagine you are about to step into a world transformed, one in which our good friends have gone and the rule of justice, peace and plenty begins. And what if that promise has been snatched from you just at the moment you were sure of it being kept? Snatched away by the most obvious, predictable and undeniable promise-keeper of all: death. That's what happens when you set up as king of your people and you've got a pedigree proving you're entitled to do so.

Then Yakoub spoke.

"It's Yehuda's, that. It's the bastard's ball of twine."

"What do you mean?"

"It's his twine. I told you. It's the purse-keeper's twine. He was always fiddling with it."

"What do you mean, fiddling with it?"

"We want to know what he used it for," said Saul.

Iosefos from Arimathea sighed and stretched out his arm to beckon silence and attention from his guests.

"My brothers, be patient." Then he turned to Shimon. "Do you recognise it, my friend?"

"Well, see, he used it for tying them purses. He was always giving the money away, Yehuda. Like the master told him. He always tied them up with that twine, eh?"

"Who taught him to tie knots?"

Shimon smiled and shook his head. Yehuda looked at us with derision in his eyes.

"Come on. You're fishermen, aren't you?"

"You think that we could teach that bastard Yehuda?"

"None of us could teach him anything, that one. Except the master. Not even the master, sometimes."

"The master was the only one he ever listened to."

"Yeah, and the master listened to him."

"Him and bar Ptolemai."

"Enough, Yakoub," said the Twin. Then he stood up and spoke to me. "What he means is that my brother would tell him what to do. And he obeyed. Always. He was always helpful, Yehuda. Always did what my brother asked him to. 'Do what you must do, Yehuda.' And he did it. Like he always did."

"Perhaps you could tell me what happened to Yehuda's purse. He kept your common purse, didn't he?"

"They have no common purse, as you put it," Iosefos said. "They have nothing. Do you understand? None of them have anything at all."

He took a folded papyrus from his tunic.

"How much do you think that it costs to purchase one of these from your good friends?"

14th Nisan. To the duty officer, day watch. For the release of the body of the executed criminal Iesos Nazarenos to the bearer of this receipt, who will identify himself as Iosefos president of the woodworkers' synagogue.

Beneath it was what must be the Prefect's signature.

"And you ask if we are rich. Have you any idea how much I had to bribe the Prefect's secretary just to get a chance to speak to His Excellency on Preparation Day? That was nothing compared to the sum I had to give Pilatos himself to sign that chit. Then there were Quintus' men. I know them – their corruption is decent and restrained. They begged me to take the body – one less for them to dispose of. But I still had to pay them. And that, my friend, is where the common purse of Yeshua and its contents went. His brother and I will ensure his mother and her daughters are not exposed to the humiliation of beggary. And his wife and their son too."

They were all on their feet now. Iosefos spread out his arms.

"Brothers," he spoke in Aramaic. "Let us not quarrel now." He turned to me and spoke in Greek. "Yeshua told us. In the room below." He gestured downwards. "When the master explained to us what he was going to do. What he was expecting to happen." The moment lengthened into silence. "It was folly," he said. "It was madness. He led us down to disaster. To death. None of us can understand it. Especially the women. And now we cannot complete his burial and mourn him according to the Law."

Iosefos turned to the followers.

"Brothers. You should return to your prayers."

There was a loud knocking at the door below. Iosefos left the room. The followers fell silent as soon as he was gone. Only Yakoub and Yehonatan stared at us with unconcealed hostility. The other two could not meet my eyes. At last voices came from below, then a woman speaking too. The curtain behind us swung back and Iosefos returned. Behind him, two women wreathed in black shawls entered the room and shuffled uncertainly to the side of Yehuda-the-Twin. One of them was old and wrinkled. Beside her stood the woman from the pool. She held in front of her a child, a boy of perhaps six or seven years. Beside Iosefos was a young man, a slight figure, thin face, light beard and dark eyes; no distinguishing marks. I mentally thanked my good Yehuda for providing descriptions of each of the followers in his reports.

"You!" Saul cried out.

"There you are, son," said Shimon-the-Rock. "I told you he'd be back, didn't I? That's the lad you should give the linen to, see? Before you go, like."

I held out the linen, but, if Thaddeus bar Ptolemai recognised it, he showed no sign. For a moment he could not speak, but seemed as if about to burst. He stretched out an arm towards us. His mouth opened and a look of ecstasy and astonishment distorted his face. Finally, he spoke.

"I've seen him," he said. "In Emmaous. I've seen him."
Then everyone started shouting.

TOMB
3RD DAY OF THE WEEK,
10TH HOUR

Bar Ptolemai was at the centre of the followers, a look of blissful detachment on his face. The women were crying – we must bury him. Shimon was shouting at anyone who would listen that he had told them so all along, see.

Cassiel caught my arm.

"Boss, we should go. This is not our fight."

I put the linen down on the table by the long wall and we walked to the door. The last words I heard as we left were screamed in Aramaic:

"You're wrong."

"And so is he. And all of you."

"Aye," someone shouted back. "You're right there."

"No, he's not."

"Neither are you."

And finally:

"You mean we don't have to sit *shiva* for him after all?"

We had gone twenty paces in the street before we heard the lodging house door open and close. Iosefos from Arimathea ran towards us.

"You offered to examine my family's tomb. Now, more than ever, I would be grateful for anything that you can do."

He led us down to the Alabarch's gatehouse. Beyond, the dust of the road shone golden between the green shoots of the gardens and the white tombs by the city walls. Down at Akel-dama, the potters' kilns were burning. It was a bright spring day, at the time between afternoon warmth and evening chill. The time that I should be walking among the vines with Zenobia.

"There's a guard at the tomb," said Iosefos. "They threw Yephthah my gardener out and won't let him back in."

"And you want me to arrange access to the place?"

"Yes," he said, without shame or presumption. And he stopped, quite suddenly, at a gated enclosure. It was barred by the two soldiers we had seen relieving their fellows earlier in the afternoon. They stood to when we faced them.

"We've already told you, lad," the one on the right said to Iosefos. "You can't come in, see?"

"Orders of the Prefect," said his comrade. This one was taller, and spoke with a Syrian accent. He had bloodshot eyes and a deep scar across the right side of his face.

"What's your name, friend?"

"Never mind," he barked, and looked through me.

"The gardens are my property," said Iosefos. "The tomb is my family's. You cannot prevent me from performing a duty to my dead."

The Syrian spat.

"But we can, see. Prefect says so."

"Then tell your Prefect these men are from the Temple Guard and they have orders to examine the tomb."

The Syrian stared back, completely indifferent to the needs of the Temple Guard.

"My orders from the Antonia: keep out unauthorised locals."

Slowly, and with my eyes on the second soldier, I slipped my hand into my tunic with exaggerated care and withdrew the document within.

"I have the commission of His Sanctity the High Priest Caiaphas ben Ananias to go freely within Jerusalem to investigate matters of religion and observance at festival time," I told him. "The tomb within this garden is a matter of religion."

I offered the Syrian Philo's papyrus, and to my surprise he took it and stared into it for perhaps ten heartbeats. I knew by the way that his eyes stared without moving that he could not read.

"See," he said at last. "It says 'within Jerusalem' here, doesn't it?" He looked around in a self-consciously stupid way before smiling at us. "And we're outside the city walls here, aren't we?" He pushed the papyrus back into my hands. "Sorry, pal. Your priest's permission doesn't open doors here. No, not gates neither. My boss decides all that."

"This is disgraceful," Iosefos said.

I held up my hand. "I also have," I said to the older Syrian, "the authority of the Prefect's head of security to investigate the case of how this man's tomb came to be opened and robbed of its contents. His express authority."

I handed him the letter Zenobia had sent me. *Come back in three days or not at all.* The big Syrian held it up. Again, his eyes did not move. When he looked up there was the first trace of uncertainty.

"You can go and send to Marcus Ulpianus, if you like. He'll confirm the commission, if you doubt the evidence of your own eyes."

"Hermas," he said to the younger soldier.

"Boss?"

"I'm hungry, aren't I? Go and get me a pastry and cheese from Gershon's inside the gate. Go on, lad. I'll cover for you. Marcus the bastard'll never know."

When his comrade was out of earshot he handed back the letter. By now he looked satisfyingly nervous about querying an order from the head of intelligence.

"You've got till just before dusk. I don't want you lot and His Honour here when the trumpets sound. Understand? Then you get out. Like a dose."

"Thank you."

"Don't touch nothing. Not a thing, you understand?" He looked at Iosefos when he spoke these words. "Not a thing, Your Honour. I'm watching you."

He opened the gate and Iosefos entered his garden.

"Thank you. Do you always do that?" he asked me.

"What?"

"Treat our occupiers like that."

"Marcus Ulpianus really did suggest that I examine your tomb. He even encouraged me. Now, can you think of any reason he would do that?"

I paid attention to our surroundings. We were in the paradise of a rich man, a secluded garden far larger and more opulent than our retreat behind the press house in the Judean hills. By the gate there was a fountain that by some clever device concealed among the rocks – not, surely, a hidden culvert from the aqueduct above the city – played water in twelve cascades. Beyond this, a terrace shaded by seven palm trees led towards a line of tombs.

They had been cut into the rock of the hillside, where the slope curved towards the city wall. Above us there was a clear line of sight to the open roof of Iosefos' lodging house. All but one of the tombs were sealed. The third in line was open. A dark square cut into the rock above a low step.

"What do you want me to do for you?" I asked him.

"I want you to tell me who stole his body. What they did."

It seemed to me that they should look no further than our good friends for help with that. Cassiel was already bent low, peering into the darkness. Saul stood back among the palms.

"Master?"

"Saul?"

"Will I have to make a record of this?"

"That won't be necessary. This is not a formal investigation. At least not yet." I turned to Cassiel. "Commit the account of what we see and do to memory, will you? We can make a written record later, if it is needed."

"Yes, boss."

Saul turned away, more relieved than offended.

"Now, let me listen to what this place tells me, and tell you what I hear. Cassiel, would you stand to one side? Iosefos, you too, if you please."

I looked down at the ground for some twenty heartbeats. Initial impressions. The most important things that you discover about any scene. I stared at the dark rectangle. And I listened.

The stone that should seal the tomb stood upright against the natural rock of the hillside just to the right of a shuttle bush. The buds upon it were in flower. They had the soft, curled brightness of the blossoms in my vineyard. At the foot of the tomb, the plants and stones had been trodden hard by many feet. Men had come and gone to the left and the right and there were traces of the wheels of a cart. I looked away from the rock towards the road. More disturbance, torn branches and a confusion of feet, boots and other objects that I could not identify.

A few paces from the tomb, tangled in a bush, was a hemp satchel. By it, on the ground, an unstoppered amphora, its contents long since poured out onto the earth. I pulled the satchel from the branches and found within it two coarse sponges, each a mass of fibrous desiccation, and a still-sealed flask of oil.

"What is this?"

"Property of the guild," said Iosefos. "Mistress Mariam took it when she came here to wash the body."

I knelt by the rock and ran my hands across its surface. Smooth-dressed. Chisel-marks in lines slant-wards down its sides. Rough-hewn and raw upon the long and wide external sides. There were chipped scars and scuffs on the lower edges, the width of two fingers. To the left clean and sharp; to the right worked raw and flaking. I turned to the tomb's threshold: limestone dust and rock chips were trodden into the mud.

"How did you move the rock?"

"I did not move it," Iosefos said. "My servants set it firm in the doorway with an iron bar and mallets. Yehuda-the-Twin and I saw them do it. They set the stone properly."

"Where is the bar?"

He indicated the far side of the bush. An iron rod the length of a tall man's leg lay there. Beyond it, run into the bushes, there was a wooden handcart. I pushed the branches aside. A sack of spices lay unopened in the bed of the cart. The mourners had not had time to complete their preparation of the body. And whoever had broken into the tomb had not bothered to steal a sack-load of expensive spice.

"What happened here?"

"I thought you were supposed to tell us?"

"I'm asking for your account. You were here, weren't you? Tell me what you saw."

"We rushed. There was no time to finish unloading the cart. We left it behind."

I looked at the sack and pushed it upright. There was the trader's mark and name painted in red on its front. *Mariby*. And the words *The Only Genuine* beneath it in Greek. I rubbed my fingers against the sacking and sniffed the bitterness of aloes.

I picked up the iron bar and turned it in my hands. The tapered end of it was caked with the dust of the rock. A slash of raw metal glinted where it had bitten. I laid its pick to the base of the stone and leaned upon it. Nothing.

"I am an old man," I said to Cassiel. "You are young and strong."

He grasped the bar, breathed in, braced and leaned upon it. The stone lifted with ease.

I stood back. Saul had retreated along the line of palms and was standing at the gate.

"Come and observe," I called to him. He dawdled forwards.

I looked again at the chaos of footprints, markings and dust. It said nothing to me but the crowd's rumble of chaos, haste and fear. No voices cried out.

"And what happened afterwards?"

"When, exactly?"

"When you came back and found the tomb open. Tell me, exactly, what did you see?"

"It was as you see it, here and now." He spoke slowly, as if he was picking out his memories with care and examining them before speaking. "The rock and the bar. And the stone turned aside. The cart with the spices was further towards my father's resting place. We moved it to keep it out of the way of the soldiers."

"And that is all that has changed since you came here and found it open?"

"I – yes. That's all. But I did not find the tomb opened."

"What do you mean?"

"The women found it. Not I. The women, when they came to wash the body and finish the business with the spices."

"And when was that, exactly?"

Iosefos pointed up to the balcony of his lodging house, which loomed above the city walls, shrouded by the trailing branches of trees coming into bud, but barely more than two hundred paces, in a straight line, from where we stood.

"Do you see that? That is where we spent the double Shabbat of Pesach. Up there. Within clear sight."

I turned back towards the tomb. I was four or five paces from the place where the stone would have been. I stepped to the right and looked up. The tomb was obscured by the bushes of the garden and the bulging rock. But they must have had a clear view from the lodging house of the ground just outside the tomb.

"And no-one saw anything, in those days? From dusk on the first Shabbat till morning on the first day of the week?"

"Nothing."

"Do you want me to question the women? About what they saw?"

"No, I do not," he said sharply. Then he drew back. "No. There would be no point. Their accounts would be of no value."

"What is an admissible account in law and what is factual and accurate and tells us the truth are sometimes two quite different things."

He made no response.

"As you wish. Then tell me in your own words. What happened when they came here?"

"To understand that, you must understand what happened on Preparation Day."

He squatted down and placed his hands on his knees. I followed him, slowly, the pain flaring in my joints. Cassiel did so too. Only Saul stood aloof.

"Have you any idea how difficult it is to get in front of the Prefect on the afternoon of Preparation Day? I had to bribe five of his freedmen just to get to the door of his office. Marcus, his head of security, is a highly unaccommodating man. Then I had to beg. Yes, beg. And offer him a very large sum of money. Everything of my own, half the lodging house treasury and every last obol and asser of the money that Yehuda had left there. The Prefect's greed is as vulgar as his temper is coarse. I regret very much that I had to use the funds that were intended for the poor as a bribe to get Yeshua's body back. I don't think that Yeshua would have wanted me to do such a thing. Of course, he never imagined that I would need to – that was the problem. I will repay that omission, from my own hands, for a long time to come. The poor are still with us even if he is not. But we could not let them throw his body onto the spoil heap for the dogs. And we could not pollute the festival Shabbat. He had to be buried. Do you understand?"

"Of course. What happened?"

"We had no time. Young Yakoub and his brother the Twin tried to march everyone back to the lodging house. It was the women who were the problem. They wouldn't be told. We had to drag them away from Golgotha screaming. It was only when my servants arrived with the cart that we could make them move. It was already late in the afternoon. We ran through the streets with the cart. We had no time even to wash the body. I sent a friend down to the spice market. When we came to the Siloam Gate I ordered Yakoub and Yehuda to take the women up to the lodging house and then I begged the Temple guards to let us out of the city. More time lost. They were terrified: in the end they decided that leaving a body unburied in the city at Pesach must be far worse than people performing the work of burial after dusk. They let us go, and we ran here. The spices were already waiting. My friend had had the presence of mind to bring a winding sheet. It had not occurred to me that we would need one. We wrapped up the body as it was, unwashed, and spread the spices over it. Then I heard the trumpets sounding for the start of Pesach. While I was still in there. We climbed out of the tomb and my servants fixed the stone. Then we ran again and the trumpets sounded for the last time. When I got to the walls, one of my men was physically preventing the Temple Guard from shutting the gates."

I looked up to the roof of the lodging house. The two women stood there, the light of evening cast across them. Between them, the young boy.

"Then surely you had no time to set the rock in the mouth of the tomb?"

"I told you. I saw it done."

"You were in a hurry. I understand." I looked into the darkness of the tomb. "Is it possible that your people left the stone unbalanced? So that it could be easily moved?"

"Come," he said. "Look at this." He led me deeper into the garden and the next of the tombs cut into the rock. "My father's tomb," he said. "We buried him at the end of last winter. Look at it yourself. Shem and Nathan set it. Masters, both of them. They know how to work accurately, and they know how to work fast."

I looked at the stone of his father's tomb. It was the same size as the stone that I had just examined. Well set and heavy. Immovable.

"And I set my shoulder to it when they heaved. I saw the joint. It was a good piece of work."

"What else do you remember?"

"We stood back just as they finished. Then the Temple horns sounded the start of Pesach. We dropped our tools and we ran back to the gate."

"And you are sure that you locked the gate?"

"Of course, I did. I was the last to leave."

"And when you returned here once the double Shabbat was over, what did you find?"

"I told you. The women came here first."

"Then show me what you saw."

He stooped and slid through the space, legs first, with a grace that surprised me in a man so broad. Cassiel followed. Only Saul refused the invitation. He trembled when he spoke.

"No. I will not touch such a place."

It was the stench that shocked me. This was not the stench of death. The smell of ripe unguents and spices filled my nostrils. Oil of myrrh. The bitterness of aloes. The smothering, perfumed oppression of nard. And I felt the softness beneath my feet. When I moved, my feet slid upon the stone of the tomb's floor. Slowly, with the usual agony, I bent down to an uneasy squat and waited for my eyes to look into the darkness within. I am in Sheol, I thought. The world that my Benjamin and Eleazar inhabit. My sons are in Sheol. And I am here, in another man's tomb.

"Show me."

Iosefos shuffled around and indicated with his right hand.

"Nothing has changed." I followed the sweep of his arm. "The light of the morning sun was behind me and it illuminated this space." He indicated the rear of the tomb. "I could see it quite clearly. There was nothing to be hidden here. I looked and I saw what I saw."

He paused for a moment and then went on, his eyes unblinking. "I saw it all. Quite clearly. My tomb, with four slabs. Two here. Those two there. And Nicodemus' spices piled up where we had left them. There was another pile too. That one. Just there. And that was it. The place where we laid Yeshua, there was nothing. His body had gone. The women were right, as far as that was concerned."

I peered into the gloom. Forms began to resolve themselves. The lower left-hand deck of the tomb. The same position in the tomb at the farmhouse where, two winters ago, I had laid my sons together. No body was there. But a shadow, some mass, at the near side of the space.

"What is that?"

"The shroud we wrapped him in. Whoever did this, they weren't interested in anything but the body."

I turned, squatted, and peered into the vacant spaces of burial. Whoever had done this had taken the trouble to fold up Yeshua's shroud with care and leave it placed neatly at the head of his resting place, untroubled by the fear of disturbance. They had been confident, unconcerned with Shabbat and the laws of hygiene.

"And that is all that you saw?"

"That is all."

"Did you search this place? Did you move or disturb anything?"

"No. We did not."

"Not even the grave-cloth?"

"No, I won't disturb the repose of those who have gone down to Sheol. Not until it is time to collect their bones."

I looked again at the slab upon which the body had been laid.

"Again, who came here before you?"

"The women." He was silent for a long time. "The women. You must understand something. Before I tell you this."

"What?"

"They'd spent the day at Golgotha watching him die. His mother. His sister. His wife. His child. None of us had slept the night before.

None of us had eaten. Then we'd rushed to bury him, and the women were taken back to the lodging house to prepare the meal and scour the rooms for leaven. It was dusk when I returned, and Mother Mariam was lighting the lamp. I still had my cloak on, and my staff in my hand. We ate in haste. Do you know why? We were expecting, at any moment, that the soldiers would come for us. I was waiting, with every mouthful I ate, for the hammering on the doors. The previous night he had promised us that we would not eat and drink wine again until we were together, with him, living in the kingdom of the Almighty, here and now in Jerusalem. We sat down with our cloaks and our staffs, and the boy, little Yeuda, his son – he'd just watched his father die at Golgotha – looked around and he asked us the question: *Why is this night not like other nights?*

I looked down at the spices of death that oozed between my feet. There was silence in the tomb for a long time. Then voices came to us.

"Come on. Out you get. You're leaving. Now."

It was the Syrian, and Saul echoing his words.

"The day's ending."

We stirred, rose, and stumbled towards the square of light.

"What happened?" I asked Iosefos. "Never mind that evening. What happened in the morning?"

He looked up at me just as Cassiel was vanishing into the light of the upper world.

"We spent two days praying together in that room. In sight of the garden and this tomb. Two days. By dawn on the first day of the week the women were desperate to be released. They were frenzied, all of them." He knelt and stretched himself through the hole. "They tore at the latch and ran down here as soon as the horns sounded for daybreak. They begged the watchmen to open the gates and they ran down here."

He too vanished into the light. I was alone in the tomb. I looked around, at the heaps of spices, the stained slab and the folded cloth.

There was nothing here that gave me any clue to this mystery. A shadow moved across the interior wall of the tomb. I looked up to the light, and gasped. Framed by the rock, a figure stood in the garden with just the stance and attitude – head turned, shoulders dipped – that I had seen our Yehuda take up so many times. I knelt, grasped the cold rock and pulled myself forward into the fading day.

It was Saul who stood by the entrance. He was speaking to the soldiers, though I could not tell what he was saying. Cassiel walked past them without acknowledging their presence. The Syrian stared at me with stark loathing as I stood up. I turned to Iosefos.

"Go on."

"I was up in the lodging house, and I heard the scream. From down here. Screams such as I have never heard before or since. It was not just from his widow, Mistress Mariam. It was from them all. When they found that the tomb had been opened. And it was empty."

Saul turned away in disgust and strode back to the garden gate.

"Come on, lads," said the Syrian. "Don't make me have to encourage you to go home."

Iosefos held me by the arm and drew me towards him. When his lips were a finger's breadth from my ears he spoke, in a hushed rasp, urgent and low.

"That's when the trouble started," he said. He stood back and looked at me. "They've started to see things. They keep seeing him. Him. In daylight. They've half-convinced themselves that he's still alive."

He leaned close to me again.

"And now it's not just the women. They've persuaded Shimon-the-Rock that he's seen him too. And now there's bar Ptolemai."

I stood back. Men were coming back from the dead all over Jerusalem. First the man up at Beth-Anya; now the man who was supposed to have brought him back. It was the sort of thing that – if you were pious and enthusiastic for freedom – you imagined must have happened in the time of Yehuda Maccabeus and his liberation of the nation from our Syrian friends: patriots whose bodies had been mangled by unbelievers were restored to physical perfection by the Lord of Israel. The sort of thing that these days only the conspicuously pious, men like Saul, could imagine happening. And our good friends, with their customary thoroughness and attention to detail, could not possibly allow that sort of thing to happen.

I looked along the line of palms. What would be the questions you would ask of a dead man? How would you begin to assemble the evidence of what had happened to his body, or to the breath of his life? There were many times that families and business partners had asked the courts of law to declare that a man was dead. As far as I was aware, no case had ever come before a court in which a man petitioned to be declared alive.

"And what do you think?" I asked Iosefos.

"I think that Shimon will agree with anything you say to him if you say it to him often enough. And I would not trust bar Ptolemai to tell me day from night."

"I meant what do you think about what the women are saying."

"Prattling and tales," Iosefos answered at last. "A man should ignore such things."

"I grant you that I can see nothing here that suggests what they say could be true."

"Then help me to find his body and end their grief."

"But there is one thing here that I do not understand," I said to him. "Part of the truth that I do not hear."

"What?"

"You said that you did not imagine that you would need a shroud. Why did you only begin to prepare the burial at the last possible moment, late in the afternoon? Surely you must have realised that you would need to do so from the moment that our good friend the Prefect was involved?"

Iosefos stood still. Cassiel and Saul looked back.

"Come on, you bastards," said the Syrian.

"Were you in Jerusalem that day?" Iosefos asked.

"No." Before he could ask me why not, I told him. "My wife is unwell. She cannot travel for Pesach."

"So no-one has told you about what happened?"

"I've questioned a lot of people since I came to Jerusalem. Nobody wants to tell me about anything else. Except for your friends Shimon and bar Ptolemai."

He moved closer to me and spoke softly, in haste.

"We were," he paused, and began again. The Syrian was shouting. "Everyone had convinced themselves that something wonderful would happen, that a great work would be performed. They thought that it would happen when he was nailed to the cross. Or when the cross was raised. Or when he screamed. They were convinced that at that moment everything would change."

"What do you mean, everything would change?"

Iosefos looked down.

"What do you think they were expecting? They were convinced Elijah would come down from the heavens and rescue him. They were hoping for the rule of the Almighty to begin on earth. All of them were. All of us. That's why they went to watch. None of them were expecting him to die on that cross. Least of all Yeshua himself."

"And you?"

"No."

"And now. What do you think?"

"I think that bar Ptolemai is raving. Grief has sent him mad. But that makes my own despair no less easy, do you hear?"

I looked around. Cassiel and Saul were at the garden gate. Iosefos was staring at the churned mud of the garden path in humiliation.

"It was only when he died that I realised that we would need the tomb," he said. "The rest of them could not understand. And now they cannot understand what they have been left with. None of them. They have been left with nothing. Do you understand? Nothing. Not even a body."

If you were his brother, his wife, his child, you were left abandoned with the sheer horror of the manner of his death, a recollection that you could never pull from the box of your memory and destroy. And if you were one of his followers, a half-starved peasant fisherman from Galilee who had signed up for sitting in judgement over our nation on a throne rather than fishing in a leaking boat that there's no wood left to repair and the only person who can explain why you're not going to be sitting on that throne is dead, well, your despair would be total. There would be nothing in your life that you could put your hand to and say *This is mine, this is what I do*, in the name of either God or man. Nothing at all. And the idea that you could go back to your village, to face the shame, the mockery and the lifetime of contempt at your folly. It was unthinkable that anyone would do so. A man would rather die.

At that moment the horns on the Temple colonnade sounded to warn us of the end of the day and the closing of the city's gates. The Syrian bundled me along the green path, away from the tomb and out of the garden.

Then we ran towards the city. I had not imagined that Saul's short legs could move so quickly. The tassels of his shawl danced and flicked at his britches. Iosefos, Cassiel and I stumbled behind him.

"Go on. Run." Then I looked up and saw that the city gate was already moving on its hinges.

"What?" Cassiel asked.

"Go on." I stood up for a moment, clutching my sides. "Go on. Run!"

"Boss?"

"Go. I'm going to the kilns. Without Saul. Make sure he's inside the gates. Understand?"

In two strides Saul had slipped through the gate and was back inside the city. Iosefos reached the threshold and looked back.

"Go on."

I stood still and caught my breath as the gates came together and closed with a dull, hollow creaking. The last call of the trumpets announced that the moon had risen and the fourth day of the week had begun.

Then the hammering against the inside of the city gate began. Saul's voice rose above the calls of the watchmen, who were telling him that nothing could be done, not even for a fellow officer, not even for the Service. I was outside the city walls, and I would have to remain there until dawn. I smiled and turned away.

AKEL-DAMA
4TH DAY OF THE WEEK,
1ST HOUR OF DARKNESS

I arrived at Akel-dama too late – the kiln master and his men were raking the boy Levi's bones out of the furnace where, three days earlier, I had questioned him. They had seen nothing. They had heard nothing. They had returned to the kilns to find him gone and it had only been hours later, when they opened the furnaces for the last firing of the day, that they found him.

I looked at the heap of charcoal, embers and grey clinker that had once been a child, turned away and wept.

May God's great name be glorified and made holy throughout the world.

And nobody now left to describe the men who had murdered our Yehuda.

The boy's body would never be laid, wrapped tight and his face covered with linen in the long chamber of a tomb, as Zenobia and I had wrapped and buried in the rock behind the paradise in our courtyard our infants Benjamin and Eleazar. One day, if we lived so long, Zenobia and I would ask our good Stephanos to use his strength to prise open the stone that sealed the rock and we would gather the remains of their infant bones into two stone coffers with their names cut upon the sides. Benjamin son of Solomon. Eleazar son of Solomon. *For I have no sons to leave behind me any remembrance of my name.* Of course, my family had no other tomb in which to place those bones. My father and my mother, and all my brothers and sisters had vanished in the trouble when Old Herod, the monster, died. I could no more bury them than Yehuda-the-Twin, Mother Mariam and her family could finish burying their brother and their son.

I gave the kiln master a Tyrian shekel. "For the boy's *satva*."

"Keep it," he said. "Do you think I'll allow her to starve?"

I sat down in the lee of the kiln, listening to the roar when they fed the furnace, and watched the lamps of Jerusalem begin to shine. The lights merged into the lights of night-visions of our vineyard in the time of Zenobia's illness after the deaths of our Benjamin and Eleazar. The year when the rains failed and Zenobia lay sick. Stephanos and Abi had begged me to pray for rain, but I could not, and no rains came. They had sent for the circle-maker and he had arrived at the vineyard on a morning when clouds hung above the western valleys. The circle-maker sat down in the middle of the vines, and he drew his circle. We waited for three days, and no rains came. A wandering holy man came, begging for food and drink. He told us that the word of God's Law would free us. Abi begged me for a scroll of Torah, and I found in the bottom of the chest at the end of our bed a desiccated, worm-eaten scroll that had once been the property of my grandfather's father. Stephanos tore the scroll into flakes, buried the scraps in the four corners of the vineyard and the dust beneath the roots of the vines. They prayed for rain, but no rains came. Then, three days after the holy man departed, his goatskin full and bread in his sack, Zenobia had crawled from her bed and left the house, her hair a filthy knotted mat that stank of dead creatures, stale cosmetics and rank sweat, and embraced me. "You look dreadful," she said. And at that moment I felt the drops of water upon my hair and the lids of my eyes.

I woke to the dampness of dew on my beard, and the chill of night's depth. Above me, the Stream of Fire gushed onwards. Over my shoulder Kesil the Hunter had dropped through his door in the firmament and taken his warmth with him. At last, I permitted myself to think about bar Ptolemai's words in the lodging house. What, or who, had he seen? Nico had once assured me that in his view as a lover of wisdom even diseased souls do not return as spirits or demons from Sheol. Quite the reverse: it is a disease of our own souls that makes us see the recently departed whom we have loved before us in the noonday sun. Long after my boys died, Zenobia told me that she saw them before her, heard their cries, felt their hands and their lips upon her breasts, taking her milk. Perhaps it was no great wonder that the women, when they were unable to wash the body of their son and husband, had seen what it was that they had seen. But bar Ptolemai?

There was nothing I could do to help Iosefos at the carpenters' synagogue. What evidence would you look for to establish that a man had come back from the dead? The evidence of the body. You would start, I supposed, with the women of his family who had washed the body and who had laid it out. The women who had been most intimately acquainted with the revolting, disfiguring reality of death that is the only certain fact. Zenobia had washed and prepared the bodies of our Eleazar and Benjamin when they died. And she would not speak to me of the condition of their bodies. She knew, but could not speak. Women know, women whose testimony no sort of law will ever believe, unless it is corroborated by a man. Yeshua's women had not been able to wash and lay out his body – Iosefos and his men had put the body in his tomb and run back to the city as Preparation Day ended. Then the women had come and there was no body to wash. There was nothing in that tomb that could be known. Whatever had happened to the body of Yeshua, the self-made king of our people, it would not tell us who had killed our Yehuda.

There was still his torn last despatch and the dead letterbox in Gethsemane to bring together. I stumbled to my feet, the pain in my knees a sudden fire, and walked in darkness to the ditch at the end of the road. Down by the banks of the Kidron, I turned right, crossed the bridge and began to trudge up the long side of Mount Olive.

I recalled Saul's description of the arrest. *At a gatepost on the left of the road. A grove of olive trees.* The darkness of the trees loomed above me far sooner than I expected, but the gatepost and the gap in the wall were there. I turned and looked back across the Kidron at the night-city. A single light burned in the Antonia Tower. Sheol take you, Marcus. I stepped through the gap in the wall.

The olive grove air was chill. Patches of deeper darkness dappled the ground between the lines of trees. Beyond lay open ground. I counted five lines of trees and found the edge of a clearing. Where was the press house? There was no sign of any agricultural work being carried on in the open space. I stepped out from the shadow of the trees.

Not agriculture, but the sure and certain signs of human activity. Boot prints deep in mud. Churned and battered turf. A wide circle of broken stone and trampled clay. My left foot turned something soft in the dirt. I knelt and picked up a dried-out, toughened piece of gristle, alive with the movement of vile creatures. The thing was shaped in a twisted oval half the length of my fingers. I realised, in the moment that I dropped it, that it was the severed cartilage of a human ear. I stepped back lightly and re-entered the gloom of the trees.

Yehuda's tradecraft notes had stated that his postbox for despatches was in the sixth tree of the seventh row. The owner of a vineyard would count his vines from the north-eastern corner of his land, down and across. I had no idea what an olive grower would do: our own trees at the farm are too few for any but our own needs. I stepped forward and began to count the trees, six from the top of the wall, seven from the side.

It was three trees behind me from where I stood, two to my right, a smooth, low bole, breaking into two great branches just above my shoulder.

I ran my palms across the fibre of the bark, stood back, and walked around the bole. Then I leaned into it and embraced its bulk, my head pressed against the bark. Nothing. This was no Service drop-box.

I went up to the wall at the top of the grove and this time I counted seven trees down and six across from the northern side. The tree was split at shoulder height, the larger branch spreading out above the downward slope. At the root of the smaller branch, there was a dark cleft, closed off and unremarkable – a tight fold in the bark, turned away from sight.

I slipped my hand into the darkness of the cleft, and grasped what I found there.

It was at that moment that I heard the sounds of movement across the open space, and caught at the edge of my vision a shadow of darkness mobile.

He was a professional, to approach me so cleverly. And he was swift, though his gait was an unbalanced lope. At the moment that my fist curled around what it found in the cleft, a dark agony far deeper than that of the shadows above me fell upon all my senses. I knelt, released the knife that was strapped to my calf, and brought it up. He lurched straight onto the point and felled me with the force of his weight. In the grey I could see a mottled, disfigured face and I felt the putrid heat of his breath. His limbs trembled and kicked, and his eyes rolled. I reached out a hand, grasped a stone and swung it against the side of his head. A crackling eructation began to tear its way up through his windpipe, and Ev, the Lady Esther's former doorkeeper, went down to Sheol on top of me.

LOWER CITY
4TH DAY OF THE WEEK,
FIRST LIGHT

It was the cold hour just before dawn when I stumbled down the hill and crossed the Kidron bridge. The spring dew was on my coat and the chill of night bit my bones. At last, when the light above Mount Olive was sufficient, I unclenched my fist and took from it the roll of papyrus that I had found in the cleft of the tree. I unfolded it and held it up to the first light of the day. In lampblack, there was written:

> Bar Ptolemai. Not what he seems. Our good friends give him orders. He more than any of us persuaded Yeshua that he should embark upon his course of action in the Temple, and agreed with him that Elijah would save him from death at his execution.

By the pool at Siloam Gate I cast off my cloak and tunic and hid the knife beneath them. Then I hitched tight the cloth around my loins, took off my vest of Egyptian cotton and plunged into the pool.

The muffled drubbing of the waters pressed upon my ears and for seven heartbeats I heard nothing but the blood of my own body.

Then I raised up my head, clung to the stone ledge at the side of the pool and heard the sounds of the trumpets upon the Temple heights announce the end of night.

I shivered in the shadow of the wall and wrapped my tunic round my shoulders. The cloth was harsh and its fibre stiff with dirt. I squeezed the last of the water from my beard and reached out for my cloak. The knife was sitting upon it.

"You're not a murderer, are you?"

The words were Hebrew. He was a child of eight or nine years, with cropped black hair cut close to his scalp and a rent in the cloth of his too-short cloak. A growing boy. Clean feet and sandals. And pained, empty eyes. I sat down beside him on the sill of the pool and arranged the linen cloak and my tunic about me. Our backs to the waters, we dangled our feet down towards the steps.

"And what makes you think that?"

"Your cloak. And all that blood. Am I right?"

"You're a good boy to be so watchful. Your father must be proud of you."

"I do know a lot," he said, in a detached, matter-of-fact way. "My father's friends are always asking me my opinion. But only on the most difficult points. The ones they can't agree among themselves."

"And what does your father say?"

"My father's dead," he said, again in that matter-of-fact way. "I was going to be a prince of Israel. But he's dead."

The boy looked down in silence. He was staring at the blood.

"Yeuda? What are you doing?"

The woman spoke Aramaic with a Galilean peasant's accent that had a layer of refinement. She wore grey rags and within the shadow of her headscarf there was a streak of hair matted with ash. I had seen her on the stair at the lodging house. The boy looked back at her with a mixture of adoration and anxiety.

"Nothing, Mamma."

THE JUDAS CASE

The woman put down the two-handled pitcher that she carried and stood in front of us. Two fingers of her right hand were missing. The first finger of her left hand was a stump.

"Oh. It's you. You were at the house." She turned to her son. "He knows that he's not supposed to trouble people with questions. But he can't be stopped. Can he?" He laughed shyly, and rushed to her, wrapping his arms around her waist and burying his head in her clothing.

"He's not being trouble at all. He's a fine boy."

The child unwrapped himself from his mother and ran over to the pool's edge.

"Yeuda! Be careful." Yeuda looked utterly unconcerned. "His father never taught him to swim," she said. "We're fishermen. We live on a lake. And he never taught the boy to swim. Yeuda! Come here!"

He ran to her along the ledge.

"Who's my best boy? Best boy in the whole world?"

"Yeuda!" he squealed, delighted, and she took him in her arms. Her sorrow lifted for a moment before enclosing her again. She unpicked the boy's embrace, sat him down at the side of the waters and hitched the sleeves of her cloak.

"Let me help you," I said. But she turned her head away and lowered the pitcher to the pool herself. Her movement was strong, sure and solid, and she hefted the filled vessel to the pool's edge with a peasant's ease. Then she looked down at the boy, who was tugging at the hem of her cloak.

"Yeuda. Enough." She turned back to me and met my eyes.

"My man was executed by the soldiers," she said.

Yeuda pulled at the hem of her cloak again, bidding her towards the road.

"Mamma. Come on. We should go to the garden again. To see Papa."

"Yeuda, no. We can't do that, child. Not again. Do you understand? We should go back to *Satva* Mariam. She'll be wondering where we are."

For a moment the child looked dejected. Then he smiled.

"Yes. Come on." And he began to pull her back towards the city. She swayed as she lifted the water pitcher to her shoulder. Then she stopped, and the child clung to her.

"Oh no." She put down the pitcher. "Mother!" she called out.

At the gate, two watchmen were arguing with an old woman. She was wandering, hands outstretched as if begging. The child's mother turned back to me.

"Keep him with you, will you, my brother?" Then she rushed towards the gate.

The old woman was asking the men at the gate something, holding out her hand and pulling at their cloaks. A crowd was beginning to gather. Voices called out.

"It's *Satva* Mariam," the boy said after a while. "We should probably go and see if we can help."

"Mother. Let me help you," I heard the younger woman say to her, and she turned her away from the crowd. "They do not know," she said, as she led the old woman towards us. "They know nothing."

The old woman followed her with vacant docility, oblivious to the crowd. Then she saw me, but her eyes were voids. She reached out and pulled my sleeve, and began to speak in a droning whisper.

"My son," she said. "Can you find him for me? Tell me where he is. We do not know where he is. Nobody knows what they have done with him."

Then the old woman's eyes fastened upon little Yeuda.

"My boy," she said, and smoothed his hair with her hand in an odd, ungainly way. "My boy," the old woman repeated. "We should go and find your Papa. Together. You must help me find your Papa. You're a good boy, Yeuda."

"Mother Mariam," the younger woman said gently, "we should go back to the lodgings. You should rest."

The old woman turned and looked about her, distressed for a moment, her lips and jaw moving, before the certainty of her detachment returned.

"Yes," she said, "we should go." She let go of my sleeve and turned in her docile way towards the street. Then she stopped.

It was Shimon-the-Rock, shod and wrapped in a travelling cloak, holding a staff. Yeuda wriggled from my grasp and ran to embrace him.

"Shimon, brother: where are you going?" the younger woman asked.

"Going back to Galilee," he grunted. "Got a boat to fix. Got fish to catch." He stopped and looked at her. "There's no future. Not for any of us here."

"Shimon-the-Rock," Yeuda cried out. "You should stay here. We'll go to the garden again with Mamma."

"Yeuda," said his mother, "enough. You mustn't speak like that."

Shimon bent down.

"There's nothing for us here, little one," he said sadly, and touched the boy's cheek. There was more movement of people behind us on the street. Iosefos from Arimathea, the two thugs from the previous day Yehonatan and Yakoub, and finally Yehuda-the-Twin appeared. Little Yeuda squealed with delight again and went to the Twin, who held him by the shoulders, and turned him round to face Shimon and the women.

"Now, Shimon, my brother. Where are you going?"

A dispute that must have not long been suspended resumed. Shimon would return to Galilee. No-one showed any sign of wishing to follow him. The two thugs would stay in Jerusalem. Yehuda-the-Twin was undecided, trying to balance between the competing voices. Whatever the women wished to do was of no concern to the men. Little Yeuda wanted to return to the tomb. The argument grew in ferocity and the child disentangled himself from his uncle and returned to the embrace of his mother. Only Iosefos from Arimathea stood apart. At last he spoke to Yehuda-the-Twin.

"Should we not seek guidance in prayer, brother?"

"We decided we will go and pray in the House of the Lord. We will seek guidance as to what we should do, at the end of Pesach."

"Now," said Shimon.

In answer, Yehuda-the-Twin strode up the road to the lower city. Shimon followed. I watched the mother, Mariam and the boy go. Yeuda waved at me as they left. Then there was a voice behind me.

"Husband?"

I wish I could say that she came up from the desert like a pillar of smoke and fire. But my wife entered the city astride the vineyard's second donkey, led by Stephanos with Abi clinging to him. The girl looked terrified by the sights and sounds around her. Zenobia watched the old woman, Mistress Mariam and the child as they departed. Then she dismounted and looked at the blood on my tunic.

"You look as if you've been beaten up."

"I have."

"Then I've arrived not a moment too soon."

We embraced and when her fingers touched the wound on my head I flinched.

"You see what happens when you go and indulge yourself in this nonsense?"

"This is not nonsense."

"You stupid, stupid man. You abandoned us, you abandoned our vineyard. You abandoned me, your wife, and I had to come and find you. What have you done here?"

"I have done my duty."

"Your duty is to your vineyard, husband, and to me."

"And to the Service."

"And what happens when you abandon us? I find you looking as if someone has tried to murder you."

"Congratulations on your deduction. Someone has."

"I don't suppose that your Service paid you for that did they? No, of course they did not. You risked your life – for what?"

"Duty. It was my duty. You don't expect to be paid."

"Well, I always did, my love. And I made sure they coughed. Every time."

"A boy has died," I say to her. "A boy has died and I could not prevent it."

"Then you should never have taken on that duty if you could not perform it. Don't insult me like this, you hear? What about your duty to me? And the vines?"

"The vines have nothing to reproach me for."

"The vines need you. And that wound needs Nico. Where is he?"

As we crossed the square to the Service door I noticed that the Essene and his boy were gone from their place by the messengers' post. I had time to hope that whatever had happened had been quick, and then we were at the door, to the clucking delight of Zev. Nico was waiting at the inner barrier, just back from his morning consultation with Pilatos.

"A row at the Prefect's this morning," he said to me, "Marcus. Philo's expecting trouble." Before I could say anything to this Azizus began applying unguents to a streak of cuts and grazes on my left arm. "Good. That's very good. Very good indeed. You'll be fit to travel later in the day, old son."

"Fit to travel?"

"My dear," he turned to Zenobia, "I think you may wish to consult me too? Don't you?"

My wife looked utterly reluctant but was eventually persuaded to walk with Nico to the far end of the office, where they spoke together at the gate of the great iron cage. Disturbed by their presence, Micah came to me with a bundle of papers, looking fiercely pleased with himself. He spread out a sheaf of papyri and parchment that were spilling out of the satchel of a High Priest's personal messenger.

"Just come back from His Sanctity's office, these. Just the way you asked for them. Someone on his staff must like you." His expression was pleasure bordering upon awe. "First time I've ever seen it happen this fast."

They were a verbatim record of the interrogation of Yeshua that was carried out following his arrest. They had been annotated by one of the priests who must have been the man who was attempting to prepare the legal case against him. The topmost was a single sheet: a Temple genealogy, certifying Yeshua's descent from King David. But there was a curiosity to it: unlike the one that Yehuda had described, this genealogy showed the man's descent from David by Solomon, not Nathan, the more usual means by which someone anxious to acquire legitimacy would embellish their ancestry. This really was evidence of kingly authority for the educated. Most Galileans would be unable even to read the text. A priest's note at the top right: copied to Prefect's office. Had they even bothered to compare the details, I wondered? Or just sent it off to His Excellency: proof that suspect claims royal descent. Whatever else our Yehuda had done, that genealogy had been enough, as he had recognised at the very beginning.

I heard raised voices at the Service door, and the sound of Zev fussing over a new arrival – "Come in, master, the Lord Shlomo is waiting for you." It was Philo, from his audience with the Prefect. He occupied his desk, invited me to sit opposite him and picked a scroll from his satchel.

"This is from Marcus. I already know its contents. Shall I read it to you?"

He broke the seal and read aloud without waiting for an answer.

"Marcus sends me fraternal greetings, reminds me of the obligations of friendship that the Service is under to the Prefect of Judea as representative of the Augustus, and demands that I present you, the Jew Solomon Eliades known as the oenarch, temporarily attached to the Service of the Jerusalem Temple, at the Antonia Tower before the end of the day."

He dropped the scroll on his desk and leaned back in his chair. His fingers began to mangle his stylus.

"The High Priest and I may be able to find some way to make this right with Marcus and His Excellency. Because I am not going to have him demanding the lives of our people, particularly not of one as eminent as you, when there is something so transparently wrong here. But I cannot allow you to stay in the city a moment longer."

He stood up, and addressed me in formal Greek.

"Solomon Eliades, temporarily attached to the Service, I hereby relieve you of all duties in the case of Yehuda from Kerioth – and from any other responsibilities that you may have taken on in the Service – from this moment forward. Do you understand?"

I looked straight back at him and said nothing.

"Do you understand?"

"It is a duty," I said. "I understand that."

"Then your duty is to me and my orders. You are removed from this case. From this moment. Agreed?"

I sighed and looked up to the great vault of the ceiling above us.

"Agreed," I said at last.

"Good."

"Am I still under the Service's protection?"

He took another scroll from the basket beneath his table, one that I felt I should recognise.

"I asked Micah to bring this to me again. And there's something I still don't understand. Something that I'd like your help with."

"Is this an interrogation?"

"Solomon, this is an attempt to save your life. Don't you understand?"

"Of course. Of course."

"Explain this to me. A note on your personal record. No identification. It says that you should under no circumstances be assigned to any work that involves contact with Marcus Ulpianus Varro. And then you're sent off to that spice trader's in Pera to run our eastern network."

He stopped, shuffled the scroll to one side and placed his elbows on the table. Then he leaned forward.

"What is it that I'm not hearing in all this? There's a lot of noise, but no sense. Will you speak to me out of this confusion?"

Second rule of the man in the field: never lie to your controller or pretend there are things he does not need to know. I sighed and made a decent show of reluctance.

"I will tell you. But you must understand that it was a long time ago. Long before I went to Pera. Marcus and I became enemies. Unfortunately it is all as close as yesterday for him. As I have found out this week."

"There's another thing here. Except it's not here. Look at this."

My scroll had been cut in two, a section removed and the remaining parts, before and after, joined crudely back together. A part of my life given to the Service had been stolen. I took the scroll from him and held up the top end. It was still there: my name written in my own hand, on the day I joined the Service. When I had returned to Judea from school in Athens, a young man still confounded by the life that he was trying to live, and found that my parents were both dead, my brothers and sisters vanished, our house and our land confiscated by the Herodians. I looked at the damaged section. Someone had removed a hand's span of material. The scroll had been cut through, sewn together and painted with gum. A repair job that would fool no-one with an eye. I knew perfectly well what the missing material recorded.

"Help me here. Who would have removed that passage?"

"I do not know. But I can tell you that I did not."

"You're quite sure? Because I understand from the fetchers that you're in the habit of searching the box yourself."

"Was. I was in the habit."

"Then make sure that you don't fall back into old ways. Do you understand?"

I handed the scroll back to him.

"Now. For the good of the Service, I want you to tell me about the missing portion. What did it record?"

"It records how Marcus and I became enemies. And I have no idea who has removed it, or why."

"What happened between you and Marcus?"

"Don't you know? I thought that it was common gossip the length and breadth of the Service. And the Temple Guard too. They used to teach the mission to recruits. The dangers of working under cover, and what happens when you become too closely involved with the people that you are observing."

"Go on."

There was silence between us for many slow heartbeats. Then I breathed out and laid my hands flat upon the desk.

"In the 26th year of the rebuilding of the Temple, I joined the Service. Marcus had just come out from Rome as chief political officer under Prefect Coponius. The Service wanted to be sure that they knew exactly what our good friends were thinking before they even knew it themselves. It was a difficult time. The great rebellion. Thousands of our countrymen hanging from crosses by the roadsides. Tens of thousands. And one of our predecessors as Prefect's liaison had made rather a mess of things, the way they do.

"Marcus proved impossible to understand. We could not hear his thoughts by any of the usual means. Then someone decided that we needed a pair of ears in his private house. They thought that a domestic slave would be the best means of achieving this. Not a real slave, you understand, but an officer masquerading as a slave. And for some reason the Service chose me. Are you surprised?"

"Yes. I am."

"I was quite different then, when I was a younger man," I said. "I was considered handsome and well formed."

"I meant – why did we not simply bribe his secretary?"

"Someone had a new theory about the gathering of intelligence. I had to become a convincing slave, bought and sold. Impeccably authentic provenance. And Marcus had to choose me himself. He had to be fooled. So, for the sake of the Service, I became a slave. You do understand what that means, don't you? Our ancestors were slaves in Egypt. And I became the property of a Roman master. A speaking tool. A very sharp tool, but still just a tool. My task was to write and read for Marcus. Everything that passed over his desk passed through my head too, and it stuck there. And of course, he owned me."

"And did it work?"

"We found out what Marcus was thinking. I listened to his mind as it worked. There was a problem, though: something that we should have known about before I was ever sent to his household."

"What was that?"

"Not what, but who. Marcus had a wife. He'd brought her with him from Rome. She didn't like Jerusalem. Domitilla was her name. She was easily bored, and she developed a taste for servile amusements, as I believe they're known. She decided that I, her husband's secretary, was going to be her principal – though by no means her only – source of amusement."

The look of disgust upon Philo's face as understanding came to him was the most disturbingly vivid thing that I had seen him express while I had been in Jerusalem.

"What happened?"

"The inevitable. There were some humiliating events. Humiliating for everyone. And dangerous too. But I got out – with some help. My control had the good sense to prepare an exit for me to a place of safety. And I did get out. My first ever mission was over. Finished."

Philo remained silent for some time.

"And what effect did this have upon relations?"

Which was, I suppose, the sort of question you would expect.

"I believe it was a long time before Marcus realised that I was not simply a runaway slave. He really was quite a fool, for all his cleverness. The Service had the good sense to get me away from Jerusalem, and for a long time I ran our office in Pera. Then, when it was judged safe, I came back. Unfortunately, Marcus was still here."

"And his wife?"

"Domitilla died not long after I left. In childbirth."

Philo looked away, across his desk, to the memory box and then tilted his head up to the ceiling and the chambers of the priests above us.

"And that is why you and he are enemies."

"It is."

"And he wants you dead."

"Oh yes. You can be sure of that. It's also the reason that Zenobia and I never come to Jerusalem at festival times. We fail in our obligation of observance because we do not wish to come to his attention."

Philo picked up the scroll of my service record again and threw it down onto the table between us.

"And if I had known this at Pesach I would never have asked you to help us."

"I would have come anyway, whatever you had asked me to do."

He took Marcus' message from my hands, and looked at the Prefect's seals. Then he took one of the clay lamps from the head of his desk and held Marcus' warrant for my arrest over its flame until it began to burn. Within a moment, the soot and rags of the papyrus ascended into the upper air of the office, towards the altar of the Lord far above and to who knew what acceptance of its validity as a sacrifice.

"Shalom," I breathed out softly when the scroll was consumed. "Lord have mercy."

There was silence between us for a very long time after that. Philo was staring into the distance behind my head. At last he spoke.

"You must leave. Immediately. I'll do what I can to get you beyond the city walls and safely on your way to wherever you chose to go."

"Husband?" Zenobia was standing behind me along with Nico. She must have heard everything that had passed between us. "This Marcus is the man that you told me about when you left the Service?"

"Yes."

"Then there can be no disagreement between us. Philo is right. Any more of these games will see you killed. We are leaving."

Philo stared at Zenobia in unexpected and profound gratitude. At that moment there was another hammering upon the outer door. It was Marcus, or his thugs, come in person, I was sure of it. Zev's voice rose in a screech of pleasure that our visitor was very welcome, that he had come back to us at the very moment, and the Lord Solomon would be glad to receive him.

"Lord Solomon?" Philo looked at me across the table.

Zev entered the office, this time followed by Cassiel.

"Boss, you should know that—"

"There's no boss here," I said. "I'm going home. You should report to Lord Philo."

Cassiel bowed in formal High Priest's messenger fashion and recited. "The head of the duty sacrifice division of Levites sends his greetings and requests the assistance of the Temple Guard. And the Service too."

"Well?"

"Didn't you know? There's another riot. Court of the Nations. Worse than last week. The Galileans again. And a crowd of pilgrims."

"How could it possibly be worse?" Philo demanded.

"The visiting garrison. They're down from their billets and starting to restore order."

Philo ran to the stairs and called up to the barracks.

"Everybody," he shouted. "The sick and the injured too." Then he turned back to Cassiel and Nico. "Come on," he said. "I need everybody. Not," he added when he saw me stand up, "you. You're to go back to your vineyard. Immediately. Don't be here when I return."

Within moments the office was full of supernumeraries from day watch clattering down the stairs and swinging their clubs. Zev was thrilled by all this prompt action. The great days of the Service were back, he called out to me as Philo, Cassiel, Nico and Azizus rushed to the door. Cassiel leaned towards me as he went and spoke softly.

"Irakleides sends his greetings. Says he saw your man Yeshua. In the flesh. Alive. Not just him, hundreds of pilgrims did too. That's what set them off."

I was halfway to the inner door and Zev's booth before Zenobia shrieked.

"Husband! You cannot do this."

"My Service," I said. "My duty."

"We are going home. Now."

I turned to her and looked back.

"My people," I said. And I fled.

THE TEMPLE
4TH DAY OF THE WEEK,
6TH HOUR

My experience of riots is unrivalled in all Israel. When I became a man, the riots that accompanied the death of Old Herod, the monster, convinced me that my adult life, if it was to last more than a few days, would consist entirely of rioting, punctuated by brief intervals of mass crucifixion. As a student of rhetoric in Athens, I learned many tricks to provoke and to calm riots in a reliable manner. When the Greek inhabitants of Alexandria took exception to the presence of Jews in the city, I was one of those rioted against. Much later, when I was working for the Service, I would arrange a carefully managed disturbance somewhere, under cover of which we could achieve some greater end. A well-organised riot may serve many purposes. But I have never experienced anything quite so unexpected and devoid of use as the riot that broke out that day in the Temple courts.

I looked out at the Court of the Nations from the top of the stairs. The doors of the Court of Israel, with their threat of summary death for the uncircumcised, were behind us. Two Temple guards were pulling bodies from the waters of the *mikvah* at the foot of the steps. A body lay twisted beneath a wooden beam, its head a mess of blood. Our good

235

friends had indeed abandoned their porridge on the upper colonnade and come down to restore order. At the eastern end of the court, a line of soldiers five deep was facing a crowd of pilgrims. Pottery, fruit, lengths of timber and at least one new-season lamb were flying through the air between them. The crowd were between the soldiers and the steps where we stood. The soldiers were slowly, with deliberate and unanswerable strength, pushing the pilgrims back towards us.

Irakleides stood in the wreckage that had been his stall. His two guards were gone. He shouted at me.

"Behind here, Shlo. Keep your head down."

We squatted beneath a length of cedar.

"What's happened?"

"That riot, Shlo. So good they decided to do it all over again. First time was comedy. Like anything involving those Galileans. This one's serious."

"You mean our good friends?"

"They come down the moment it kicked off. About time too. I wasn't sorry to see them."

"What happened?"

"It was the same lad as last time."

"What do you mean, the same?"

"That Galilean magician. The one they put up on a cross on Preparation Day. Can't have done much of a job, now, can they? He was here again, right in front of me, real as you are. With his friends too, the same lot. Most of them, anyway – no sign of that redhead you were asking about. But their boss, it was him. Big lad, long beard, forehead like a cliff. Walking around alive as you please, stall to stall. As soon as people saw him and realised who he was, it all kicked off again. Write off your debts, lads: jubilee's come early and no mistake."

"Where is he now?"

"They left, him and his friends, soon as it started. They were off over the bridge with the women before anyone noticed."

"Didn't that put an end to it?"

"Come on, Shlo, where have you been—"

Further explanation was cut short. A plank flew through the air on my left and stones began falling behind us. People were running along the length of the portico. A stone hit canvas. The pilgrims' retreat was becoming a stampede.

"Keep your head down, Shlo," were the last words that I heard from Irakleides. Bodies came between us, everywhere voices were shouting. What they shouted, I could not tell. I reached down to the knife strapped at my calf, but my hands were pulled away by other, stronger hands.

"Come with me, boss." The voice that had been shouting was Cassiel's. The crush was pushing us towards the courtyard wall and I felt sudden terror as my feet were lifted from the ground.

"Spare me," I wailed. "I am old."

The bodies to my left and right swayed and pitched and then we were packed together into a tight crowd where I was unable to turn or to lift my arms. Women were screaming.

"Boss?" Cassiel pulled at my arm. Our good friends the soldiers were moving past the wrecked stalls.

"Where is Philo?"

"Gone looking for reinforcements. Wherever they are."

Behind us, a mob of pilgrims armed themselves with wooden sticks and last season's pomegranates. And they began to move towards the soldiers. Really, I have always admired my countrymen's refusal ever to consider the consequences of their actions.

We turned back towards Irakleides and his friendly wreckage. He had vanished, and so had the pile of wood. The crowd thickened. Ten paces and we were struggling in a press that stretched as far as the gates. On our left, the soldiers. Ahead, a mass of raised arms. The air above our heads was full of stones and planks. People around us had blood on their faces.

Cassiel pressed against me. I felt the terror of constriction and loss of control again as my feet lifted from the ground. Then we stopped, pressed close.

"Brother…" the cries came to me from the crowd. "My brothers. I cannot breathe, my brother. I am caught."

"Backwards, boss." Cassiel hooked his arm into mine. Men pressed against the rim of the *mikvah* were falling into the water, thrashing in terror. We stepped back and began our tripping, uncoordinated ascent into the courts of the Lord our God, with the encouragement from below of our very good friends. When I felt the first step against my heel, I fell backwards. My arms waved free and I stared at them as they cut through the air in unwilled, jagged terror. Cassiel was there with the steadiness of his bulk.

At last we stood beneath the doors of the Court of Israel. I set my feet wide apart upon the steps and Cassiel held my shoulders. The soldiers were now four or five paces from the steps. Down in the courtyard to our left the riot, confined to a cauldron by our good friends, was continuing with no sign of losing either enthusiasm or energy. There was still no sign anywhere of Philo, the Temple guards or of any of our eyes and ears.

At the foot of the steps stood a man in a white tunic, his red skin looking even more suffuse and angry than usual.

"Oh," he said, "it's you. I should have known."

"Hello, Marcus."

On Marcus' left was a big bruiser of a common soldier, shaved head and a scar down the side of his face. I had seen him at the tomb. Demas, as Quintus had identified him. The real surprise was the man standing to his right. He looked uncomfortable and was rubbing the left side of his chest, the place where I had bruised him three days before in Curds and Whey.

"Shalom, Saul," I said. He did not respond.

"I hoped it would not be," Marcus went on. "Really, I did." His lips twisted into a phantom smile. "Something that needs my attention, and the meddler Eliades has mixed himself up in it."

"And what are you doing here?" I asked Saul.

"Young Saul," said Marcus, "has been extremely helpful to us today."

"What do you want, Marcus?"

"You're making a nuisance of yourself, Solomon. I don't want you in my way. It's not you that I'm looking for. I can find you whenever I want."

Saul stared at the ground and closed his eyes again. This time when he looked up his face was full of serenity. Any pretence of the casual vanished from Marcus' voice.

"Where will I find Yeshua from Nazareth? Your holy man. You do know where he is, don't you?"

I struggled to control my laughter. Cassiel grasped my arm.

"Don't you understand, Marcus? Don't you know that he's dead? Let me think. Who told me? Oh yes. It was you. Three days ago. At Curds and Whey, when we reacquainted ourselves."

Marcus stepped towards me. "Where is he? Our people have sighted him three times in as many days. He was seen in a crowd of hundreds, just now."

"Are you quite sure of that?"

"I want the co-operation of the Service on this, Solomon. And you will give it to me." The slack skin beside his eyebrow was throbbing. "Solomon, you need to understand that I am serious about this. Let me speak plainly: I'm not having dead men walking around Jerusalem, do you understand? He's a fugitive from justice, and I'm going to make sure that I find him, and, when I do, I'll send him back to Golgotha and nail him back up on that cross till our job's finished and he's really and truly dead. Do you understand?"

"The man you're looking for *is* dead."

"Do I believe someone who's still a runaway slave? You've betrayed me once, Jew. Look at what your friends have done today. I can hardly stop a disturbance like this from coming to the attention of the Prefect, can I? And you know what he'll do if he gets to hear about this and thinks that he's being made a fool of? It won't be some hairy-arsed boatwright from Galilee that'll be to blame. It will be your High Priest and it will be your colleagues in the Service. None of you will be safe. So, if you see your friends from Galilee, you should tell them to talk to us. Do you understand?"

It was at this moment that Saul finally spoke. His eyes were closed and the words poured out as if without deliberation or thought.

"Don't you understand? It will be like the days when Herod our king died. Thousands of us, lashed up and nailed down. He'll execute us and sell us into slavery. Do you really want that for our nation? How can we help you, Marcus? Because we must help you. Even Solomon the Oenarch knows that."

"Thank you, Saul." Marcus turned to me. "He's been extremely helpful to us in understanding what you have been doing, a model of the sort of co-operation that our services should be enjoying. We know that you've had contact with them, Solomon. Demas tells me you went through a pantomime of being puzzled by the absence of a body. After you'd spoken to the man's followers in their lodging house."

"Well, I congratulate you on the efficiency of your spies, Marcus. I'll have to find another occasion to admire your reasoning and deduction." I grasped Cassiel's arm. "Help me, please. We should go."

I stepped backwards two paces, pulling Cassiel with me. To his credit, he smiled at Marcus and gave a reasonable impression of assisting an old man with a whimsical decision.

"Solomon," Marcus said, "I've decided that you're obstructing me and my men in their duties."

We reached the top, directly beneath the lintel of the great doors.

"Solomon, it's time you gave up this line of work. Do you understand? You're a danger. To all of your people."

Cassiel and I were almost within the Court of Israel. Marcus, Saul and their soldiers were mid-way up the stairs. Saul was staring at the inscription above our heads. *Anyone who is not a Jew who is found within these courts has only himself to blame for his death.* Marcus was staring at me.

"Arrest them," said Marcus. "Both of them." Saul's look of serenity turned in an instant to one of appalled distress and he clutched his side again. I spoke to Saul.

"Of course, you can come with us, Saul. If you choose." The appeal, simple and direct. My former assistant looked at me, then at Marcus. At last he stepped back, and looked down in shame.

"No," I said. "I didn't think so."

Marcus shouted at Saul.

"Well? Go on, then," he said. "Go and arrest him. You said you would do it, didn't you?"

Saul lifted up his face to the heavens, his eyes closed for a moment, and then they opened wide. Only the whites were there: his pupils must have been staring into the depths of his own skull. Then his fists clenched, his arms locked rigid by his sides and he fell to the ground, a white froth bubbling on his lips.

The shock to Marcus and his soldiers was palpable and it spread out in an instant among the angry crowd behind the cordon. At the top of the steps, the men behind me shuffled backwards.

"Spirits," someone shouted. "Demons."

"He needs Nico," I said.

Cassiel pulled me under the shade of the lintel.

"Come on, boss. We should go in. We'll be safe in there, yes?" And he pulled me into the Court of Israel.

Below us, Marcus was looking down at Saul in disgust. His men had stood back and were staring down at him too, unwilling to touch a man so obviously possessed by spirits in a holy place. Two priests appeared from out of the crowd, looked at Saul and stood back. They conferred, then one of them vanished behind the line of soldiers. No-one gave Saul help of any sort.

"Come on, then, Marcus," I called out. "You're not going to take another step towards me, are you? Look at the words up there, Marcus."

Cassiel tugged at my arm. "Boss. Come on."

"So come up here, if you wish to, Marcus. Please do."

Inside the Court of Israel a crowd of my fellow countrymen had gathered just behind us, diverted by this confrontation. "Come on, then," someone shouted. "Come on – if you think that you're Jewish." Laughter moved through the circle of men. I looked back at Marcus. He was no longer smiling.

"He needs Nico," I repeated.

"Come on, boss," said Cassiel. "We're finished."

I turned my back on Marcus, and on Saul, and entered the courts of my fathers.

"Runaway slave?" Cassiel asked as we walked across the Court of Israel.

"A story from long ago."

"Boss, you need to get out of Jerusalem. Right now."

LOWER CITY
4TH DAY OF THE WEEK,
10TH HOUR

To pass unknown through the city in full sight of your enemies, to know them and their acts, and with that knowledge to undo them: that is the craft and secret art of my calling. The journey from the Service door to the Alabarch's gatehouse at Siloam Gate and the slopes of Mount Olive was the most perfect realisation of the idea that I could hope for life to offer. To act, yet to leave no trace of your actions in the world.

Cassiel and I returned to the Service office by the staircase from the Temple barracks. There we found Zenobia barely restrained by the solidity of Stephanos and Zev's good-natured soothing.

"Husband, we are going home! Immediately."

The remains of the riot might, I supposed, keep Marcus from vengeance for a summer-hour at most. There was neither time to dress for the journey, nor ask questions, no time even to eat in haste. While my wife berated me for further delay, I sat at Philo's desk and wrote him a short despatch.

You can assume that the man who murdered our Yehuda is Marcus' Syrian friend with the bald head and scar. Name of

Demas. And that matter that you could not possibly ask me to investigate. Saul is Marcus' man. Though I would guess that you already suspected that when you asked me to observe him. If you've not already done so, send Nico to attend him.

I sealed the folded papyrus: *Solomon Eliades. Oenarch. My vineyard is my own to give.* In any other circumstances I would not have been so foolhardy to commit such information to writing in plain, but there was no time for encipherment. Then I embraced Micah and Zev, called the Mariby boy for mugs of sour milk and lemon, and thanked Cassiel for his service and protection.

"What do you mean, boss?"

"I mean that you're free of the burden of following me around and running messages for me. I hope that it has, as Philo said, been a change from the usual."

"Boss, Lord Philo may have relieved you of your duties, but he said nothing to me about mine. My orders are to act as your messenger."

"Husband, this nonsense is putting us all in danger. Bring him with us if you must, but we must leave, now."

"Cassiel, I want you to go to the carpenters' synagogue. Tell Iosefos that his guests have got to leave Jerusalem immediately. It's not a place of safety for them. Don't wait for them to argue with you. Come straight down to Siloam Gate and meet us on the road to Beth-Anya. We'll need your protection until we are that far from the city at least." I turned to Zenobia. "Wife, let's go home."

As we left, Micah took me to one side and spoke softly.

"There's one thing you should know. My oppo at Records tells me they finally found what they were looking for."

I left Jerusalem with my wife and my servants, like any other pilgrims walking back to their lodgings outside the walls. We were surrounded by a jam of citizens crammed into the narrow streets below the Temple. There were no Service eyes on street corners, and no sign of either Quintus' men or Marcus' Syrians: still busy restoring public order to Pesach. As I guided the donkey on which Zenobia sat I was seized not by the relief of escape from the city's dangers but by the melancholy of failure. No mystery can be considered solved until all those involved have been brought to light and every secret revealed. The men who killed our Yehuda still walked free in Jerusalem and breathed the city's air. If there was any further truth in the city, it remained hidden. We waited for Cassiel outside the Alabarch's gatehouse, but he did not come. At last, Zenobia insisted that we must move.

"Stephanos will protect us."

Neither Stephanos nor even Cassiel could do anything to save us from a troop of Marcus' men. We walked on, then I looked up and saw the keystone of the Siloam Gate pass above us. I left the city a free man.

At the third bend in the Mount Olive road I drew the donkey aside, halted and looked back at Jerusalem. The shadow of Mount Zion and the Upper City was already halfway up the walls. I stared down at the dark bastions of the Antonia Tower and permitted myself the luxury of deriding Marcus for the blunt stupidity of his incompetent vengeance. I had escaped him, I had chosen life and I would live. Back down the road a fast horse was beginning the ascent of Mount Olive. There was no mistaking its rider. Cassiel caught us at the next turn of the climb.

"There was no sign of them, boss. The boy told me that they'd cleared out. He didn't know where. Said they were still arguing about Galilee."

By the time we came to Beth-Anya the lodging houses were full of pilgrims, but Zenobia came to an agreement with the woman who ran the village's only brothel, a run-down two-room hut a decorous distance from the synagogue. We could, along with a family from the land between the rivers, sleep on the roof while the business of the house was conducted below us, where a long line of pilgrims stood waiting. When I asked the owner if she knew where I could find the man who had died, she shrugged.

"In Sheol."

"No, I mean the man who died and was brought back to life."

"He died," she said. "Again. His family are mourning him."

"Where can I find them?"

"They live at the other end of the village. Opposite the poorhouse. They're sitting in mourning for him."

"Husband," said Zenobia, "let them mourn their dead in peace. We should eat and sleep."

We descended from the brothel's roof before dawn and I breathed the cold air of the hill-country morning. The beast that Zenobia rode was a gentle, pliable thing on the rein.

"Home," she said, "and by nightfall, my sweet. The vines need us."

At the north end of the village the path took us past olive groves and fields of pomegranate trees. Then cultivation ceased and we moved through fields of uncleared stones. The beast lurched when it heard the bellow of an ass tethered by a wrecked hut. My sides ached with sudden pain. We moved north.

And, of course, we found them. Just as the sun was at its fullest height behind us we came to a great bend in the road. A group of peasants was standing by the roadside, shouting at each other. Their women stood a little way ahead, showing every sign of the weariness of delay. They looked northward, silent in their impatience. We had already passed the men, and were passing the women, when the boy recognised me.

"It's him," he called out, and ran out towards us. "My friend from the pool. With a donkey. Am I right? I'm tired of walking," he said, and he tugged at the hem of my cloak, his smile pleading. "We're going back to Galilee," said the boy. "My father said that we would see him there. Am I right?"

We halted, with reluctance. We were still far from the cut that led up into the hills and the narrow path to the farm. Hours of walking at a countryman's pace.

"Yeuda!" his mother called out to him. The boy turned back with reluctance. "Don't be bothering the gentleman." The men's voices rose in anger.

"They're arguing again," she said. "That's all they can do now. Even the Twin. I wanted to stay in Jerusalem and find out the truth about what happened to my man's body. But they'll not listen to us. They'll not listen to anyone."

"We're going to Galilee," said the boy. "To see my father. Am I right?"

One of the group strode out towards us, pulling his shawl tightly around his shoulders. It was the Rock. He stopped and looked at me.

"I'm going back to Galilee," he said.

A voice came from the group, directed at no-one but loud enough to be heard by all.

"Running away. Again."

"I'm going back to Capernaum. I've got a boat that needs work. I've got mouths to feed. I'm going back to the boats. That's all." He looked at the child and the women. Then he started to walk north along the road.

The boy's mad grandmother, eyes still cavernous with grief, reached out and touched my Zenobia's face, as a child might. Zen took her hand, gently, and smiled.

"Let me help you, mother," said Zen. "Lean on my arm."

The young boy's mother was at her left hand, instantly.

"Thank you, my sister," she said. "Now, mother, be calm. We will help you, together."

The woman showed no awareness of where she might be, not of the road nor of the arguments and ill-temper of her son's former followers. The vacancy of her gaze was unchanged, but her face softened, and Zenobia laid her hand upon the old woman's arm again in reassurance. I looked back at the little group of angry peasants.

Beside me, Cassiel looked back too, but his eyes were on the distant line of the road through the jagged hills.

The men resumed their argument. Nine, turned inwards in a circle, their backs to the road and to their people, their backs to everything. I looked ahead, up the road. Shimon-the-Rock was vanishing round the bend. I touched Zen's shoulder.

"We should be moving on."

"In a moment, husband," she agreed. "What are those men doing?" She crouched down, hands on knees, addressing the child.

They were shouting at each other now. Cassiel and I approached them.

"Your friend has gone," I told them. The argument continued. "I said, your friend the Rock has gone back to Galilee."

They turned and looked at me, in disbelief. Thaddeus bar Ptolemai was with them. He wore his mud-stained and tattered linen. But his eyes were pits of blissful unknowing, staring straight ahead without any sign of sense.

"Shalom, my brother."

He smiled, oblivious.

"Shalom. Are you going to see him too? He told me I would see him in Galilee."

His mind must already be there. Only his body was dragging itself along the road. If this man had ever worked for Marcus, then he'd crossed the river long ago. Not just crossed it but journeyed on deep into whatever territory lay on the other side. No night at Esther's would ever be enough to bring him back to his true self.

Yehuda-the-Twin walked through the group, moved an uncomprehending Thaddeus out of his way, and greeted Cassiel.

"Shalom."

With Yehuda-the-Twin was a youth of about thirteen or fourteen. Thin wisps of a beard over too-pale thin-stretched skin. His eyes were sunken, almost lost in their sockets, but with a sharp, constricted intensity when you found them. It is not good for a child to starve himself out of devotion. This one was barely a man.

"My little brother Yakoub." Yehuda-the-Twin spoke. We greeted each other.

"Thank you," young Yakoub said to Cassiel. "We were grateful to receive your warning."

"You did? Then you have my boss to thank for it." Cassiel turned towards me.

"Thank you, my brother," Yakoub said with a simplicity and reverence that made me wonder what point he could have been arguing so strongly a moment before.

The brothers Yakoub and Yehonatan were standing by my side now. Yehonatan spat on the ground.

"The Rock's off again, eh? And the priest-boy's away with the goats. Always knows more than us."

"Let's go to Galilee," the child Yeuda announced. "Come on. We're going." Then he turned to me, beaming with sudden confidence. "We'll see my father there. Am I right? He told me that we would."

I turned to the road and took the donkey's tether in my hand. "Let's go," I announced to no-one in particular. Zenobia and Mother Mariam started to walk along the road after Shimon-the-Rock, arm in arm, the old woman supported on the other side by her son's widow. At last the men began to stir. After a few paces, Cassiel stopped and looked back. My head went down. We were still hours from the safety and seclusion of the vineyard. To travel with the women and the child was one thing. But to be waiting at every bend in the road for these fractious, argumentative followers without a leader risked bringing us to immobility and a night on the open hillside. Whatever might hold Marcus' attention in Jerusalem, I had no wish to spend another night away from my home. My bones, skin and muscles all ached with seven different kinds of agony. I pulled on the donkey's lead. To my relief, it followed and I strode after Shimon-the-Rock.

Yakoub and Yehonatan came up to my shoulder. They patted the beast admiringly.

"You got a good beast there, master."

"Don't you worry. We'll catch him soon enough, see, that one. Walking off like that, eh?"

"Never sticks to nothing, him. He'll be back dawdling at the women's heels before we're past that tree there."

"We've got two swords, master. Can help look after you on the road if you like. There must be bandits here. What do you say?"

"Thank you," I said. "But Cassiel and Stephanos will look after us all. There'll be no trouble while they're with us."

Stephanos, who had heard this exchange, moved his considerable bulk closer to me, and I turned to speak to my messenger.

"Cassiel?"

Silence. I looked back. He was on the road, fifty paces behind us, looking back to the distant ribbon that stretched across the Judean hills. Dust rose where the road was widest just below the ridge of a distant hill. And something was moving down the hill. It was moving slowly, and to the side of the road. Cassiel turned and looked towards me, and I waved him over.

"What do you see?"

"Soldiers" he said. "Ten of them. And a man on horseback, to one side."

I looked up the road. Shimon-the-Rock was far distant. The rest of the followers were standing, quite aimlessly, to one side. Zenobia disentangled herself from Mother Mariam's arm and came to me. The old woman watched her go with a look of abandonment. Then she began to wail softly, and work the cloth of her robe with the fingers of her right hand.

"Husband. We must go."

I watched the dust rising for some ten or twenty heartbeats.

"They're slow. What's happening?" I asked Cassiel.

"They've stopped a group of travellers. They're picking them out and taking them aside."

"Solomon. Husband! We must go."

"Describe them. My eyes are old. There is a white horse. The rest – I cannot tell."

"Now they're marching forward. They're on the road."

I watched the dust until it became clear, even to my eyes, that people were moving within it. And the horseman beside them was a shard of white against the hills. There could be no doubt.

"It's Marcus, isn't it?"

"Yes, boss."

Zenobia tugged at my elbow. "Solomon, we cannot wait. We must go. Now."

"How far," I asked her, "are we from the track up to the farm?"

"An hour. If we go alone."

I looked at the holy man's former followers. They were arguing again. Closer to the road, the women and the young boy were watching us, and looking back to the horizon.

"And what do you think that Marcus is looking for?"

I walked over to the donkey and pulled on its lead. This time it screeched in protest.

"Tell them to stop arguing," I said to Yehuda-the-Twin. "Tell them that, if they want to be safe, they're to go and catch up with Shimon-the-Rock. Tell them to run after him if they want to live." He looked back along the road.

"Who are they?" he asked. "Why do they follow us?"

"It's the Prefect's head of intelligence."

"His what?"

"His spy. Do you understand? I know that man. The last time I spoke to him he said that he was going to seek you out and do to you what his people did to your brother at the beginning of Pesach. Do you understand me?"

Mistress Mariam grabbed the child and held him to her. The mother began to wail and slap her hands against her cheeks. This got the attention of the men, who stopped their argument and turned back towards us. Young Yakoub tried to calm his mother.

"Listen to me," I shouted, "all of you." At last I had their attention. Even Yehonatan looked round.

"We have to move. Quickly. There are men back there, soldiers, who mean us harm. Now. Your friend Shimon-the-Rock is ahead of us. We need to find him and take him with us. Not far ahead, there is a track on the left of the road. If we can reach it, it will lead us to a place of safety."

They looked at me with the dullness of bullocks in the Temple courtyards before the knowledge of what is to come strikes them.

Yakoub and Yehonatan came up to me by the roadside.

"We've still got two swords, master, if that will help."

I turned to Yehuda-the-Twin.

"Make them understand. We move now, all of us, or we die."

JUDEAN HILLS
5TH DAY OF THE WEEK,
9TH HOUR

There is a cleft in the rocks at the side of the Damascus Road, a half day's journey north from Jerusalem. A track leads through it, up into the hills. The road turns sharply just south of the place, and the landscape gives you a glimpse eastwards down into the desert and the broken lands that lead to Jericho and the river. Travellers pass by in ignorance of the path: it is a misdirection of the landscape, a happy deception.

We passed through the cleft. Cassiel stood sentry at the road, Stephanos a little way above him. As we began to climb into the hill-country I spoke to Yehuda-the-Twin.

"You and your family are welcome to my house. Your companions too. All of you."

"Thank you."

"There's a track that goes north, above my vineyard, further into the hills. If you leave at dawn tomorrow you'll be out of the rough country before the end of the day."

"Are there bandits here?"

"You see that ridge there?" I pointed ahead. "The land to the north and east of my vineyard belongs to a relation by marriage of Eleazar ben Ananas."

"The old High Priest?"

"His father-in-law. Bandits keep away. They've more sense than to maul the hands that feed them."

We came to the crest of the hills in the late afternoon and looked down upon my vineyard and the farmhouse that nestled beneath the great rocks. When we walked through the upper blocks the air was cool and I saw that the blooms on the vines had begun to shoot. I trailed my fingers against the leaves. At summer's end the grapes they bore would in their turn reach out to me and say, *Choose me. Choose me, for I am a better bunch. Choose me, for I will make the finest wine.*

We halted beneath the shade of the olive tree. I tethered the donkey, then Zenobia and I embraced.

"We are home." Her voice softened. "Thank the Almighty. Now rest." The trellis that shaded the press house was shining in the light of evening and its leaves cast cool shadows across the wooden benches. Behind us, the followers and the women picked their way between the vines. Last of all came Yakoub and Yehonatan and Shimon-the-Rock. They were arguing again.

I went through the house and into the courtyard of our paradise. I knelt, pressed my face against the cold stones of the tomb of our sons Benjamin and Eleazar, closed my eyes and wept. I put the palm of my hand against the rock and I whispered the words of Kaddish. At last the words came, though it seemed to me there was no will or purpose in me that made them. I spoke, but my mind was dumb. Long after silence enclosed me, I felt a hand upon my shoulder.

"You've brought work and duty back to our home, haven't you? All that you told me was in the past, in Jerusalem. Now it's here. No, don't say anything. Just promise me something, will you, my love? When they leave in the morning, that's the end of it."

I opened my eyes and found myself staring into her own wide-open eyes, our faces pressed together, her lips parted, as if we were huddled together for the first time back in her room at Esther's.

"Come," she said after the silence. "Come. We have guests."

They had settled themselves on the benches beneath the trellis. The young child was sprawled across his mother's lap deep in the sleep of exhaustion. The Twin sat by them, his head on the table. Yakoub the younger brother lay on the bench next to him. The others were looking at the vines and the trellis, the farmhouse and the press with the sort of curiosity you see in peasants at a market. They were, I realised, sizing me up for my wealth.

"Stephanos," I said. "Broach one of the old amphorae at the back of the press house. Bring it out and ask Abi to serve our guests."

I turned to Cassiel.

"It may be the last opportunity we ever have to drink it."

"There was no sign of anyone following, boss."

"I'm setting a watch tonight. You, me, Stephanos, some of the guests. Not the two that are always arguing. The Twin and one of the reasonable ones."

Zenobia passed us as she went into the farmhouse. She squeezed my arm as she went and looked back at me. "Rest," she said. "Rest, my love."

Stephanos returned from the press house: butchery for so many, so late in the day, was out of the question, would meal porridge, cured meat, dried fruits and the wine be sufficient?

It was at that moment that Yehonatan and Yakoub finished another argument with Shimon-the-Rock. They looked at each other, each indicating that one of the others should act. At last, fury on his face, Shimon-the-Rock walked towards the farmhouse door and raised his hands. Then he looked back at the other two. Go on, they gestured.

"Peace be upon this house," he said at last. Yakoub and Yehonatan smiled in approval. Yes. Whatever this was, he had done it. Then he turned to Zenobia.

"Well," he stumbled through his words, "you see. It's this. We were wondering, mistress, as we're here and you're kindly offering us food and drink. Would there be anybody in the house who needs healing? Healing of anything? Anything at all?"

My Zenobia smiled and said "No. You're our guests. Eat. Drink. Rest. That's all that we can ask of you."

The Rock looked back at the others. He bobbed his head and thanked my wife for her hospitality. Yakoub and Yehonatan clasped him by the shoulders, congratulating him for having done what was expected. Then the blank misery of grief and resentment returned to his face.

Cassiel came to me with Stephanos, Yehuda-the-Twin and one of the other followers, the tall, thickset man with scars on his neck and forehead.

"He says he knows how to use a sword."

"Unlike those two," the new man offered, glancing back to Yakoub and Yehonatan. "They just talk. Phillipos," he said. "At your service, master."

So, this was the former enthusiast for armed insurrection in our Yehuda's reports. Stephanos and I led Cassiel, Yehuda-the-Twin and Phillipos down through the vines. One man who would act with the certainty of professional violence when required; two whose behaviour was unknowable. We paused at the bottom of the home field.

"These," I told them, "are the first vines we planted when the rootstocks arrived from Tirazis. The ones that survived. Now they give us the best grapes. The best grapes give us the best juice. The best juice makes our best wine. With some help from the press. This block's on sabbatical. Six years of growth, so no pruning, no cutting, no irrigation, no cropping in the seventh year. They're supposed to come back with a richer and fuller crop the next year. I'll believe that when I drink the wine that we make."

We climbed the bluff above the third block on the north slope, where the sun bakes the vines from early morning, and I showed them the spot where there is a line of sight far down through the lower hills. Anyone approaching from the direction of the Joppa Road can be seen long before they are even aware of the existence of the vineyard above them.

"Stay here till second watch," I said to Stephanos. "We'll send you food before then."

We left Phillipos at the top of the southern slopes. Cassiel, the Twin and I walked northwards through the upper block till we came to the spot where we had first looked down at the vines in the sun of late afternoon. I pointed out a spot on the side of the ridge to Yehuda-the-Twin.

"That's the place. Between those two rocks. Beyond them there's a great thorn bush. Keep it on your right. After a thousand paces you'll pick up the start of a trail that takes you north. I'll lead you there myself in the morning," I said when I saw the doubt in his eyes. "You'll be safe."

Cassiel and I descended through the short block to the north of the farmhouse where the grapes are always the first to ripen fully. I left him at the far end of the third row of vines, where the gatehouse can be seen across open ground.

"If you see anything down there, anything at all. Come to the house immediately."

Then I walked through the rows of vines, the leaves leaching to darkness, and returned to my house.

Yakoub, Yehonatan, Shimon and the rest of the followers had vanished.

"The men are praying," Zenobia said. "Abi's made porridge and I've told her to put tomorrow's bread in the oven. You could cut down some of the dried meat if you want to be helpful."

The old mother and the young widow, busy with the bowls on the table, glanced up, first at me, then at Zenobia.

"Come on," I said to little Yeuda. "You can help me." I took one of the clay lamps and led him to the press house door.

The air within had a harsh, deeper cold than the hills outside. The child stared in wonder at the great stone tanks and the amphorae full of last year's wine propped up in ranks that stretched beyond the low circle of lamplight.

"That's where we tread the grapes."

"Like this?" He clambered over the stone rim and jumped down into the first tank. Then he mimed great strides of trampling down whatever was beneath his feet. His arms were pumping and look-at-me joy, eager for my approval, was on his face.

"No, no. We do it gently. You don't just pull off your wolfskin boots and go in there stamping and kicking. The grapes are soft, they're delicate. They need our care and our love. All they want to do is become the very best wine that they can. We have to let them do that."

He grinned at me and mimed a gentler, softer lifting of his feet and a squirming, slow trampling of the stone floor.

"Like this?"

"Like that."

I hauled him out of the stone tank and we moved deeper into the press house, past the amphorae that contained the lees of our first vintages, the wines we had never been able to sell. Even the first ones had the seal: *Solomon Eliades. Oenarch. My vineyard is my own to give.*

"Look at them," and I held the lamp close below the necks of the first in the row, and brushed the dust from their shoulders. The marks upon it read "North Block. Unblended. 42nd Year of the Temple."

"Is that good?"

"That was when we were still learning. We're still learning today. I think that we should try this one, don't you?"

Yeuda seized hold of the handles and heaved. He crumpled against it, laughing at his own weakness.

"We'll bring it out later and serve it to your uncle and his friends. Now we go. This way."

We came to the back wall. Here there hung from hooks in the ceiling beam the haunches of cured kids' meat that Zenobia and I had salted and stored at the end of summer. I found the stool by the light of the lamp and released the knife that was still strapped to the inside of my calf. Then I stretched up, cut down a haunch and passed it to Yeuda. He took it clumsily, clutching it to his chest.

"Good boy."

When I cut the second haunch, the light flickered across the fibres of the twine by which it hung and I wondered what Saul and his ropemaker's eye would have made of the plait and the knot that I had tied around the kid's hock last autumn. I held the haunch in one hand, untangled the string with the other and slipped it into the fold of my tunic.

"Come on."

The men had returned from wherever they had gone to pray and were sitting beneath the trailing vines where the day-labourers ate their meals during grape-harvest. Thaddeus bar Ptolemai was at one end of the bench, the blissful peace still upon him. Zenobia, Mistress Mariam and the old woman brought boards of dates, dried fruits, porridge and the morning's fresh bread from the farmhouse. Voices rose in approval and pleasure when the boy placed the haunch of cured kid-meat on the table. Well done, lad, someone said. That's the stuff. Abigail was at the far end of the trellis, with Yakoub and Yehonatan. They were trying to convince her that she must be unwell in some unspecified way and that they would be able to help her, that they would pray for her and lay hands upon her.

"Abi," I said, "would you help the mistress, please?"

She went into the house, looking down. The women gathered their bowls and were ready to move into the farmhouse for their meal. Mistress Mariam beckoned to little Yeuda.

"Come, my boy. Come with us."

"I should stay with the men, mother. I'm old enough now. My father let me."

There was muttered agreement from the far end of the table.

"It's good for the lad," a voice spoke, unsteadily. "He's made friends with our host. It's good for him." It was the old grandmother. Little Yeuda squealed with delight and sat down on the bench next to me.

"He'll be no trouble," I said to his mother. "I promise you."

I cut slices of smooth-grained meat from the inside of the haunch and passed them down the table. Then Zenobia came with a jug of our wine, her hand brushing against my arm. She poured, and the women withdrew to the farmhouse with their food. The company fell silent, intent upon their meal.

When I had finished with the haunch and the white sinew between the cured flesh fell sheer to the bone all along its length, I reached into the pocket of my tunic. The string that I had cut was there. So was another, wound in a ball and knotted close. I took this second string out: it was the twine that Saul had cut from the wrists of Yehuda when we found him hanging on the tree. I looked down the table at bar Ptolemai. I had an opportunity that would never come again to establish the truth about something that had troubled me ever since Saul first examined the knot. I sat in silence for a long time chewing on the last of the meat. Then I began.

"Yeuda. Let me show you a trick." I took three clay mugs from the end of the table, upended them and tied the string with a loop. The boy was by my side, eager in his fascination. I coiled the string around the three mugs, in and out, in the way that any trickster in a marketplace will do, and I looked him in the eyes.

"Now. Which one of the mugs has the string around it?"

He looked down at the mugs and then back at me.

"Is it lawful?"

"Of course it is. You have to use your skill to find out the truth. You're a clever boy."

He seemed reassured and tapped his finger upon the middle mug. I pulled the string. It unravelled and the loop tightened around the left-hand mug. The child looked up in equal parts of disappointment and delight.

"Again?"

"Again!"

The men began to pay attention. Andros-the-Man, Yakoub and the other Shimon leaned over. I looped the string in another simple arrangement that is known in the marketplaces as "the ass and two corn-shucks". Little Yeuda watched the movement of my hands with care. This time, he picked the right-hand mug.

"Am I right?"

I pulled the string away. Middle mug.

"You'll need to be smarter than that, lad," a voice said from down the table.

"Again!"

"Aye, again."

Again I wrapped the twine around the mugs, he touched, and I pulled. To my relief, he got lucky with the middle mug, and we played on, Yeuda with all the confidence of the fortunate beginner. On the sixth or seventh turn he began to watch my eyes, not the mugs. Smart boy. And he began to win.

"Now, you try," he said at last. I pretended just enough reluctance when the men cheered and I handed him the string. He looped it with care and I watched his eyes.

"Go on. Choose!"

Middle cup. Wrong. The boy pulled the string and it closed on the left-hand mug.

"I can do it too!"

We played on and I made sure that I lost often enough to encourage him. He was a sharp, intelligent boy. I watched him understand the game, work out the way to loop the string, weighing complexity against guile. I took back the twine and set some more complex arrangements for him: the sideways snake; the fig-tree and the rocks; the goat and two dogs; the deception of the pigeons.

After I had pulled the string around the leftmost mug three times in succession I stopped, took the string and held it up.

"I think we need another length of twine, don't you? This one's too easy for you."

Little Yeuda looked unsure, but reached out to the mugs.

"Andros-the-Man, Shimon-the-Rock, brother Yehonatan." I had their attention. "You're fishermen, aren't you? Don't you have a length of twine about you?"

The two thugs looked at each other and began a mimed search of their cloaks. Andros-the-Man stirred. His eyes were bleary with my wine. Shimon-the-Rock shook bar Ptolemai.

"Come on if you're still with us. Lend the man your twine, brother..."

Bar Ptolemai came back to the present and he searched the folds of his linen coat. He pulled out a plait of twine from somewhere within.

"Aye, mate. There you go," said Shimon, pushed it down the table and went back to his conversation with Yehonatan.

I unwound the new twine and examined it, held it up in front of the boy as a conjuror would. Look: it's good rope, one length, no knots, no tricks or imperfections. I forced myself to look at it as Saul, a man raised in the tent-maker's trade, would look at a piece of rope. It was thick, with a smooth, tight-wound weave that barely bristled. Laid next to the twine that had bound the wrists of our Yehuda, it was quite obvious: both had been cut from the same length.

"Again!" Yeuda was impatient. I took the twine that Thaddeus bar Ptolemai had given me and laid it around the mugs in the arrangement known as the path to Masada. He picked it without hesitation. Left-hand mug.

"Well done."

We played a few more games, for the sake of the show, but by now the men had lost interest and were arguing about what they should tell people when they came home to Galilee. Shimon-the-Rock wanted silence. Yakoub told him that that was no surprise and the argument began again. Yeuda and I played the disguised eagle, the antelope in the bush, and the reversed goat. He chose them all, without hesitation. After we had swapped roles again and played a journey round Mount Gerizim, En-Gedi road, and the needle gate, his eyes began to drop and his head became heavy.

"Enough?"

"Enough," he conceded with reluctant longing.

I went to the press house and carried out the old amphora of unblended wine we had found. My oldest, long-overlooked vintage. Then I took the mug that Yeuda had last chosen, turned it upright, filled it with my own best wine and emptied it. It was rich and round, the fruit of the grapes filled my mouth, each one calling out to my tongue. *Take me, for I am a better grape.* When I swallowed the taste of it was like fresh plums of the finest picking and I could not believe that the wine we had made could possibly contain so rich a scent and such a stew of flavours. I wondered if Zenobia had ever tasted this wine from the far end of the press room. Next spring, she would take it down to Caesarea and allow Ariel on the Cyprus Wharf to taste a drop of it before she named her price. I drank again, and the fruit followed its path through the limbs of my body till my hands and feet shone with the sharpness of its pleasure.

Then I leaned back against the bole of the vine-tree, gave thanks to the Almighty for his mercy and benevolence, and forced myself to consider what I must do now that the two ropes in my hand had turned out to be the same. The scar-raked face of the Syrian soldier rose before my eyes. The Service had been betrayed by our very own good friends. Why Marcus should have done this was now a mystery that Philo could try to solve. I had identified the man who had murdered our good Yehuda. I had done my duty to the Service. Whatever state of deluded bliss Thaddeus bar Ptolemai might be in now, he and his companions were guests in my house, were sleeping under my roof as a refuge from clear danger. I could not in any conscience act to avenge myself or the Service on behalf of our Yehuda. To leave the case to Philo's judgement would be absurd. This left me with one choice, as revolting and bereft of responsibility to my wife, my people and my vines as it was possible to imagine.

I unfastened the knife from the strap at my calf and slipped it into the folds of my vest.

"Yeuda, you should be asleep by now." Mistress Mariam came to us from the house. The women must have finished their meal.

"Lord Shlomo has been teaching me his trade."

She looked at the mugs and the loops of string as if they might at any moment come alive and start moving of their own accord.

"Master, you're a good man taking us in like this, we're in your debt, but you shouldn't be teaching the child such things," she said quietly. "Yehuda from Kerioth, that bad man – he was always playing that game with the child."

Of course he was, I thought. I taught him the game myself when he too had been a boy.

"If he should be learning anything, he should be learning Torah."

"Mamma…"

"Your father taught you Torah. You should study, for his sake. Look at your uncle Yakoub." The young man put away his writing tablet and was at the boy's side before he could respond.

"Come on, sleepy Yeuda," he said, lifting the boy into his arms. "We've got a long way to walk home tomorrow."

The child hung on to his uncle and leaned out with his free arm to embrace me.

"Go on," I said, "I'll walk with you some of the way tomorrow. I promise."

I took a goatskin of water and a satchel of bread and cured meat and walked the perimeter of my land in darkness. Down at the bottom gate Stephanos was squatting back on his heels, staring out into the darkness, all steady attention. I squatted beside him and passed him bread and meat in silence.

"Nothing," he said without stirring or taking his attention from the darkness beyond. I stared until the rough outlines of rock and stone lost their form, shifting into the mass of the hills and the clouds. The darkness stared back at me.

I walked through the upper block, trailing my fingers against the vines. To end my life in my own vineyard would be something for a man of the soil. I felt the blade against my side. To use it against myself would be difficult, agonising, messy and prolonged. Our friends had two swords. Cassiel was a trained professional who could act with speed, accuracy and competence. I had no doubt he would do so if I asked him.

I came at last to his watch station. He had seen nothing. I gave him some dried fruit and slices of kid and waited until he had eaten.

"Cassiel, my friend."

"Boss?"

"When we have seen our friends safely on their way tomorrow, before you go back to Jerusalem, there is something that I want you to do for me."

We sat and stared out into the darkness, down into the great bowl of the vineyard and beyond, across the hills towards the lowlands and the Western Sea. At last Cassiel spoke.

"Boss?"

"I said there's something—"

"Out there. Look." His arm dragged a curve across the unseen horizon. "Do you see?"

I peered out.

"My eyes are old."

"Down there. Lights. Moving."

I strained again. Deep in the lower darkness I saw a distant speck of fire that was not starlight.

"Joppa Road," I said. "Or further off."

"It's moving." And then, "It's gone."

I stood up. "Come and tell me if anything changes." He thanked me for the food. "I'll come when Kesil the Hunter leaves heaven and watch for you." I left him the water-skin and walked back up through the rows of vines to my farmhouse. Looking up, I saw that Zenobia had set two lamps in the high window of our chamber.

The men were stirring now, beginning to gather their waterskins and their satchels, shuffling towards the press house where they would spend the night. On their faces once more was the look of utter defeat, of grief and the burden of despair that they had worn when I first saw them in the room at the carpenters' synagogue. The return to Galilee weighed upon them, the shuffling back to the narrow villages and the families they had left behind. What could they tell their people of what they had seen and experienced in Jerusalem, of the disaster to which their master and teacher had led them?

Inside the press house, the men spread out in the space between the first tank and the new amphorae. An eye winked in the darkness and from somewhere close to my feet I heard Yakoub whisper.

"The master: do you remember? He always came round and locked up the boatyard, last thing. Made sure we were all safe in the night."

From the deeper darkness, a voice told him to be quiet and to sleep.

"All right. All right. Peace."

I closed the press house door and returned, at last, to my house. The boy was sleeping on the bench by Abigail's hearth. There was no sign of the women. I lit a lamp and mounted the stairs to the upper floor. Then I heard Zenobia's voice, mixed with soft laughter and the voice of the old woman coming from our chamber. And I opened the door.

Zenobia sat before the great burnished sheet of copper, her hair stretched out to her side. It shone in the dim light of the oil lamps placed around the polished metal. Mother Mariam was combing it out for her with the brush of ivory and antelope hair that Zenobia had bought in Caesarea. The old woman's movements were quick, but gentle and precise and did not snag. Abigail was watching her actions with the attention of a student. The boy's mother sat beside Zenobia, examining her cosmetics, jewellery and brushes.

"Your wife has the most beautiful hair, master," the old woman said to me. "I've not handled hair as beautiful as this since I was a young woman in Egypt. She is very lucky, your Zenobia."

"Mother Mariam has been showing Abi how to do this. She knows so much. Learned it all in Egypt."

Mother Mariam's face softened. The look of concentration passed as she put down the brush, and let Zenobia's hair shimmer and cascade through her hands.

"When we were in Egypt," she said, "and my Yussuf died, I had to bring up my boys alone. I found work with a hairdresser in the rich part of Byblos, not far from the little Temple our people have there. You know it? Yes, of course. I swept the floor and collected the cuttings." She turned to Zenobia, "After a few months the mistress showed me how to wash and how to cut. Soon I was her second girl and she let me build up my own list of regulars." Zenobia nodded in agreement. "You know? By the time the boys were five, I had women from all over Byblos coming to me. Of course, it could not last."

"What happened, mother?"

"After a time, when things changed again in Judea, we were told that we could go home if we wished to. I so wanted to see my Nazareth again, our street, and the olive tree by our workshop. I so wanted to go back." She looked down and her hands ceased moving through Zenobia's hair.

"So we came home at last. There are no fine women in a place like Nazareth. None in Cana neither. No-one in our Nazareth ever needs their hair cutting. Not even the synagogue president's wife. So I went and opened a shop in Sepphoris. That was after we'd got my late husband's workshop back from the Herodians who had stolen it from us. They're vultures, those people. Preying upon widows and taking bread from orphans. My second husband, my Yussuf's brother Alphaeus, he had to go to the Temple archives and pay them to trace the descent of my sons to prove that they were my Yussuf's boys, before the court would even let us plead for his workshop to be given back. And then that lawyer lied about it. They lied about everything, the Herodians. They're foxes and vultures. So my Yeshua would have a trade like his father. And my Yehuda too. All so that my boys would have trades, and their families would not have to starve like the peasants do."

"Mother Mariam…" The younger Mariam put her hand upon the older woman's arm. "It's over, long ago, all that. And it's late. We should rest." She placed the brushes and the cosmetics back upon the table with her maimed fishwife's hands.

"Keep it," Zenobia told her. "The pot of kohl – it's best Peran. None better north of Arabia." The younger woman looked at the gift with horror and regret.

"I cannot," she said. "My man is dead."

The old woman became agitated again, and a blankness passed over her face.

"And my Yeshua. Where is he? Where is my boy? Why can I not see him? Why can I not? We have done all this for him. For my Yeshua."

"And we have a long journey over the hills tomorrow, mother. And we will be back in Nazareth soon. I promise you, mother, soon. We will be home, and it will all be over, all this."

She lifted the older woman up by the arms and my Zenobia came to assist her, holding the mother's elbow and whispering to her as they walked with care and painful slowness to the door. The old woman was weeping silently as they went, her head bowed. How would they carry her across the hills and down to the valley tomorrow? I would give them the donkey, and send Stephanos with the cart.

Zenobia led them down the steps to the room at the back of the house. When she returned to our chamber, she closed the door behind her and stood for a moment, her hands upon the clasp. Then she breathed in and opened her arms to me.

"Solomon ben Eleazar," she said. "My old goat. Come home to us." I took her hand and she drew me to her against the door. Her breath was hot on my cheek. "Come to me, my love. Come inside. Come in to me."

Her eyes were huge, her lips full and smiling, in just the way they had been when she first looked at me in her room at Lady Esther's, when we sat together so close and listened to the girl in the next room, long ago.

"Do you know what she told me, the younger one?" she whispered, and her breath was wet on my ear. "She and her carpenter husband had kept away from each other since their child was born. Look at the age of the boy. She purified herself after he was born but that carpenter of hers had other ideas. He told her that they had to prepare themselves. Prepare themselves for what? Look what happened to him. In the end, he never came home to his woman, did he? Well, that's no good, is it? This is the only life we have, here and now. Come to me, my love."

Her voice trembled, and she smiled as she drew her fingers down my cheek.

"You may kiss me," she said.

I moved towards her and we embraced.

"Yes," she said. "Yes—"

At that moment a hammering of blows sounded upon the door behind us. Two blows. A moment's silence. Then three more.

JUDEAN HILLS
6TH DAY OF THE WEEK,
6TH HOUR OF DARKNESS

Stephanos stood at the door.

"Torches," he said. "Down below the bottom field. Coming this way."

"Wake the guests. Get them out of the press house and ready to go up the hill."

Zenobia gripped my arm. "You bring work home from Jerusalem with you. And this is what happens."

"Get the women and the child ready. Put the old woman on the donkey. Untether the beast, put a rope on it and bring it round. As quietly as you can. We leave in silence."

I went to our bed and took out the bag of Tyrian gold and silver I kept beneath it. When I looked back at Zenobia she was stuffing the Isis brooch, the antelope brush, her gold earrings and the great necklace into a leather pouch.

"Come on."

Downstairs, the child was stirring, sleepy and confused. Mistress Mariam was speaking to him, pulling at his sleeves and holding his chin. She looked up at me as I passed, terror on her face.

Outside, the followers were making far too much noise as they stumbled from the press house. Cassiel appeared from among the vines.

"The lights, boss," he said.

"Show me."

Stephanos led us to the outcrop at the high end of the home block. Below us, a line of torches danced in the night air. Then the movement stopped, but the lights still flickered. Whoever they were, they had a purpose. It was deep night, but they were not entrenched and posting pickets. I looked down into the darkness and listened to my own heart beat slowly. After what seemed far too long a time to be standing, exposed and motionless on the rocks, with the men and women unguided and chaotic behind us, a new line of lights emerged, somewhat to the right of the first line.

"Boss?"

"There's a *tel* down there where the wild goats gather in the evening. They've gone round the back of it on the mountain path. We had a leopard down there last winter."

"We dealt with it," Stephanos said. "It was old, and sick."

"How far?" Cassiel asked.

"Down there? Five thousand paces."

"Master, we should go. They'll be at the bottom gate soon."

At the farmhouse the followers were staring out into the night, without purpose. Only Zenobia and Mistress Mariam were struggling to get the old woman up on the donkey. Mother Mariam was oblivious, unable to help herself, and stared vacantly at my wife while leaning over as if about to slide from the beast. The old woman was repeating, over and over in a rasping whisper: "Yussuf, help me. Where is my Yussuf? He will help me. My Yussuf will help. Where is he?" Zenobia tried to calm the beast, but it kept stepping away from her. The men did nothing.

Without a word, Stephanos took control of the beast, looped a lead-rein round its jaws to silence it, steadied it with his free hand and pulled it round.

The old woman stared at us. Her eyes were caves. She leaned forward and grasped my hand. "Are you my Yussuf?"

"No, mother." Zenobia said, holding her arm steady. "He's still my husband."

"My boy," she went on, "You will take me to find our Yeshua? We will find him, won't we? You will know where to find him."

"Mother." Yehuda-the-Twin gently untangled her hands from my arm and placed them on the beast's neck. "We must go." She looked away without a word, her eyes still cavernous, and at last the donkey moved.

The followers picked up their satchels, their goatskins and their staffs and began to shuffle forwards. Zenobia tugged at the donkey's halter, her hand closed upon its nostrils to damp the sounds of its snuffling, and she encouraged Mistress Mariam and little Yeuda to follow. Stephanos walked ahead.

"The goat-track to the ridge," I told him. "And keep them quiet."

I stood at the upper gate and counted them as they moved past me. Shimon-the-Rock trudged in silence, head down. Yakoub and Yehonatan glared, their eyes full of fear. Bar Ptolemai was cheerfully oblivious. At last, they were all out and on the mountain. Finally, Phillipos came down from his post. I looked down into the darkness, at the blocks of vines that were coming into bud and whose grapes would, in the months of Elul and Tishrei, give us our vintage. Below us the lights moved up to the lower gate.

"Let's go."

That we found our way to the ridge at all was thanks entirely to Stephanos' skill. To follow from below a trail as slight as the one that rose to the scarp above us without losing your way is challenge enough in daylight. To do so by night, with a train of slow-witted, sleep-confused followers unfamiliar with the terrain, and an enemy at your heels, is the deed of a man. The air cooled to a thin mantle of mist that chilled me and cut into my lungs as I laboured upwards. We were still moving far too slowly. Every footfall, every breath or rough snag of clothing upon branch tumbled down the slopes below like the clatter of falling rocks. I spoke no words, and hoped that whatever noises the carriers of those lights were themselves making would envelope them in ignorance of our flight.

Above us, the darkness itself vanished into vacancy. The stars were gone. The hillside was gone. The followers, the donkey with the old woman, the mother and the child, all had vanished. And my Zenobia too. The mist enshrouded the hillside of the spring night, settling its damp into the deepest crevices below and vanishing into the air above our heads. I looked back. The farmhouse had vanished. But I could still see the line of lights dimly, at a distance that was impossible to guess. There were two lines now, and both of them still moving: one to our left, the other to our right.

"They're following the walls," I said to Cassiel. A pursuit that was careful to keep off my land. We turned to the hill, and moved deeper into the mist. Stephanos appeared by my side, urging us on in hissed whispers. At last, at the crooked rocks, we saw the backs of the followers crowding together. We had found the place where we had stood late in the afternoon before our descent to the vineyard. Somewhere, two hundred paces distant, were the beginnings of the goat-track that led north.

Zenobia was by my side. "Where have you been? Slow, slow, slow. You're so slow," she hissed, and wiped her eyes. "You'll kill us all, husband."

"Go," I said. "Go on. Take them." I pulled on the donkey's halter. The old woman lurched forward over the beast's neck, a look of incomprehension and terror, her mouth an O, her eyes vacancy. Abigail was speaking urgently to Stephanos, weeping. They embraced, and then she turned towards the path, and was gone.

"Go," I said again to Zenobia. "Go with her."

"Boss." Cassiel's hand was on my shoulder. I turned. "Lights. Down there. They're close."

"Go," I said to Zenobia again, and kissed her. "Go now."

The donkey started and skittered between the rocks. Instantly, without thought, complaint or reproach, the followers went after it. The child and his mother vanished too into the mist, warded by the tall back and long arms of Yehuda-the-Twin. And they were gone.

I turned to Cassiel and Stephanos.

"Well?"

Before they could speak, we heard it. The clank of iron and leather, and the breath of men in cold air. Close. They were far too close. And then we saw the lights, dull and jewelled in the night mist, bobbing.

I knelt and slipped my knife from the strap at my calf. Raising myself from that crouch was an agony; the joints of my legs clicked and scraped in the damp air.

I stood and looked back into the darkness where my wife had vanished a moment ago. Cassiel and Stephanos were by my side with drawn swords. I kicked hard at the dust of the mountainside with the ball of my foot, to mark the spot. I looked across at them. Then we walked towards the lights. Soldiers appeared on the left and moved towards Stephanos and Cassiel. Men ran towards me, empty-handed. In the instant before they seized me I had long enough to be puzzled by why they were unarmed and dressed in a manner that I remembered from long ago – the livery of Marcus' domestic slaves.

GEHENNA
DAWN

A jolt and I was rolled onto my left side. The end of all things. I was rolling through the earth to Mount Zion. Odours danced across me. The sharp brown warmth of beasts. Husks of the dead blew before my eyes, croaked and rattled, shivered on the dark wind, and were gone. Out of the darkness, arms raised me, then cast me down into mud. A pair of boots planted themselves a hand's breadth from my eyes. The fleshly stench of Gai Hinnom cut my nostrils. This rank *mephisis* could be nothing else. A fist punched my shoulder and I was dragged upright again.

"I'm old," I groaned. "You should show some respect."

"Bring him here."

Marcus stood on the edge of the Gai Hinnom ravine. Behind him, five domestic slaves in his family's livery. Saul stood to Marcus' left. Further off, I recognised Iosefos from Arimathea.

"It's down there," Marcus announced. "The body's down there, somewhere."

The vein in his head was throbbing again and his face glowed pink.

"Where else would it be?" he added.

Is this an interrogation or a rhetoric class? I wondered, but said nothing.

"And it will be found."

The domestic slaves looked terrified. One of them stepped back from the edge and was gushingly sick onto the roadside stones.

"It won't be any of you. Not even Saul." He turned to my former assistant. "You should be grateful I don't order you down there again. Oh no, not now the lost slave has been found." He turned to me. "This can be your first task now that you're back with us. You met his twin brother so you'll be able to recognise the body. Won't you?"

From deep in the mist the howling of dogs arose, first one, then two, three, four others harmonising a mode out of Sheol that echoed around the ravine. I looked down into Gai Hinnom and the chill of early morning bit into the bones of my arms and legs. The mist of my arrival in Jerusalem had returned. Behind me, sunlight cast a long shadow down the slope.

Marcus pushed me. "Don't come back up here without the body."

The noise of the dogs returned, now directly below us, deep and angry. They were fighting.

"Mercy," I groaned. "I am old." The ground beneath me slid away as I tumbled into the grey void of Gehenna. When I opened my eyes the right side of my head was thick with a vile slime. My feet were above me. My left arm ached with a dull cold deep in my bones. The stench was stronger than any I had imagined possible.

I began to arrange myself into a sitting position. From somewhere above, Marcus' voice: "Quintus informed me the bodies from last week were dumped to the right."

Shapes moved in the mist. The howling returned. I slipped deeper into the dirt. Two eyes and a snout loomed, instantly close. I scrambled to a place where the slope seemed gentler. To get out. To refuse this degradation. To face death at Marcus' hands rather than this filth. The creature snapped and I fell back against the filth of the slope, the white mist tumbled and I slid deeper into Gehenna.

Human skin, close to my lips and nose. I jerked backwards. My hands trembled. Toes, and a foot. Flesh hanging from bones. Above the foot, a heel and the remains of an ankle. The ankle had a single iron bolt through it. Tendons and a mess of sinew were spread around. I heaved myself to my feet.

The shins were broken and the rest of the body was bent so that it faced down the slope, covered in filth. Worms crawled across green and yellow meat. The man's ribs had been gnawed. The eyes and the soft tissues of the belly were gone. A wooden board lay by his shoulder bone, dark with blood. I drew my sleeve across it. Letters, daubed in lampblack: GESTAS. THEFT OF A LAMB.

I limped along the slope until I slipped against a plank, keeled over into the filth of Gehenna and closed my eyes.

The dogs' snarling returned. The noise of a beast whose food is threatened. I stood up. The dog lowered its body, tensed. A single sharp bark. A wooden board was stuck in the filth by my feet, a knotted rope threaded through a hole in the wood. I heaved it up, took hold of the rope and swung the board at the beast. On the third flail it came close enough for the dog to feel the breath of the board's passage. The beast howled and edged back. I clasped the board to me. It was smeared with filth and blood. Beneath, scratched in the wood was a line of letters in Greek, another in Aramaic. I wiped the filth away from the Greek. IESOS. TYRANNOS TON IUDEION.

The rope vanished into a heap of rags and filth. I pulled it, and the earth began to move.

An arm and a line of ribs. There was something that might once have been a pelvis, covered in filth, half-exposed. Two thigh bones. A shoulder blade. The dogs must have been at the guts and lungs, and the ribs were smashed on one side. I looked away into the mist and then forced myself to look back. The birds had been at his eyes and the scalp and skull were a blood-caked mess. No sort of identification by anyone who had set eyes upon the Twin was either possible or necessary, whatever lunatic idea Marcus had. The words on the plank would, I supposed, be enough. I remembered Iosefos' words about the chaos of Preparation Day when they had first managed to bribe our good friends to give them his body. There was one thing that I could do that Iosefos and the family would thank me for, and it delayed the loathsome business of gathering up the body, or whatever parts of it I could bring together, and making some sort of attempt to drag it up the slope out of Gehenna. I dropped the plank and stood still for a moment before I spoke.

Let God's great name be glorified and made holy throughout this world that he created by his will.

I faltered and looked up the slope and then addressed myself to the remains of the body again.

Let him set up His kingdom in your lifetime, during the days of your life, within the whole nation of Israel, quickly and soon. Let us say Amen. Let his name be blessed forever and to all eternity.

And I went on, to the end.

He who creates peace in the heights of heaven let him, let him create peace for us all, and for all of Israel. Amen.

I stretched out my arms and began to gather Yeshua's bones and sinews and the remains of his flesh together into some sort of arrangement that I could embrace and lift up in my arms. The first movement disturbed the flies and the creatures that were covering him. The dogs kept their distance.

I could have told off the mourner's prayer another dozen times before I despaired. What I was attempting was impossible. I tried to hold the body parts together in a way that allowed me to heft and carry them, either in my arms or across my shoulders. It was a task of filth, disgust and impossibility. I sat down by the plank and the skull and bowed my head between my knees and wished for the dogs to come and find me.

The howling returned. One of the dogs approached. I could not move. When it snapped at my tunic, I swung the plank at it. The beast whined and retreated.

I looked at the tunic and pulled at the frayed end. I stood, slipped it over my head and tore at the rip the dog had left until the stitching began to part. Then I laid it out on the slope and clawed at the bones and sinews until they rolled over onto the cloth. I gathered up the four corners and heaved it off the ground. I staggered and fell backwards, but kept hold of my burden. I studied the side of Gai Hinnom and tried to find a route that a man could walk when he was pushing before him a burden as huge and unbalanced as the bent and splayed body stuffed in my improvised sack. I clutched it to me and leaned forward. It was still unmanageable. I was naked except for my loincloth and sandals. I stepped forward again, balanced the ungainly bolus of bones, flesh, sinews, wood and filth and began to stagger upwards. I stopped and called out. My words fell dead in the mist. Another step upwards, another cry. I pushed the burden upwards. Then the voices of Marcus' slaves came to me, above and to the right of where I crawled.

The mist fell away and the slaves appeared at the rim of the ravine. They reached down and hauled me up. I fell down, cut and bloody, covered in mud and filth. They shrank back in disgust and refused to touch my burden. At last I tugged at the cloth and drew it back to reveal a shoulder, ribs and the stained wood of the headboard.

"He's not walking around Jerusalem, that's certain. But you didn't really need me to identify him, did you?"

Always end on a counter-question during interrogation, they had taught us at Caesarea years ago.

Iosefos from Arimathea knelt by the remains and picked at the fabric, weeping. Marcus looked down.

"You paid the Prefect a lot of money to release this body to you on your Preparation Day. How much will you pay me to give it back to you now that we've found it again?"

I looked up at Marcus.

"Please, Marcus, can I go back to my vineyard now?"

"Your vineyard? Solomon, do I understand you correctly? You still believe that it is your vineyard?" He turned to Iosefos. "This man deceived you earlier in the week. In reality he is an escaped slave who once worked in my household. After many years my property has been returned to me, with some help from my good friend Saul. Tomorrow, Solomon, you are going to tell me everything you know about the business of Yeshua's body and his followers, in particular where the one called Thaddeus bar Ptolemai can be found. And then we'll have a conversation about your time as my household slave, and about Domitilla."

Marcus beckoned the big, bald Syrian with the scar down his face.

"Demas, take him away. He's one of my slaves again. We've got him back. At last."

The big Syrian grasped my arms and spun me round.

"Mercy," I croaked. "I am old."

He laughed. The last sensation I had among the stench of Gehenna and the odour of the remains spread out upon my ripped tunic was the stink of the Syrian's breath and the rank *mephisis* of his sweat. He had been drinking cheap wine and eating dried kid and chickpeas, I could still tell that much. The stench overwhelmed me and I vomited on his cloak. He grunted and threw me onto the ground.

SHEOL

The darkness that I lay in was surely the darkness of Sheol, the place of the dead. I had gone down, and I was lost. When I opened my eyes, the darkness I saw was deeper than the darkness of sleep. The stones on which I lay bit my kidneys and the bones of my back. An icy sweat lay on my brow. When I moved, all my limbs trembled. I lay in silence and turned my head. Darkness above me. Darkness at my side. Darkness beneath. No shadows fell upon the walls of Sheol, telling me of anything that lay beyond its bounds. I knew nothing. Touch, sight, hearing, taste, smell were faint tracings of my senses in the upper world. This was the land of the dead.

The smell of Sheol was the smell of human filth, a stench of dried rottenness that went deeper into my nostrils than any scent of the upper world. I shivered and turned in darkness. Sleep. The sleep of darkness and oblivion. Surely, it would come. Whatever dreams I had in Sheol were visions of darkness. No forms or hollow shells of humanity came and spoke to me. There was nothing. I lay without movement, and I knew nothing.

Sheol was the length of a tall man's body. There was a mess of excrement by the right-hand wall. Not mine. I could crouch, barely, the palms of my hands still flat upon the stone, before the dust and flakes of Sheol's roof caked the hair of my head. The hole through which I had entered Sheol was covered by a metal plate. The braces upon it were rusted. When I swung my fist at it the sound was deep and dull and died in an instant.

Let me, I told myself, understand Sheol by constructing a series of logical propositions. When my good friends dragged me here, the stones my feet scraped across and the walls they threw me against had lines of rough-chipped gouges made with the blades of chisels. The stone of the Temple and the Service rooms was limestone, dressed with marble. Conclusion: Sheol is beneath the Antonia Tower.

The men who dragged me through that passage wore the uniforms of our good friends. The bigger of the two, the one without the breathing problems, spoke with a Damascus accent. He was bald, and had a deep scar across his face. Conclusion: Sheol is beneath the Antonia Tower.

I lay still, and my mind moved. My body would not move again from the land of the dead until my bones would roll through the earth towards the summit of Mount Zion, rearticulate themselves, and stand up before the Lord on the last day. If I was beneath the Antonia Tower, then my Sheol was some hundreds of paces east of Mount Zion. My bones would be among the first to arrive and be judged.

Even in Sheol, would these bones live? My soul lay shrouded in dust. I lay in Sheol and I heard nothing. I emptied my mind of words and thought, and then I evicted every idea of prayer from my heart. My cry would come to no-one.

I stared upwards into the darkness of the metal plate. At some point in the morning it would open. Marcus would ask me questions to which I could not provide answers. I lifted my right hand and traced the line of the metal. Whatever was to happen when that hatch scraped open was not to be thought upon. I emptied my thoughts again and told myself that there is nothing so dreadful that can be done to the human body that the contemplation of it is more injurious to the mind than the moments in which it is actually endured. Then I emptied myself of this thought too.

At that moment, in the confines of Sheol, I was well. My lips were bloodied, my mouth an aching mush, but I was otherwise uninjured. Most of all, I had not been flogged. And my mind, my thought, my memory, my spirit was at my own command.

I stared up at the darkness of the hatch. I fixed its limits in the blackness and fitted them to the borders of my land. Here was my map: the walls of my vineyard, the blocks of my vines. From the lower gate to the east wall: seventy-seven paces. From the eastern corner to the middle block: one hundred and forty paces. Here was the gap in the wall that led to the broken hillside. In memory I walked to the upper block and the place where the rocks changed their colour: sixty paces. These had been the first we had set when the great caravan had come over the hills from the east with the most prized rootstock in Tirazis. They were withered in their baskets when we took them down from the beasts' sides. This was where the big irrigation channel snaked eastwards from the cistern. The earth was dark, the vines old, the fruit small and shrivelled. From the channel end to the culvert way: one hundred and ten paces. Then I turned.

The dampness of the shooting vines brushed upon my fingers. The grapes reached out to me upon the vines and they spoke to me – *Pick me, for I am a better bunch.* As I walked the lines I became aware that someone was walking behind me: I heard the tread of her feet upon the stones, the sound of her shawl brushing against the leaves. I knew the rhythm and movement of my wife as I walked. Zenobia. I turned at the end of the middle block and went up to the terrace wall. I would lead her home. There, at the place where the shade of our olive tree darkened the stones in the morning, I turned away from the door of my house and began to walk the borders of my vineyard again.

I walked my vineyard in the darkness of Sheol until I was sure that the night had passed. Perhaps the sound of the trumpets of dawn upon the Temple's high place would come to me through the stones of the Antonia and down into the depths of the earth. I walked my vineyard again. Then I slid the latches upon the box of memory, made fast the straps that bound it up and closed it, so that I could be sure of taking it with me.

At last, when sufficient time must have passed for Marcus and the Syrian to come for me, when I had prepared myself and had put off the necessity of prayer with the comfort of memory, when at any moment I expected to hear the rasp of the latches where they moved and the groan of the hatch into Sheol, I allowed my limbs to relax, my breathing to soften, and I began to drift into a half-aware semblance of sleep in which the lines of the vineyard returned to me and which, as I moved between the blocks, deepened into unknowing.

I cannot tell for how long I slept. I woke to find myself still in Sheol, still alive. No sounds or cries came to me. Nothing. No words, no hands of men. No light. I slept again. Again, I woke in Sheol.

I woke to hunger and the hugeness of my tongue in my mouth. The eyes of none are upon me, oh Lord. My belly was empty, my bowels full, my mouth and lips dust. No sound came from beyond the darkness of the hatch. I turned on my side, faced the dark wall of Sheol a hand's breadth from my eyes, and once again emptied myself of thought, memory, hope, anticipation, knowledge and despair.

When I awoke, the gouging pain in my belly had passed and a sweat drenched my chest and neck. Any sense of the time of the world had vanished. I rolled over to the right side of Sheol and made water, regretting the dust on my tongue and the desiccation of my mouth. Then I rolled my body back to the filth on the other side of Sheol and slept again.

I woke to the urgent pain of my bowels. Again I rolled over. Again I slept. No dreams came to me. I had neither the hope that

Marcus and his men would never come for me nor the despair that I had fallen out of human memory and been entirely forgotten.

Fire fell into Sheol from above. A torch thudded onto the filth of the floor. I screwed my eyes closed against the agony of the light and dragged my arm across my face.

Then I saw the walls of Sheol around me. They were crowded upon me, black with soot. A voice spoke in Sheol.

"Catch hold of it, can't you?"

A wooden pole hit the left side of my chest. It was strung between two lengths of rope and had a metal hook driven into it. The hook swung from side to side, trying to catch the crook of my arm. Two faces looked down from above. One was a soldier. Quintus, centurion of the Jerusalem guard. The other was a well-fed, grizzled face, with the traces of a beard and smiling eyes, and a rasping, wheezing breath.

"Nico," I whispered and the words fell dead from my mouth.

"Old son."

"Bless you," I whispered, and was surprised that any sound came at all.

They dragged me from the pit of Sheol and then they pulled me along the passage until my legs gave up and I sprawled in the dust. I was pleased to notice that the walls above Sheol were still of dark stone, well dressed and close-fitted. Quintus forced me upright in the way that centurions do. A pail of water appeared and the water drenched me. I screamed. This reassured me. My tongue and my throat could still make noise. My hands were smearing the splashed water on my face into the dust of my mouth. I hawked filth from my mouth and my nostrils and breathed out, a long, racked, stertorous, moaning in three different registers that ended in a hacking cough and an agonised inrush of breath that tore my lungs.

I looked up at Nico, and I wept.

"Marcus?" I said at last.

"Damascus by now," said Quintus. "Awaiting the attention of the pro-praetorial imperial legate. Whenever he arrives to take up his post."

"Prefect's orders," said Nico. "I wish I could say it was all on his doctor's advice. Now. How do you feel?"

"Dreadful."

"Good. And you look dreadful too, by the way. Here. Hold on to me. Can you stand?"

I stood with Nico's hands under my arms. Slowly, he released his grip and I sat back down in the dust, hard.

Quintus unslung a goatskin from his shoulder.

"Drink this. Gently."

After some time, I stood. Then I spoke.

"What has happened to Marcus?" I asked at last.

"Later, old son. There's something important you must do first."

I rubbed water from the goatskin into the dirt of my face. Then I pulled my hair into some sort of order and smoothed my beard. It seemed superfluous to ask them for oil and perfume.

"Come on," said Quintus. "The old bugger won't be kept."

They led me towards a narrow stair, Nico behind, his hands on my waist, pushing me upwards. I had never imagined that the Antonia's dungeons stretched so far beneath the ground. At last, I was pushed into a guardroom. My legs were trembling and my hands danced across my neck, my brow, the sodden, filthy folds of my cloak.

"Now," said Nico, "listen to me. Stay still. Just agree with everything he says. If he asks you a question, say yes. And sign whatever he puts in front of you. Do you understand?"

I stared at him. "I have to listen?"

"Solomon, do you understand me? You just say yes to everything."

"Yes."

"Agree to everything. Never refuse. Never hesitate. Never try to explain."

"Yes."

"Good. Now go."

"It's that way," said Quintus, pointing to the guardroom door.

"Shlomo."

I turned and looked back at Nico.

"Remember. Just do whatever he says. And don't touch anything around him. Especially anything that he's already touched himself. He's fastidious, and you'll set off his choler. Do you understand?"

I had never imagined that there could be light like the light that I walked into when the guardroom door swung open. I staggered, and began to weep. My nostrils stung and I sneezed – once, twice, three times. I bent low as my breath caught and I gulped air. Then I sneezed again. And again. Seven times. At last, I looked up.

"Approach!"

I was standing outside the Antonia Tower on the edge of the pavement that lay to the west of the Temple wall. Ten paces from me, at a table beneath a canvas awning, a man was sitting at a desk. The desk was bare in the manner of the desks of powerful men. A clerk was arranging a pile of scrolls on a portable cabinet that moved on wheels. At any other time I would have wished to investigate the workings of such a clever device. The clerk had a white tunic, short hair, barely respectable beard, and a large red wart beneath his right nostril.

"Name?"

"Solomon Eliades." I sneezed again.

"The oenarch?"

"What?"

"You're late. You've kept him waiting. Go on. Stop when you're three paces from him. Bow. Keep standing. Only sit if invited. Only speak when spoken to." I hoped that I would be able to stand upright long enough for any speaking to be over, whatever the subject.

"And don't sneeze," he added. "He hates it."

I stood filthy and cloaked in rags. Whatever odour I gave off was enough to keep the clerk four paces from me. I must be the entertainment, the overlooked amusement saved for the end of the morning's business. Today's oddity, dragged up from the dungeons.

I remembered Philo's words when I arrived in the city. He has two ways of dealing with problems – summary execution, or else they're sent to rot in the dungeons of Damascus, awaiting the imperial legate's arrival. The Prefect would not drag me away from rotting in a hole in Jerusalem in order to send me off to rot in another hole in Damascus. So, it must be execution.

"Approach!" The secretary was addressing me. I stepped forward and bowed.

The Prefect of Judea looked up at me. I had never set eyes upon this one before. He had been appointed some years after my departure from the Service. I wondered what he had done to secure the office. Some of his predecessors seemed to have been appointed more as a punishment than a reward, they had so obviously resented the people and the land over which they exercised power. I had encountered two of them, Rufus and Valerius Gratus, in the course of my work – the latter I had known well. This one was taut. Livid, thin-lipped and with ears that looked sharp enough to pare the hairs on his head. The skin of his face was stretched thin across his bones and his eyes burned red in fine filaments. Perhaps he was a drinker. His hands trembled as he shifted the papers away. The bundle was scooped up by his secretary and vanished into the little cabinet. Then he gave me his attention.

"And what in the name of the gods is this?"

I bowed, and hoped that I did not spread the dust of Sheol upon his pavement.

"Solomon Eliades, Excellency. At your service," I added, without optimism.

He frowned and leaned back. Then his secretary leaned forward and whispered to him. I heard the word "vineyard" and my heart descended back into the dust. The Prefect looked up at me. He was smiling.

"Oh. The oenarch. Sit." The Prefect's Greek had a thick, western accent. He gestured with his left hand and the secretary produced a three-footed stool from behind his cabinet.

I sat.

"Bring it." The secretary bowed and withdrew. Pilatos turned to me.

"You're the man that my former head of intelligence has been keeping locked up down there? Eh?"

"I have that honour, Excellency."

"Well, you look a disgrace."

The secretary returned with a silver ewer and a wine bowl. Just the one. The Prefect watched as the secretary wiped and polished the bowl. The slightest hint of an inclination of the head signalled to the secretary that he had laboured long enough. Then Pilatos took the bowl and the cloth of Egyptian cotton himself and cleaned it, turning it twice leftwards and then twice rightwards in his hands. This last turn was impelled with a savage force, as if he wished to inflict hygiene upon the metal through sheer violence. When he had satisfied himself that any trace of his secretary's attentions had been removed from the surface of the bowl, he inclined his head again and the secretary raised the ewer. When he poured the wine I knew from its colour and the scent that rose from it that it was the wine Zenobia and I had made three years earlier. The long vintage of the 45th Year of the Temple when the harvest had started early, finished late and the grapes had fermented on their skins for a week longer than in previous years. The wine had a depth to its darkness that was unlike any other. Its scent was dark too: ripe dates and the skins of beasts that had tanned for days. I knew it for my own long before the last of it had left the ewer and splashed into the Prefect's bowl.

Pilatos drank. Decorously, not with the ignorant enthusiasm of the bibber, nor with the alertness and attention of the adept.

"If you're wondering about Marcus Ulpianus' men – I've removed them from your vineyard and he will pay for the damage they have caused. He is on his way to Damascus for due process at the hands of the imperial legate when he arrives."

For a moment, a glorious vision opened before me. But I have long observed that the prospect of some favour or act of generosity on the part of our good friends rarely turns out to be as just and reasonable as it may first appear. The hope of some future vindication, even the chance of an unexpected reprieve, is a very foolish thing at which to rejoice.

"My physician assures me that this wine has the most extraordinary properties. It could have been made with my own constitution in mind. I like that, don't you?" He drank again. "Nicanor from Alexandria and that preening Egyptian assistant of his tell me that it works wonders upon choler, promotes clarity of thought and eases the action of my stomach and my bowels." He paused, suddenly fastidious, and looked down into the bowl and across at the ewer. Then he picked up the cloth and rubbed the ewer's lip for longer than anyone might imagine necessary. "Quite unlike the effects of ordinary wines." He drank again, paused, and then continued.

"I had often wondered where this wine came from. It can be bought here in Jerusalem, in Caesarea, even in Damascus – at a price that is beyond reason for a local vintage. The deputy legate in Damascus serves it to his guests. Young Herod keeps it to himself. Ungenerous of him, I've always thought. He's supposed to have ten thousand amphorae of the stuff hidden away down in Machaerus." I said nothing in response, not even to point out that the quantity Herod supposedly had in store far exceeded the capacity of our vineyard to produce, let alone to sell to Ariel down on Cyprus Wharf in Caesarea. It occurred to me that Ariel might be adulterating our product, watering it, or passing off some other farmer's wines as our own. What the Prefect had in his bowl was very obviously our own work, the true and genuine product of our labour in vineyard and cellar. He drank again and dabbed his lips repeatedly with a studied, trembling revulsion.

"There's a mystery about where this wine is made, and my secretary, Libanius here" – the man actually bowed to me in a self-congratulatory fashion – "consulted the Temple records and established that the vineyard was up in the hills, half a day's journey from Jerusalem. And then my physician also tells me that the man who makes this wonder among wines has been thrown in a cell by my head of intelligence. And that he has sent a detachment of soldiers to take possession of the man's vineyard. Now, what conclusion do you think that I should reach?"

"I cannot tell, Excellency."

He looked up at me sharply.

"Come on, Eliades. Don't be obtuse. For someone who apparently used to be the High Priest's own head of intelligence, you're suddenly trying very hard to be very stupid. What do you think?"

"I would think, Excellency, that something needed to be set right."

"Would you? Really?"

He reached out towards one of the water bowls at his desk and rubbed his hands together. Again, this went on far longer than cleanliness required. At last, Libanius handed him a square of Egyptian cotton, barely breathed the word "Excellency", and stood back. The Prefect mangled the towel till it was sodden and threw it aside.

"I've done you the goodness, Jew, of sparing your life. I have dragged you out of the darkness below for a purpose. I've long been sure that ownership of a vineyard that makes such estimably health-giving wine must be a good thing. Why not? If the divine son of Augustus can own every balsam plantation from here to En-Gedi, then why should his friend not benefit from a vineyard of my own? One whose wines will give me health?"

I looked back at him. His hands were twitching. It would, I supposed, be an act of instant peril to explain to him the craft that was necessary in the press room to make such wine. And he would simply buy the expertise from Cyprus or Tirazis. His actual acquaintance with the vineyard would not stretch beyond enjoying the consumption of its produce and the monopoly profit upon its sales.

"It must be freely given, of course. Any suggestion that you are offering me an inducement to spare your life is not admissible. Libanius?"

The secretary produced a scroll from his wheeled cabinet, unrolled it and placed it, corners weighed, on the desk between us, its lower end towards me. It was a Temple scroll, from the records office. The hunt that Micah had told me about had indeed brought down its prey. I recognised the upper part of it: the passage recorded, in Hebrew, the sale of the vineyard by Yephthah ben Yoachim to Solomon ben Eleazar, on 8th Ab of the 41st Year of the Temple. I recognised my own signature, and those of the witnesses, including Nico's. Below this, Secretary Libanius had already prepared the next transaction upon the property. The undersigned, Solomon ben Eleazar, known as the oenarch, makes a gift, freely and without compulsion, of the said vineyard, its vines and crops, its retained stock, its cisterns and their waters, its press house and living quarters, and all the slaves and domestics of the property, to the Prefect of Judea. It was a straightforward, unconditional sale, recorded in legal Greek. Someone knew what they were doing. Sealed this day, the 25th Nisan, at Jerusalem.

Is it really 25th Nisan? I asked myself. Had I been in Sheol so long? The transaction had already been witnessed by seven men, none of whose names I recognised. Secretary Libanius walked around the table with a fresh stylus in his right hand. He leaned over me. His beard had an aroma of sandalwood. The Prefect wiped his hands, another over-elaborate performance, and sipped my wine. His hands were still trembling.

"Excellency, may I request something?"

He looked up, neither light nor anger in his eyes but sheer cold.

Only speak when spoken to, I remembered. There was the slightest inclination of his head.

"My domestics, Stephanos and Abigail. May I humbly request their freedom?"

Pilatos glanced upwards at Libanius. Whatever signal passed between them was impossible to understand.

"I will make the arrangements," Libanius said. Then he leaned over me and spoke softly.

"If you would sign there, there and there, sir."

And he placed the stylus in my hand.

"My vineyard," I said, "is my own to give."

The Prefect stood up, dabbing his lips and wringing out the square of cotton. It was over. He turned away from the desk without the slightest indication that he was still aware of my presence. Secretary Libanius touched my shoulder as he relieved me of the stylus and handed me my copy of the contract.

"You may go."

I turned away and walked across the pavement towards the Antonia Tower. And I rejoiced. Somewhere, my good Stephanos and Abigail were alive. Which meant that somewhere my Zenobia still lived. And I was a free man. Free to go. Free, and destitute. Of course, I had signed. I had signed away my vineyard and made a gift of it to our good friends.

At the door to the Antonia Tower, the soldiers blocked my way.

"You don't want to be going back in there." I looked around. "The street gate," one of them said. "That's the one you want." He turned and indicated an entrance in the curtain wall, and a flight of steps that led down into the city. I walked to the gate barely aware of what was happening around me. My body ached, my tongue clung to my mouth and I was speechless. I had no words. I stepped down into the streets of Jerusalem alone, destitute and free.

My vineyard is my own to give.

JERUSALEM
26TH NISAN,
DAWN

I woke beneath the canvas of Nico's roof, my beard soaked with the dew of morning. It was a little while before dawn: the sky above Mount Olive was moving between the orange and the bleached-out blue that it has on fine spring mornings. My bones ached. I was chilled to the stiff, dried-out marrows of them. By the other couch, the last amphora of my wine that Nico possessed lay on its side, unstoppered and empty. We had finished it. Sosthenes stood over me and bowed.

"The master sends his greetings and says: will you join him downstairs before he has to depart?"

I stood at the second attempt, and looked out across the roofs of Bezetha, past the walls of the Temple, to the distant potteries at Akel-dama. I had to get out of Jerusalem. I should have left yesterday. Instead, I had accepted Nico's hospitality.

Downstairs, he was preparing his satchel with Azizus, fussing over the vials and the little case of instruments.

"Old son." He embraced me. "My house is yours. But you cannot stay in this city. Now, what will you do?"

"I'm going back to the vineyard," I said. "The grapes need me."

"Solomon…"

The latches on the box of memory snapped. Of course.

"Zenobia," I said. "I must find her. Wherever she is."

"How can I help? Can I give you money? A horse? Food and drink? Can I give you Sosthenes?"

I sat down, utterly defeated, and leaned forward till my head touched my knees.

"Nico. That would be a kindness. All of that. But no, thank you."

Last night, as the trumpets sounded from the Temple's high place to mark the rising of the moon and the start of the new day, we had gone up to the roof with the last amphora of my wine, and three bowls. Azizus had joined us. Nico embraced him, and then turned to me.

"I'll tell you what I'm going to do, old son. At the new year, I'm going to do something quite shocking and unexpected." His eyes glittered and his tongue licked his lips with an anticipatory slyness.

"What?"

"I'm going to emancipate my Azizus, and then I'm going to adopt him as my heir." Azizus beamed, while Nico waited for my reaction.

"Congratulations," I said to Azizus. "Congratulations to both of you. I'm delighted."

"And I'll tell you what else I'll do. I'm going to take him into partnership in the practice. He's an outstanding diagnostician – he should be, too: I've taught him everything I know. And he's got a gentle way with the clients. They trust him and he'll do well. He'll make a very good physician, won't you, my dear?"

"Nico, I'm delighted for you," I said. "That sounds like an excellent way to leave your mark."

"It's not entirely selfless. We may have to live quietly together in the country but I'll be well looked after in my old age by someone that I know will be the best doctor in Syria and Judea."

Later in the evening, when Quintus arrived from the Antonia barracks, I stood with him and Nico at the far end of the roof and watched the lights of Jerusalem begin to be extinguished.

"I owe you my life," I said to the soldier. "Both of you. How did you know where to find me?"

"Quintus got wind of it," Nico said. "The duty guard reported that Marcus had bundled someone from the Service down into the cells with orders that no-one was to go near his hole."

"Splendid way of ensuring more than the usual interest in the prisoner's identity."

"And what about the Prefect? Why did he send Marcus off to Damascus? I can't imagine it was any concern for my well-being."

"It wasn't at all. I was there when they had their argument about it at the end of the morning audience the day after the riot."

"What happened?"

"It was our young friend Saul who started it all. You'd think that the boy would have shown more sense. He was foolish enough to refer to Marcus' search for the body of the man the Prefect had executed. Pilatos must already have heard about this search, I think, but suddenly there it was, in the open. He asked Marcus what he thought he was doing and was it true that he had one of his people placed in the holy man's entourage? I really can't imagine where he'd heard about that. For once, the only time that I've ever seen it, Marcus was lost for words. The Prefect went into one of his episodes of sheer rage. It wasn't pleasant or funny, old son, I was sure we were going to lose him to a fit. And how would that look if he dropped dead while his doctor was in attendance? What, Pilatos demanded to know, did Marcus think he was doing running someone who was encouraging a country faith healer to set himself up as king of Israel? Treason and conspiracy. Incandescent anger, and a lot of wiping his wine bowl. At last, he calmed down enough to order Marcus to produce the man. Thaddeus bar Ptolemai? Yes, that one. Saul was sent off to find him with a couple of soldiers."

"Was one of them a big Syrian? Scar down his face?"

"That's him. Marcus was ordered to remain, and he stood there all morning, looking as if he'd rather swallow a pot of poison presented to him by Old Herod than see Saul come back with his man."

"And how long did it take?"

"All morning. At last our young friend came back. With the two soldiers, but no bar Ptolemai."

"Where had they gone to find him?"

"The woodworkers' synagogue. All spectacle. This did my patient's temper no good at all. He ordered Marcus to go and get him, wherever he was, and not come back without him."

"And Marcus came back without his man?"

"Two days later. Pilatos' anger was the most extraordinary display I've ever seen in a disease of the soul. It exceeded anything I'd ever witnessed. He was incoherent. The veins on his head really were throbbing – something I've rarely actually witnessed myself. Eventually, I persuaded him to swallow a sedative draft, mixed up with a cup of your wine. It really does have the most remarkable properties. He wanted to know all about it."

"Nico…"

"Yes, he recovered enough to stand and to speak. First thing: Marcus is taken down to the holes to await an armed escort mustered to take him to Damascus. Saul is thrown out of the presence and told to present himself to Philo with a clear message that its bearer is never to be allowed to bring his meddling anywhere near the Prefectorial office again. Then he asked me about the wine. Did I know where more of it could be found? After that he wiped his drinking bowl rather a lot before he looked up and asked me why I was still there when I should be finding the man who made that wine. Luckily for me, Quintus knew just where to find you. I do wonder what its properties really are, old son. But after last night, I don't suppose I'll ever be able to find out."

"You'll have to ask the new owner to sell you some. I'm sure he'll oblige if it's good for his health."

My vineyard is my own to give.

While Nico and I ate bread and honey, Azizus brought me a tablet and stylus. I wrote greetings to Ariel on Cyprus Wharf at Caesarea and instructed him that, when the boat returned from beyond the Pillars, he was to turn my share into gold, hold half of it himself and give the other half to the bearer of this message. I went to seal the tablet, and reached automatically for the ring that was no longer on the middle finger of my right hand. My vineyard, my self. I scratched my name, crudely, in the wax. *Solomon Eliades, Oenarch*, and gave Nico the tablet.

"In spite of the outright lie in the wax, I am not completely destitute. I rented ten square *amots* of space in the hold of a ship that is trading beyond the Pillars. If it ever comes back, I may even be able to buy a patch of land somewhere across the river and plant some vines. This is my instruction to the ship's agent at Caesarea. Will you take it to him? He will give you half the profit."

"Old son…"

"Take from it whatever you wish, Nico. Don't insult me, I insist. Then take the rest of it to Pera, over the river. The spice merchant there can be trusted and he knows my name. He'll hold it for me."

"Of course, old son. Of course I will."

He called Azizus from the courtyard and told him to fetch two purses from the chest in the inner room. He gave both of them to me.

"Take them," he said. "No, please. Don't you insult me. Pay me back when you press your first grapes."

And then he was gone, borne up by Azizus, Sosthenes and the rest of his domestic slaves, to inspect the excretions of His Excellency and interpret the dreams of his wife.

I left Nicanor's house and went down into Jerusalem. I bought a satchel and a goatskin from a traveller's stall just inside the Damascus Gate, some flat loaves, hard cheese and half a *kab* of dates. At a stable by the gate I bought a donkey that was docile enough to let me ride it at the first attempt. The groom had a row of red fox-brush charms for sale, which did not reassure me about the steadiness of his mounts. The cost of a charm far exceeded the price he was asking for the donkey.

"With that beast, it'd be a good investment. Trust me."

"I'd rather trust the beast and my own good sense."

He overcharged me, but I did not care. He threw in a stick to goad the beast when it grew tired, and I pretended to be grateful. Then I rode out of Jerusalem for the last time, and I turned the beast's docile nose to the Damascus Road.

It was mid-afternoon when I reached the great curve of the bluff and found again the narrow cleft that led up into the hills. The beast beneath me hesitated when it faced the rocks, but at last it went up the path without the need of the goad. After a while I dismounted and led him till we came to the crest of the ridge. Beneath me, I could see the blocks of the vineyard, the farmhouse, the press and the paradise where my boys are buried.

Soldiers were moving between the blocks of vines. Four of them, naked from the waist, were sunning themselves beneath the olive tree on my terrace. I began to descend the path towards the back gate. Ten paces from the entrance, a soldier with a drawn sword barred my way. He spoke sharply in Syriac and ordered me off. I bowed, muttered apologies to him in Aramaic, and tried to seem harmlessly stupid. He was sufficiently convinced by this charade to spare my life and order me back up the hill. I bowed, stepped back, and walked away from my vineyard for the last time.

At the top of the ridge I led the beast along the rough trod that passed through the rocks and thorns. At the place where the path that leads north begins, I stopped and drank from my goatskin. Below me, the rocks fell away into the eastern desert and the valley of the river. I knelt and examined the dust, but there were no traces visible to my eyes of the passing of the followers or my beloved Zenobia.

Before me, the path led north to Galilee, and to the cross-roads that ran down to Jericho and Pera across the river. I stood the beast in silence for time out of mind, thinking of my beloved. What would she have done? At last I tapped its side with the stick, and we began our journey in search of my Zenobia.

Continue reading for a preview of *Solomon's Vineyard*, the next novel from Nicholas Graham in the *Jerusalem* series . . .

Much later, when Nico found me in Damascus where I was, at that time, living a life of blameless but necessary obscurity writing letters for the illiterate spice-traders in the warehouses on the banks of the Golden River, my old friend described to me exactly what had happened below the city wall.

"It was just off the Caesarea Road, old son – "

"– Yes, below the walls, where the road curves round to the Jupiter Gate," Azizus interrupted him. Nico frowned.

"Yes, of course it was. At first we didn't think it was a man, still less that he could be alive."

"– Nothing but a bundle of rags, covered in dust."

Nico frowned again. "Azizus, dear, let me tell this one. He's become terribly pleased with himself since I freed him, haven't you?" The frown again. Azizus laughed.

"We would have passed him by, we were about to go up to the gate, but I looked back and it seemed to me that the dust stirred, as if the rags were trembling."

They had turned back to the tattered sack, almost indistinguishable from the stones around which it was draped. Dust-clogged hair, and a foot sticking out from beneath a torn cloak. Azizus had knelt down and brushed away the dirt from a human hand. The man was alive, but his limbs were as rigid as the first day of death. Spittle mixed with dust caked his mouth. His eyes had rolled back, staring deep into the darkness of his own skull.

"The Sacred Disease," Azizus said. "His god was beating upon the doors of his body."

They had taken a jar from Nico's portable cabinet, mixed the contents with a little camphor and kneaded the paste into a ball that Azizus had forced into the man's mouth.

"You escaped with all your fingers, though, didn't you dear? That's the mark of a good physician," he smiled at me this time. "Never let the patient bite you."

They had waited for the trembling to diminish and a forced, throaty moaning began to come from deep in the man's lungs.

"He was calling on the Almighty," said Nico. "I thought, for a long time, that he really would die there in the dust outside Damascus. I've seen it happen, old son. Their god visits them – if you believe that a god will do such a thing – and it batters the pathways and the organs of a man's body when it leaves them. It can break their bones, twist their limbs, tear their muscles to shreds. I put my ear to his lips when I heard him moaning. "My god, my god," were his words."

"This one was lucky," said Azizus. "He lived."

"That paste-ball you put in his mouth, it must have worked a wonder. What do you use?"

"Camphor, and the blood of a dead gladiator. Freshly spilled, when I can get it," Azizus said. Nico's face was sheer embarrassment.

"You're supposed to be a diagnostician, dear. He's dragging me back to the bad old ways," he said to me. "Our patients don't need that sort of country nonsense."

"Well it seems to have worked for your patient. I must say I'm impressed by your resourcefulness. It must be difficult to maintain such a well-stocked cabinet of drugs, if that's really what you use." Azizus smiled and looked down in modesty.

"Don't be so philosophical, old son. I'm relieved to say it's usually impossible for him to get hold of the real thing unless there's a reliable supplier who's well-disposed. For some reason Damascus is drenched with the stuff this spring."

"You've got the new imperial legate to thank for that. Or so I'm told. Apparently he's making a point of celebrating his arrival.

They usually do it by freeing the prisoners in their gaols or bringing Imperial clemency with them. Not this one."

"That's exactly why I'm here old son." I stopped and looked up at him.

"What? For the chance to re-stock your medicine case?"

"No."

"He's consulting you?"

"Can't say, precisely." I raised my brows, gently encouraging, but he smiled, shook his head and changed the subject. Better entrust your secrets to a doctor than to a spy.

"And do you know, the most extraordinary thing about this patient that we found by the roadside? When it was safe to move him without setting off another set of tremors, we carried him into the city and set about cleaning him up. The most extraordinary thing when we washed the mud and the dust from his face. What do you think?"

"I have no idea."

"It was our young friend Saul from the Temple Guard. He looked straight up at Azizus and thrashed around as if he was about to be possessed again. And then he started wailing about falling into the clutches of Sodom." Azizus laughed softly. "Well, old son, I thought it was typically graceless of the young man after all that we'd just done for him."

"And what happened?"

"Steady. If you're concerned about his wellbeing, he's laid up at the lodging house of the Drug-makers' Synagogue. I gave him a mild dose of narcotic and he's sleeping it all off. He'll be on his feet tomorrow."

"You mean he's here in Damascus now?"

"Of course." Nico patted the sides of his cloak. "Don't look so worried. If we'd not found him I'd've been here sooner to give you this."

He took a purse from inside his cloak and placed it on the table between us.

"There you are. Compliments of Ariel at Cyprus Wharf. I had to wait a long time for him – he spent the winter in Rhodos and only came back when the shipping season started. That's on account until he can get the rest of it transported safely to wherever you want it sent. Don't look at me like that, old son. Don't you realise? Your ship came back. After two years beyond the Pillars. You're a rich man at last."

After two years beyond the Pillars. I slumped in my chair and reached out to the purse. Tyrian gold. Good in any town between the sea and the two rivers. I was a rich man again.

We were well into the contents of an amphora from Anemos' on the corner of the Straight Way – it was a too-sweet red from somewhere down in the valley below Mount Hermon – when the soldiers hammered on my door. The military beat of the military fist: somehow you never quite become used to the shock of it.

There were two of them. Short-armed, muscle-bound Syrians from the city garrison. With knuckle-dusters on their hands.

"Are you Solomon, the *grammateos*?"

Solomon the Writer. *Grammateos*. Solomon the *Oenarch* no more. I looked down at Nico's purse. My purse. I was back on my feet. The *Oenarch* again.

Until Nico arrived I had been making a living in my destitution as the paid writer of the obscure little community of foreigners and Jews in the poorer side of Damascus, at the wrong end of the Straight Way where I had finally stopped when the search for my beloved Zenobia wore me out. Letters to distant families, bills of trade and business instructions, whenever one of my neighbours among the Damascus poor needed to make a formal complaint or petition the magistrates, Solomon *Grammateos* was the man to whom they came. Last greetings on death-beds. Confessions and life-testaments a speciality. The dying who wished to leave a scant record of their deeds, however modest, in witness that they had passed through this world, so that they would be remembered by their sons when they lay below in the long grey-shaded attendance of Sheol. They sought me out, they begged me to make them remembered.

"Sorry lads," I said to the soldiers, "if it's a love poem for one of your girls at Thais' place – or for one of your boys – I can't help you. I'm done with all that. And your girls too."

"That's not what we come for," said the taller one, and shifted his weight.

"We was told to ask for you special."

"And you are Solomon, right? The *Grammateos*?"

"Only there's someone who wants a word."

"And who sent you?" I asked, imagining it must be one of their officers, too embarrassed or reluctant to approach me in person.

"One of the prisoners."

"He wants to have something in writing," shorter one said. "Can't understand why."

"*Go and get the Writer called Solomon to come and do it for me*, he said. *He'll want to, Solomon will, when he hears.*"

Oh will I. I put down my cup. They were eyeing the purse, anticipating their reward.

"And why would he think that, this prisoner?" I asked. "What's his name?" A vision of Marcus Varro's corpulent, puffy-eyed face, haggard and hollowed-out by two years of lightless confinement, rat-bites and sickness, came unbidden into my mind.

"He's another one of you Jews," said the short one. "So he asked for you. Thaddeus is his name. Thaddeus bar Ptolemai."

I dropped my cup, spilling wine across the stone ledge I used as a table. Azizus breathed deep, whistling in astonishment. I said nothing, but looked across, first at Nico then at Azizus, and then back at Nico.

"You'd better hurry if you're coming," the shorter one said.

"He said he's got a lot he wants you to write down for him," said the taller one.

"And you've not got long. We're executing him tomorrow."

ACKNOWLEDGEMENTS

The seeds of this novel were planted in conversations with the late Theodore Hines, whose intellect and wisdom illuminated everything he addressed. I owe him and his wife, the late Lois Winkel Hines, an enormous debt of gratitude. Andrew Biswell, Peter Davidson and Jane Stevenson have been consistent sources of encouragement and insight over many years. Stephen Badsey shared numerous conversations on how history and fiction can come together. Nicholas Royle and my classmates at the Writing School of Manchester Metropolitan University were unfailing supporters of first steps. Finally, Ashley Stokes, Henry Doss, Christine Arvidson and Ken Powell have all been careful and sympathetic readers of *The Judas Case* at various stages of its development. I am grateful to them for their criticisms and suggestions.

I would also like to acknowledge the support of a 2016 Northern Writers' Award from New Writing North, supported by the Literary Consultancy, Northumbria University and Arts Council England.

For writing and publishing news, or
recommendations of new titles to read,
sign up to the Book Guild newsletter: